The Green Man of Bamberg

a novel

NORMAN BEAUPRÉ

CAJETAN THE
STARGAZER

For Lis with my very best
regards
Norman R Beaupré

Llumina
Press

ISBN: 978-1-60594-927-7 (PB)
      978-1-60594-928-4 (EB)

Printed in the United States of America by Llumina Press

Library of Congress Control Number: 2012907673

For my wife, Lucille, who has been most supportive in my career as a teacher, in my passion for travel and in my efforts to write, *Merci!*

From the same author:

1. *L'Enclume et le couteau, the Life and Work of Adelard Coté, Folk Artist*, NMDC, Manchester, N.H., 1982. Reprint by Llumina Press, Coral Springs, FL, 2007.

2. *Le Petit Mangeur de Fleurs*, Éd. JCL, Chicoutimi, Québec, 1999.

3. *Lumineau*, Éd. JCL, Chicoutimi, Québec, 2002.

4. *Marginal Enemies*, Llumina Press, Coral Springs, FL, 2004.

5. *Deux Femmes, Deux Rêves*, Llumina Press, Coral Springs, FL, 2005.

6. *La Souillonne, Monologue sur scène*, Llumina Press, Coral Springs, FL, 2006.

7. *Before All Dignity Is Lost*, Llumina Press, Coral Springs, FL, 2006.

8. *Trails Within, Meditations on the Walking Trails at the Ghost Ranch in Abiquiu, New Mexico*, Llumina Press, Coral Springs, FL, 2007.

9. *La Souillonne, deusse*, Llumina Press, Coral Springs, FL, 2008.

10. *The Boy With the Blue Cap---Van Gogh in Arles*, Llumina Press, Coral Springs, FL, 2009.

11. *Voix Francophones de chez nous, contes et histoires,* par Normand Beaupré et autres, Llumina Press, Coral Springs, FL, 2009.

12. *La Souillonne, Dramatic Monologue*, trans. from French by the author, Llumina Press, Coral Springs, FL, 2009.

13. *The Man with the Easel of Horn---The Life and Works of ÉMILE FRIANT*, Llumina Press, Coral Springs, FL, 2010.

14. *The Little Eater of Bleeding Hearts*, trans. from French by the author, Llumina Press. Coral Springs, FL, 2010.

15. *Simplicity in the Life of the Gospels*, Spiritual Reflections, Llumina Press, Coral Springs. FL, 2011.

16. *Madame Athanase T. Brindamour, raconteuse, histoires et folleries*, Llumina Press, Coral Springs, FL, 2012.

CONTENTS

AUTHOR'S PREFACE

In the spring of 1989, I was invited to a National Endowment for the Humanities Summer Seminar by Professor Stephen Murray of Columbia University. The seminar was held in Paris, France and the title was "Gothic Architecture in the Île-de-France." My project was "The Green Man." It dealt with what is called in French, *la tête feuillue or le masque feuillu* and in German, the *Blatte Masque*. I had previously chosen the stained glass windows of Chartres Cathedral with the artisans and their crafts depicted in some of them. However, when Professor Murray suggested that someone choose the Green Man as a project, since it was a subject that few people had chosen to research and write about, I jumped at the challenge. I've always loved challenges. I got to love the topic, and eventually wrote my paper on the subject after much reading, research and deliberation on the foliate head that appears in corners, cornices, capitals and sometimes shadowy places in Gothic cathedrals. Although I had never seen the Green Man of the Bamberg cathedral, I became fascinated with it when I happened to glance at it in William Anderson's book, "The Rise of the Gothic." I thought that the acanthus-leaf Green Man with the somewhat savage eyes peering through the mask of leaves was captivating. I wanted to learn more about what was called the Green Man. The result was that I melded the study of Gothic cathedrals with a concentration on the Green Man. The foliate head became my passion in the study of Gothic architecture and the building of medieval cathedrals.

I was very enthused with Professor Murray's on-site visits to cathedrals that he had gotten to know well such as, Notre-Dame d'Amiens, Notre-Dame de Chartres, Saint-Denis de Paris, Notre-Dame de Laon, Notre-Dame de Reims, Saint-Étienne de Bourges, Saint-Pierre-et-Saint-Paul de Troyes and even Saint-Étienne de Beauvais, whose 153-meter central tower collapsed in 1573.

I was intrigued by the Gothic cathedrals that we visited, and took copious notes on every aspect that Professor Murray talked about. It was a fascinating subject for me since I had never approached Gothic architecture with a meticulously close observation as we were invited to do. Professor Murray talked about the height of piers, their girth and their design. He also talked about vaults and arches. He really knew the architectural structure of cathedrals. It was evident to me and my colleagues that Professor Murray had spent a lot of time studying Gothic architecture. He was a true master of his academic discipline. But most of all, what I retained from his views was the term "Gothic space." I learned to look up and not a minute downward when I stepped into a cathedral from the main portal. It gave me vertigo after a while, just keeping my head held high and staring into "Gothic space" but it was exhilarating, like flying in a vast unobstructed space high above my head. I truly felt a sense of being carried upwards in the high Gothic vaulted ceiling.

I also liked the stained-glass windows, those kaleidoscopic colors catching the light from the exterior. I had seen the rose windows of Notre-Dame de Paris, and was awed by their huge roundness and color design. Why, even today when I go to Paris, I always stop at Notre-Dame and stand in front of the south rose window admiring the subtle colors of violet-mauve-rose. I also got to see the windows at Chartres, the windows that I was to study for my project where one can see windows offered by medieval craftsmen such as, the butchers, the furriers, the vine growers and innkeepers, the coopers and the carpenters, as well as the masons and stone sculptors. These are the indelible and tangible marks of direct involvement by town dwellers who worked at their crafts knowing full well that they counted for something. They were the backbone of the town, and kept it vibrant and economically stable.

I also learned that an architect's role in the construction of a cathedral was of utmost importance, for his design and plans were the basis for all of the work to be done in that majestic project. In the case of the Gothic cathedral, the architect's plans were to elevate the vaults of the cathedral to new heights, and allow more light to penetrate its thin walls pierced with large windows that drew light from the sun, and gave the interior of the cathedral a resplendent luminosity not seen in the Romanesque churches. The thin walls were made possible by the help of the flying buttresses, *les arcs-boutants*, a much more accurate hyphenated word according to Professor Murray, because there is nothing "flying" about buttresses in Gothic architecture.

One last thing I learned about Gothic cathedrals was the vast sums of money needed to build them, and the great difficulty bishops and their chapters encountered in their campaigns to raise funds. That's why the construction often took much more time than previously expected. That's besides the many difficulties that several cathedrals underwent. Such was the case for the Cathedral of Reims that went through four architects, sporadic work due to political strife and a disastrous fire. It was never completely finished, at least not with the crowning glory envisioned for it, a spire on the cross and six other smaller spires, standing on the towers of the façade and the transepts.

Finally, I got really reacquainted with medieval literature, its romances, fabliaux and poetry that I studied during my graduate years at Brown University, when I was drawn to it. So much so that I had initially planned to write my doctoral dissertation on some of the romances and the role they played in the life of the people who read or listened to them. Somehow I turned to 17th Century classical theater and Corneille. Let's just say that it was done for expediency and money. I needed to get a teaching job. Doctoral dissertations are often written to meet a requirement in the doctoral program, the final requirement. They are not always done with joy and a sense of fulfillment. Rather, they're done with the guidance of an advisor whose field matches the chosen dissertation. Mine was the expansion of a paper that I wrote for which I had gotten an "A". I never liked the subject of my dissertation. My heart was still with the medieval romances.

Partially because of my fondness for medieval studies, I have decided to write a novel about an architect named Cajetan who rises from the ranks of the apprentice and journeyman to become what he had dreamed of since childhood, a master builder of cathedrals. Cajetan the Stargazer, I call him, because he likes to gaze at the stars like his grandfather, the stone cutter, did before him, and who wondered what the stars had in store for him. Follow me in my efforts to bring you back to the Middle Ages, and wonder how you yourself would have gazed at the stars and thought about the wonders of a majestic and imposing Gothic cathedral.

« Il n'y aura jamais de construction noble si l'architecte est ignoble »
Alain Erlande-Brandenberg, "Quand les cathédrales étaient peintes"
[There will never be noble construction if the architect is ignoble.]

THE YOUNG APPRENTICE

Cajetan looked up at the sky on a bright sunny day in September and wished he were with his Master back in the Kingdom of France. The year was 1263 and he longed for his native soil. He had been in England for two and a half years now, and although he loved his work as an apprentice with the Master Architect, he much preferred his first Master in France, a robust and gentle man in his early forties. He was Maître Albert de Chaussoyes, now a Master Architect in Reims. He had been a Master of the works in the building of cathedrals in a few selected *chantiers* although he had not built too many since the completion of a cathedral took many years. Some, over thirty years or even forty years due to a severe lack of funds, or certain insurmountable obstacles or difficulties. Maître de Chaussoyes was much celebrated and even revered in his field. He himself had been an apprentice under the well-known Maître Sigismond de Montfort who had worked for seven years under the tutelage of the Architect, Maître Edmondin de Chasteigne, first as an apprentice, then as journeyman. Maître Edmondin de Chasteigne and his craftsmen had completed the Cathedral of Chartres in the time span of thirty years, thanks, in great part, to the energy and indefatigable drive of Bishop Fulbert who worked tirelessly at raising funds among the many merchants, money lenders and high-placed members of the nobility that he knew well. He had spent years developing good relationships with them, wining them with the finest of champagnes, serving them the choicest of meats on large platters, and especially flattering them with his smooth and silvery tongue while they swallowed both food and compliments drinking heartily the bubbling wine of the Champagne region. Bishop Fulbert had an unsurpassable strength of character that allowed him to confront any possible donor with courage and dignity and, of course, with just the right offerings for the palate. Donors just could not refuse his plea for funds. It was, after all, for the cathedral dedicated to the Most Blessed Virgin Mary, Mother of God, and of all the faithful who prayed to her constantly to come to their assistance in time of need.

Cajetan's Master in England was the Architect Sigismond de Longchamp. He was an intelligent, willful but knowledgeable architect. He knew what he wanted and managed to get it in whatever way he deemed appropriate, be it through discreet bribery, some arm-twisting or simple convincing. He was himself a skillful craftsman and had managed to win over Archbishop Tintamarre into naming him Chief Architect. Archbishop Laurence Cyrille Tintamarre was the Archbishop of the region of Exeter and had fought hard to gain funding for his cathedral. The chapter fought him tooth and nail, for the members of the chapter did not want such an extravagant Gothic cathedral, flamboyant, they said, built in the diocesan *chantier* of Devonshire. He had won the chapter over once he himself had raised sufficient funds from his close friends and merchants to begin the rebuilding of the old Norman cathedral in the Gothic style. He always referred to it as his cathedral.

Master Architect Sigismond de Longchamp, originally from le Vendôme, had risen through the ranks in France and then managed to be incardinated in the English diocese of Wells, due to his fluency with the English language, but especially by his contacts with Cardinal Archbishop Abelard de Mornay of the Norman province of Fontenay-sur- mer affiliated with the Devonshire region in England.

Archbishop Tintamarre had anticipated the cardinal's red hat to be conferred by Pope Urban IV at a consistory proclaimed by the Vicar of Christ. This new pope had been elected in 1261 and was recognized for his education, his self-reliance, his ability to strike negotiations among the rulers of his day, such as the one with Charles of Anjou. The Archbishop did not hide the fact that he had expected this high honor, and that such an honor would redound on the clergy and the faithful of his diocese who had supported him in his efforts to build a cathedral. He had pulled strings to get to this point, and he did not want his determination to become a cardinal be spoiled by unwarranted or indeterminate factors. He was the type of man who planned every move and every calculation in his life. Everything, but everything, it seemed, happened according to his will, desires and plans. He considered himself to be a person blessed by good fortune through the good graces from God. And so, within a year of his papacy Urban IV had convoked a consistory and created fourteen new cardinals. Of these fourteen, seven were Frenchmen among who was Archbishop Laurence Cyrille Tintamarre. That was the year after Cajetan arrived in England.

Long before he had been made a cardinal, Cardinal Tintamarre had considered the fact that he would be given the red *galero*, this large broad-brimmed hat with elegant tassels, a ceremonial hat that would be on display in his cathedral after his death. It would hang in his cathedral in tangible memory of his tenure as Cardinal Archbishop where everyone could see it hanging way up there like a huge scarlet floating bird. He had formulated plans for his installation as cardinal with all of the pageantry associated with it. The *galero*, the *capa magna*, this very long cope of some fifteen meters in length, the ermine hood and, of course, his cardinal's coat of arms with the red *galero* on top, and with fifteen tassels on each side along with the motto and escutcheon. He had already formulated both in his mind: *Incarnatus sum in Domine,* and the blazon with azure, enté en point gules, a double-headed marten proper beneath a six-pointed star on a peninsula vert holding a vase pouring water into the sea argent beneath a crown proper with bands Or. He had taken his ideas for a blazon from the heraldic book of Vaticanus Proprio. Archbishop Tintamarre was a builder of high extravagance and a man of immeasurable appetite for vainglorious ideals. His cathedral was to be his mark of character set in stone.

Cajetan considered the Archbishop a little too haughty and somewhat capricious, but he went along with his wishes as carried out by Master de Longchamp. After all, Cajetan was a guest apprentice in the *chantier* of Devonshire. He had been sent to England by his Master in France with whom he had worked as an apprentice since the age of thirteen. Cajetan had been very fortunate to have had the privilege of sponsorship by Sir Knight Évrard de Châteauloup who held Cajetan's father in high esteem since, Philippon, Cajetan's father, lived in Sir Knight's domain, and had become favored by Sir Knight due his patience and diligent work with many of the serfs and laborers of the domain of Châteauloup. Philippon had mentioned, one day, to his master, that his son, Cajetan, had been dreaming of becoming an architect but that he lacked a worthy sponsor. Sir Knight took Cajetan under his wing and sent him to be educated and formed by the monks of Clairvaux in mathematics, geography, philosophy, and astrology enough to be trained as an apprentice later on. Cajetan was eight years old at the time. His mother, Grisoulda, thought that her child was much too young to leave home and live among an unknown group of men who prayed all the time. Philippon assured her that it was in the best interest of the boy, and that the parents had to start thinking about the future of their son. After all, Cajetan was going to a monastery where the finest of educators could be found, said Sir Knight Évrard de Châteauloup. Philippon had accepted his word as one who accepts the word of God.

Grisoulda Sansouterre was born in the family of the Sansouterres, father, Hubert Sansouterre and mother, Lydia de Rochefort from the town of Vénizerey. They lived in the domain of Sir Knight Henri de Sansouterre. Hubert came to be known as Hubert the Stargazer because he was a dreamer and liked to gaze at the stars at night while reminiscing about the sweet days of his youth when he loved to walk across the meadow and dream of becoming a builder of cathedrals. He did become an apprentice to Master Stone Cutter, Jéhan de Beauce, who taught him the craft of stone cutting. Hubert Sansouterre, the Stargazer, became known through the years as one of the best stone cutters in all of the Kingdom of France. He knew how to coax the stone into the shape that was in his head, and according to the architect's designs that were engraved in his creative mind. "Look at that," the other craftsmen would say, "Hubert cuts stone as a woman who cuts into butter, so easy and so well done that the carved stone seems to emerge out of its dull hard rock shell as a beautiful stone carving. He is a Master Stone Cutter, that one." It seemed that every architect wanted Hubert the Stargazer for his *chantier*.

Sir Knight Henri de Sansouterre had lived on his domain for thirty years and had sired three sons and one daughter. The oldest son was named Roland de Sansouterre while the other two sons were, Armand and Olifant, and their sister, Félicité. Their mother, Réjeanne de Valois, delighted in her children, except she had a hard time understanding her eldest son who seemed to exercise his strong will on everything from the way he would dress, the responses he would give her when she asked him for something and, worse, his entire attitude toward all of the laborers who worked on the domain. He was simply gruff and intolerant with everybody. Of course, he would tone down in front of his father, but he never ceased to be the rough and coarse man that he turned out to be. Even his own mother could not stand him. His brothers tolerated him as long as they were left alone, and the sister shied away from him and his antics.

With time. Roland de Sansouterre fell into disrepute and shamed his family with his wasteful deeds of plundering, thievery, perjury, venality and, worst of all, the disdainful treatment of maids, servants and all whom he wanted to do away with. He was truly a dissolute person. His mother called him, *mon fils, le débauché*. His father, Sir Knight Henri de Sansouterre, died when Roland was twenty-seven. Roland was to be his father's inheritor, but the Duke de Grainsaint, the domain's overlord, did not want the domain to be in the hands of Roland, the spoiler, as he became known. So the Duke decided to manage his own domain until such time he would find a reputable knight he could trust to manage the Sansouterre domain. Since Sir Knight Henri de Sansouterre was dead and his son was not to inherit the fief of the domain, Duke de Grainsaint changed the name of the domain to Hoguedonnay, the name of a favored maternal ancestor. Grisoulda's father, Hubert de Sansouterre, became known simply as Hubert Hoguedonnay.

Grisoulda's mother, Lydia de Rochefort, had been taught by the nuns of the convent of Marie Mère de Grâce et de Pureté in the valley of the Loire river. Lydia's family moved to the domain of Sir Knight Edmond de Tranchemontagne, a domain nearby the former Sansouterre domain. It was there that Lydia met Hubert Hoguedonnay, and they were married not long after. The mother had wanted a solemn wedding in a large church, or better, a cathedral, but it was not meant to be since the bishop did not want to be involved with a domain tainted by the Sansouterre name. So, Hubert and Lydia were married on the *parvis* of the little church of Sainte-Eulalie where relatives and friends congregated to celebrate the joyous occasion of a wedding.

Lydia's mother did not want her daughter to marry a stone cutter because she wanted someone more worthy of her daughter, she said. A stone cutter stargazer was not good enough as a spouse for her daughter, she told everyone. Lydia tried to convince her mother that a stone cutter's trade was a dignified and worthy craft, and that Hubert was an honest man, a person everyone trusted. When Hubert and Lydia Hoguedonnay set themselves up in their own abode, Hubert did not see his wife's mother too often. He liked it that way.

Lydia gave birth to a lovely girl the following spring. She had bright blondish-red hair and pink cheeks with deep blue eyes, and she smiled all the time. They gave her the name of Grisoulda after Hubert's grandmother who was the love of her grandson's life. It was she who raised him and his three siblings after their mother died, and the father had remarried to a woman who did not want the children. Hubert never liked his father after that. Lydia had three more children after Grisoulda, a daughter whom she named Marie Julienne after her understanding with her husband that she would be the one to name the second child. This one was truly a gift from God since Lydia had had a hard and difficult pregnancy with her second child. Next came a boy whom they baptized Antoine Joseph after Hubert's uncle, a writer of fabliaux and a troubadour of sorts. He entertained people, and they loved him and his art of working with words.

The fourth pregnancy was a most difficult one for Lydia, and when it was time to deliver the baby, the child was a still-born and the mother died not too long afterward, extremely fatigued and exhausted due to a loss of blood. Hubert was terribly grieved by this death. He so loved his Lydia, the woman of his life, the one he loved and cherished as a beautiful and precious star of the night. He did not want to remarry, and could not take care of his three children, so he farmed them out to relatives. Grisoulda went to live with Hubert's aunt Mistaine, in upper Picardie, Marie Julienne went to live in a town far away with a cousin who had no children, while Antoine Joseph was taken in by a close friend of Lydia, the Bernardins, who wanted to help out the best they could. Hubert was satisfied that he had done right by his children, and wanted a good future for all three of them. He would miss them, he said, but a man without a woman cannot bring them up the way a woman could. He told himself that he would help provide for them because he felt a certain responsibility to his daughters and his son.

Grisoulda never blamed her father for giving her to a relative, for she never felt abandoned by her father. Hubert had to do what he had to do, give all three of them a home and some comfort. She knew deep inside that her father loved her and would always have a place for her in his heart. That's what really made a family, she told herself, the love among father, mother and children. She told herself that when she married, she would make sure that her husband had enough love in his heart for her and an entire family. She wanted to have children that she herself could love and nourish with her own love and understanding. They would grow up bright, healthy and honest. Honesty was a cherished virtue for her, and she modeled it in her life, and especially in her struggles. With time, she became known as Honest Grisoulda.

Honest Grisoulda grew up to be a beautiful young woman who loved people and cats. She had a cat that she named Minou, a male cat, whom she dressed up in tiny clothes and paraded him around the village where she lived. Her father's aunt with whom she stayed, was a kindly old woman who thought that so much care lavished on a cat was a bit extravagant, but she enjoyed having Grisoulda with her, and supported her every whim. Grisoulda loved her great aunt Mistaine and did everything in her power to please her.

The old aunt wanted so very badly to have her niece, Grisoulda, meet a dignified and handsome young man when she grew up, and perhaps marry in the process. Above all, she wanted a young man who could provide for

Grisoulda. He had to be above-board, hard-working and a craftsman, at least an apprentice to one. In the meantime, Grisoulda met a Franciscan monk, Brother Abélard Marie, who became friend and confident. She used to go to the monastery chapel to pray every week, and talk to the monk who offered her sound advice about her life. He was a simple monk, always cheerful and humble in his own way. He did illuminations on the pages of certain manuscripts dealing with sacred scriptures and other holy texts preserved by the monks of the Franciscan community of Combry-sur-Falaise. One manuscript that Brother Abélard Marie liked to work on was the one about the life and good works of the founder, Francis of Assisi. He knew every detail of the saint's life, his stigmata, his living in poverty, his deep love for all of creation, great or small, and above all, his detachment from all worldly goods. That's why Brother Abélard Marie had joined the order called the Franciscans because he wanted to imitate the virtues and the life of Brother Francis of Assisi. He told Grisoulda that the saint had been canonized just two years after his death by Pope Gregory IX.

Grisoulda asked Brother Abélard Marie if he could show her some of the illuminations he had worked on. He answered her by a slight frown saying that no woman had ever penetrated inside the cloister since it was considered to be private and sacred. However, recapturing his sense of good cheer and humble pride in his works, he told her that he would get permission from his superior to bring some of the large texts in the chapel, and then he would be able to reveal to her the beautiful illuminations he had done. The following Friday after Tierce, Grisoulda sat in the quiet chapel of the Franciscans and awaited the coming of Brother Abélard Marie with his illuminations. While waiting, she uttered a short prayer to the Virgin Mother of God and asked her to guide her in the meeting and selection of a man who would become her husband. Grisoulda was now seventeen years old past the usual age of young women already married. Why, she thought to herself, even the Virgin Mary was married by the time she was fifteen.

Brother Abélard Marie finally arrived shuffling along in a bit of a hurry for he wanted to show Grisoulda the illuminations he had brought with him. He carried two big oversize volumes in his arms, and was a bit out of breath. He whispered to Grisoulda,

----Here they are, my dear friend in Christ. I have here two books, *Livre des Évangiles* and The Life of Saint Francis of Assisi, my very favorite.

----Why, they're so big, Brother Abélard Marie.

----All books dealing with illuminations are large, and sometimes very heavy. Take for example, the Bible, that's quite a heavy volume because there are so many pages. Many illuminations in that one. I like the one with Noah and the Flood as well as David and Goliath. Do you know the story of David and Goliath?

----Some of it because I see part of it in stone in the cathedral.

----Yes, in stone in the cathedral. That's a nice way of instructing the faithful about the Bible. Some call it the Bible in stone.

----I go there several times during the week just to be instructed in my faith because I have no one to teach it to me. I thank you for teaching me some of the things that I have learned so far.

----I will do my best to teach you, my child, for you need to know more about your own faith and the Church.

----I know.

----Well, let's see what we have here. The first one is about the gospels, you know, what the priest proclaims every Sunday at the pulpit. This is an illumination called "Christ in Majesty." It's the beginning of the gospel by John. "*Au commencement était le Verbe et le Verbe était avec Dieu, et le Verbe était Dieu. Il était au commencement avec Dieu.*" It's in French because the entire book of the gospels is in French. We have some in different languages, many of them in Latin. Of course you understand French. It's your language as taught to you by your mother, Lydia, and your father, Hubert the Stargazer. I like to call him that for he was indeed a stargazer and a dreamer.

----Yes, I remember. I love them both. I wish I was back with my father.

----Someday, perhaps. Now, as for the meaning of the words I have just given you in this gospel, they're quite simple and complex at the same time. They speak of Jesus as the Incarnated Christ, God the Son born of flesh and the Son of Mary. However, Saint John goes way back to the very beginning to what we call Genesis in the Bible, and speaks of the eternal presence, Christ, even from the very beginning of creation. Do you understand that?

----Yes, I do.

----Well, the gospel of Saint John uses the word "*Verbe*" because it's a word that denotes action and the power of coming into being. You see in Latin it's, "*Et Verbum caro factum est.*" The Word was made flesh. That's what we hear in our churches.

----But what does "made flesh" mean?

----It simply means being born, like you and me, we were born of flesh. We're human as He was human but He was also divine. He had two natures.

----I see.

----Moreover, all through the gospel of Saint John we see the theme of light and darkness. Out of darkness, we come to step into the light with Christ the Redeemer. Christ dismisses the darkness of sin, you see. The darkness of evil.

----Exactly what is evil?

----That requires a long explanation, and I'm not prepared to give it here and now. Later, we'll talk about evil. All I can tell you now is that evil exists, and it's the contrary to the good. You're a good person, Grisoulda. You're not evil.

----Is evil linked to the devils we see on the stones of the cathedral?

----Yes, in a way it is. At the beginning the devil tempted Eve and she tempted Adam so they fell into sin. They went against the will of God. That's what sin is.

----What is the will of God?

----That's another question that takes a long explanation.

----You see nobody ever gave me those explanations. I wonder about things all the time.

----I'll do my best to give them to you someday. Right now, I have these two books with illuminations that I will show and explain to you.

----Yes, please.

----First, here's the one called "Christ in Majesty." You know that He's the King of heaven and earth, His royal kingdom. Well, this represents Him in all of his majesty and royalty. He's surrounded by angels and their wings are all pointed upward, towards heaven. Christ is seated on his long blue throne, like a bench, and his right hand is lifted as in a blessing or as a teacher. He holds a gospel book in his left hand. He has a blue under robe and an over-mantle in red. The background is gold. We have to be careful how we handle the gold leaf for it's very delicate. The red is called cinnabar or vermillion while the blue is ultramarine or azurite. We, the scribes, work in a scriptorium each next to a window to have enough light to see what we are doing. On a cloudy day we work by candlelight. It's very fine work, meticulous work, and you need good eyes to do this. Some older monks go blind over the years doing this work. But, it's the work of God and we don't mind. Whatever happens is the will of God.

----Are you going blind?

9

----No, my child, I'm not. I'm not a full scribe. I only fill in when it is necessary. They appreciate my work. Well, the next one is part of the life of Saint Francis. There is still much more to know about him. Not everything about his life has been recorded yet. This book is the beginning of a master plan to record everything we, his brothers, know or will get to know about our saintly founder and brother in Christ.

----Was he a great saint?

----Yes, he was Grisoulda. One day the whole world will know about him and his humble work.

----Oh my! The whole world?

----Yes, the entire world. You see here in this illumination first his face. It's a saintly face, radiant with the light of the divine presence and in the fellowship of all the saints in heaven. That's what you can see here with all of the tiny faces surrounding Saint Francis. He shows his hands and the stigmata. His eyes are fixed on the crucifix that appeared to him in a vision.

----What are they, these stigmata?

----Stigmata? They're the marks of Christ's suffering on the cross, the places where the nails were, and where the Savior bled. He suffered a lot, Grisoulda.

----I know, I know. Sometimes standing in front of a crucifix I start crying for I know that he suffered much for us.

----You're a gentle and compassionate soul, Grisoulda.

----Everyone must feel something when they look at Christ crucified, don't you think?

----Not everyone does, my dear friend. Not everyone.

----Why not?

----Because not everyone recognizes the pain and suffering on the cross, and they could care less about religion and our faith.

----I care.

----I know. Now, let's see. Next we see the lead white of his garment. That's because we picture him as a saint in heaven. Do you like these two illuminations?

----Oh yes, very much. Are there many more?

----Yes, many more. I can't show you all of them. You're fortunate to be able to see these, for not everyone is allowed to see illuminations. These are on calf vellum, an expensive parchment to work on. We would not want anyone to steal these cherished manuscripts.

----Do all monks work on them?

----No. Just the trained and talented scribes.

----Oh, I see. Then you must be talented, Brother Abélard Marie.

----I'm just an ordinary man with a few humble talents. It's part of my duty as a Franciscan brother. Listen, Grisoulda, you had asked me about getting to know a good Christian man who would make a fine husband, and I believe I have a very good lead for you. Philippon is a good man, and he's looking for an honest woman to make him a home to which he would like to return every day.

----Really? Tell me about him. I want to get to know him as soon as I can for I am in a hurry to find a husband who will give me a home and a family.

----Wait a minute there, Grisoulda. Things like that don't happen in a flash, you know.

----But, if I can start right now, then I'll be saving time.

----First of all we have to arrange a meeting between the two of you. That will take some strategy on my part, but I think I can do that.

----What's his name again?

----Philippon, Philippon the apprentice to Master Joffre, the carpenter. In no time, they say, he'll be a journeyman. He's twenty-three years old.

----I'm seventeen. Will he have an older woman?

----You're not old, Grisoulda.

----But I'm past the ordinary age of getting married. I'm an old maid.

----No, you're not. You're vibrant and full of vigor. Besides, you're Grisoulda, the Honest woman, as they call you. You have the qualities of a good woman who will make a very able wife and mother.

----When can I meet him?

----Not so fast. I have to make arrangements. I'll let you know.

----Oh, I will pray the Blessed Virgin Mary with all my heart. The one in the cathedral, Our Lady of Succor.

----Saint Francis too.

----Yes, Saint Francis also.

2

GRISOULDA AND PHILIPPON, THE PARENTS

Grisoulda and Philippon were married in the chapel of the monastery where Brother Abélard Marie served as sacristan, sometimes porter, and part-time scribe. He had made the arrangements for them with a dispensation from his superior to be able to have the couple get married in the Franciscan chapel. Ordinarily, no one was admitted there especially for weddings and funerals, except members of the immediate Franciscan community. It was a quiet and lovely wedding with Grisoulda wearing her aunt's wedding silk garment with over lace, and a long magenta scarf that covered her head and shoulders. She carried fresh flowers from the fields that she herself had picked. There were mirabelles, red poppies, blue cornflowers and dainty lilies of the valley. Philippon wore his Sunday best and carried the staff of a Master Carpenter that his Master had lent him for the circumstance. He was so proud of the staff that he gleamed with joy simply looking at it. Grisoulda and Philippon were two proud people standing in front of the monk priest officiating at the marriage. Brother Abélard Marie stood next to them as an official witness.

Brother Abélard Marie had arranged for them to meet at the church fair in early May. Grisoulda met Philippon on the church grounds. It was a small church called Saint Agnes in upper Picardie. It was renowned for it's annual fair, and they both found each other compatible and friendly. Philippon was a man of dignity and trust, she thought after meeting him for the first time. He in turn thought that Grisoulda, Honest Grisoulda, was a woman worthy of him and he decided to see her again a second time, and offer her the story of his life. He then told her he was born in a small village beyond the mountains in the southeastern part of France, but that he did not remember too much about it since his family had moved away when he was but two years old. They moved to Laon, and at the age of thirteen, he started to work as a carpenter's apprentice, but soon found himself out of work since the Master Carpenter had failed to renew his contract with the guild. He floundered around and fell into the wrong crowd and began to steal money from rich people who hired him as a tender of their wares. He then moved to the outskirts of Amiens and there he met Brother Abélard Marie who took him under his wing. He watched over Philippon like a mother hen, and gave him advice about turning things around in his young life, and even introduced him to Master Carpenter, Joffre Jeffroy. He vouched for him and begged some of his friends to give the boy enough money to begin his apprenticeship. Brother Abélard Marie had a way about him that made people listen to him and fulfill his requests. He was a people convincer. It was never for himself, always for others. Philippon was fourteen at the time.

Within a year after their marriage in 1246, Grisoulda gave birth to a son that the father insisted on calling, Cajetan, after his grandfather, Cajetan Léon, the mountain climber. He always was reaching for the heights, and died a happy death after many years of mountain climbing. He would tell his grandson, Philippon, tales of mountain climbing and adventures of braving the raging wind and the conquering of new heights. Philippon loved his grandfather and wanted his son to bear his name. Grisoulda had wanted to name him Dieudonné, since she thought he was truly a gift of God as the name indicates, but she yielded to her husband since the naming of the first-born son was the father's prerogative.

When the second child arrived, Grisoulda lost no time in naming her Marie Dieudonnée. The child was a Sunday's child, a child filled with grace, and destined to become a woman of endless gifts and talents. She will be my gift to God and I will offer her up to Him as *une obole de graces et de simplicité*, an offering of graces and simplicity, she told herself. Surely she would be destined for a renowned monastery or a convent where she could flourish in the sight of the Lord and under the tutelage of Mary the Mother of God. Grisoulda convinced herself of the idea of the gift-giving mother who is grateful for giving life by reciprocating and giving it back to the Lord Creator. Grisoulda was grateful for a good husband, a good marriage, a good home and two children. What more could she ask for, she thought over and over again. Her husband adored the two children and seemed to favor Cajetan, for he saw in him a bright future as a Master Carpenter or a Master Mason, someone with a dependable craft. Grisoulda, on the other hand, wished for a more idealistic future for her son. She wanted him to grow up like her father, Hubert the Stargazer, an honest man and a man of ideals and dreams. When she told her husband about her thoughts and Cajetan, he smiled and told her that she was dreaming, and was not realistic enough with young people's lives.

"Dreams are just that dreams," he told her. "You have to face the reality of things, Grisoulda. Dreams don't put bread on the table." Grisoulda then realized that she could never convince her husband of the marvelous gift of dreams in one's life, and that her father was a splendid example of both dreams and reality. Hubert the Stargazer, Hubert the Stone Cutter of cathedrals. She told herself that gazing at the stars does not mean that one is foolish, but that one is filled with the graces of the Lord who created the stars and put them in His heaven. Those who gaze at the stars are those who go beyond the reach of human destiny, she told herself. She was convinced of that. Cathedral builders were somewhat like that, she mused. Dreamers.

After the birth of Marie Dieudonnée, Grisoulda had two other children. However, one died in childbirth and the other, a little girl, died just after two weeks of her birth. She had a strange disease that contorted her little body and made her scream all night long. They were both buried in the church cemetery. Grisoulda cried for days for she had wanted another girl. A year or two after the death of her fourth delivery, Grisoulda conceived another boy and she named him Abélard François, after Brother Abélard Marie and Saint Francis. Cajetan had a brother and Marie Dieudonnée a playmate.

Cajetan grew up with vim and vigor. He sprouted like a tall weed that one notices in the fields, first short and out of sight but then in the wink of an eye, a tall stalk that one cannot fail to see. Although Cajetan was his father's chosen delight, Marie Dieudonnée turned out to be her father's favored child, a young and pretty girl, the delight of his soul. As for Abélard François, well, he was *un enfant à part*, an independent child who played by himself and never bothered with others. Grisoulda wondered what he was to become this son of hers who was "apart." Philippon used to reassure her that there was nothing wrong with the youngest child, he simply was like that, "apart" and he would find his way some day. Every child finds his way somehow or other.

One night after a very hard day's work, while everyone was sleeping, Grisoulda got up, went to the kitchen and got herself some hot water in which she put some herbs and honey. She had gotten the herbs from the local healer, Geneviève la Guérisseuse. Both she and la Guérisseuse had created a bond between them and Grisoulda trusted implicitly this healer. That night Grisoulda felt awful. She was very sick. She had not been feeling well for days but had ignored it thinking that it would go away. No one knew about it, not even her husband. Now it had gotten worse. She could hardly swallow her drink. Everything spun around in her head. She became faint and dropped to the floor. They found her in the morning lifeless. Philippon went to get the local healer, and having looked and examined Grisoulda, she pronounced her dead.

Philippon grieved over Grisoulda a very long time. He stopped eating and even stopped his work with the carpenter until two weeks into his grieving, Joffre the Master Carpenter threatened Philippon to take him off his roll. The children felt very sad having lost a mother with a father who had become hollow inside. The neighbor, Anne-Marie Delasanté, came every day to take care of the children. She fed them while encouraging Philippon to come out of his shell of mourning. She scolded him and made him realize that he had to take charge and go back to work for the family needed the money to live on. Brother Abélard Marie came several times to pray over Philippon, and urged him to think of his children first, for there was nothing to be done about Grisoulda, except to pray for her soul. Finally, Philippon snapped out of his mournful torpor and returned to his work as a journeyman carpenter.

Knowing that he could not raise a family of three alone, Philippon called on his cousin, Eugénie, to take care of his three children. So that no impropriety could even be sensed or attributed to this move, Philippon moved out of the house and went to live at an inn not too far away so that he was able to visit the children quite often.

Cajetan loved the cousin and as he grew up, he tried to help her out as much as he could. He swept the house, brought in the firewood and kept himself clean and tidy. She told him stories about cathedral building since her brother was a journeyman to a Master Architect in Laon. Cajetan confided to her that cathedral building had been his dream ever since he was a very young child, and that he had told his mother about it. The cousin encouraged him to continue dreaming since dreams are often realized. "Pray, Cajetan, so that your dreams of building a cathedral will, one day, be fulfilled." "But how will I be able to get a sponsor to become an apprentice?" he asked her. "By being patient and asking God to help you. Go to the cathedral and pray in front of the statue of Our Lady of Succor as your poor mother did so often."

One day, a year after Grisoulda had died, Philippon visited his son as he usually did every week, and asked him what he wanted to do in life. Cajetan replied that he wanted to be a builder of cathedrals, an architect, but that he had no sponsor and did not think he would ever be able to get one since he had no important contacts, and he was the son of a poor but worthy man.

----But I am not poor, my son, replied the father. I have my family, my craft as a carpenter and I will someday become a Master Carpenter, Master Joffre told me.

----When, father?

----Soon, my son, soon, I hope. Then I will be earning an honest wage better than the wage I earn as a journeyman, and support my family as a man should. Thank God for your mother who worked so hard to help me support our family. She washed clothes for others, made jams from the fruits she collected during the spring and summer months, and candies with honey and nuts that she sold at the church fair while practically begging for enough money to live on at inns and public houses. I did not like her doing that but we were living poorly. I got a few coins from Master Joffre since he knew I needed more money to support a family. And thanks to your sweet mother, who has now passed on, that we survived.

----Some day, I'll be an apprentice and then a journeyman too, and I'll help out, father, I swear by the sacred wounds of Christ.

----Listen, my son, I have great news for you. I know how badly you have been desiring to have your dream fulfilled, that of becoming an apprentice to a Master Architect. You're still young but I did some work, some excellent work, if I may say so, for Sir Knight Évrard de Châteauloup from the manor of his lord, the Duke of Blanford. He was so pleased with my work that he asked me if there was something he could do for me. I told him about you, Cajetan, about your dream of becoming an architect and getting an apprenticeship with some Master Architect. He asked me how old you were and I told him eleven going on twelve. Am I not right?

----Yes, father. But, is he going to follow through?

----Of course, Cajetan. He's going to contact his very good friend, Maître Albert de Chaussoyes. He's a well-known architect. He's presently at work in the Reims *chantier*. Would you like to work with him and study under him?

----Of course, yes, indeed, that would be my opening to the world of the cathedral builder, the world of my dreams.

----I have seen you dream and gaze at the stars just like your grandfather, Hubert Hoguedonnay. You are indeed a stargazer, a dreamer. Just make sure that you keep your head screwed on well and tight. You must learn to be a practical man besides being a dreamer.

----I know father, but mother always told me to hold on to my dreams. I was quite young when she died, and I don't remember everything she said to me but I remember that.

----Yes, your gentle mother, God bless her soul which is now in heaven. Your mother was a good and honest woman who had all of the generosity of a kind person has in her heart, a saintly woman.

----I know that mother is looking down from heaven on me and is guiding me on my path to being an architect. Her father too, the Stargazer.

----Yes, the Stargazer like you.

----Oh, father, I'm so excited about the news that I don't know if I'll be able to sleep tonight.

----Don't lose sleep over it. I'm sure that Sir Knight de Châteauloup will get you the apprenticeship. He has many contacts, and is well placed to get what he wants. But, it will take time.

----Thank him for me, father.

----You will be able to thank him yourself when you meet him.

Within a year and a half, Cajetan learned from his father that Sir Knight Évrard de Châteauloup had gotten Cajetan the apprenticeship that he so wanted. He even supplied the money to get him started since an apprentice did not earn any wages. All he got was his food, his clothing and housing in and around the *chantier*. Sometimes an apprentice slept in the master's attic and was fed by the mistress. Cajetan finally met Sir Knight and thanked him profusely, so that Sir Knight had to stop him and tell him what he had to do next. First, Cajetan had to prepare himself for the journey to Reims and then gather his belongings, which were few, and find a way to get there. First, he said goodbye to his sister and to his younger brother, then to his father. Of course, he did tell cousin, Eugénie, how much he appreciated the care that she had given him, and the encouragement to become an apprentice to a Master Architect. Once he had said his goodbyes, he then went to see Brother Abélard Marie, his mother's Franciscan friend, and told him how much he enjoyed his friendship, and how well he retained all of the advice Brother had given him since Grisoulda's death. Brother Abélard Marie wished him well and gave him his blessings. He told Cajetan that he had met Archbishop Aubry de Humbert, who laid the foundation stone of the Reims cathedral in May 1211. That was before he joined the order. He also remembered well the destructive fire of 1210 that had burned down the second building that was the cathedral. The fire had also partly destroyed the town center of Reims itself. "What a tragedy," said the Brother to Cajetan. "What a terrible incident in the history of the building of cathedrals. But you must remember that those old and dried timbers catch fire very easily."

Cajetan found himself a ride to the Reims *chantier* when this old trader of wares offered him transportation since he was going that way. Cajetan quickly jumped on the cart, and since he had very few belongings, he placed himself very easily alongside the old driver of the cart. The horse trotted away, and the old man was very talkative so that Cajetan could hardly put a word in edgewise. Cajetan ate his lunch, and later on his supper while the cart was in motion. The old man hardly stopped along the way except to answer to the call of nature. They got to Reims in fourteen hours and Cajetan was overjoyed to see the cathedral of Notre-Dame de Reims.

There had been many struggles before the cathedral was finally rebuilt. In 1233 , a long-running dispute between the cathedral chapter and the townsfolk boiled over into an open revolt. It was a question of taxation and legal jurisdiction. Several clerics were killed or injured during the resulting violence, and the entire cathedral chapter fled the city, leaving it under interdict thus effectively banning all public worship and sacraments. Work on the new cathedral was suspended for three years, only resuming in 1236 after the clergy returned to the city, and the interdict was lifted following mediation by the King and the Pope. Construction then continued but more slowly. When Cajetan arrived there in 1259 the nave had not yet been roofed.

Having just arrived on the *chantier,* Cajetan wasted no time to introduce himself to Master Architect, Albert de Chaussoyes, and proceeded to find himself lodging with the help of Maniple Chrétien, the clerk of the works. He was going to share part of a small dwelling with another apprentice, Rielbert Hardgrave from Canterbury. He found Rielbert not too friendly and closed-mouthed. Cajetan did not care what the other fellow did or how he behaved as long as he, Cajetan, was free to roam about and learn the trade of architect from the Master. Rielbert told Cajetan, in no uncertain terms, not to get in his way for he wanted first priority in the learning process from the Master. Cajetan told him that he did not mind that, and that he would follow whatever instructions the Master would give him without interfering with Rielbert. Cajetan found the other apprentice mean and distrustful after only a few hours with him. He himself had learned to trust others and be trustworthy and honest, and he could not understand why a person like Rielbert was so hard of heart.

After a good night's sleep, Cajetan was ready to go to work. He was brimming over with enthusiasm and pride in the *métier* that was going to be his. When he left the house, Rielbert was still sleeping soundly. Cajetan wondered if he should wake him, but on the other hand, did not dare do so for he was afraid that he would be yelled at. Maître de Chaussoyes was an affable young-looking man in his late thirties with reddish hair, brown eyes and a warm smile on his lips. Cajetan liked him as soon as he first met him. He felt somewhat at home. Better than the reception he had gotten from the apprentice, Rielbert. The Master Architect showed Cajetan around and made him meet the other masters of trades such as, the carpenter, the mason, the sculptor and the stone cutter. Cajetan told the Master Stone Cutter that his grandfather on his mother's side was a stone cutter, and that they called him Hubert the Stargazer. The Master Stone Cutter told Cajetan that he remembered his own father talking about such a man since the father had worked on several *chantiers*. It was then that Cajetan realized that his grandfather was well-known among the craftsmen of the guilds.

After a short while, Rielbert came running out of breath and yelled at Cajetan, why he had not woken him before he left. Master Architect de Chaussoyes stopped Rielbert from chiding his *confrère* since getting up on time in the morning was his responsibility.

----Besides, he told him, if you had been nicer to Cajetan, I'm sure he would have bothered to wake you.

----How did you know how Rielbert treated me?

----He does that to all of my apprentices. I lost three on account of him. I only keep him because I made a promise to his uncle whom I know personally, and who's not at all like his nephew.

----How long has Rielbert been at this *chantier*?

----Three years.

----How much longer before he becomes a journeyman?

----I don't even know if he'll make it. He doesn't have the will nor the determination to become an architect, not to mention the skills.

----Then, why is he an apprentice architect?

----Nobody else will have him, and because his uncle is the one who is financing him.

----That's too bad. Such wasted talent and time.

----Not wasted talent, just wasted time and energy. He will self-destroy with time, wait and see. Stay away from him, Cajetan.

Cajetan went back to his work mindful of his own sense of pride and passion for the *métier d'architecte*.

The following day, when the sun had just risen in the east, Cajetan went to the front of the cathedral and saw that the men were working on the façade, specifically on the central portal dedicated to the Virgin Mary that was to be surmounted by a rose window framed in an arch decorated with statuary in place of the usual tympanum. Maître de Chaussoyes explained to Cajetan the meaning of the terminology associated with cathedrals such as, the tympanum, the recessed space, usually triangular, enclosed by the slanting cornices of a pediment often ornamented with sculpture.

----Above the statuary will be the "gallery of the kings" showing the baptism of Clovis in the center, flanked by statues of his successors. The façade of the North transept will have a representation of the Last Judgment and a figure of Christ as *Le Bon Dieu*. That's all in the plans, my plans as architect of this cathedral. However, I'm not the only planner and designer of this building. There's also four Master Masons who contributed significantly to the construction of Notre-Dame de Reims. They're Jean d'Orbais, Jean-Le-Loup, Gaucher de Reims and Bernard de Soissons. Great masters in their trade. You will find their names in the labyrinth built into the floor of the nave.

----What's a nave and what's a labyrinth? I'm afraid I'm new at this. I don't know all of the terms associated with a cathedral.

----Well, a nave is that part which is between the side aisles and extends from the chancel to the principal entrance. A labyrinth is a maze, an intricate enclosure containing a series of winding passages hard to follow without getting lost. The model of all labyrinths is the one in the Greek legend designed by Daedalus for King Minos of Crete to house the Minotaur. Are you familiar with the Greek legends?

----No. I'm afraid I'm ignorant about many things known to educated people.

----Of course you're not familiar with such things. I shouldn't have asked you that. However, later on, I'll tell you all about Greek myths and legends. They're my favorites. I will also show you the labyrinth of Reims cathedral a little later on. You will see how intricate the pattern is.

----Why a labyrinth in a church?

----No one really knows. There are some like Chartres Cathedral and others I'm not familiar with. Some say that the labyrinth is linked to pilgrims and pilgrimages. It's a way of finding God in a maze of challenges, like the intricate paths in all of our lives. It's good that you ask questions, Cajetan, you have an inquisitive mind. I like that.

----Thank you, Master. You are so kind to teach me and be patient with me.

----You're also polite and well behaved, Cajetan. You must have had a good mother to teach you how to behave properly.

----Yes, her name was Grisoulda.

Cajetan truly liked the Master Architect for he was open and friendly. Cajetan felt assured that he would certainly learn much from him. There was so much to learn and so much to see. He was glad that his mother had taught him how to read and write. She had done the same with Marie Dieudonnée. What a clever woman she was. Now he could take notes about everything in his notebook that cousin Eugénie had given him as a going away present. So much to learn and so many terms, and so many ideas about cathedrals and Gothic architecture. I'll have to take time at night to write down everything I learn during the day, he told himself.

The months went by and spring turned into summer, summer into fall. Cajetan was by now quite conversant with the trade of the architect as well as the mason, and even the stone cutter. What he wanted to do next was to find out more about stone sculpture. The sculptor in a cathedral is a very important craftsman since he embellishes and gives life to almost everything he touches. He's a true artist, not that the architect isn't, Cajetan thought. The sculptor turns stone into shapes and forms, figures and faces of saints, Prophets, angels, statues of Mary, tympanums with God the Creator and Jesus at Judgment time. He even carves out devils and monsters to induce fear in the people who study the cathedral as Bible. With his chisel and his hammer, he makes stone come alive like *le Beau Dieu* on the façade of North transept. What a marvelous figure of Jesus that is, he said to himself out loud. What a marvelous work of art!

Cajetan then went to that part of the *chantier* where the stone cutters and sculptors worked. He introduced himself to a man who looked to be in his forties or fifties. Cajetan could not make out his age. He knew that the man was old, for a person in his forties or fifties looks old to a thirteen and a half year old. Cajetan looked older than his young years and had a remarkable maturity for his age. He was open and honest and spoke to anyone and everybody. He had an inquisitive mind and learned fast. His bright smile opened up many a conversation be it with a friend or stranger. People back home said that he was like his mother, Grisoulda, always frank, open and honest with people. The man asked him who he was and what was he doing in the *chantier*. Cajetan told him his name, his being an apprentice under Maître de Chaussoyes, and that he was very interested in sculpture.

----Well, my young man, I'm Timon Chenovert and I'm a stone sculptor. I'm in the process of carving this tall piece of stone that will become a full-length angel. It will go in the Northern doorway. I'll not only give her wings but a beautiful smile. She'll have a mantle with a clasp over a long flowing robe. She's going to be a really nice lady angel.

----But I thought all angels were men. That's how I saw them in and out of our cathedral back home.

----I know, and that's how most sculptors make them out to be, males. But I believe that there are lady angels, and they're beautiful messengers of God. That's what angels are you know. Messengers of God.

----Oh, I didn't know that.

----How old are you?

----Thirteen going on fourteen.

----Did you ever have a special relationship with a girl?

Cajetan blushed a little before he answered the man.

----No. I was too young. None except my mother who was a very special lady. I do have a sister named Marie Dieudonnée. She's a pretty girl and I love her. She's my sister.

----Well, someday you'll have a girlfriend and you will probably fall for her and perhaps marry her someday. You do like girls, don't you?

----Yes. But first of all, I have to go through my apprenticeship and then go on to being a journeyman. That takes time, you know.

----I know, I know. I've been through all of that. I'm a Master Sculptor and I have been working with my chisel and hammer for some twenty-two years. I had to create a masterpiece as a journeyman in order to qualify for my admission into the *corps de métiers,* the guilds. Did you know that it takes two to seven years to become a journeyman. Usually, at least seven for most apprentices.

----I plan to qualify for the journeyman status in less than six years. I'm going to work real hard at it, and I have a good Master.

----An apprentice can use the tools that are provided by the Master but the journeyman must provide his own tools and materials. That costs money.

----How much?

----A lot for the small wages he earns. But later, he'll be able to earn more as he gets more and more experience. A journeyman can travel taking with him a letter of introduction from his Master, stating that he can learn skills related to his craft from other masters. He can farm himself out.

----I see.

----With time the guild's members rate the talent of a journeyman by evaluating his masterpiece. This showcase project often takes years to complete since only Sundays can be used to pursue personal work.

----How many Sundays did it take you for your masterpiece project?

----Many, many Sundays, too many to count them. At least two years and a half of Sundays. It was a long project, but I loved it.

----What exactly was your project?

----It was an angel. You see I love angels, and they love me because they look down on me and watch over me. I remember once I got into an accident. A huge stone fell right next to me injuring my right foot. It could have fallen on my head and killed me. I'm sure that my guardian angel was protecting me. Judith, I call her. Have you given your guardian angel an name?

----Why, no. I know I have one because Brother Abélard Marie, he's a Franciscan, told me I had one, but he never told me I had to give him a name.

----Are you sure he's a he and not a she?

----What do you mean?

----That your guardian angel is a woman rather than a man?

----I never thought of it that way. It might be a woman. Then I would name her Grisoulda like my mother. She's in heaven, you know.

----That's what I'm going to name my angel with a smile, Grisoulda. When she's all done, you can come and visit her on the Northern doorway, tall, proud, beautiful and smiling.

----I certainly will. By the way, where's your masterpiece angel now?

----At Notre-Dame de Paris. I couldn't give her a smile because my master insisted that all angels had to be serious. Serious business, angels are, he told me. However, I did put her left hand up in a sort of a wave, as if she's waving to people who look at her. The Master thought it was a hand lifted toward heaven, but I knew better.

Rielbert was mad, real mad. He had lost the tool that Maître de Chaussoyes had provided him for a study of a miniature cathedral, a compass used in drafting a plan for a cathedral. Rielbert yelled at everybody and specifically at Cajetan. Maître de Chaussoyes told Rielbert to calm down and look in his possessions to see that it wasn't there, somewhere. Possibly had he misplaced it? The Master knew that Rielbert had a temper, and often lost it like he did with things. He told himself that Rielbert could not be trusted with any tool. That was evident to him. A week after Rielbert claimed to have lost the compass, he then accused Cajetan of having stolen it. He went to the clerk of the works and told him to search Cajetan's possessions. The compass must be there, he was sure. When Cajetan heard about this, he incessantly proclaimed for all to hear that he swore he had never set hands on the instrument, and that Rielbert was lying. Cajetan had searched all of his own possessions the night before and did not find any compass. He told the Master and the clerk about it. "Search for yourselves if you don't believe me," he said. The Master sent the clerk to search Cajetan's possessions just to render justice to both Rielbert's and Cajetan's word on the matter. The clerk went to the lodging where the two apprentices lived, and started looking into Cajetan's belongings. Lo and behold! He found the missing compass in a pouch where Cajetan kept his Bible and a silver broach that his mother had given him as a memento of her affection for her older son.

----No. It wasn't there last night. I did not steal it. I did not. Someone must have put it there when I wasn't looking...and he kept looking at Rielbert.

----Don't look at me that way. I'm not the one. This proves that you stole it from me.

----I did not steal it. I'm an honest person, I'll have you know.

----You mean like your mother, Honest Grisoulda? Sure, she was as honest as a thief in the night.

Cajetan's face got red, as red as a cockscomb. He was angry, oh, was he angry. It showed in his eyes. Cajetan never got angry but when he did it showed all over his face. Seeing this mêlée of words, Maître de Chaussoyes insisted that the two apprentices quiet down and ordered them to each go to the Master's quarters, one after the other, because he wanted to talk to each one of them separately. Rielbert walked away with a grin on his face, a grin of contempt and triumph while Cajetan walked slowly, sheepishly, with his tail between his legs, and with tears in his eyes.

Maître de Chaussoyes met with Rielbert first. Rielbert appeared to be miffed by the fact that the Master dared to question him since he was the accuser and not the accused.

----Rielbert, I've had you with me for three years now and I've yet to see good things coming from you.

----What do you mean?

----Everyone with whom you come in contact, tells me that you're an insolent, jealous, dishonest young man. If I'm to believe everything that was said to me on your account, I'd have you thrown in jail. I have not done anything as of yet on account of your uncle who is a very good friend of mine. You know that.

----Are you accusing me of something? If so, tell me and stop playing the game of rumors about me.

----I'm accusing you of stealing a compass and planting it in Cajetan's possessions while my compass remains in yours. You deliberately lied to me and, who knows, you probably intended to rob me of my compass since it's made out of silver with a crown as a hallmark right beneath the pivot. I know my compass, and that's not the one in Cajetan's possession. It's another one. How could you deal with me that way, and how could you blame poor Cajetan for your mischief? You're a coward and a thief. I'm dismissing you right now. Get your possessions and good riddance.

----My uncle will hear of this, I'll let you know. You're the coward for letting a fraud like Cajetan work for you. He's a dirty Frenchman and Frenchmen don't know how to really be craftsmen. The English are better at it. I'm better than Cajetan, the little brown-noser.

----I'll have you know that many Frenchmen are terribly good craftsmen, and all you have to do is to look at their accomplishments in Chartres, Paris, Amiens and so many other centers of culture.

----I, I.....

----Not a single word from you. I've had enough.

Reilbert stormed out of the Master's quarters letting the door slam behind him. The Master then talked to Cajetan privately and told him the entire story, that the compass in Cajetan's possessions was not the Master's compass but one planted there by Rielbert. The Master's compass had a hallmark that the other one did not have, and that this one was in Rielbert's possession. Hidden in his trove of stolen goods discovered by the clerk.

----You're an honest young man, Cajetan, and you should be proud of that. I'm going to keep you under my tutelage because I admire you and I want you to succeed.

----Thank you, Master, thank you very much.

----Now, go to your lodging and get some rest because tomorrow we're going to Paris to view Notre-Dame de Paris cathedral. Maybe, if we have time, we could then go to Amiens. Would you like that? Notre-Dame de Paris is not essentially finished yet, but there is enough there for us to see and appreciate.

----Oh, yes. Oh, yes, I'd love to see it.

And Cajetan had stars in his eyes.

----You'll make a good architect, Cajetan because you have dreams and cathedrals are made of dreams. I know.

3

NOTRE-DAME DE PARIS
AND NOTRE-DAME D'AMIENS

Notre-Dame de Paris stood majestically on its own site of l'Île-de-la-Cité. The site was filled with the radiance of roses and the newness of a Gothic cathedral being built by master craftsmen. Groundbreaking was held in 1163. Several houses were demolished to make room for the construction, and a new road was built in order to transport materials to the construction site. Both Bishop Maurice de Sully and Pope Alexander III were present at the laying of the foundation stone. Bishop Sully spent the rest of his life raising funds for the cathedral and promoting its splendor-to-be. Master de Chaussoyes went on to explain to Cajetan that the choir took from 1163 to around 1177, fourteen years, and the high altar was consecrated five years later.

----You see, Cajetan, a church is built in the form of a cross and the head of the cross must face east. It's customary for the eastern end of a church to be completed first, so that a temporary wall can be erected west of the choir, allowing the chapter to use it without interruption while the rest of the building slowly takes shape. That's what happened here.

----Did Bishop Sully see the completion of the transepts?

----No, he died in 1196 and his successor finished that work. The successor then pressed forward with the nave, which was nearing completion when he died in 1208. As for the western façade, it was completed around the mid 1240's.

----What happened then?

----The most significant change in design came in around the 1250's when the transepts were remodeled in the latest Rayonnant style. You know what I mean by the Rayonnant style? We talked about it just last week.

----Yes, I do. It means that the style is much more elaborate and ornamental with motifs that flourish and captivate the artistic imagination. Isn't that right, Maître de Chaussoyes?

----Precisely the very words I used. You're sharp and with a very good memory. Now, in the late 1240's Jean de Chelles, I knew him, added a gabled portal to the north transept topped off by a spectacular rose window. That's the one we're standing in front, right here. See the splendor of this window? Magnificent! I only wish we can put one like it in our cathedral.

----You think so?

----I hope so. That's if the chapter can find enough funds to finance such a project.

----You keep telling me that the Archbishop will find the money for whatever he deems important to his cathedral.

----Yes, I did say that, but the Archbishop has other problems right now. I'm not at liberty to tell you about them.

----Are they big problems?

----Big enough. Let's get back to Notre-Dame de Paris. Shortly afterwards, around 1258, that was three years ago, Pierre de Montreuil executed a similar scheme on the south transept. Both these transept portals are richly embellished with sculptures. The south portal features scenes from the lives of Saint Stephen and of various local saints. The north portal features the infancy of Christ and the story of Theophilus in the tympanum. Do you know the story of Theophilus?

----No.

----Remind me to tell it to you someday, a very interesting tale about a saintly man and a pact with the devil.

----Oh!

----In 1250, the Western Towers and North Rose window were finalized. That's what you see today. The cathedral is not yet completed and it may take several years to finish it, because there are many elements to be completed.

----Like what?

----Like the remaining sculpture program and the rest of the glaziery.

----You mean the windows with colored glass?

----Yes. Now, let's look at this North Rose window up close. You want to?

----Yes. I love the colors and the shapes of the many pieces of glass. It must be quite a puzzle to put all the pieces together to form one whole unit.

----That's the craft of the glaziers. They're a pretty exclusive bunch of men for they just don't let anybody in. You have to be quite talented to join their guild. Besides, it's not an easy craft, you know. You have to know glass blowing to begin with. Then, you have to rotate the blown glass to make it flat. And first of all, you have to know how to make glass. They take vegetable ashes and mix it with sand from the river and some potassic element to make the mixture strong. Then they fire it until it comes out as glass. I've only seen the procedure once. It's really a challenge. Then, comes the cutting. They used to put it on a large table covered with chalk and proceeded to mark the patterns. But, now they use patterns made of cloth. It's much easier that way, and not so messy. Once they have the desired patterns, they cut the glass very carefully according to the patterns ready for the paint. It takes a real artist to do this work. One who can paint designs, faces and figures of the human body with garments. They put the pieces on a large glass in order to assemble them in the right order, and then they proceed to paint them. After the procedure is done, all of the painted pieces have to be fired in an oven of some 600 degrees. Then, once it's done and cooled, the lead is prepared for the assembling and positioning of the pieces on the windows. It's a long and, at times, difficult process, but what a wonder of glass and light.

----What's a potassic element?

----It's a strong white crystal used in the making of glass.

----Are there many glaziers in the *chantiers*?

----In ours, we have about eighteen. In others, there may be up to twenty or even twenty-four.

----When we get back, I want to go and look at our glaziers working.

----The Master Glazier's name is François Bellicourt. He's truly a master at his craft.

----I love to watch all of the craftsmen doing their work. That way, I learn about the making of a cathedral.

----That's a wise thing to do, Cajetan. A prudent thing since one has to prepare for it, not just one's specific task as a craftsman but all of the crafts utilized in the building of a cathedral, especially if you want to become an architect, a Master Architect.

----That is my dream.

----Keep gazing at the stars and the wonders of cathedral building as you are wont to do.

Maître de Chaussoyes and Cajetan then proceeded to go and stand in front of the rose window of the north transept, the first one to be installed at Notre-Dame de Paris.

----Amazing! said Cajetan.

----Yes, a truly amazing grasp of light although, at this time of day, the brightness of daylight is subdued. Look at the filtering of colors with a definite color scheme, the highlight of the color violet and mauve. Although there are several colors in the patterns, the colors of violet and mauve seem to dominate the lancets. In the center oculus, that's Latin for eye, you can see the image of the Virgin Mary enthroned holding the Christ Child. Surrounding them are Old Testament Kings and Prophets. We could stand here all day and try to identify them.

----I'd like to do that but I know we don't have too much time.

----Let's look at the south rose window now.

They crossed the nave to stand in front of the south rose. Once again, they were awed at the sight with a brighter daylight luminosity coming through the window, and casting a wondrous ambience.

----Look at that, Cajetan. Isn't it marvelous? What a wonder of light, color and awe-inspiring intensity. The glaziers have truly succeeded in replicating the mystery of colored glass in a Gothic cathedral. Not that the north rose isn't a wonder, but I prefer the hues of coloration in the south rose. Notice the ambience that's produced by the rose and the blue, a delicate and captivating essence of coloration. Every time I come to Notre-Dame de Paris, I never miss coming here in front of the south rose and stare at it for a long time, if not for hours, sometimes. I'm so captivated by it that I feel as if I'm in a trance.

----I love it too. It's become my favorite now that I see it, although I haven't seen too many rose windows.

----Let's examine this one closely. It's dedicated to the New Testament. It's divided in four circles. The twelve apostles are part of the first circle. In all of the four circles we can see saints and martyrs as well as the wise and foolish virgins.

----Who are the wise and foolish virgins?

----They're the ten virgins of the parable in the gospels. Five who were wise and five who were foolish because they forgot to bring extra burning oil for their lamps awaiting the coming of the Master.

----I see.

----You see also Lawrence, the deacon, holding the grill he was martyred on. Then there's Denis, the first bishop of Paris holding his head.

----Holding his head?

----Yes. He was martyred, and his head was cut off, but he rose from the river carrying his head. It's a legend.

----Oh.

----Then there's Marguerite and a dragon, then George, Ambrose and others. I don't know them all, and you certainly don't know them either.

----There must be a lot of saints in heaven, and the builders of this cathedral know many.

----Yes, of course.

----In the fourth circle, you see over there? There are around twenty angels each carrying a candle, two crowns and a censer, as well as scenes from the Old and the New Testaments: the flight into Egypt, the healing of the paralytic, the Judgment of Solomon, the Annunciation and more. At the edges, there are two corner pieces, the one to the east represents the Descent into Hell, surrounded by Moses and Aaron and the temptation of Eve.

----I know about the temptation of Eve by the devil.

----Yes. Then, the Resurrection of Christ to the west with Saints Peter and Paul and Sainte Madeleine at the top.

----I see. Wow! There's certainly a lot to learn about the Bible and the saints.

----Yes, there is. But you will learn about them gradually as you go along in life on your path of the stars, and the way to becoming an architect. Keep reading your Bible, Cajetan.

----I do, every day.

----A good builder of cathedrals knows his Bible. Now, a final thing about this rose window is the central medallion, and that's God in majesty. Do you see Him?

----Yes. He's beautiful in all of that light and colors.

----Light and colors, now that's two of the main tenets of Gothic architecture. If we have time, I want to show you Abbot Suger's Gothic masterpiece, the first in Gothic churches. It's here in Paris. He was the first one, the founder, so-to-speak, of Gothic architecture by his inspiration and determination to make everything rise to the heavens and proclaim the glory of God with light and majesty.

----Oh, I hope we can make the time to go there.

----If we don't make it on this trip, we'll do it in our next trip to Paris. I do want to show you the beautiful and very elegant Cathedral of Amiens, *la grande rayonnante*, as I like to call it.

----That will be a great delight for me. I'm learning so much from you and these cathedrals.

----The cathedrals, as you can see, are the Bible in stone and glass.

----I can see that now, more than before.

----You're only fourteen now. Wait until you're my age.

Maître de Chaussoyes was referring to the fact that Cajetan had just had his fourteenth birthday, the week before on April twenty-four.

Maître explained to Cajetan, before leaving Paris for Amiens, that the great city also had a jewel of a church in the Sainte Chapelle, not too far from Notre-Dame. That this church held the sacred relics of the crucified Christ, the crown of thorns and they say, a fragment of the True Cross as well as the Holy Lance and the Holy Sponge.

----I haven't seen all of the relics. King Louis IX had the Sainte Chapelle built to house them. The church was consecrated in 1248, and I was here to witness it, but there were so many people here for this great event that I wasn't able to see all of the relics, only the Sacred Crown. That's when I was in Bourges overseeing the final phases of the cathedral's nave as assistant Master Architect.

----What's a relic?

----A relic is part of a saint's body, such as a bone fragment or an object to be venerated like the True Cross, and the Holy Crown of Thorns. Every church and cathedral has some relic of sorts. There has to be one in the altar stone in order to say mass. Others are much bigger relics and are placed in a prominent place so that pilgrims can come and venerate them. That's a very big attraction for pilgrims and usually a money-maker.

----A money-maker?

----Yes, relics attract people and people bring money with them, and spend it on holy objects or food for sale around the churches and cathedrals. It sometimes becomes too business-like, too commercial for my taste.

----Can we avoid it?

----No, it's part of the construction and physical realization of a cathedral. People are people and priests are priests, and bishops are bishops looking for funds to built their precious cathedrals or churches. Take Cardinal Archbishop Tintamarre, for instance, he's really one to proclaim the importance of sacred relics, and his goal is to get the most, or, at least, one of the most prestigious relics around for his cathedral. Yes, his cathedral, as he always puts it. His, not ours, his. I shouldn't talk like that but sometimes it makes me mad, Cajetan, it makes me mad.

Cajetan said nothing.

After spending three days in Paris, Maître de Chaussoyes was bringing Cajetan to Amiens. It was early evening and they could see the sun setting on Notre-Dame de Paris in a subdued but resplendent muted deep golden light. The two of them hitched a ride on a farmer's wagon. The farmer, Médard Sauvetel, was returning to his farm after unloading his produce at street markets in Paris. He lived in and around Amiens. He preferred having someone with him at evening hours, and especially at night for there was the ever-present danger of thievery and assaults. It turned out to be an uneventful trip, and all three of them were pleased that things had gone so well. When they got out after a long ride, the two riders were tired and a bit sleepy since it was now after Vespers. They had left Paris the night before.

Cajetan and Maître de Chaussoyes found themselves in the middle of the city, right in front of the Amiens cathedral. It was dark and they decided to find shelter for the night. The following morning, in full sunlight, they found themselves in front of the cathedral facing the huge *rosace*, the rose window in the Gothic Flamboyant style. They were both looking upward at the rose window that had just been completed, and under it stood the main portal with its tympanum with a relief that depicts a lively description of the Last Judgment. In the center is enthroned Christ flanked by the Virgin Mary and John, whereas the two-part lintel below shows the resurrection of the dead and their judgment with Saint Michael, the Archangel, who weighs their sins and piety on a pair of scales.

----Do you see the final Judgment, Cajetan?

----Yes, Maître. Is this what we have to go through at the Final Judgment? Judged by Saint Michael and sent to heaven of hell?

----This is but a representation, a creative adaptation of the Bible stories concerning the final ends. This comes out of the genius of the stone sculptors and the master plan as presented by the architect in charge. When we die we must all face our Creator for judgment, and this is represented in cathedrals, usually with Christ as the grand Judge. Saint Michael is not the judge but the one who is represented as being in charge of the scales of justice. Either one is found to be wanting and awaits damnation or at the opposite end of the scales, he is weighed in the fullness of grace. All of our sins are weighed as well as our works of piety and charity.

----During an entire lifetime? That's a lot.

----Yes, that's a lot. But there is room for conversion for those who need it. Like Saint Paul or Theophilus.

----There's that name again, Theophilus.

----Yes, and I'll tell you all about him later, as I told you before. Next comes the left side where we find Saint Peter who has opened the door of heaven with the keys given to him by Christ on earth. Remember that passage in the gospels?

----Yes. *"Tu es Pierre et sur cette pierre je fonderai mon église,"* You are Peter and I will found my church on you, the Rock. He gives him the keys to the Kingdom. Brother Abélard Marie taught me that.

----He taught you quite a bit this Brother Abélard Marie.

----Yes, he did.

----Now, back to the tympanum. While the just get into heaven on the left, to the right there's a devilish creature and angels with flaming swords who drive the damned into the mouth of hell, depicted here with the gaping jaws of a monster. Do you see that, Cajetan?

----Of course. It's terrifying.

----Well, now direct your attention to the trumeau where a statue of Christ blesses the faithful as a gesture of compassion and love.

----Maître is there such a thing as hell?

----Now that's a real and difficult question. We find the notion in the Bible and bishops, priests and monks talk about hell all the time. The nuns too. Is it a real place? I don't know how to explain it to you. A priest once told me that it was more of a condition than a place. The damned feel alone and without the goodness of God. They wallow in their own sins of gluttony, avarice, lust, pride and so on. There's no more redemption for them. They're damned for eternity. That's how he explained it to me.

----That's terrible. I certainly don't want to go there.

----You're saved, Cajetan. You're a good soul.

Cajetan looked at his Master and smiled contentedly.

----Cajetan, let's go to the south transept before we go inside to look at the rose window. I want to show you the statue of the *Vierge Dorée*. This is a recent addition to the south transept. Before that, there was a statue of the bishop-saint.

Both of them walked over to the south transept and stared at the Gilded Virgin.

----Notice the Virgin's smile and her animated features as well as the softer treatment of the drapery folds. This indicates the influence of the Parisian courtly style now in vogue.

----What do you mean?

----Well, it means that her mantle if more flowing, and has a greater sense of folds especially up front. Here the sculptors have captured the elegance of the courts and the ladies wearing the flowing garments.

----Have you been to court, Maître?

----No, not yet, probably someday.

----I'd like to go. My sponsor, Sir Knight Évrard de Châteauloup who lives in the manor of the Duke of Blanford offered to bring me to court but it never transpired.

The two of them penetrated inside the cathedral and started looking around until Maître de Chaussoyes told Cajetan to go to the front portal, the west one, and enter from there not looking down at all but only looking upwards. Cajetan asked him why, and he answered him, "Gothic space."

----Of course, Gothic space. I should know better.

Cajetan hurried to the front portal while Maître de Chaussoyes cautioned him not to run in a church, "It's sacred space, Cajetan, it's sacred and one must not defile it with irreverence."

Cajetan started coming down the center aisle slowly, down the nave ever looking upward, never looking downward. A big smile covered his lips and his face seemed to radiate with joy.

----Gothic space, Maître, Gothic space! I feel like I'm floating on air.

----See, I told you that when you only look upward in the Gothic space, such as here in Amiens, you fly. You're uplifted by the terrific energy of angelic space in a Gothic cathedral. You fly like the angels, like the spiritual beings they are, you fly, Cajetan, you fly!

----Yes, I fly on the wings of angels. Do angels really have wings?

----That's the way we represent them. They're messengers using their wings to greet someone, like the Virgin Mary at the Annunciation or deliver God's message as in the case of Abraham with his son, Isaac.

----So they fly.

----Yes, at least in art and architecture.

Maître brought Cajetan to the nave and looking upward he told Cajetan:

----The verticality of this nave is accentuated by the extreme height of the arcades which measures half of the nave's total elevation. The arcades with 126 pillars are crowned by a foliated frieze running around the entire church. A marvel, in my opinion as an architect. The three architects of this cathedral are Robert de Luzarches, Thomas and Renaud de Cormont. All three are Master Craftsmen in their artistry. They know architecture as a true art. I admire them greatly. Let them be your models, Cajetan.

----But how?

----By observing their work and capturing the essence of their designs and plans as executed here in Amiens. The Amiens cathedral will go down in history as one of the greatest Gothic cathedrals. Mark my word.

----I can see that. I hope I can measure up to them in the future.

----It will take time, patience and, above all, skill. You have all three my friend the dreamer. Keep reaching for the stars. This cathedral is almost completed, and we shall come for its dedication when it's time.

----Oh, yes, Maître. It will be a great event in my life as an apprentice architect.

----Maybe as a journeyman.

----Really?

----Really. We'll see.

Maître de Chaussoyes and Cajetan left Amiens the following morning, and the sky was pinkish mauve with the birds singing and the River Somme flowing with a swift current past the cathedral as if it was mirroring the energy emanating from this architectural giant on its banks.

4

FINDING THE SISTER AND THE BROTHER

O n their way home back to the *chantier,* Maître de Chaussoyes told Cajetan that he was pleased with Cajetan's openness to cathedral architecture and his attitude toward work in general. He liked the way Cajetan took advantage of every little bit of information that was presented to him. That meant that Cajetan was willing to learn and retain things.

----If you continue the way you have been, studying hard and doing your work as an apprentice, I'm willing to bet that you will make journeyman sooner than the usual time it takes to attain that level of skill as a craftsman. I'm sure that the guild would be open upon my recommendation to promote you. That would mean wages and your ability to purchase the tools you need, as well as the ability to live in a more adequate lodging for a young man your age. It would also mean that you could be looking for a young girl, and start courting her. Later on, it might lead to marriage and the establishment of a family. Isn't that what you want?

----Yes, but not now. I'm only fourteen going on fifteen. Later, I'm sure.

----By the way, I did not forget your birthday even though I'm late.

Maître handed Cajetan something wrapped in a piece of cloth. Cajetan thanked him and stood there with the gift in his hands. Maître told him to open it. It was a compass.

----It's similar to mine. You won't have to borrow mine now. This is the start of having your own tools.

----Thank you ever so much.

Cajetan ran out of words to say what he wanted to tell Maître de Chaussoyes, which was unusual for him, since he normally had the facility to speak and hold a conversation. He really felt at that moment that he was part of the fabric of cathedral building, and he was learning more and more every day about cathedrals and his craft. He had Maître de Chaussoyes to thank for he thought he was the best master and teacher to have at his side. Without a good teacher, the craft becomes a useless exercise, he thought.

The following day, Cajetan decided to go and see his friend, the sculptor, Timon Chenovert. He wanted to tell him all about Notre-Dame de Paris and Notre-Dame d'Amiens, and their sculptures that he had seen. He ran over to the stone cutters' and stone sculptors' area. Timon was busy finishing his sculpture of the smiling angel.

----Good morning and the Lord bless you, Timon.

----And may the goodness of the Lord rest upon you, Cajetan. I've been wanting to see you.

----What for?

----To wish you a happy birthday which I forgot when it was time, and also to give you something.

----What?

----First, tell me about your trip to Paris and Amiens. Aren't those the places you went with Maître de Chaussoyes?

----Yes, and did we see marvelous things, Timon.

----Tell me all about it. I haven't seen these cathedrals since their walls were barely begun some time ago, and now they're in the process of completion. I was very young then.

----Well, we looked at them and Maître de Chaussoyes explained to me many things about them, the architecture, the vaults, the pillars, the sculptures and the glass. Timon, what beautiful glass windows are the rose windows. They're still vivid in my mind.

----And the sculptures?

----There are so many that I cannot describe them all to you. But, there are a few that are simply splendid.

----Like?

----Like the *Vierge Dorée* of the Amiens cathedral and the Christ on the trumeau at the front portal. He's blessing the faithful, it seems. But the *Vierge Dorée* with her smile reminded me of your smiling angel here.

----It's nice to see that other sculptors enjoy the smile on some of their statues.

----What was most fascinating for me was the notion of Gothic space, especially at Amiens. What a thrilling feeling to walk down the nave and feel as if you're floating on air. You know what I mean.

----Yes, I know just what you mean.

----Isn't that a thrilling feeling?

----Yes. That's because you're in the craft of cathedral building more so than simply a visitor.

----What is it you wanted to see me about?

37

----It's this…and he handed Cajetan a package.

----What is this?

----It's your birthday gift. Happy fourteenth. You were away so I wasn't able to give this to you in time.

----What is it Timon?

----Open it.

Cajetan opened the package and saw a small carved stone head that resembled his own features with a star on the forehead.

----It's you, Cajetan, it's you with a star, the dreamer's star. That's the way I see you and many others see you since we often see you at nighttime lying on the grass gazing at the stars. Cajetan the Stargazer. That's what we all call you. We admire your tenacity to dream. So many people give up on their dreams. Many craftsmen simply do their work almost mechanically. They do their work, get paid for it, and then jump to another task leaving their dreams behind. But, you hold on to them and you are so right to do that. Dreams are the stuff cathedrals are made of.

----Thank you, for your kind words. Thank you for this bust with a star on the forehead. It's me, all right, Cajetan the Stargazer.

Cajetan had tears in his eyes and remained there speechless. Timon, the Master Sculptor, looked at Cajetan with a broad smile on his face, happy to have pleased the young man.

The weeks went by and it was late fall, mid-November, when the morning chill makes the craftsmen hold on to their gloves, and those without them, rub their hands together to get some heat from the friction. Everyone realizes that winter is coming, and that the work will slow down soon and then stop, for most of the masons go home for the winter because mortar work cannot be done in cold weather. Come November, the finished stonework is covered with straw and dung to prevent the frost from cracking the mortar before it has completely dried. However, other work continues for temporary workshops are built against the finished walls of the choir to house the stone cutters who can no longer work outside. They await the return of spring when the masons come back.

After the Christmas season ending with Candlemas in early February, Cajetan went to see Maître de Chaussoyes and asked him to take a leave from his work as apprentice, since he wanted to go home and visit his sister Marie Dieudonnée. Besides, work on the cathedral was really slow. Cajetan had not seen his sister since he had left for his apprenticeship two years before. He had not heard from her either. He would try to find her.

On the day of Candlemas, Cajetan went with Maître de Chaussoyes and other craftsmen to the local church where they went every Sunday for mass and communion. There, on this day, the feast day of the Purification of the Blessed Virgin Mary was celebrated with the traditional blessing of the candles with procession after Tierce. The celebrant dressed with stole and purple cope, stood by the epistle side of the altar, and blessed the beeswax candles. He sang the five *orisons* and sprinkled the candles with holy water, and then incensed them. The candles were then distributed to the clergy and the faithful. Cajetan held on tight to his candle. He was going to bring it with him when he left the church, he told himself. His mother used to do that every year just to have a blessed candle in the house. The antiphon, *"Lumen ad revelationem gentium et gloriam plebis tuae Israel"* was repeated after every verse, as was customary. The procession followed. Everyone sang *"Gaude Maria Virgo"* to honor Mary. Cajetan loved these ceremonies, not just this one, but most of them, ever since his mother had brought him and his sister to church for those special liturgies, such as this one. The mystery of them stayed with Cajetan never to be wiped away from his memory.

Cajetan left the following morning traveling with some butcher who had to go on business to the town right next to where Cajetan was born and lived for a while. It was in the eastern part of Picardie, not too far from Reims, and the small town was called Rumigny. He was hoping that Marie Dieudonnée still lived there with the father and Abélard François. When they arrived at their destination, it was late afternoon, for the butcher's horse was old and terribly slow. Cajetan told himself that he could have walked there just as a pilgrim walks to his sacred destination. Cajetan walked fast, had endurance and was filled with high energy. Once in Rumigny, Cajetan went to the house where he used to live. There was nobody there. He asked around and found out that Marie Dieudonnée had moved far away to a town called, Cambrai, in the Artois. He knew that he had too far to go if he wanted to go to Cambrai, so he decided to stay overnight in Rumigny. He slept in a little inn and shared a room with another traveler. The following morning he had a light breakfast right before dawn, and left for Cambrai.

He walked for two days before he arrived in the town where he was going. He had to ask several people before he could get a lead as to where Marie Dieudonnée lived. Someone knew her by the little candy she sold at the fairs in and around town since everybody, he was told, knew about the *bêtises de Marie Dieudonnée*. Cajetan then walked over to the place where people said she lived. It was a very humble dwelling with climbing roses around the door. He knocked at the door but no one answered. A neighbor came to talk to him and said, *"C'est Marie Dieudonnée que vous cherchez?"* And he answered her, *"Oui, femme."* She replied, *"Elle est à la bonneterie. Elle rentre vers les dix-huit heures."* Cajetan thanked her and sat on the stoop of the little house where he would wait for his sister until she arrived home. The neighbor told him that she was at the bonnet shop and would not get back until six o'clock that evening. It was three o'clock in the afternoon, so Cajetan had to wait three hours for his sister to come home. He dozed off several times since he was very tired from walking.

As Cajetan was glancing over and beyond the road, he saw this young woman with reddish blond hair walking briskly up the road. She appeared to be in her teens. Marie Dieudonnée was, after all, just a year younger than Cajetan. Cajetan hid behind the roses wanting to surprise her, for he was sure it was his sister. She had a dog walking beside her, and her attention was given entirely to the dog. From afar, it seemed to be a shepherd's dog. What is she doing with a dog? asked Cajetan to himself. Surely, she doesn't do shepherd's work, he told himself. He waited for her to get closer to the house, and then he rushed out and cried loudly, "Marie Dieudonnée! Marie Dieudonnée!" The young girl was caught by surprise and shouted with an emotional voice, "No, it can't be Cajetan. It cannot be! Lord in heaven and Blessed Mary Mother of God, you have brought him here!" And she ran to him. They embraced each other very hard and kept hugging each other until both of them were out of breath and words.

----Where did you come from, Cajetan?

----I came from Reims where I work as an apprentice.

----I never knew where you were, so I could not get in touch with you.

----I've been there ever since I left home almost two years ago. How are you?

----I'm fine. I live here in a small room. The concierge is very nice to me. There are four other women living here. We all work somewhere around here. I work at *la Bonneterie Valenciennes* owned by a Madame Valois. She's kind to me and let's me walk her dog, Pomme Dorée, that you see here. I'm going to return him to his home after supper. I've been living here in Cambrai ever since papa died a year and a half ago.

----He died?

----He died some months after you left. He was exhausted and worn out from his work, and from the fact that you were gone. He missed mother so very much too. He never got over it. He continued with his stone cutting but with time, he relinquished his craft and started to lose weight and fell into deep depression. I took care of him. And after he died, I moved here from where we used to live. I could not afford that house anymore. I worked the best I could but no one wanted to give me work, except washing clothes and taking care of young children, and that did not pay very well. Besides, I wanted to be close to Abélard François. He's in a monastery, here in Cambrai.

----Too bad I wasn't around to help out.

----You had your apprenticeship and you were committed to becoming an architect. I would not have wanted you to separate yourself from your dream.

----But you were in need and we're family. Family comes first.

----I know but I'm not in misery. I can take care of myself. Besides, I do sewing, make candies, sweet berry jams, herbal medicines and people are kind to me. Brother Abélard Marie, poor old Brother Abélard Marie, is getting old and he shows it. He's the one who told me about Cambrai since Abélard François wanted so desperately to enter a monastery. I sell my wares and candies at local church fairs. People come from everywhere to taste my honey and nut nougat and my *berlingots* that I call *mes petites bêtises*. It's a hard candy made with honey and mint, mint that I grow myself in pots. People also buy my jelly made with the rind of lemons and a touch of cloves. I can't always find this spice but I manage to get some here and there. It just takes a touch to get the flavor I seek. You can say that I manage well by myself. I'm seldom sick, and if I do have a fever or some other kind of malady, why, I make my own herbal remedies. Geneviève la Guérisseuse taught me how. You do remember her, don't you?

----I certainly do. She helped mother so much. Tell me about Abélard François?

----After papa died, he went to see Brother Abélard Marie and asked him if he could join the Franciscan order. He was told that he was too young, and that he would need his parents' consent to leave home, but both our parents were dead. He wanted desperately to live in a monastery. He kept telling me that he had the vocation, the calling. I tried to console him, and I went to the Franciscan Monastery myself to plead with the superior, but he would not listen to my plea. I did not know what to do. I was too young to effect the demand. I wish you had been here.

----I should have been but I didn't know papa had died, and Abélard François wanted to leave home. Poor you. You must have felt alone and powerless.

----Alone, yes, but powerless, no. I came here to Cambrai where there was a Carmelite monastery that took in boys, and educated them for future placement in their order. They said it was cultivating a vocation, as they explained it to me. After I got the local priest's permission on paper and he signed it, I returned to the monastery with Abélard François and they took him in. They charged nothing, no dowry, nothing. Of course, he wasn't a girl entering a convent.

----Does he like it there?

----Yes, I think so. I go see him once in a while when I'm permitted to enter the monastery. It's a cloistered community. I can only see him twice a year, and I talk to him through the grille. I hear him but I can't see him. He told me that he had grown healthy and strong. He asks about you sometimes. The monks do a very good job with him, I'm sure. He's on his way to being well educated. He's learned Latin, Greek, theology, philosophy, mathematics and meta, meta or something.

----You mean metaphysics.

----Yes, that's it.

----Well, at least he's well fed and has a roof over his head. And, he's secure in the hands of the Carmelites. The important thing is that he's going to have an education, and that's very important for a man.

----For a woman too, Cajetan. Don't forget. But, Abélard François never wanted to get an apprenticeship like you. Remember how he was *un à part*, a loner? He simply wanted to lead the life of a solitary person like a monk. Well, he has what he always wanted. Do you know anything about the Carmelites?

----Very little except that it's a very strict order.

----Well, I found out about them through Brother Abélard Marie. The Carmelites are associated with Mount Carmel and the Prophet Elijah, he told me. The Order is considered by the Church to be under the special protection of the Blessed Virgin Mary, and thus has a strong Marian devotion. Abélard François is in a very good place.

----As long as Abélard François is happy where he is, then I'm glad for him. I think mother would have been happy too.

----Perhaps if you come when it's time to see him, then you could accompany me. I can't see him alone, not a woman. I always bring someone with me, a man, of course. A friend. The first time I went to see him was when he pronounced his vows, and I had asked Brother Abélard Marie to come with me. He received permission from his superior. We were on the side aisle of their chapel at the priory with the other visitors, family, of course, and I was able to glance at him, tall and lean in his long white mantle with black and brown stripes. After he pronounced his vows with a promise of obedience to his Prior, they placed a scapular over his head and tied it to his shoulders. The scapular, I was told, is made up of two pieces of cloth and was given to Saint Simon Stock by the Blessed Virgin who promised him that all who wore the scapular with faith and piety and died with it on would be saved. Simon Stock, who became the Order's general at eighty years old, served the community for twenty years until his death. I wear a miniature scapular every day. I should get you one. Abélard François looked so serious at his profession. I didn't get a chance to speak to him for they observe a deep silence. It's part of their rule. I wouldn't want to live like that. Too strict for me. I must say though, that I found our brother to be a little too lean and even ashen. Probably the fasting and penance of the Carmelites got to him. I do hope he gains in strength and vitality.

----That's a genuine concern. I suppose there's nothing I can do for him.

----Not much, for he lives with his vows, his holy rule, his contemplative life and celibate existence.

----That means that you are truly alone, all by yourself, here in Cambrai, now that father is dead.

----Yes, all by myself. But you're here now, and I don't want to lose touch with you even though I can manage by myself and do my work at the bonnet shop. I sew ribbons that are tied to the bonnets. Beautiful colored ribbons.

----I'll stay in touch with you as often as I can. It should be easier when I become a journeyman and earn a wage. I'll have more freedom and money. I'm sorry that I cannot offer you anything now, but later, I'll see to it that you get something, a small income from me.

----I really don't need anything from you, Cajetan. Keep your money when you get some. I get along very well.

----How about marriage, a dowry and sufficient clothing and wares to start a household and a family?

----I don't contemplate getting married. I don't want to give up my life as a woman of freedom. I don't want to be anybody's serf or slave. Mother always thought that I would join a community of religious women, but I really don't think about that right now. Maybe later. I'm torn between married life and celibate life.

----You don't have to be. You're young, beautiful, and talented and you deserve a family besides me. Marie Dieudonnée, Marie Dieudonnée, you're my sister and I want you to be happy. I'll take care of you somehow.

----How? You'll leave your apprenticeship and come here to Cambrai as a simple peasant, poor and without a trade? No, Cajetan. I don't want the responsibility of your being without a future and your dream of becoming an architect. That would be terrible. I could not live with that guilt.

----You can come and live with me then.

----Live with you as an apprentice? You have nothing, and live completely dependent on your Master until you become a journeyman. I know about these things. No, Cajetan, I have my own life and I'm happy that way. If I should decide to marry, I'll let you know somehow. There's time for that, there's time. After all, I'm only fourteen going on fifteen.

----Many young women your age are married.

----I know but that's not for me right now.

----Anyways, I'm so very glad to see you again and I promise that I won't wait this long next time. Please know that I have not abandoned you.

----I know, Cajetan, I know.

----Where is papa buried?

----He's buried with mother in the church cemetery.

Cajetan stayed with his sister two days, and they both enjoyed their company. Marie Dieudonnée cooked for him, sewed his tunic where it needed mending, repaired his shoes and gave him the necessary care he needed. They went to mass on Sunday at the local church, and Cajetan left that afternoon. Marie Dieudonnée put some of her honey and nut nougat in his traveling bag. He thanked her for his visit and her good deeds towards him. He left her in the road next to her house with a very large smile on her lips. She waved goodbye and with her right hand she pointed to the sky. He knew what she meant and gave her a smile. He was pleased that the visit had worked out so well. He would keep the memory of it for a long time, a very long time.

As he took the road to Reims, he could hear his mother, Grisoulda, whispering to him, " My Cajetan how God is good to you, my dear boy, and my Stargazer." Back at the *chantier*, Cajetan got ready to help Maître de Chaussoyes assemble his tools and place them in order so that he would not have a hard time to find them when he wanted to use them. Maître was an orderly man.

The weeks went by and the months also. Cajetan went through another winter in Reims and saw the dawning of a new and bright spring season. He loved spring. There was talk that the cathedral roof would finally be done since the king had lifted the tax on lead used for that purpose. Things looked bright indeed, said Maître to his men.

One day in June, it was the feast of the Nativity of Saint John the Baptist, Cajetan sat down with Maître and asked him to talk about Abbot Suger and the foundation of the Gothic cathedral. Maître had been promising Cajetan this talk for quite sometime, ever since the two of them had gone to Paris and Amiens. The time had finally come to have this talk, and Cajetan looked forward to it. He loved Gothic architecture, and wanted to learn more and more about it, especially about its very beginning.

----Please tell me all about Abbot Suger and the rise of the Gothic.

----I can't tell you everything but I'll give you the highlights of his contribution to Gothic architecture and the Saint Denis church in Paris.

----Too bad we could not visit Saint-Denis when we were in Paris.

----We could not do everything, Cajetan, too little time.

----I know.

----Some day, you will go and explore the site yourself. I'm just going to give you the important details about Abbot Suger's historical contribution in the building a Gothic church.

----Good, I've been waiting for that a long time.

----I know. You have a gullible ear for whatever is Gothic. First of all, Abbot Suger was a great devotee of Saint Denis, the patron saint of Paris. At the age of nine or ten, he was dedicated as an oblate or lay novice to Saint-Denis, and became identified with the Abbey Church. He was appointed Abbot in 1122 and Suger's main goal was to honor God and Saint Denis through the beautification of his church. Abbot Suger's great ambition led to the thorough remodeling of the Abbey Church of Saint-Denis. This made his name synonymous with the beginning of Gothic art and architecture in France.

----I see.

----No one really knows how much influence he exercised on the design plan of Saint-Denis, but we know that he was an active participant. The rebuilding of the west façade seemed to conform to Abbot Suger's philosophy of *anagogicus mos*, "the upward leading method," as it is known. Ever higher towards the heavens. His great motivation was to try and reach the light of heaven and of the stars. He reminds me of you, my dear Cajetan, in your constant reach for the stars through your passion and dreams .

Cajetan smiled and touched Maître's shoulder in a friendly gesture of warmth and admiration.

----I will never give up my dream of building a cathedral someday.

----Well, Abbot Suger had his plans, and his great desire to generate light and more light in his church, and the west façade served as a stepping-stone on the way to Heaven towards the light of God. However, the style he innovated had huge stained-glass windows and used pointed arches and ribbed vaults to create high, soaring ceilings. To accomplish this new look, the Master Masons had to resolve some staggering architectural challenges. The main problem was to buttress the outward thrust of vaulted ceilings built of stones and bricks. Abbot Suger's Master Masons solved this problem by creating huge buttresses that stood at a distance from the thin window pierced walls, and transferring the outward thrust of the heavy vaulted ceilings to the outer buttresses, *des arcs-boutants,* as we know them.

----Thank God for good masons and good thinking.

----Yes. Furthermore, contrary to Bernard de Clairvaux's ideas on the simplicity, if not the stark severity of monasteries, churches and the religious cult, Abbot Suger believed that ornamentation had a place in the cult of God and his saints. Abbot Suger justified his extravagant taste in gold and precious stones as a way of honoring the Lord with the most precious materials available as Solomon had done in the Temple at Jerusalem. Abbot Suger had a definite taste for splendor and beauty, and filled the church with golden vessels, stained glass, lustrous vestments, and tapestries. By his death in 1151, Suger had renewed Saint-Denis from its very foundations, and made his church one of the most resplendent in the Western world. His influence on the Gothic is certainly unsurpassable.

----Do you believe in all of that splendor in a church, Maître?

----I believe in light, thinner walls that let in the light through its windows, and the majesty of the religious cult in its simplicity and religious grandeur. Not in gold, silver or precious things that glitter and attract thievery and stirs the temptation of haughtiness. Besides, the gold and the precious stones, Abbot Suger replenished the choir with holy relics thus reacting against the order of Saint Bernard. You know why?

----To attract pilgrims and their money.

----Of course. Abbot Suger was not a monk to go against the wishes of his order and the Church, but he loved grandeur and resplendency. He loved the magnificence of the Christian cult and in doing what he did, he became the founder, as such, of a magnificent style and design: the Gothic as it came to be known. Some people may object to this way of describing Abbot Suger and the Gothic, but he certainly played a very important role in the promotion of the Gothic style. When Saint-Denis, the remodeled church, was rededicated on June 10, 1144, no less than King Louis VII and Queen Eleanor of Aquitaine and the dowager Queen Adelaide as well as members of the royal court joined the throngs of pilgrims in attendance for the ceremony of consecration. They all thought that the architectural daring and stunning luminosity of the new Saint-Denis was a fitting tribute to the Capetian royal power. It was King Louis himself who bore on his shoulder the silver reliquary containing the bones of the martyred Saint Denis, patron saint of France that had been housed in the crypt of the old church. The King deposited the reliquary reverently in its new bejeweled shrine. We are told that the King was greatly moved by the ceremony of dedication as was Bernard of Clairvaux who was there also.

----Were you there?

----No, that was in 1144. I was not yet born.

----Oh, I see. That must have been a tremendous ceremony celebrating such a church with its Gothic splendor.

----That's the brief history of Gothic architecture and Abbot Suger's Saint-Denis, the best I can relate it to you. All I know is that there is still the twenty-foot crucifix on the high altar and the Oriflamme, the sacred banner of Saint Denis and standard of the kings of France remains on the same altar.

----Thank you ever so much, Maître. You know so much about your craft as an architect, and I admire your knowledge and skills. That's why I'm here to study under you.

Maître de Chaussoyes looked at Cajetan and held his hand in his.

----Cajetan, my apprentice, I have good news for you. I have made arrangements for you to go to England to pursue your apprenticeship with a very good and honorable Master Architect, Master Sigismond de Longchamp. I've worked with him before. He's a good teacher and architect. You'll like him.

----Why now? I don't think I'm ready for this. Besides, I'll be leaving my beloved France.

----It's now because you have not learned about excavations and foundations, the cathedral from scratch, the very first beginnings. I could not show it to you here since the foundation had already been built.

----Isn't there another *chantier* here in the Kingdom of France where I can learn?

----Not at the moment. You have to go to England with Maître de Longchamp. I've already made arrangements with him, and he's prepared to receive you. Not everyone has a chance to work with Maître de Longchamp. He's highly respected in his field. You have to go where the opportunities lie, Cajetan.

----I know, but leave you?

----You have to leave me someday, so it may as well be now.

----How will I get to England and where will I live? Where is the *chantier*?

Cajetan prepared his belongings and put them in a large leather bag that he could carry over his shoulder. He did not have many belongings. A few clothes, his compass and the bust of himself in stone with a star on the forehead that Timon had given him. He said farewell to all of his friends, Master Masons, Master Carpenters, Master Stone Cutters and Master Sculptors. Then, he went to see Maître de Chaussoyes. It was a difficult parting for Cajetan, but he forced himself to be brave and strong under the circumstances. His heart was pounding and his head felt weak with the idea of leaving Reims behind. His first *chantier*.

5

THE EXPERIENCE OF ENGLAND

Standing on the beach at Calais, Cajetan felt a bit nauseous. His stomach felt queasy and his legs weak. He felt the fear of crossing the channel in a sailboat. He had never set sail before. All of this was new to him. It was September 1263 and Cajetan was looking forward to a bright future where opportunities would open up for him and his dreams. But now he had to face the challenge of going to another kingdom and progress in his quest of becoming an architect. He was determined to succeed. He had to. Success meant the willingness and capability of accomplishing his dream of building, one day, a cathedral, a Gothic cathedral.

Cajetan only had the chance to send a few words to his sister before leaving France. He told her that he was going to the region of Exeter in England, specifically at the *chantier* of Devonshire. He tried, the best he could, to orient her geographically, hoping that she would understand where he was going. Marie Dieudonnée is intelligent enough and has enough resources around her to figure out where exactly the *chantier* is situated, he told himself. He was hoping she would be able to contact him from time to time. He promised himself that he would take the time to do the same.

The crossing was uneventful, but the arrival across the channel through the Strait of Dover was somewhat confusing for Cajetan. He had no sense of direction at sea. He had left Calais in France with a few men who were also crossing the channel, and they all weathered well the twenty-one miles of crossing. They had left very early in the morning, before dawn, and made it across in the evening. The wind was brisk and helped them to reach their destination in good time. However, at the landing site, Cajetan saw no one that he knew, and certainly not the man who was supposed to be there to greet him. Maître de Chaussoyes had promised him that someone would be there to guide him along to his destination in the Exeter region. But there was no one. Cajetan was greatly disappointed and wondered where he could find someone to lead the way to the *chantier* Devonshire. He felt lost, cold and lonely. He was also hungry. He found a small inn after he had walked from the beach in Dover to a small village called Langley.

He stayed overnight at the inn, and early in the morning, after a quick breakfast, he readied himself to take the road with some instructions from the innkeeper. As he was stepping outside, a young man greeted him and asked him if he was Cajetan, the apprentice architect from France. Cajetan was caught by surprise. Could this be the man who was supposed to meet me on the beach? he thought.

----My name is Peter Mallory. I'm an apprentice carpenter from the Devonshire construction site. I'm here to lead you to it. I'm sorry I was not able to meet you yesterday because I had problems with transportation, and the road to Dover was unknown to me. So, I finally found someone to bring me here. I looked for you on the beach and around it until I came here to this inn, and here you are.

----Yes, here I am. I'm very glad to see you. Is the *chantier* far from here?

----Not too far. It's about some eighteen miles west of here. We can walk the distance if you don't mind. I know my way now.

----Why not?

They started walking with a steady step, and they talked about their individual skill, one as an apprentice carpenter and the other as an apprentice architect.

----My master is Journeyman Carpenter, Timothy Smiles. I originally come from London but I moved when I was ten. My father died when I was nine, and we went to live with my mother's sister, Aunt Polly Langshere. She stayed in and around Exeter. There's a lovely cathedral there. When I reached eleven I got to liking carpentry. I worked for this man who was an all-round person, and he mended things like furniture. He had been a member of the guild, but they threw him out when he insulted the head of the Carpenter's Guild. I worked for him a little while. He did not pay me much. My aunt thought that he was treating me life a slave. So, she went to the guildhall and informed herself about my becoming an apprentice carpenter. They told her that the guilds were responsible for the vocational education of town's children, and that they would look at my possibilities as a carpenter and my level of intelligence and skills. And that's how I got into the guild program. I was then sent as an apprentice to Master Smiles at the Devonshire cathedral construction site. You Frenchmen call it shantiey-ey.

----Yes, *chantier*. I was working at the *chantier de Reims,* when I left France to come here.

----That's a pretty nice site, I am told.

----Yes, a very nice one. I was fortunate that I had a sponsor by the name of Sir Knight Évrard de Châteauloup.

----God Almighty! That's class, Cajetan. Nobility. I'm of the low class.

----So am I, Peter. My father was a journeyman stone cutter. A good one too. My mother was a good woman who worked hard and took care of the family. I have one sister and one brother. They both live in Cambrai, and my brother is in the Order of the Carmelites. My grandfather, my mother's father, was a stone cutter too. They called him Hubert the Stargazer.

----Why the Stargazer? Did he like to look at the stars?

----Yes, you might say that. But he was a dreamer as well. Like I am.

----What do you dream of?

----I dream about becoming a Master Architect and building a cathedral someday.

----Wow, that's a big dream. My dream is to be a carpenter and go beyond cathedral building and timbers. I want to own my own shop and produce quality furniture.

----Oh, I see.

----When we get to the site, you'll come with me and I'll introduce you to my Master. Then I'll introduce you to your Master, Master Architect, Sigismond de Longchamp.

----Maître de Chaussoyes told me all about him. He comes highly recommended.

----He's an excellent architect, and everyone sings his praises, masons, stone cutters, stone sculptors and carpenters. Even Archbishop Tintamarre praises him and his work. I should say Cardinal Archbishop.

----Who's Archbishop Tintamarre?

----Why, he's the head of the diocese of Devonshire, the Archbishop in charge of the building of the cathedral you'll be working on. Except he's a Cardinal Archbishop.

----A Cardinal?

----Yes, a red hat Archbishop.

Both young men started laughing.

Cajetan and Peter reached the *chantier* by Vespers and they went directly to the two Masters, Smiles and de Longchamp. Afterwards, Peter took Cajetan to the quarters where Cajetan was to live as an apprentice.

----All of the apprentices at the Devonshire site live in designated quarters. This is yours right here. You're thirty in all. I don't know all of the apprentices. There are too many of them, all in their fields of craftsmanship. I think you're the only apprentice architect here. All of the apprentices here in this dwelling are nice and they all get along well together.

Cajetan thought of Rielbert back in Reims, and he shuddered a bit.

----Show me my place and I'll put my belongings there.

----Right here.

----That will be just fine. I'm so glad that we met, Peter.

----We're friends now, Cajetan. We're friends in the guilds of the cathedral makers.

After settling in, both boys went to have something to eat, and then they went to bed because they were exhausted from the trip. The following morning, bright and early, with the rising of the sun, Cajetan rose, quickly washed himself at the outdoor water fountain and then got dressed. He had made sure that his compass and the stone bust were well hidden in his bundle and placed under the bed. Those were his little treasures. After a quick breakfast of bread and something hot, he didn't recognize but liked, Cajetan ambled off to see Master de Longchamp. Peter had pointed him out to Cajetan while not introducing him to the Master the day they arrived from Dover. He was on site near the foundation. He greeted his Master and he, in turn, started explaining to Cajetan that there was not any need for a full excavation since they were rebuilding on the old site of the former church.

----But Master de Chaussoyes sent me here because I was to learn about excavation and foundation. I did not learn about those in Reims because they were already done just like here.

----The excavation is done but we have to rework the foundation. It's weak and we have to strengthen it. You'll certainly learn something about foundations here, my boy.

Cajetan wondered why Maître de Chaussoyes had lied to him. Not lied, but somehow misrepresented the work here at Devonshire. Maybe he wanted to get rid of me, he thought. "No, he was my friend and I trusted him," he said out loud.

For the next several weeks, Master de Longchamp explained to Cajetan how excavations were done prior to the foundation of a church.

----Once the design of a cathedral is approved by the bishop and his chapter, work on the excavation is begun. While the carpenters are being sent to the forest for the cutting of timber for the construction of scaffolding, workshops, and, later on, the roof, the Master Quarryman is sent to supervise fifty or so stone cutters with apprentices and two hundred laborers in an area known for its limestone.

----Where is the limestone quarry here, Master?

----Not very far. It's in Waterford, some fifteen miles away from this site, although it's far enough for the transporting of the stones. Then the laborers help the stone cutters lift large pieces of stone out of the quarry. Then the stone is cut, chiseled and hammered so it can match the patterns or templates supplied by the Master Mason.

----Who's the Master Mason here?

----Samuel Feldstone. Each stone has to be marked three times, once to show its future location in the cathedral, once to show which quarry it comes from, so that the quarry man can be paid for every stone extracted, and once to show which stone cutter actually cut the stone, so that he can be paid as well. So you see, everyone who deserves to be paid, is paid the proper sum.

Master de Longchamp pointed to a cut stone showing three marks.

----See this one, you have a mark for the quarry man, μ, a second one for the cathedral location $\yen$, and a third one for the stone cutter, $\pm$.

----Do they chose marks out of a list of them?

----In a way. We have a system created by our craftsmen, and that's what we use. Some masons or stone cutters choose unusual marks, sometimes based on the zodiac. Now, as you can see, since we already have our foundation in place, we don't need to lay the foundation stone with the blessing of the Archbishop. However, our Archbishop Tintamarrre insists on blessing the foundation since we are rebuilding his new cathedral . You'll see that tomorrow.

----You mean, I'll see him tomorrow?

----Yes, in all of his majesty and pomp. He's a man of colorful ceremony.

----I'm looking forward to seeing that.

Morning came and around noon, Cardinal Archbishop Tintamarre all dressed in his best ecclesiastical garb, red cassock, white surplice with subtle appliqué, pectoral cross and gold embroidered miter, stood tall and erect before the far side of the foundation for the blessing. Cajetan was watching him closely. The Cardinal Archbishop took the aspergillum from the gold urn and sprinkled profusely the foundation uttering some prayers. At the end, people said, "Amen." After the ceremony, the Cardinal Archbishop looked around to see if he could spot his Master Architect. Master de Longchamp went to him dragging Cajetan behind him. The Master Architect kissed the Cardinal Archbishop's amethyst and gold ring and beckoned Cajetan to do the same.

----I need to speak to you, Master Architect.

----About what, Eminence?

----About the plans and design.

----What about the plans and design?

----Not here, not here. Tomorrow morning in my cabinet. Who's this? he asked pointing to Cajetan.

----That's Cajetan, my new apprentice. He's from the *chantier* of Reims in France.

Seeing that the apprentice was French, the Cardinal Archbishop smiled benignly at him and told Cajetan,

----*Bienvenue, mon enfant,* welcome to England, boy. How is the work on the majestic cathedral of Reims coming along?

----Well, sire.

Looking sternly at Cajetan, Master de Longchamp repeated to him,

----Eminence. Eminence.

Cajetan looking at the Cardinal Archbishop said in a rather humbled voice,

----Eminence, The cathedral looks great.

----A beautiful Gothic masterpiece just like mine is going to be. Who's the architect?

----Master Architect Albert de Chaussoyes, sire... Eminence.

----He's a good man and a splendid architect.

The Cardinal Archbishop looked at Master de Longchamp in the eye and said,

----I wish I could have gotten him for my cathedral.

Then the Cardinal Archbishop went away without saying anything else. The air was dry and almost lifeless.

----That's Cardinal Archbishop Tintamarre, Cajetan. A bit imperious but he's a doer and a go-getter. He'll have his cathedral come hell or high water.

----I don't know if I like him. He's so...

And the Architect cut him off.

----You don't have to like him, Cajetan. Only if he likes you enough to keep you on the job.

The weeks went by, and Cajetan met most Masters on the *chantier*. He also met many apprentices like himself. He realized he could not get to know all of the toilers and craftsmen since there must have been hundreds of them all working in different areas of construction, all helping the Masters, and all anticipating that, one day, they would climb the ladder in the guild to which they belonged. What with the laborers who did the menial jobs, the apprentices, the journeymen and the Masters, there must have been close to eight hundred people working on the *chantier*. That was an entire village for Cajetan.

With the experience that Cajetan had already acquired in Reims, and with the skills at his command, Cajetan grew into a handsome and intelligent young man that everyone liked and admired. They admired him for his keen sense of things, his firm grasp of architectural principles, his sharp learning skills and his enviable personality strengths. Even the Cardinal Archbishop noticed that Cajetan was very well liked by all, and he told himself that the *chantier* had acquired a desirable asset, that of attracting women, young and old, who admired beauty and talent in a man. The Cardinal Archbishop himself admired not only qualities in a man but greatly admired feminine qualities in a woman, such as beauty and sensuousness. Though celibate by vocation, Cardinal Archbishop Tintamarre knew his penchant for the feminine qualities that would probably lead him to embarrassing moments in his life, but he told himself that he would deal with that when the time came. Right now, he was more fascinated with the construction of his cathedral, its intricacies and challenges.

One day in the spring after Cajetan first arrived in Devonshire, Cajetan woke up with a severe headache and fever. He felt terribly sick. He had no appetite for breakfast and his palms were sweaty. He started shaking inside of himself and his legs were limp and cold. He was almost breathless at the thought that he might be really sick, sick enough to be sent home away from the work he loved. He started thinking back at what he had the night before: bread, almost stale, some pork, legumes, a handful of pine nuts and a tall glass of ale at the local tavern with the boys of his dwelling. They were celebrating his birthday. Cajetan had just turned fifteen. Peter tried to allay his fears but recognized that it might be more serious than he thought it might me. Cajetan lay on his bed trembling and cold. Peter put his blanket on Cajetan and went to fetch the Master Architect. In no time, Master de Longchamp was at Cajetan's bedside.

----What did you eat this morning, Cajetan?

----Nothing, I wasn't hungry.

----And last night?

----I ate pork, legumes and pine nuts.

----Did you have ale?

----Yes, but not much, no more than I usually have when we go out.

----How do you feel now?

----I feel miserable. I'm going to throw up.

Cajetan vomited bile and some black liquid that smelled foul.

----I had better get the physician, said the Architect.

----Do you want me to fetch him? asked Peter.

----Yes, and hurry.

Master de Longchamp was worried about Cajetan and his present condition. Things did not look good. When the physician arrived, he looked at Cajetan and checked him all over. He asked him all kinds of questions, and then he asked to see the vomit. Then he asked Cajetan,

----Did anyone give you anything strange or bitter sometime last night or this morning?

----What do you mean, sir?

----I mean some medication, some herbs or something like that?

----No.

----Well, it looks to me that you have been poisoned by something or someone.

Everyone around Cajetan's bed let out a gasp of utter surprise. In the meantime, Cajetan was getting worse with every minute that went by.

----If we don't do something now, he may die.

----But what, physician Donatus?

----I'm going to give him some emetic hoping that it will clean out his stomach and eject the poison, whatever it may be.

Later in the day, the physician came back to visit Cajetan and he found him in a worse condition. He tried some other remedy but it would not work. Scratching his head, the physician told Master de Longchanp that he no longer knew what to do. He had tried everything in his power to heal the young man. It is then that Peter suggested that Cajetan's sister be brought in for she was a healer. A very good one, Cajetan had told his friend.

----But she lives in France, said one of the apprentices who knew Cajetan.

----I know where she lives. She lives in Cambrai not too far from Reims. I'm going to get her right away.

----But you'll have to cross the channel to bring her here, and it may be too late. Poor Cajetan, poor sick man.

----But it's worth a try, said Peter.

Peter Mallory went to see Master de Longchamp and got his permission to go and get Cajetan's sister. It seemed to be the last resort. Peter convinced the Master that Cajetan's sister was considered a master healer since she had studied under a well-known healer called Geneviève la Guérisseuse. Master de Longchamp gave Peter some money to finance his trip.

Peter left right away and lost no time in getting to Dover where he took a boat with a couple of other men to go to Calais. Thank God there were no incidents in the crossing. From Calais, Peter proceeded to go to Cambrai, sometimes riding in a farmer's cart or climbing on a horse with its rider. He begged, he coerced, he shamed people into giving in to him, so determined was he to get Cajetan some help. When he got to Cambrai, he did not know where to go, and he started asking people for Marie Dieudonnée, the candy maker of the *bêtises de Cambrai*. In no time, he found Marie Dieudonnée. He explained to her Cajetan's condition. She knew right away what was wrong with her brother. She gathered her healing herbs and medicines, put them in a large pouch and was ready to go. They immediately left for Calais.

As ill fortune would have it, the return sailing was difficult what with the storm and the high winds they encountered. Except for being afraid of the sea, Marie Dieudonnée conquered her fears and remained calm during the entire crossing. As for Peter, he vomited three times while Marie Dieudonnée gave him some medicine to alleviate his vomiting. He was terribly glad when they reached Dover.

When Marie Dieudonnée saw her brother in the sad condition that he was, she immediately began to prepare some medication. It had taken Peter and Marie Dieudonnée almost four and a half days to get there. She felt dejected and started losing hope for Cajetan's recovery. But she did not tell either Peter or Master Architect de Longchamp. She thought they were worried enough.

----He's been definitely poisoned. Do you know who or what? she asked.

----No, we don't know who would do such a thing.

----Perhaps vengeance or jealousy?

----We cannot say, replied Peter.

----Do you think you can cure him? asked Master de Longchamp.

----I will do my very best. After all, he is my brother and I feel a great affection for him. He and my other brother are my family. I have no one else. He's been ill for well over a week and I do not know if I am too late with my healing medications, but Il try. I will try the best I can.

Marie Dieudonnée worked tirelessly at trying to heal her brother while Cajetan kept sinking lower and lower. The priest even came to give Cajetan the last rites. Everyone's spirits were low, very low. Marie Dieudonnée decided that she would try some of the incantations that Geneviève la Guérisseuse had taught her. She had told Marie Dieudonnée that these incantations should be used only when necessary, and with great care and diligence for some would interpret that as possible sorcery. La Guérisseuse had told Marie Dieudonnée that one had to fight sorcery with sorcery. Marie Dieudonnée did not care at that moment, and she told herself that she would add some of her own prayers that her mother, Grisoulda, had taught her when she was young. She was willing to try whatever would pull Cajetan out of the dark hands of death. Cajetan was now ashen and his breathing was heavy and labored. His fever had not ceased for his forehead was burning and his hands were terribly cold.

Marie Dieudonnée stayed at her brother's bedside four days and four nights. She was utterly exhausted and dejected in spite of the fact that she somehow clung to some hope in the Good Lord and especially in Blessed Mary's intercession. The fervor with which she recited her incantations and her prayers made her observers feel as if she were a saint come down from heaven. She impressed some of the observers with her dedication to her brother while she inspired others to pray with her. Cardinal Archbishop Tintamarre came one early evening after Vespers and blessed the sick Cajetan. He had genuine concern in his eyes, thought Master de Longchamp.

On the fifth day, right before sunrise, before the cock crowed, Cajetan's fever began to subside and he opened his eyes. He was thirsty, he whispered. He was so terribly surprised to see his sister at his bedside that he uttered a small cry. Marie Dieudonnée who was sensitive to the least sound, being on edge for days, woke up and started to cry tears of joy. Her hopes had been met; her dream of her brother's recovery had been realized, and her prayers answered. She took Cajetan's hand in her own and squeezed lightly. He squeezed back. Master de Longchamp and Peter, who both had been keeping vigil over Cajetan, woke up to find Cajetan speaking in a low voice to his sister. They were both excited about the good news. Cajetan had made it; he was going to live.

A few days later, Cajetan was up and about eating and wanting to get back to work. Master de Longchamp told him to take it easy and enjoy the company of his sister. Master de Longchamp was still concerned about Cajetan's poisoning. Who had done such a thing? Was it poisoning ot not? Cajetan told him not to worry about that since he was going to be just fine. However, Marie Dieudonnée had told her brother in secret that she thought that his serious malady was sorcery and that a curse need not be put on someone near. It can be done from a distance, she said. Cajetan thought of the only person who would wish him wrong…Rielbert. But was it him?

----I'm going to look into this issue of poisoning as much as I can. There has to be an answer to it, said the Master.

----Please don't waste your time on that issue and on me. You have important things to do. I have caused enough worries and problems for so many people.

----People love you, my friend, and they have a right to worry about you when you're so close to death.

----Was I?

----Yes, Cajetan, replied Marie Dieudonnée. You were this close to death. I tried everything that I could, herbs, other medicines and incantations given to me by Geneviève la Guérisseuse, and nothing seemed to work. Remember what I told you. I really think that a hex or a curse was put on you by someone. Thank God that our prayers were answered. The Blessed Virgin Mary took good care of you. She's the one who has replaced our mother, Grisoulda, you know.

----Don't say curse, Marie Dieudonnée, for someone may hear you and think that you're a sorceress yourself with your incantations.

----Rest, Cajetan. Be quiet and rest. I'll stay with you until you are completely well.

----But what about your work back home?

----It can wait. I sent word to the bonnet shop, and alerted the owner that I would be gone for some time to take care of my sick brother, and that it was truly serious.

----I've caused you so much pain and worries. I'm sorry.

----Don't be. Besides, I'm with you and I'm enjoying my visit. You can show me your cathedral later on.

----It's not up yet, only the foundation.

----Then you can explain the whole process of building a cathedral to me. I'm afraid I know very little about the construction of a big cathedral.

----A Gothic cathedral.

----Yes, a Gothic cathedral.

Once he got out of bed and started walking again, Cajetan was quick to show his sister the *chantier*, the various workshops, the Master Craftsmen and the foundation of the proposed new cathedral. She thought that he really knew quite a lot about Gothic cathedrals the way he explained everything, and she told him so. He also told her about his trip to Paris and Amiens with Master Architect de Chaussoyes, and the magnificent sculptures in stone as well as the glorious stained-glass windows, especially the rose windows that he saw at Notre-Dame de Paris and Notre-Dame d'Amiens. She told him how she envied him for the learning he was experiencing, and that she wished she could profit from learning too.

----But you can learn, Marie Dieudonnée. You can attend some school or convent somewhere in your vicinity.

----Yes, but it costs money and I don't have it.

----As soon as I'm made journeyman, I'll send you some. Promise me you'll take it and get some education.

----I'd like to learn how to teach children. I think I'd be good at it.

----Then do it. Learn and teach.

----I don't know if I want to get married though, Cajetan.

----You don't have to. You're still young.

----Not so. I'm sixteen, Cajetan, an age when other young women are already married and have children. Besides, an unmarried woman my age sticks out in society. People pass remarks on her.

----You don't have to follow the rules, my dear sister. You never did.

----No, I didn't, didn't I?

----You were your mother's daughter, Marie Dieudonnée.

----Yes, I was. Mother was her own woman. She made her own way in life. Not that she was a rebel but she learned how to fend for herself. Papa was her steady rock on whom she leaned for encouragement, but she was the master of the house, she made us children in her image. Too bad she died so young.

After a few more days, Marie Dieudonnée decided it was time to head back home. She knew that Cajetan was well now, and that he could make it on his own. The curse had been lifted, she thought in her heart, but she did not dare pursue the matter any longer. Let matters that deal with evil lie. She told herself that evil existed in the world and that it sometimes manifested itself in mysterious ways. That sometimes the devil was out to get any young person who was God's chosen one, and tried to poison him in any way he could. That's what Geneviève la Guérisseuse had told her, but she had never told anyone about it. She did not want to admit to such beliefs for fear of having to contend with serious breaches in her own Christian faith.

She said her goodbyes to Cajetan and made him promise that he would visit her in the fall. With the help of Peter, she got onto a boat in Dover, alone, for she didn't want Peter to lose his time chaperoning her to France. She knew her way, she said, and she could very well fend for herself, she told him. There was smooth sailing aboard the boat, and she reached Calais in complete safety. Then she proceeded to find transportation to Cambrai. She was glad that she had spent some time with Cajetan but not in that situation of illness and worries. She never wanted to experience that again. Never. The following day she was back at work in *la bonneterie*.

Cajetan lost no time to get back to work with Master de Longchamp. He explained to Cajetan how the foundation had been closely examined for fissures, and how the masons had assured its stability.

----The foundation of a cathedral, my dear Cajetan, has to be solid and without fissures so that the rain, snow and ice cannot seep through it. Cold and ice expand and endanger the mortar on the stones. Any threat to the stability of the foundation is a threat to the cathedral, remember that.

----I will.

----The Master Mason will inspect once more the foundation for the horizontality of the stones, and use his plumb line to make sure that the wall will be perfectly vertical. Any deviance in the foundation could endanger the wall to be built on top of it.

----I understand.

----You understand everything well, Cajetan. That's why I enjoy having you with me. You're a very good learner.

----Thank you.

After that, the two of them moved to one side of the *chantier* where the first wall was to be built. The Master explained to Cajetan that the walls of a Gothic cathedral consist of piers that support the vault and roof, and space between the piers are filled for the most part with tracery.

----Tracery?

----Yes, tracery. That's the stone framework of the windows.

----Like Master de Chaussoyes and I saw in Paris and Amiens.

----Precisely. My design shows that the piers of this cathedral are going to be one hundred and seventy feet high and seven feet thick.

----Those are big piers.

----Yes. They're to be constructed with hundreds of pieces of cut stones. You can see why we take out so much stone out of the quarry.

----I see.

----The walls will be much thinner than the old Romanesque walls, as you saw in Paris and Amiens.

----At Notre-Dame de Paris and Notre-Dame d'Amiens.

----Yes. You also know why we will need buttresses on the outside.

----Yes, to buttress, reinforce the walls with the arched vaults tending to push the piers outward. In Gothic architecture, everything needs to be balanced and the weight distributed. Right?

----Right. You've learned that lesson well, Cajetan.

----Then, the glaziers must be working on the stained-glass in preparation for the large windows. Will there be rose windows ?

----Yes, four of them. One above the main portal, one above the south portal's tympanum, one at the north portal's tympanum, and one above the high altar that I reserve for myself. The Cardinal Archbishop has already elected to design, with the glaziers, of course, the other three rose windows. He has his hand in everything, you see.

----What is your rose window going to be like?

----You'll have to wait and see.

Another year went by and Cajetan was learning fast about the various components of a cathedral. He was ever hungry for details and ways of doing things. Having explored the workshops of most of the craftsmen, Cajetan then went to that part of the *chantier* where the glaziers were. He looked around and then saw Master Glazier, Thomas Morand.

----Are you making preparations for the windows, Master Morand?

----Oh, so you're ahead of the game, aren't you. They haven't raised the walls yet.

----But they're going to, soon. I know.

----Of course, I'm in preparation for those windows. I've been preparing for those for the last six months. Stained-glass takes time, and so does the preparation of the lead. It's like a giant puzzle, my young friend, like an enormous prefigured design that one has to assemble. When we've reached that point, I'll let you know.

----Thank you, Master Morand.

After a few more weeks when Cajetan had regained all of his strength, Master de Longchamp told Cajetan to go out more and enjoy himself, for, after all, life is not meant to be at work all of the time, he told him.

----Go to the tavern at the Inn of the Green Man. Have an ale or two. Take a look at the barmaids. Enjoy a good evening at my expense. Here's a few coins.

----Thank you, but I don't want to spend money on entertainment and ale.

----Yes, you need to do that. I order you to do it. You need to lighten your mind of architectural problems and designs. Things will fall into place, you'll see.

And so, that evening, Cajetan went to the Tavern-on-the-Square. He ordered a tall ale and sat at the bar looking around to see if he might recognize anybody. He did not see anyone that he knew except the journeyman from the carpenter's workshop. As he was sipping his ale and sort of daydreaming, a young woman came to tap him on the shoulder and introduced herself as Maureen Coveneigh.

----You're a barmaid here aren't you?

----Yes, I am. I saw you there sitting by yourself not talking to anyone, and with your mind lost in the clouds.

----You might say that.

----What's your name?

----Cajetan from France.

----Cajetan from France. Well, Cajetan from France tell me about yourself.

----There's nothing much to tell. I'm an apprentice to Master Architect Sigismond de Longchamp right now and previously an apprentice to Master Architect Albert de Chaussoyes in Reims. I've been an apprentice since the age of thirteen. I've just turned sixteen.

----Well, that's quite a personal history, Master Cajetan.

----I'm not a master yet.

----But you are to me. You look like a master of what you survey and guide.

----You're teasing me.

----A bit. You look like you could enjoy some fun.

----Tell me about yourself, Maureen Coveneigh.

----Well, I was born in Ireland and stayed there until I was sixteen. My parents were poor. I mean very poor, and they had a hard time taking care of us all, me and my brothers and sisters. We were thirteen in all.

----That's a large family.

----Oh, yes. And so I decided to come to England to spread my wings and earn a living. It wasn't easy to get here alone, so I asked my cousin, Eberly, to accompany me, and that I would give him the first two weeks of my wages if he did that for me. He agreed and here I am.

----Weren't you afraid?

----Afraid of what? I was more afraid of being poor and staying that way all of my life. Poor like dirt. Even poorer, like being without honor and dignity. Now, that's being poor.

----I'm poor but I have my honor and my dignity as a man.

----Yes, it's easier for a man than for a woman. My mother was a woman without any shred of dignity left after giving birth to fifteen children. She lost two at childbirth. She was treated like a slave by my father who had no honor himself. No dignity either. He was a tramp, my father. He was a stinking, drinking tramp.

----Don't say that about your father.

----I sure as can. That's what he was. I hated him for it. Hated him for what he was doing to my mother. The priest kept telling my mother to endure him and offer her sufferings to the Lord for her sins and my father's sins. What sins? She had no sins except of staying with my father for so many years. What did the priest know about endurance and suffering? He stayed in his comfortable rectory and said mass in his comfortable church. I hate priests. Do you go to church, Cajetan?

----Yes, I do. I'm building a cathedral, and I want to follow the Church's teachings and her example.

----What teachings, except to mire the minds of the faithful and reduce them to mush? Obedient slaves, they are.

----You are certainly harsh on priests and the Church, Maureen. Don't you have anymore faith left?

----I've seen too much and experienced too much. People who suffer and are caught up in poverty begin to lose faith, not in God, but in the priests that tell you to suffer all the time. It's good for you and your soul, they tell us. Good for the soul, my eye! A soul without dignity and sense of trust.

----My experience with family and the Church is different than yours. I was born in a family of three children. Both my parents were good and kind people. My mother, Grisoulda, bless her soul, was an honest and generous person to all and especially to us her children. And to my father. My father was a stone cutter. A very good one. He was like my grandfather on my mother's side, a stone cutter and a believer in dreams. As a matter of fact, they used to call him Hubert the Stargazer. Do you believe in dreams, Maureen?

----I don't know.

----You don't know?

----Well, I wish I could believe in them but I'm often disappointed. Dreams seldom come true.

----I dream of becoming a builder of cathedrals. I mean an architect who designs and makes plans for a cathedral.

----Aren't you doing that now?

----No. I'm just an apprentice.

----Well, you're on your way to becoming one, aren't you? Then your dreams are coming true.

----You might say that.

----As for me, I have no dreams. That way I won't be disappointed.

----But a life without dreams is a life without sunshine and light. You live permanently in the dark. In the shadow of things.

----My, you're the philosopher, Cajetan from France. You see things in a different light than me.

----Some day I'm going to bring to life your dream, Maureen.

----How can you if I don't have one.

----Oh, you have at least one. It's hidden, and you don't know about it.

----If you say so, Cajetan from France. If you say so.

Cajetan met Maureen again for the next couple of evenings at the tavern. They enjoyed their conversations together. Cajetan felt attracted to her. She had red hair, the color of bright copper, green eyes, hardy complexion and freckles on her nose, and high cheek bones. Her smile was congenial and her laughter, hearty and engaging. He really liked her. She put a spark in the ordinariness of his life. She was a very good worker and greeted all with a warm disposition unless the guest was mean to her and the others in the tavern. Then she showed her Irish, as she called it, with bright glints in her green eyes and, at times, flashes of fury. That's when Cajetan told her to hold her temper and cool her head. It made her laugh.

After several weeks of tavern encounters, Cajetan convinced Maureen to go to church with him Sunday morning and attend mass. At first, she did not want to do it, but after some gentle coaxing, she relented. So they met in front of Saint Agnes church on the knoll, not far from the *chantier* and they both went inside the church that Sunday morning. When they came out followed by the other faithful, they went to sit on a stone bench right outside the church in a little park to talk and tell each other about their week, and what they had done and what they had seen. The following week, they did the same thing, attend mass and sit outside on the park bench. Suddenly, there appeared the Cardinal Archbishop strolling along the road leading to his residence. He stopped in front of the couple and started to talk to them. He looked proud and affable at the same time. Cajetan had never seen him so approachable, even kind in his manner.

----Good morning, Cajetan. Who is this young woman with you?

Cajetan got up and introduced Maureen to him.

----This is Maureen Coveneigh from Ireland, Your Eminence.

----I'm glad to meet you. You look bright and charming this morning my child. Nothing as beautiful as an Irish lass. Irish beauty is to be treasured.

----Thank you, sire.

Cajetan corrected her, Your Eminence, Maureen.

----Your Eminence.

----How old are you, Maureen? asked the Cardinal Archbishop.

----I'm eighteen, Your Eminence.

----You're not married yet?

----No. I have time to get married when it's time.

----Oh, I see. Then Cajetan is your special friend?

----You could say that.

----You're a lovely young woman, Maureen. I trust we'll see each other again.

----I suppose, Your Eminence.

The Cardinal Archbishop departed with a certain gleam in his eye.

----Who is that, Cajetan?

----He told you, the Cardinal Archbishop Tintamarre. He's in charge of our new cathedral.

----I find him a bit too sugary in his approach to women and a bit haughty too. I did not like his approach with me. It made me feel nervous. I don't know why.

----Probably because he's an Archbishop and a Cardinal on top of that.

----Archbishop, Cardinal or not, he's a man like any other man. I know the kind. Why did he stop to greet us, Cajetan?

----I don't know why. He doesn't usually show any kind of friendly overture with me. Only with Master de Longchamp.

----What do you suppose he wants?

----I don't know. Do you think he wants something?

----Not from you but most probably from me.

----What?

----What men want from women. Favors.

----No. He's not that kind of a man. He's celibate and an Archbishop on top of that.

----That's the worst kind, Cajetan. I know them all.

----What do you mean?

----I mean that people like him use their power and position to gain favors.

----Here you go again with favors.

----Favors, favors from women like carnal favors, Cajetan. You're so naïve. You've had so little worldly experience in your young life, Cajetan.

----I've been around.

----Not around much.

----But the Cardinal Archbishop would not even dare touch you. He's admired and adulated by everyone.

----That's precisely the kind I'm talking about. I stay away from them.

----I think you're exaggerating, Maureen. I think you're just making things up.

----Wait and see, Cajetan. Wait and see.

Several weeks went by. Cajetan and Maureen met at the tavern as usual during the week nights and on Sunday morning at Saint Agnes church. The last time they saw each other, Maureen looked somewhat peevish. She seemed irritable and a bit cross. Cajetan asked her what was wrong, and she answered back abruptly with a bit of sarcasm. He didn't know what to make of her sudden irritable behavior. Then, one evening when Cajetan visited the tavern, Maureen took him by the hand and brought him outdoors and sat him down on the corner of the large flower container. She told him that she was leaving Devonshire, and that she had had enough of everything.

----Enough of me?

----You too. Men are all alike.

----Why are you mad at me?

----I can't tell you.

She started to cry.

----What's the matter, Maureen?

----You and your Archbishop, he's no better than all the others.

----What?

----Yes, he approached me and forced me to go with him in his residence telling me that if I did not go, he would make sure that everyone knew about me and my reputation.

----What about your reputation?

----I was a prostitute once. Not for long. Just to survive. Are you ashamed of me, Cajetan?

----No, but how did he know that?

----It's his business to know things.

----What did he do to you?

----He had his way with me. When I resisted, he forced me to lie down with him using all the power of his strong arms. He had his way with me, Cajetan. He had his dirty ways with me.

Then, she started sobbing. Cajetan did not know what to do or say. He put his arm around her left shoulder.

----Cajetan, I'm leaving. He gave me some money to keep it quiet. Enough money to help my mother for some time. I'm going back home.

----Is that all you're going to do about it?

----What else do you want me to do? I'm caught in his web, the ugly spider that he is. I'm caught in his web and so is my dream of becoming your wife some day.

----You want to be my wife?

----Not anymore. I can't. I'm soiled by the very man you serve. You and your cathedral.

----Wait a minute now. I don't approve of his actions, especially with you. That's not at all appropriate.

----Appropriate or not, there's nothing you can do. He has you in his evil power too, except he hides it in a very cagey way. Beware Cajetan, just beware, because he knows that you know. He'll want to get rid of you also.

----He can't do that. I have my Master who will take care of me and vouch for me. I haven't done anything wrong.

----He's got the power, Cajetan, he's got the power to rid of what bothers him. Nothing gets in his way. Men like that know how to exercise power over people.

----I'm so sorry, Maureen. I'm going to talk to my Master.

----Please don't. You'll just make matters worse.

Maureen left the following morning right before dawn as if she wanted no one to know she was leaving. There was shame in the air, the shame of a Cardinal Archbishop shaming a young woman.

Cajetan felt low and sad. He could not overcome the frustration that gnawed at him. He decided to go and see Master Architect de Longchamp. As he arrived to his workshop, the Master told him with a curt and joyless voice,

----You arrive at a good time, Cajetan. I want to talk to you.

----And I want to talk to you too.

----I have some good news for you. You're now seventeen going on eighteen and you are to be promoted to journeyman. I've talked to the guild and the members agree, upon my recommendation, to give you the rank of journeyman. You're practically eighteen now and it's time you earned an income. You have shown your skills and your intelligence here at this *chantier*. You've been here for close to three years. Congratulations.

----Thank you, Master. I have something…

Master de Longchamp cut him off.

----I have some more news for you, Cajetan.

He said it with an awkward smile on his face.

----What, Master?

----In a few days you'll be going to Flanders to a new *chantier*.

----Why Flanders?

----Because you've been wanting to see an excavation and a new foundation. It will be from the ground up.

----But I've seen an excavation and a foundation right here.

----The excavation was already done as well as the foundation. Now you'll be able to see everything from the very beginning of construction.

----But I prefer staying here with you. I don't really want to go to Flanders. It's too far.

----You have no choice in the matter. It's been decided for you, Cajetan.

----By whom?

----I'm not at liberty to say.

There was a cold moment before Cajetan was able to speak again. Like frost had covered the relationship between master and apprentice.

----Is it something I've done?

----No.

----Is it my qualifications as an apprentice?

----You've just been promoted to journeyman.

----Then what?

There was a long silence, then Master de Longchamp told Cajetan authoritatively,

----Do what you are told, Cajetan.

----Am I being punished for something?

----No.

----Then what? I want to know.

----This is all I'm going to tell you.

----You're hiding something from me, is that it?

----Please do as I tell you, Cajetan, or else…

----Or else what?

----You risk losing not only your job but your trade and any future that goes with it. Your dream, Cajetan.

There was a very long pause, then Cajetan said reluctantly and with a tinge of sad submission.

----How do I get there and where is it?

----The clerk will tell you all about it. And you will have money to travel. Besides you will start earning a salary as soon as you get to the new *chantier*. Your new master architect is Master Architect Kurt Marquardt, a most capable man with superior skills as an architect. I know him personally.

----And the Archbishop in charge?

----He's not an Archbishop yet. It's Excellency Bishop Romuald van Artevelde.

----I hope he's nothing like Archbishop Tintamarre.

----Cardinal Tintamarre.

----I forgot. Do you think I could appeal my case to Cardinal Tintamarre?

----No. Absolutely not.

Cajetan felt as if he had been cheated out of something, probably waylaid or even violated by an act of treason. That's how he felt. He felt helpless.

----But I wanted to talk to you about Maureen Coveneigh.

----That's a dead issue.

And with that, Master de Longchamp walked away without turning around for one final glance at his beloved apprentice now journeyman.

Cajetan did not sleep all night. He tossed and turned. Got up and went back to bed several times. Peter asked him what was wrong, but Cajetan did not want to talk about it for fear that it had the potential of implicating Peter, his friend. Cajetan now knew that the Cardinal was directly involved. He had to be, and that his Master would not stand up for him for fear of losing his position as Master Architect. The Cardinal had that power, and he would use it too. Cajetan knew all too well that this power held by the Cardinal was very strong and damning. It all made sense to him now. Maureen was gotten rid of and now the one person who knew about the incident was being sent away, far away to another kingdom where he could not talk about the Cardinal in any way shape or form, and be listened to. Cajetan was being exiled, so he thought. Was he right?

Cajetan was to leave the following Friday morning. Everything was prepared for his departure. He was going to Ghent in Flanders. He said goodbye to Peter and tried to say farewell to Master de Longchamp but could not get to see him. At each attempt, the Master was not available, he was told. The day before he left, he happened to meet the Cardinal on his way to the *chantier*. The Cardinal gave him the hardest and coldest look a person could ever give. It was just a glance but a glance that penetrated to the heart like an icicle. "What did I do to him?" asked Cajetan to himself. Cajetan left very early at dawn for his destination. He would have to write his sister about the change. As he was leaving, Cajetan was able to spot Peter from away waving to him and pointing to the morning star. The year was 1265 A.D. as written in Cajetan's diary. He had begun to keep one.

6

MARIE DIEUDONNÉE AND ABÉLARD FRANÇOIS

The journey was long, arduous, tiring and cold. It was late October. Cajetan could not understand why he was submitted to such an ordeal. He thought of Maureen back in Ireland, and wondered how she was managing things in her life. He felt deeply sorry for her. Why did things happen that way? he thought. Why did Cardinal Archbishop Tintamarre behave like a deranged man? Why could he not restrain himself? After all, he was a Church leader of high position, Cajetan said to himself feeling utterly confused. He just could not make any sense out of this. Cajetan had the habit of matching responsibility with correct ethical behavior. He allowed for no deviance. For him. men were bound by reason and moral behavior to make the right choices. He thought of Brother Abélard Marie, the good and honest churchman that he knew and trusted just like his mother did. How different from that pompous Cardinal, he thought. After a while, he stopped questioning things and started to think about his new position as journeyman at a new *chantier*. That brought him relief from the burden of questioning things and getting no answers.

When they crossed the border between England and France, Cajetan was told that he would have a new guide all the way to Flanders. His name was Mathieu Delamarre. He was a fat little man with wisps of hair sprouting out of his hat. He looked like a jester. He was funny like a jester and he laughed with a loud voice that took over all or any conversation in and around him. He laughed so loud that people turned around just to see where the laughter was coming from. Cajetan liked him. He was a jolly man, and Cajetan needed cheering up. He had put behind him all of misery of the bad experience in England in the last few weeks. He was now ready to look to the future and to his new status as journeyman. He was hoping that the new Master Architect Marquardt would accept him and his accumulated skills as a cathedral designer. Besides being with two Master Architects, he had studied on his own the planning and designs of a cathedral. Cajetan had an probing mind and a voracious appetite to learn. He lost no opportunities to learn be it his encounters with master craftsmen, journeymen, even laborers. He firmly believed that everyone could instruct him in some fashion. Cajetan was not a haughty person nor a self-centered individual who only trusted the learning of higher placed individuals. Everyone, he said, had intelligence and gifts from God that could be shared with others, if only one received them honestly and without any sense of self-centeredness. Cajetan's personality was an open one; he was opened to everyone and everything. He liked people and people liked him, a gift from his mother, Grisoulda. Of course, there were some who did not want to admit in their midst anyone not associated with their respective guilds. They called them spies or snoopers, and they were not open-hearted enough or not secure enough to accept what they called outsiders. But Cajetan had managed to ingratiate himself with almost everyone on the *chantiers* where he happened to be. They knew he was a dreamer and dreamers are not always considered a threat to anyone or any craft or trade.

Mathieu explained to Cajetan what route they would take to go to Ghent. He also instructed Cajetan about the large city of Ghent, an esteemed city by all who lived there and visited it. Cajetan was glad that he was going there to build a cathedral, part of the dream of his life. However, Mathieu told him that the new cathedral would not be in Ghent proper but on the outskirts in a town called Zelzate. Ghent already had an Episcopal seat, and because Ghent was growing so fast, it was decided by Archbishop Alexander van der Goes, with the consent of Rome, to form another diocese, and build a new cathedral, a Gothic one. A new bishop, His Excellency Bishop Romuald van Artevelde had been ordained and enthroned in his newly formed diocese.

The *chantier* was called *le chantier* Saint Amand, he told Cajetan. You're going to like it there. I come from there. I am a guide and a craftsman. I repair timepieces, like hourglasses, sundials and the likes. No more telling time by candles.

----Are you good at your trade?

----Of course. I'm getting better at it. I'm looking into the clock. That's a new concept of telling time. It may take some time, but I'm going to invent a clock that will not only tell time but also it will feature automated figures that go round and round when the clock tolls time. I'm going to have roosters crowing, tiny people ringing bells and angels sounding trumpets and even jugglers.

----That's quite something. When will your clock be ready?

----Oh, I don't know, Perhaps in twenty years or more. It's not done yet. I have to work hard at it, and I have very little time since I do repairing and serve as a travel guide. But it's still in my mind and my imagination, for, you see, I too have dreams, dreams of inventions.

----Too bad that we could not put one in our new cathedral.

----We'll see, Cajetan. We'll see.

The two of them took to the road and walked until they were completely exhausted. Then they rested for a while. Once in Flanders, Mathieu got a room for the night at a local inn since he did not want to go any further without having a good meal before retiring. They were in a small village called Rumbeke. Mathieu knew the proprietor, and told him that he wanted the room upstairs with a window facing the road that accommodated two people. He knew the inn well. Mathieu and Cajetan climbed the stairs to their room, discharged their belongings and got ready for the evening meal. Cajetan wanted to wash the road dust off of him, but Mathieu told him that it was good dust, and that a little bit of road dust never harmed anybody. However, Cajetan insisted, and he went outside to wash up in a large basin filled with cold water.

Sitting at a wide oval table with two other guests, Mathieu and Cajetan looked forward to the evening meal. They were served helpings of *stoverij'*, a meat stew with lots of meat that Cajetan liked as soon as he put a spoonful in his mouth, *mastellen* called Saint Hubert bread, and a tankard of strong brown abbey beer.

----My grandfather on my mother's side was called Hubert, Hubert the Stargazer, said Cajetan while chewing on a piece of bread.

----Why Stargazer?

----Because he liked to look at the stars, just like me. He was a stone cutter.

----You like to gaze at the stars?

----Yes. There's nothing like a nice cool and clear evening when the stars glimmer in the dark sky, and I lie down on the grass and look at the stars dreaming that, one day, I will build my own cathedral.

----Your own cathedral?

----Not mine, actually, but one that I plan and design as a Master Architect.

----That's your dream.

----Oh, yes, Mathieu.

----Well, I hope you have your dream come true some day.

----It will happen, Mathieu, because it's not only in the stars but the Lord will see to it that it happens if he wants a cathedral in the Gothic style that elevates its arches, vaults and spires to heaven in praise and glory to Him.

----*Le Bon Dieu.*

----*Oui, le Bon Dieu.*

----So, you like Gothic architecture, Cajetan?

----Yes, there's nothing like it. Unlike the Romanesque with its thick walls and small and narrow windows, the Gothic lets in a lot of light through its large stained-glass windows. And the rose windows, what a sight, a real wonder, Mathieu. Have you been to Paris and Amiens to look at the cathedrals there?

----Not yet, Cajetan but I've been told they're fabulous pieces of Gothic architecture.

----Not only fabulous but marvelously fabulous if I may say so, and filled with wonder like magic. They are truly the Bible in stone and stained glass.

----You are truly taken with the Gothic cathedrals, aren't you?

----Of course, who would not be, Mathieu?

After they had eaten, Cajetan stepped outside in the cool air to look at the stars while Mathieu who gorged himself with the bread, stew and beer, went straight upstairs to bed, and began snoring right away. Cajetan stayed outdoors for quite a while since the air was mild and mellow. He told himself that he was going to like this new place called, Flanders. Here, he would learn much more, from the ground up, from excavation to spires, the art and craft of architectural design put to execution with a Master Architect. He could not wait to get started.

Cajetan went upstairs to the bedroom, and even before he could reach the top stair to the room, he was astounded by the loud snoring he heard. It was so loud that Cajetan dared not penetrate inside the room, for he did not want to sleep with such noise. However, he rushed inside, grabbed a pillow and blanket and went to sleep outdoors under the stars and the soft whisper of the breeze in the trees.

The following morning, Cajetan woke up feeling a bit chilled for the dew had settled on his blanket and the air had gotten colder. He got up, washed his face and hands, straightened his clothes and carried the pillow and blanket upstairs to the bedroom where Mathieu was still sound asleep. Cajetan did not want to wake him, but he knew that Mathieu wanted to leave early that day.

----Wake up, sleepy head. It's time to get ready for the road.

Mathieu, woke up slowly with sleep still in his large brown eyes. He rubbed his eyes and saw Cajetan with a pillow under one arm and a blanket under the other.

----Where have you been, Cajetan?

----I slept outdoors. Impossible to sleep here with your loud snoring.

----I'm sorry. I didn't realize that my snoring would push you outdoors. Please forgive me. My mother always said that I snored too loud, loud enough to wake the neighbors. I don't know, I've never heard myself snore.

And Mathieu laughed out loud.

----I enjoyed the outdoors under the stars.

----Cajetan the Stargazer. The man who looks beyond the heavens.

----Yes, I've been called that before.

After breakfast, Mathieu and Cajetan set out for Ghent. They were on the last leg of their journey. Mathieu explained to Cajetan that Ghent lay some distance away but that they should reach it by nightfall. Mathieu informed Cajetan on the way that Ghent started as a settlement at the confluence of the Rivers Scheldt and Lys. He told Cajetan that Saint Amand founded two abbeys in Ghent, the Saint Peter Abbey and the Saint Bavo's Abbey. As it grew as a city, Ghent became an important center with the two abbeys and the commercial center. He went on to say that Louis the Pious, Charlemagne's son, appointed Einhard, Charlemagne's biographer, Abbot of both abbeys. Since the last century, Ghent flourished with the trade of cloth made from sheep's wool and became the biggest city after Paris. Along with spices, wool cloth was one of the great staples of long-distance commerce, Mathieu said. He added that Flemish wool manufacturers bought fine wool fleece from England which produced the best wool. This wool was put out to weavers who, in their own houses, and their own families, spun and wove it into cloth. The very best cloth around, Mathieu said.

----Really?

----Yes. I know, because my sisters and two of my brothers-in-law are spinners and weavers. They make excellent wool cloth which they sell to the manufacturers. Besides the herding of sheep on the *meersen*, the water-meadows, and the many attractions offered to visitors and the many scenic places, Ghent is a very popular place for people to settle with a family.

----When did your family come here?

----I was born here. I'm fourth generation Delamarre. My great-grandfather came from France, Delamarre from the region of Lille. He was a sheepherder.

----And your father?

----A wool merchant.

----Your mother?

----A seamstress. She mends clothes and makes clothes for others and her family. She was very good at it.

----Do you have any brothers and sisters?

----One brother and three sisters. My brother lives with my mother, and my sisters are all married with children. My father died seven years ago.

----How about you?

----I live with my sister, Gertrude, since her husband died four years ago. He died in an accident. He was plowing his land when the harrow struck some rocks and the horse got frightened and he kicked my brother in the head. He died instantly. My sister was left with three children. I help out. How about you?

----I have one sister and one brother who's a Carmelite brother in a monastery in Cambrai. My sister, Marie Dieudonnée, is not married yet. She lives in Cambrai too. Both my parents are dead.

----Marie Dieudonnée, that's a lovely name.

----Come to think of it, I have to get in touch with her soon because she doesn't know I'm not in England anymore. She will worry when she does not hear from me. You see, I was very sick, close to death, and she came to take care of me for several weeks. I hope I can find a courier to send her a letter.

----You won't find one that's fast enough. It will take weeks if not months for your sister to receive any mail from you. But, I'll tell you what. I'm going that way next week, and I'll be glad to deliver your message to her in Cambrai.

----You know where Cambrai is?

----Of course. You're talking to an experienced guide and traveler. I know where Cambrai is.

----Thank you so very much. That's a load off my mind. I can never thank you enough.

----Well, go on dreaming and build your cathedral.

----First I must help build the one in Zelzate at the *chantier Saint Amand*.

----Yes, my friend.

Since it was mid-November, nightfall was coming in faster than late September or early October. It was getting dark. Mathieu told Cajetan that they were approaching the city of Ghent and not to feel apprehensive. Ghent was a friendly place, and crime was very low. Thievery and killing were not usual happenings. People were busy with their own affairs, and the poor and the destitute were being taken care of by charitable organizations such as the local convents, hospices and centers of mercy.

----What are centers of mercy, Mathieu?

----They're groups organized by men and women who feel the need to care for the downtrodden and those who suffer the vagaries of life.

----Vagaries?

----Yes, vagaries. They're the caprices of life's happenings such as bad luck, sudden mishaps, a lack of money due to theft, an illness of some kind, and many other unexpected happenings that come and reverse someone's good fortune. According to the people who deal with those who suffer from the reversals, these poor souls need mercy. Just as the Lord brings mercy to all of us sinners, the people working in these centers bring mercy to those who suffer in pain. It's not pity, it's mercy. We are asked to be merciful as God is merciful.

----This is a great idea. Are you part of this movement? You seem to know a lot about it.

----Yes, I'm part of it. I do what I can.

----I'd like to be part of it myself.

----I'll help you to join.
As they approached Ghent, Mathieu felt a tug on his left sleeve. It was a young boy with his hand out, begging.

----Please sire, help me. It's for my sick mother. Help me.

----He's really not in need and neither is his mother, Cajetan. I know the kind. They're gypsies, wanderers out robbing people. The older ones send the children out to beg and keep the person being solicited occupied, and unaware while someone in hiding robs and runs away. Some deserted streets are crawling with them. We are not in a good section of the city right now. But, we have to go through here because I want to bring you to an inn that is perfectly safe for the night. I think it's too late to go to the *chantier,* don't you think?

----I agree.

The two men spent the night in a humble but clean and safe inn for travelers. Mathieu knew that Cajetan was running out of money, and he did not want to make him spend money for nothing. The following morning, after breakfast of *mastel* and a hot beverage, possibly made of barley, the two of them headed for the construction site.

The *chantier* was in an area that was huge and open. It looked like the land had been cleared of trees and shrubs. It was on a knoll overlooking the river. Perfect as a cathedral site, thought Cajetan. Mathieu said goodbye to his traveling companion and told him where to go to find the Master Architect. He did not have the time to introduce him to his Master, not that Mathieu was without courtesy but he had to be somewhere to meet another man who needed his services. Cajetan smiled at Mathieu and thanked him warmly, for he felt he had had an excellent guide and found a new friend. They parted company and Cajetan walked toward the workshop marked Master Architect.

Master Architect Kurt Marquardt was a personable man in his early forties. He had blondish hair with streaks of grey, blue eyes that seem to drill into your soul so deep and intense were they. His face was slightly scarred on the right cheek, and his hands were the hands of an experienced craftsman, so thought Cajetan. The young journeyman saluted his Master and introduced himself. He handed over the letter of introduction given to him by Master Architect Sigismond de Longchamp. Master Marquardt looked at it quickly and told Cajetan to sit down. He had already heard about this young man named Cajetan recently promoted to journeyman. He told Cajetan that he looked forward to working with him and teaching him what he knew about cathedral building and design. Cajetan thanked him and told him that he was proud to be his journeyman. With the formalities over, the Master Architect brought Cajetan to the excavation site. Now, Cajetan was going to experience the construction of a cathedral from the very beginning. He felt excited about that.

Master Architect Marquardt told Cajetan that the Bishop wanted desperately to get started on the foundation as soon as possible for time was of the essence for him. He was a man of time consciousness. Everything had to be done fast and on time, if not ahead of time. He wanted the cathedral built in less time than usual, not forty years, not thirty years, not even twenty years but sixteen to eighteen years. The Bishop was still young and he wanted the project completed when he wasn't too old to enjoy it, said the Master Architect.

----You see here the deep and wide hole that's been dug by excavators. It was done in less than fourteen months. The Bishop wanted it done sooner but the laborers had a hard time removing the large rocks implanted in the ground.

----How many laborers?

----Four hundred and sixty.

----That's a lot of men. A lot of time for each man.

----I did not count the hours. They labored ten to twelve hours a day.

----When will the foundation begin?

----The day after tomorrow. The Bishop wants to get started, and he's very nervous about it. He makes everybody nervous.

----Are you nervous?

----No. Someone has to remain cool-headed.

----I would like to be here at the ceremony.

----You will be. From now on, you will be involved in every step of the construction since you want to learn. It takes much training and many hours of work to become a Master Architect. That's what you want to be, isn't it?

----Yes, of course.

----I am told that you are an intelligent young man, and that you have an inquisitive mind, and you learn well and fast. Everything fascinates you, and you do not hesitate to explore various crafts in order to learn more about the construction of a cathedral. You worked in Reims, and you visited the cathedrals in Paris and Amiens.

----I was going to go to Chartres when I was sent here.

----Well, I think that you are a well-rounded journeyman, and that this experience here in Zelzate will crown your learning and your experience in Gothic architecture.

----Thank you. What you say about me and my experience is true. I never get enough of learning about Gothic cathedrals. It's all so fascinating and glorious.

----Well, keep at it and we'll see about your future development as an architect. I am willing to share with you all that I've acquired over the years.

----That will be great, Master.

----Now, let's continue with the excavation and the foundation, shall we? The excavation went well, even though the Bishop didn't think so, but it went well. The men worked very hard. Now, we've arrived at the foundation. It must be as solid as a rock for on it will rise the walls of the cathedral. It will be made of thick walls, built twenty feet below ground level. The usual depth is twenty-five, but, again, the Bishop wants to save time. I told him that this was not the time to save time. Remember the foundation must support the building and prevent it from settling unevenly.

----So, the Bishop did not listen to you?

----No. He never listens to me. But, I make sure that the necessary critical measures needed for the construction of the cathedral are met.

The following day, a cold November Friday, the Bishop appeared in his crisp new vestments and his violet zucchetto. His pectoral cross of filigree gold with a large amethyst in the center hung on a gold chain around his neck. He stood proud and imperial in front of the foundation stone he was about to bless. Cajetan thought to himself that he hoped this Bishop would not be like Cardinal Archbishop Tintamarre in his haughtiness and spiteful bearing. The Bishop recited a few prayers after he had said, "In nomine Patris et Filio et Spiritui Sancto." Then he took the aspergillum from the gold urn filled with holy water held by a young boy dressed in black, and sprinkled the stone with the holy water. He then handed over the aspergillum to the server. "Amen," said the small crowd surrounding Bishop van Artevelde. The Bishop then turned to his Master Architect Marquardt and said to him in a low voice, but loud enough to be heard by those close to him, "Let's get started." Cajetan heard it and looked at Master Marquardt with a gleam of exhilaration in his eye thinking that, finally, he was going to experience the full building of a cathedral.

The foundation got to a start that very afternoon. Master Architect Marquardt and Master Mason Hilaire Desautels, formerly from Valenciennes in northeastern France, thought that November was too late in the year to begin a foundation, but the Bishop wanted it that way. Save time and gain an advance of the work before spring was the word of the day. However, come late November when the first snow started to fall, the foundation came to a halt, to the great disappointment of the Bishop. As in every previous winter, the finished stonework was covered with straw and dung to prevent the frost from cracking the mortar before it had time to be completely dry. Most of he masons went home for the winter because mortar cannot be done in cold weather. The few that remained were those who lived too far, and could not afford to travel long distances. There was also a cadre of craftsmen like the carpenters, the stone cutters, the sculptors and the apprentices, along with the journeymen living on site and managing the cold weather. They worked in temporary workshops built against temporary walls for the winter months. Everything was quiet in the *chantier Saint Amand*. The hush of winter had begun.

Cajetan asked his Master if he could leave the *chantier* for a while in order to visit his sister in France. He had not seen her in a long time. Master Architect Marquardt granted him his leave, and Cajetan set out to find Mathieu Delamarre to serve as a guide, at least, to the border of Flanders and France. He had heard from Mathieu the week before when Mathieu told him that he had delivered his letter to Marie Dieudonnée, and she had given him a letter for Cajetan. Cajetan had read the letter in which she told him that she heard from the monastery that Abélard François was not well. She was not permitted to take care of him with her herbs and other medicines. The monks would use their own therapies, she was told at the visitors' portal. She was worried, she said. Cajetan was worried too, and that's why he had decided to go to Cambrai.

Cajetan reached Mathieu and the two of them started out on their journey to France. It was cold and windy with blasts of wind that penetrated any clothing one was wearing. Fortunately, Mathieu and Cajetan were wearing several layers of warm woolen cloth under their long tunics. Cajetan had wrapped both of his hands with long strips of woolen fabric. He could not stand having cold hands. Mathieu was all bundled up. Cajetan could barely see Mathieu's face under the cloth he had twisted around his head. He looked like a swami or a diviner with a turban. They left very early in the morning, and only stopped twice for rest and something hot to drink. As soon as they approached the border of France at Lille, Cajetan told Mathieu that he did not need a guide any longer, and that he could make the rest of the journey by himself. Mathieu argued with him about the security of being alone on the road rather than being two. Cajetan told him that he did not want to impose on him any longer. He had done quite enough for which he was very grateful. Mathieu would have none of that, and insisted on going with Cajetan to Cambrai, no matter what Cajetan might say. Cajetan ceded to his friend's wishes and left with him, glad in his heart for the companionship.

Once in Cambrai, Mathieu went his own way to visit friends and have some ale at the local tavern. Cajetan left him and went to his sister's house. He was somewhat apprehensive about what he might hear from her about Abélard François. He knew that his brother never had a strong constitution, and was prone to illness. Cajetan was especially concerned that the monks did not allow his sister to exercise her medicine on Abélard François. She was, after all, a good healer, a very good one indeed. He knew by experience. Cajetan had a hard time accepting all that cloistered secrecy that prevented families from seeing and talking directly to their own, and taking care of them when it was needed. He would see to it that Abélard François got the care he needed and the comfort of family, even if he had to infringe upon the rules of the cloister. He was determined to rescue his brother from the silence and concealment of the monastery.

Cajetan knocked on Marie Dieudonnée's door. She opened and was caught by surprise since she had not expected him so soon after receiving a letter from him telling her he was coming to see her. She welcomed him, and invited him to take off his hat, the strips of cloth around his hands, and some of the layers of woolen cloth under his tunic. It was quite warm and comfortable by the fire. She served him a large cup of some warm beverage. He sipped it and gave a long sigh.

----I'm so glad to be here. There wasn't much doing at the *chantier*, so I asked for a leave from my Master, Master Marquardt. Winter is upon us, and many of the men have returned home until spring.

----I'm glad you came. It's always so good to see you and chat with you. I don't get to see you too often. I miss you. You're my family now since Abélard François is shut in this monastery, and I seldom get to see him except once or twice a year. Even then, I never get to see his face, always do we have to speak through a curtain covering a grille. It's so cold and inhumane, this rule of the cloister.

----I truly wonder if Abélard François is really happy there all enclosed within those monastery walls never seeing the real world outside.

----But that's of his choosing, his vocation, Cajetan.

----Do you really think though that's God's choosing?

----What do you mean?

----I mean did our brother have the freedom to choose? He probably was forced into his calling by the soft, honeyed talk of the monks. They have a way of making young men think they have the vocation.

----All I know is that Abélard François insisted that it was his choice. He wanted to enter the cloister and spend the rest of his life in the monastery. I could not refuse him his choice. I did what he told me, lead him to the Carmelite priory.

----But, Marie Dieudonnée, how could you know that he was not coerced into it?

----As far as I knew then, he went of his own free will.

----All right if you say so, but I do want to go and visit him.

----You'll have to ask the Prior. He's a very stern and stiff man who doesn't listen easily to anyone's plea. I know.

----Well, I'll see to that. I'm not one to bend too easily to someone's dictates if they're not humanly sensitive to someone else's condition.

----We'll go tomorrow. First, let's have some food that I've prepared already. I wasn't expecting you but there's enough for the two of us.

Marie Dieudonnée talked about her usual daily chores and undertakings in mending and sewing while eating. Cajetan talked about the progress in the construction of the new cathedral, and the fact that he was now a journeyman earning a wage.

----I can now afford to give you money towards your dowry.

----I don't need your money. I manage very well by myself as I've already told you. Keep your money. Besides, I'm not ready to get married. There's plenty of time.

----But, you're not getting any younger, and men don't want old maids as their wives.

He had a mild smirk on his face while Marie Dieudonnée gave him a small push on his shoulder.

----When are you getting married, Cajetan? Any girl yet?

----I had one in England but she went back to Ireland.

----Oh, an Irish girl, hein?

----Yes, but she left without my knowing why.

----Did you do anything to offend her?

----No, not me. Anyways, I don't want to talk about it.

----I'm sorry about that. You're bound to meet another one. Probably a Flemish girl. They say they're very pretty.

----I haven't had time to meet anyone else but the men on the *chantier*.

----Then get out of the construction site, out of the architect mode and meet people. Make friends and have some fun. You're not just a craft, a job, Cajetan.

----I know.

A day or two after Cajetan arrived in Cambrai and had enjoyed his sister's welcome and good food, he told his sister that he wanted to go and spend some time with Abélard François at the monastery. He insisted that he go alone because he did not want to explode in front of her if tempers started to flare. She insisted on going with him just because she did not want tempers to inflame. That would not be the way to ingratiate himself with the Prior, she told him. Cajetan accepted her argument.

When they got to the monastery, Marie Dieudonnée rang the small bell outside the visitors' door. Someone slid the piece of wood covering the small opening in the door, and all that one could see was an eye through the grille.

----What do you want ?

----My name is Marie Dieudonnée, and I'm here with my older brother. We want to visit with my brother Brother Abélard Marie du Carmel.

She turned to Cajetan and told him that was Abélard François's name in religion.

----It's not time yet to visit with your brother. It's not the appointed time.

With that he closed the hatch. Cajetan started to get angry and told his sister to step aside. He then knocked on the huge oaken door with his fist. Nothing. He knocked repeatedly until the hatch was opened again.

----I told you it's not the appropriate time.

----Appropriate time or not, I'm going to enter and visit with my brother. I come from far, and I'm on a *chantier* in Flanders on a cathedral construction site. I don't have time to argue with you. Where is your superior?

----You mean our Prior.

----Yes, your Prior or whatever.

----He's Brother Ethelbert de la Cape.

----What is your name?

----Brother Cajetan Bellefort.

----My name is Cajetan too. Please be kind and get your Prior. Please.

----Please wait.

The hatch was closed one more time, and Cajetan and Marie Dieudonnée had to wait in the cold for a long time before the door itself was opened. They were ushered into some kind of bare room with very little furniture. It smelled of beeswax and incense. The Prior asked Cajetan what he wanted.

----What I want is to see my brother, Abélard François.

----Brother Abélard Marie du Carmel.

----Yes.

----But it's not the appropriate time for visitation.

----When is the appropriate time, Brother?

----We have set appropriate times for proper visitations by the families of our resident brothers. We do not make any exceptions.

----Never?

----Hardly ever.

----Well, you can make an exception for me and my sister.

Cajetan was getting hot under the collar and his sister could see it.

----Please, Brother Ethelbert, this is a kind of emergency. My other brother is here, and he's from far away. All we want is a brief visit with my younger brother who we know is very sick.

----Who told you that? Oh, you're the one who wanted to come and use some kind of medicine on Brother Abélard Marie du Carmel. Now I know who you are. We do not accept outside therapies from unknown sources, Mistress Dieudonnée.

----But my sister is a well-known healer and she's very good at it.

----Where did she get her healing instructions?

And Cajetan blurted out,

----From Geneviève la Guérisseuse.

----Oh, a gypsy healer most probably.

----No, replied, Marie Dieudonnée.

----In any case, you cannot break our rules.

----What rules? asked Cajetan.

----The rules of our community as written by our founders a very long time ago.

----You mean to tell me that your rules will not allow you to do an act of kindness to family members of a brother of yours, who, by the way, is also our brother, and let us see how he is?

----Those are the rules.

----Well, rules without any sense of charity are worthless rules.

----Sire, you are speaking to a representative of the will of God Himself. I'm here as Prior and I direct souls. How dare you say that our rules are worthless.

Cajetan kept getting closer and closer to the boiling point. Marie Dieudonnée tried to restrain him from blowing off his anger at the Prior. She tugged at his sleeve to remind him of his promise not to get angry openly.

----I'm really not condemning your rules. I'm simply here to see my brother. That's all. I'm sorry if I seem angry, and I mean no offense to you and your rules. If only Cardinal Archbishop Tintamarre would see me now, he'd be ashamed of my behavior.

Cajetan was trying to throw in a name with a certain ecclesiastical importance attached to it that would impress the Prior.

----Cardinal Archbishop of Devonshire, England?

----Why yes. Do you know him?

----Do I know him! He's out great benefactor. He claims that he gives us his munificent donations in repentance of and satisfaction for his failures. A man like that cannot have too many failures in life, I tell you. Yes, I know Cardinal Archbishop Tintamarre. Quite well.

Cajetan had the temptation of telling the Brother that he did not know the high cleric as well as a woman known as Maureen Coveneigh, but he refrained, knowing very well that such a statement would only inflame the situation.

----Well, on the other hand, I can let you see your brother for a very brief time.

He said that with a honeyed, if not hypocritical smile.

After a while, Cajetan was led to another room, called the parlor. He had to go alone while Marie Dieudonnée had to wait for him in the room where they had just been talking with the Prior. Cajetan waited a long while before the Prior came to him and told him that his brother would be there soon, and that he would be behind the curtained grille.

----You mean that I won't be able to speak face to face with my brother? I won't be able to see him?

----Those are the rules of the cloister. I don't make them up.

----But you have the authority as Prior to dispense with a particular rule, don't you?

----But, I don't want to exercise my privilege precariously.

Cajetan could see that the Prior was playing with him. He wanted him to beg. To show who had the preeminence of power.

----Please, Prior Ethelbert. Cardinal Archbishop Tintamarre will hear of your graciousness when I meet him again.

Cajetan was saying that knowing full well that he would not see the high cleric again, not if he had his way, but he said so knowing full well the mention of the Cardinal's name would sway the Prior's mind towards a more favorable inclination.

----I'm going to bend the rule and allow you to see your brother face to face, but just for a little while, mind you.

Two Carmelite Brothers brought Abélard François out to Cajetan. They were both holding him under his arms. He appeared very weak and his face was ashen. He was emaciated and looked downcast as he walked slowly to the chair given to him. When Cajetan greeted him, Abélard François started to look up in Cajetan's face, and slowly began to recognize him. He started to whimper, and huge tears dropped on his cheeks. Cajetan was stunned at the condition his brother was in.

----How long has he been that way?

----You know that your brother has always been of weak constitution, and probably our lifestyle with fasts and abstinence, mortification and daily prayers was not necessarily meant for him.

----Didn't you know that?

----He's under vows in our community, and we cannot dispense him from his vows at will. It takes a higher authority.

----You mean that he cannot leave here and go somewhere where he can find solace and good care?

----No. It's the rule approved by the Vatican. Besides, he gets all the necessary care here in our monastery.

Cajetan winced at those words coming from the Prior.

----Well, I'm going to take him out of here come hell or high water. Rules are meant to be broken.

----Not ours, sire. Not ours.

----Then, I'll make it happen even it means going to the authorities.

----Oh, please, don't make trouble for us. Please don't. Your brother is of no use to us as a community. He's so weak and sickly that he's become a burden for us. You would be taking him out of our hands if we were to let him go.

----Then let him go now.

----Not right away. I cannot do that.

----When?

----I have to prepare the papers for the dispensation of vows, and it has to be approved by the Abbot and then the Vatican officials.

----All of that bureaucracy?

----It's a serious matter.

----Yes, it's a serious matter for my brother. He's dying. If you don't set him free right now, I'm going to take him forcibly. Try me.

----But...

----Don't but me. I can do it, and I'm going to do it.

Cajetan turned to his brother and said,

----Abélard François do you want to come home with me and Marie Dieudonnée? Do you want good care with good food and comfort by the fire?

Abélard François nodded his head in the affirmative.

----I suppose that I can release him in your custody, family custody, until such time we can get the necessary paperwork done and signed. He did not come with a dowry so there's nothing coming to you.

----I don't care about the money. I care about him.

Marie Dieudonnée was elated when she saw her younger brother being supported by Cajetan, although she was aghast at the sight of him.

----Let's get out of here, out of this hellish place, said Cajetan in a low voice so as not to be heard by the Prior.

The monastery doors opened, and three persons, one holding the arm of another, while the third person was holding his hand wrapped in some cloth. Cajetan had put his own cloak on Abélard François's shoulders, for he had none. They had not even given the poor creature a cloak to go out in the cold. Such was the condition of being a discalced monk being sent home away from the monastery.

Marie Dieudonnée worked tirelessly with her younger brother in order to bring him back to good health. Cajetan watched her grinding herbs, blending some medication, and making some potions to cure the sickly young man that both of them knew as *un à part*. The sister lost no time looking in her notes given to her by Geneviève la Guérisseuse. She boiled and she mixed, and she waited until the right consistency and the right potency were reached. Cajetan marveled at her skills as a healer at work. It was a craft, he told himself. A genuine craft that some called the art of healing. She fed Abélard François the finest of meats and vegetables she could find at the local market. Cajetan kept giving her money for the food that his brother needed. He was running low on money, and he had to go back to Flanders soon. After several days of unimpeded care, Abélard François came around slowly and began to show some color in his face and hands. He was more talkative now that he saw himself out of the monastery. He had been under the rule of monastic silence for close to two years. He told his brother and his sister how much he appreciated their loving care, and how much he appreciated what Cajetan had done for him with the Prior. He did not recall all of the details, but he knew that Cajetan had really forced the Prior into submission, for the Prior had no mind to release his minion. The days went by and Abélard François was getting stronger and stronger. Cajetan then realized that he had been away for three weeks. It was time to go back. He bid farewell to his siblings and went away knowing full well that what he had done for his brother was indeed a blessing for himself, his brother and his sister, and that he would never regret what he had accomplished. He had saved a life.

7

THE GOTHIC EXPERIENCE IN FLANDERS

When Cajetan returned to the *chantier,* he saw how desolate the site was. He went to the excavation and there he saw how everything was frozen and covered with snow. He circled the excavation site and saw in his mind a cathedral rising up into the sky like Notre-Dame de Paris and Notre-Dame d'Amiens. The consummate craftsmen of both cities had built those cathedrals just like the craftsmen at Devonshire were building theirs, and how the cathedral builders of the *chantier Saint Amand* would build their own, and he was so very proud to be part of a group of dedicated craftsmen in the building of cathedrals. He could not believe that he had come this far, a journeyman architect. He was excited, he was happy, he was filled with glee, and he marveled at the winter sky so pure and so crystal clear that one could easily get lost in it just by looking upward toward the heavens. It was like Gothic space way up in the sky.

Cajetan wondered how he would celebrate Christmas and Twelfth Night this year. Like any other year when he was alone, celebrating by himself and sometime with a few friends. He had enjoyed celebrating with Maureen when she was still in England. He also enjoyed celebrating with Peter. Those were enjoyable times, he thought. He had gone to the Christmas mass with Maureen and then twelve days later, Epiphany, when they had exchanged gifts. They were small and simple gifts but meaningful ones. They had eaten well and had sung joyous songs that enlivened the season of joy commemorating when Jesus was born in Bethlehem. He still remembered when he celebrated these special days with his mother and father. Maman always made Christmas and Twelfth Night memorable, he thought. She and papa made lovely gifts out of practically nothing. It wasn't the gift, he thought, but the memories that those gifts generated for such a long time. That was the true gift.

Cajetan felt the chill in the air and decided to return to his dwelling place. He decided then and there that he was going to celebrate Christmas and Twelfth Night the way his parents had celebrated them when he was a child with his sister and his baby brother. So, on Christmas day, Cajetan went to mass in the local church and saw many people with what he called festive faces. He remembered the time in Devonshire when he had gotten to know this couple, Goodman Crayer and Goodwife Crayer, who were always gracious with him, and he had enjoyed their company whenever they were together somewhere like church, the market or in the park. Cajetan liked them and they liked him. For Twelfth Night, Cajetan had gone to the Cayer house and had brought two small gifts with him. He had given one to the man and the other to the wife. They, in turn, had given him a gift. When he opened it, he saw that it was a miniature polished wooden wheel on which had been carved the twelve signs of the zodiac. "It's all about the stars," the man had told him. Cajetan had kept it with his *petits trésors,* with his compass and stone sculpture.Pleasant memories, thought Cajetan.

The winter months went by, and the early signs of spring came out of the earth with crocuses and the bright daffodils. It was mid-March and the craftsmen were returning to the *chantier,* one by one, until they were all back ready to get to work on the foundation. Master Architect Marquardt summoned Cajetan to review his plans and design for the cathedral. Bishop van Artevelde had told his Master Architect that he wanted higher walls than had been planned.

----You know, Cajetan that the walls of a Gothic cathedral consist of piers that support the vault and roof. I designed the piers of the choir to be one hundred and fifty-five feet high and five to seven feet thick. The Bishop wants piers of one hundred and seventy feet high and six to eight feet thick. He wants walls higher than most cathedrals because he wants to rival the best of them, I know. I've discussed this with the Master Mason and he agrees that those dimensions are extravagant and too high for the foundation. The foundation would not sustain such height and weight even with the outside buttresses.

Both the Master Architect and Master Mason were ready to talk to the Bishop about their reservations, and Architect Marquardt wanted to inform his journeyman about the situation with the Bishop. He trusted Cajetan and wanted him to back him up in his decision.

----But why do you need my approval, Master Marquardt?

----Because I need confirmation of my decision. I know you and I trust your knowledge about pier and wall construction. You have been studying it for a long time, I know. You have made it your specialty. You have a keen mind, Cajetan, and you grasp things very well. What do you think?

----You're the expert in architecture, Master. What do I have that I can teach you? I'm just a young journeyman.

----You have wisdom and the practical sense that I need. I'm not always practical about things sometimes.

----I'm the one who's called the Stargazer, the dreamer, not the practical one.

----But you are practical when it comes to the science of cathedral building, and I want to hear your opinion on this.

Cajetan started to scribble some figures on a piece of paper and added a geometrical drawing with mathematical factors and did some calculations.

----Well, let's take a look at the geometry of the case in point. If I look at the geometry and mathematics of the construction of these piers and walls with the dimensions that the Bishop wants, I would say that you and the Master Mason are right, and that the Bishop is wrong. I may not be an expert mathematician and geometrician, but I know a few things from what I have studied, especially during the past few months when I had time on my hands. My learning goes a long way back when Sir Knight Évrard de Châteauloup sent me to the monks of Clairvaux to study. I was very young then but I learned fast, and my teachers were some of the best at that time. What I learned about mathematics and geometry stayed with me. I learned to build upon that on my own. I tell you, that foundation will not sustain such height and weight.

----That's what I thought. But how do you tell the Bishop that he's wrong?

----Give him the evidence. I will gladly put everything down on paper, every configuration and every calculation, and that will make it official. You can sign it and then give it to him. Don't worry, I don't want credit for it. I'm here to serve.

----Thank you, Cajetan.

With the evidence of mathematics and geometry at hand, Bishop van Artevelde was resigned to the fact that science had proven the Master Architect right. He congratulated Master Marquardt on his studies with facts and figures. Master Architect was quick to point out that his journeyman, Cajetan, had helped tremendously with the details of the presentation. From that day on, Bishop van Artevelde held the journeyman, Cajetan, in high esteem.

With the straw and the dung out of the way, the laborers finished the cleaning of the foundation that had been started last fall, and gave way to the masons to finish their work. The foundation was planned to be made of thick walls, built twenty-five feet below ground level which would support the building and prevent it from settling unevenly, but the Bishop had insisted on a depth of twenty feet in order to save time, energy and money, he said. Master Architect knew very well that the decision was made primarily for the essence of time. The Bishop wanted to get his cathedral as soon as it could be done, and cutting corners was his way of doing it. Master Architect had argued with him, at length, but he got tired of arguing with the Bishop. However, it must be said that he did stand his ground on the height of the piers.

The masons got busy and the mortar men prepared the exact mixtures of sand, lime and water. Laborers carried the mortar down the ladders to the masons as they had done before. The masons lay the stones on top of each other, troweling a layer of mortar between each stone and each layer of stone. It was done with so much proficiency that the foundation walls were finished in no time. All that remained was the drying of the mortar. The Master Mason had checked continually with his level to make sure the stones were perfectly horizontal, and with his plumb line to ensure that the wall was perfectly vertical. Any error in the foundation could endanger the cathedral walls that were to be built on top of it. Bad enough that the foundation depth is not sufficient, thought the Master Architect, that we need to face flaws in the stone walls of the foundation itself.

In the meantime, the Master Carpenter had to think of the construction of the roof. Timber had to be ordered from Scandinavia. He needed large pieces of wood, some sixty feet long. Soon the wood for the roof and the stone for the walls would float down the river to the city's port where they would be hoisted out of boats with derricks and windlasses built by the carpenters.

The construction of the Bishop's cathedral was now into full swing. Bishop van Artevelde was overjoyed at the prospect of seeing the walls of his cathedral go up reaching to the skies. His dream would be fulfilled, that of raising a cathedral on a site that once was brush, trees and a few huts. So was Cajetan's dream of helping to build a cathedral from the beginning. His own cathedral, as an architect, would have to wait until he was a Master Architect and craftsman. That dream would materialize someday. He knew that dreams take time and patience. He had learned that from his mother, Grisoulda.

Once the foundation was completed and the mortar had dried, Master Architect Marquardt told the Master Mason who, in turn, told the mortar men that the time had come to erect the walls of the cathedral. Cajetan was filled with excitement because he wanted to watch every step of the way. With the building of the walls begun, the Master Architect knew that planning for the buttresses had to be done right away. An architect is always one step ahead of the present operation, said Master Architect Marquardt to Cajetan.

When the mortar in the foundation was completely dry, the work on the piers and the walls began. It was late April and the sun was shining brightly. It appeared that spring was in full force. The birds were singing, the puffy clouds high in the sky seemed to float and build upon themselves until they became huge puffs of clouds. The trees were burgeoning, and the smell in the air was fragrant. Everyone was under the spell of spring for good cheer reigned. It was heartwarming to see the piers being elevated one by one, section by section, stone upon stone. The masons were as busy as bees in a hive. The mortar men had a hard time catching up with them. It seemed that the lull of the winter months had reenergized the craftsmen and given them the élan they needed to work faster and faster. The Bishop was very pleased with the pace of the work, day after day when he visited the *chantier*. The tracery, all of which was cut from templates, was cemented into place along with iron reinforcing bars as the piers were being built. Every day the piers grew in height until one could almost see the vaults appearing over them. It was as if the architecture of the walls was being fashioned right before your very eyes.

As the walls grew higher, scaffolding became a necessity. The scaffolding was made of poles lashed together with rope. The scaffolds also held the work platforms for the masons which were mats made of woven twigs. They were called hurdles and could be easily moved. Cajetan watched with keen interest all the movements of each craftsman, so fascinated was he with the work being accomplished day by day. He was there early in the morning until late afternoon when the craftsmen were ready to leave the site. The scaffolding for the walls above the arcade did not reach to the ground. It was hung from the walls and lifted as construction progressed. Ladders were not necessary to reach it, as several permanent spiral staircases were built into the wall itself.

After much movement and work, the time had come to build the temporary wooden frames called centerings. Master Architect Marquardt explained to Cajetan how these centerings were important because they were made to support the weight of the stones, and maintain the shape of the arch until the mortar was dry. The centerings were made by the carpenters on the ground, and then they were hoisted into place and fastened to the pier at one end and to the buttress at the other.

----Watch how it's done, Cajetan.

----I'm intrigued by the skill of these men who seem to know exactly what to do and when to do it.

----That's called experience, Cajetan.The centerings will act as temporary flying buttresses until the stone arch is complete.

----Why are they called "flying" buttresses? They do not fly.

----They're really buttressing arches, *arcs boutants,* as they are called in French. They buttress the piers and relieve the pressure the vaults place on them. No, there's nothing "flying" about them.

----The real problem is in the vaults, isn't it?

----Yes, Cajetan. You see in Gothic cathedrals the arched vault tends to push the pier outward. This force is transferred through the flying buttress to the buttress itself and then down to the foundation. You see how very important it is to have a good solid foundation?

----Yes, I see.

----With the buttresses, the piers can remain quite thin in proportion to their height, allowing more space for the large windows between them.

----That's the miracle of Gothic architecture, isn't it?

With time and much disciplined work, the piers went up, the arched vaults went up, the tracery went up and the choir was well formed. Cajetan was staring at the finished work when, all of a sudden, he felt a presence next to him, a presence dressed in a long purple robe, the Bishop.

----Beautiful isn't it?

----Yes, Excellency. It's marvelous just standing here looking and staring at the Gothic style in evidence. It makes me feel joyous and satisfied with the work being done by our men. They're such good craftsmen. They make the cathedral sing with joy. I know it's not finished yet, but I can see it now in my mind, upright and majestic pointing toward heaven.

----That's what Gothic architecture does for a cathedral, elevates it upward to glorify God in all of His majesty. That's what my cathedral will do.

----Have you ever seen Saint-Denis's church in Paris, Excellency? That's what Abbot Suger did for his Abbey church, he was the first one to elevate his dream towards the heavens in the form of a Gothic church. I did not see it personally but Master Architect Albert de Chaussoyes brought me both to Paris and Amiens. Those two cathedrals are magnificent. He's the one who told me about Saint-Denis.

----I know Master de Chaussoyes, a good architect. You worked under him? Why, you're the journeyman working with Master Architect Kurt, my Architect.

----Yes, I am. They're both good architects, and I've learned a lot from them.

----I hear good things about you. We are pleased with your service.

The Bishop was using the "we" often used by members of the royalty or high clerics especially the Vatican.

----Thank you, Excellency.

----You know, Master Architect Marquardt, who is in my own Episcopal service as architect is somewhat worried about the foundation, and still keeps thinking that's it's not solid enough because of its depth. He thinks it's too shallow, but it's really not. We saved time by not adhering to the standard measure of depth. I'm satisfied with it. What do you think, journeyman?

Cajetan knew full well that the Bishop was testing him if he would take his word, the word of the Bishop, or his master's word. It was a delicate situation, and he knew it.

----Excellency, I'm not the one to make such decisions. I'm a humble servant of the Master Architect and of the Bishop in charge of the building of the cathedral, which is you, Excellency. Although I respect Master Architect's word on everything concerning the building of this cathedral, I realize that your word is the last word, and I fully respect that. Who am I to get in the middle of such decision making, Excellency?

Cajetan felt that he had delicately walked the fine line of diplomatic answers.

The walls of the choir were constructed in three stages. First was the arcade of piers that rose seventy-three feet from the foundation. Above them was the triforium, a row of arches that went up another eighteen feet in front of a narrow passageway. The last stage was the clerestory, which consisted of fifty-five foot windows that reached right up to the roof. Between 1268 and 1271 the walls of the choir and aisle were completed and work began on the roof.

Cajetan had been in the *Saint Amand chantier* five years and had enjoyed every minute of it. He had learned so much about cathedral building, and Master Architect Marquardt was very pleased with him and his diligent work as a journeyman. In the meantime, Cajetan had amassed quite of bit of money because he had been frugal in his tastes for food and ale, his pleasure seeking and his overall expenses. He had been concerned over his sister and her dowry, and his brother who had recovered quite well but, as far as he knew, was without employment and craft. Cajetan knew full well that his sister could not remain all by herself without her own family for long. She had to make a move. As for Abélard François, it was clear to Cajetan that idleness was the devil's workshop, and that, as an older brother, he would have to step in and convince him to get an apprenticeship somewhere, and with someone who could help him build a future. Cajetan had been keeping in touch with both his sister and his brother, but had not been able to visit them too often. There was too much work to do as journeyman. During the last winter break, Cajetan did visit Cambrai and talked at length to both Marie Dieudonnée and Abélard François. Abélard François told his brother that he was interested in becoming part of a troupe of players that organized and acted mystery plays, and even new plays in the vernacular. Liturgical plays and mystery plays had become *passés*, said Abélard François.

Miracle plays had been the domain of the clergy for a very long time. Early on, they were performed in front of the churches right on the square. However, ever since Pope Innocent III, suspicious of the growing popularity of miracle plays, had issued an edict some years back, forbidding clergy from acting on public stage, the clergy refrained from doing any public entertainment. Abélard François's parish priest invited the young *désoeuvré*, the idle one, to join a troupe of players and perform a play out in public. Abélard François had gotten more and more out of his shell, and had become less of an *à part*, as Marie Dieudonnée put it. Public entertainment fascinated him and drew him in. He had recovered his health, thanks to his sister, and now he wanted to be a part of life. He told Cajetan that his plans were to play a part in Jean Bodel's Arras's play, "*Jeu de saint Nicolas.*" His friends were urging him to become an actor and join their troupe. There were troubadours, actors, poets and romance writers in the group of friends. Marie Dieudonnée thought that this was a good idea, a way of engaging Abélard François in something he could enjoy, and thus forget his bad experiences with the Carmelites. Cajetan agreed and gave his brother some money to live on until he could earn his own. Cajetan told his sister that the money he gave the brother was part of the money he was reserving for Marie Dieudonnée's dowry. She told him not to worry about her dowry. She had no immediate plans to get married.

Cajetan and Marie Dieudonnée had a long conversation before he returned to the *chantier*. It was late March and it was time to go since the carpenters would be getting ready to hoist the roof on top of the walls. Marie Dieudonnée told her brother that being alone and knowing that Abélard François had found his way in life, she would like to explore the life of the cloister herself. It was a good life, she said, if you find the right monastery and the right people who live there.

----What do you mean by right? asked Cajetan.

----Right, you know, right like proper and fitting. A monastery that abides by love and caring, and not strictly by some established rule. Any community needs rules, secular as well as religious. I know that. We as humans need guides to follow in order to become better persons and better Christians. But, the strict rule becomes inhuman when applied carelessly to human beings. That's not what Saint Benedict wanted.

----All right, I agree with you on that.

----You have rules, don't you, rules in your guilds?

----Of course.

----Then, we all need rules, wouldn't you say?

----Yes.

----Not rules for the sake of rules, mind you, but rules to govern our lives like the ten commandments. I can live with the right rules, the fair and honest rules like the rule of Saint Benedict. Now, there's a rule for all, honesty, charity, simplicity and wisdom.

----How do you know that?

----I've been studying it with Mother Veronica, the nun who lives in the convent next to the local church. I go to her to study and learn.

----She's been filling your mind with great ideas about monastery life, I'm sure. Just like the Carmelites did with Abélard François.

----No, no, no. She's not forcing anything on me. It's me, Cajetan, they're my ideas and my wish. I think I have the vocation for monastic life. It draws me in, it fascinates me and it leads me to God through the Blessed Virgin Mary's' intercession.

----Now you're talking like a priest or a nun.

----Believe me, Cajetan, I'm not making it up. I believe in it, and I'm convinced that it's my path in life. Maman, Honest Grisoulda, is interceding for me up there.

----If you really think that's your calling, then I'll support you in your efforts. Didn't you feel the call when you were younger?

----In a way, but I was afraid to pursue it and, besides, I had responsibilities to myself and to Abélard François who relied on me. Not you, you already had your path carved out for you, Cajetan the architect, the Stargazer. You had a dream in life and you never once deviated from it. Some people are lucky that way.

----It's not luck, Marie Dieudonnée. It's hard work and determination.

----I know.

----Where do you think you'd like to go?

----I've been thinking of Fontevraud Abbey.

----Isn't that in the Loire Valley?

----Yes.

----That's far. Besides, you will need a dowry. I know you don't have one. You've been too generous with others just like our mother.

----Papa was generous too, Cajetan.

----I know. They were both generous people.

----Keep your money and when I need it, I'll get in touch with you. I'm not leaving right away. There are things I have to do.

----Things?

----Yes, things. You don't have to know everything about a woman's life, Cajetan.

Cajetan left the following day full of anticipation for the roofing of the cathedral. He said his usual goodbyes, and went on the road to Zelzate. When he got there, the carpenters had already started to assemble each individual truss on the ground. After test assembling every part, the truss was dismantled and hoisted piece by piece to the top of the walls. "What a complicated operation," thought Cajetan out loud. Then the truss was reassembled and the entire frame was locked together with oak pegs. The first few beams were then hoisted to the top of the walls using pulleys hung from the scaffolding. Once the beams were in place, a windlass was set on top of them to hoist the rest of the timber and help in setting up the trusses. This went on for many days, day after day until the carpenters were done doing what they had to do for the start of the roof, and the Master Carpenter approved of the wooden structure on top of the walls. In the meantime, on the ground, the roofers were casting lead sheets that would cover the wooden frame, protecting it and the vaults from bad weather. They also cast the drain pipes and the gutters.

Cajetan walked with Master Marquardt around the construction site looking at the progress that had been made on the cathedral.

----Aren't you glad about the progress that has been made so far?

----Yes, I am Cajetan. Very glad and very proud. However, I'm still concerned about the foundation and its tolerance and ability to sustain the weight of the walls and the roof once the stones have all been laid and the roof closed. I hope it does, especially before we finish the buttresses and the gutters. The buttresses will help for sure but we're only half done. Building a cathedral is a slow process and with every step comes a delicate balance between weight and thrust. Architecture deals with simple problems as well as more complicated ones like the balance and harmony of the parts that make up the entire structure. This is your lesson for the day, Cajetan.

----Thank you, Master Marquardt. You're a good teacher. A wise one.

----The Bishop doesn't always agree with me but he keeps me on the *chantier*. I suppose he trusts me.

----He does. He told me so. He likes, you and expects great things from you.

----He told you that ?

----Yes.

----I wonder what great things he expects from me.

----The completion of his cathedral in record time.

----Oh, yes, the time factor. I had forgotten about that. Well, he'll have his cathedral but I don't think it will be in record time.

The days and the months went by, and Cajetan was anticipating the summer months when he could enjoy the nice weather and the long walks along the river. He often went along the river bank to meditate and simply think about things, things like his dream, his sister's plans and his brother's involvement in the theater troupe. He was glad that his younger brother was finally enjoying life and kept himself preoccupied with the art of performing before a public. He was eager to see him and hear him in a play that entertained people and gathered crowds. This was good for his heart and soul, thought Cajetan. It nurtures him and elevates him just like a cathedral does for me, he said out loud.

One September afternoon, a Sunday when the leaves were still, the flowers majestically upright and colorful, little children danced around an old weather beaten maypole and parents watched as their children had fun and were full of laughter, Cajetan was gazing at the sky, motionless and daydreaming as he often did. Suddenly someone went by him and brushed his shoulder. He looked at the young woman that had just gone by him and touched him ever so lightly, and he wondered who that could be. It wasn't someone he had seen before. She was light on her feet, had reddish blond hair and a radiant complexion of the inner deep pinkish quality of apple blossoms in early spring. Cajetan was caught by surprise and delight. He hesitated whether he should follow her and speak to her. He just stayed there perplexed as she vanished around the corner. Her face remained fresh in his memory for days. He would be working on something, and suddenly her face would reappear in his mind like a haunting desire never completely dismissed. Cajetan would force himself to return to work and not think about her. She interrupted his thoughts, and he did not like to be interrupted in his train of thought when he was trying to solve a problem or think something through. Cajetan loved mathematics, the science of exactitude, he called it. He relished numbers and he understood why architects used mathematics in their craft. They relied on it because it was the science of numbers that gave them the confidence of being exact and precise in their planning and design. Some even called architects magicians with numbers.

Cajetan often thought of Maureen and how she was kind to him, and how she could make him laugh when he felt downcast. She had vanished from his life suddenly, never to return. She was but a lost memory to him now. What a miserable man was that Cardinal Archbishop Tintamarre for having destroyed a relationship that Cajetan was so earnestly trying to build. Except for his mother and his sister, he did not have any other real relationships with women. He had no time for relationships nor did he pursue them. His dream, his work and his learning were what was of utmost importance to him. If he wanted to achieve any measure of success in life be it in architecture, cathedral building or mathematical endeavors, he knew that he had to devote himself entirely to the goal that he had mapped out for himself. No time for frivolousness; no time for relationships that did not correspond to his dream. Whatever was worth in establishing a dream did not, in any way, suffer interference or distraction. However, attraction to a lovely woman did not suffer from prevention. Cajetan had learned to prevent himself from what he called wasteful thinking and sometimes daydreaming. Daydreaming was not always dreaming for a useful or ideal goal such as cathedral building, he told himself. But he realized that daydreaming could have its own purpose. Notwithstanding idle thinking and daydreaming, the force of attraction was a powerful one that Cajetan could not reject nor defer. It happened. It was a human phenomenon and Cajetan found himself to be integrally part of it. That he could not deny. As much as he struggled with it, he knew that he would fall prey to the force of attraction some day. He had already felt it with Maureen Coveneigh, and now he realized that he was slowly getting under its spell.

The following Sunday, Cajetan met the young woman that had brushed his shoulder in the local park a few days before. He was sitting on a bench reading. He had dropped his zodiac wheel that the Crayers had given him and it lay there next to the bench on the ground. He had brought it with him intending to study the twelve signs. The young woman bent down next to him, pick up the wooden wheel and, with a smile, asked Cajetan if the wheel was his.

----Why, yes. Thank you for picking it up. It means a lot to me. It was a gift from dear friends.

----I'm only too glad to retrieve it for you.

----May I ask your name?

----It's Wandal.

----Where are you from?

----From Germany originally but I've been living here in Zelzate for the last eight years.

----What do you do? Are you a seamstress, a cook, a laundress or something like that?

----Oh, no, my dear man. I teach young children at the Visitation of Mary Convent. My father is a Master Mason and works in the *Saint Amand chantier* .

----So do I. I'm a journeyman under Master Architect Marquardt. My name is Cajetan.

----I'm so pleased to meet you, Cajetan. I heard your name before. It must be from my father.

----What is your father's name?

----Werner van Schlaus.

----I don't know that name although I'm sure that I came across your father at work in the *chantier* , but there are so many masons on the construction site. Many are needed to work with the mortar and the stones.

----How long have you been in Zelzac, Cajetan.

----Five years. I'm originally from France. I went to England to work on a cathedral for a while, then I was sent here in Flanders.

----Do you like it here?

----Yes. It's a charming place and the people are generally friendly.

----I like it too.

----Do you have a family? I mean do you have brothers and sisters?

----I have one sister, Anna, and two brothers, Berne and Helmut. And you?

----Well, both of my parents are dead, but I have one sister, Marie Dieudonnée and one brother, Abélard François. Marie Dieudonnée lives in Cambrai in France. As for Abélard François, well, he's part of a troupe of performers, and he moves around.

----That's very interesting. I adore plays. I wish that women were permitted in the troupes, but we're not. Not yet.

----Do you think that some day they will?

----I know they will.

Cajetan and Wandal met again in the park the following Sunday. They talked about anything and everything. Cajetan just loved to talk and be with Wandal. Wandal admired Cajetan for his knowledge and skills as a journeyman as well as his dream of becoming an architect. Besides, she thought he was a handsome and vigorous man with dazzling blue eyes, blond hair and ruddy cheeks that mirrored good health. On some occasions, at evening tide, the two of them would lie on the grass in the park until twilight and the darkening of the sky and gaze at the stars. Ever since Wandal learned that Cajetan was called the Stargazer by others, she nurtured that thought, and tried to share the Stargazer's delight of simply looking up at the deep dark sky pinpointed with stars. Cajetan tried to explain to her the zodiac signs and some particular stars that he named. Wandal thought that his knowledge of the stars was fascinating. With the weeks falling into months, the relationship between Cajetan and Wandal grew serious. Cajetan was twenty-one years old and he thought that it was time for him to get married and raise a family. He had found the right woman, he told himself. Honest, kind, intelligent and hard working was Wandal. He liked those qualities in her. He met her parents several times, and he liked them, and they seemed to like him. Cajetan talked to his sister about the possibility of getting married, and she told him that it was about time. She wished him happiness and contentment with the prospect of a family. So, between Cajetan and Wandal's family an agreement was reached that the young couple would marry the following fall. Master Architect Marquardt congratulated Cajetan on his decision to marry, and told him that it was time for the journeyman to start thinking about his masterpiece to qualify for full architect in the guild. That was the next step in his craftsman's life. Cajetan was getting closer to the accomplishment of his dream. First, he was getting married.

The wedding took place on a Sunday afternoon early September when people did not have to work. Wandal's father took Cajetan aside and confided to him the expected dowry. Cajetan thanked his future father-in-law and put the money away. The young couple had invited all of their friends and relatives with some of them coming from far away. Master Architect Albert de Chaussoyes surprised Cajetan by showing up. He told him that he had heard about the wedding from other architects and journeymen, and wanted to be there with him on this festive occasion. He called Cajetan his favored apprentice.

Cajetan was glad to see his old Master again. They did not talk about Cardinal Archbishop Tintamarre. He had died the year before. Marie Dieudonnée was there as well as Abélard François who looked healthy and proud to be a performer. He could not stop talking about what he called his craft to anyone who listened to him. Wandal certainly listened to him when she wasn't talking to the other guests.

Cajetan and Wandal held the wedding ceremony on the *chantier* with permission of the Bishop, who wasn't there, but who promised to bless and register their marriage as was the custom. Friends had decorated a small area of the site with fresh flowers from the fields and colored ribbons. The bride wore a blue gown, the color of the Virgin Mary and her virginity, Wandal said. She had a garland of tiny flowers on her head. Cajetan had on his best clothes, his Sunday clothes. Marie Dieudonnée had on a yellow gown that she had made herself. It was the color of sunflowers, and she looked radiant in it. Cajetan told her so. She did not mention to Cajetan about her entering a monastery, and he did not mention it either. When the time comes, we'll talk about it, Cajetan told himself. If ever the time comes, he pursued. When the couple had exchanged their vows, Cajetan gave his bride half of a broken coin while keeping the other half as a token of their wedding bond. It was the custom to do so, and Cajetan followed the custom with faithfulness. Later on, they would go to the Bishop to bless their marriage and register it to make things proper. But first, they would celebrate with a wedding feast prepared by so many of their friends and relatives.

There was a kind of meat made from fowl and other wild birds. There were dark heavy loaves of barley and rye bread that people tore apart to eat. Everyone ate with their fingers and licked them, once in a while, to savor the juices of the meat. Many people brought little cakes and piled them one on top of the other as was the wedding custom. Of course, ale made from barley was brought in, for all were delighted in the drinking of the brew. As a matter of fact, Cajetan began to be a bit tipsy early on. Wandal did not care since she knew that this was Cajetan's day to be happy and carefree. She was hoping though that he would not get drunk like so many of the men did after drinking too much ale. The two Master Architects had long conversations broken by eating and drinking. Wandal's parents talked at length with Marie Dieudonnée for the feeling was that they were now family. Abélard François talked with Wandal about the stage and the performances of several plays. He told her that the troupe was coming to Flanders in October. All were having fun when the singing and the dancing started. There were a few musical instruments being played. Wandal's brother, Berne, played the recorder while her sister, Anna, played the horn. Wandal's other brother, Helmut, just stood there watching and enjoying the musicians. Some friends of the bride and groom beat the drums, and others had whistles and bells that they used as interval instruments. Of course, there was singing too. Wandal herself sang some melodies bringing back memories of her youth in Germany. It made her mother cry. Another lady sang a few songs of spiritual cadences that she had learned in church. Marie Dieudonnée sang a Marian hymn, and Abélard François recited three dramatic tropes. Cajetan tried his best to sing some melody that he had learned as a boy with Grisoulda, but his voice failed him and he started to whimper like a little dog. His wife told him to stop because it was not time for sadness but for joy. Everyone had fun and many danced until darkness set in. Then it was time to go home. Cajetan brought his wife to his small dwelling where he had been living as journeyman. Truth be told, it was friends who helped to bring Cajetan home, for he was on the verge of drunkenness. Sad to say that the marriage bed did not know much marriage frolic that night.

Wandal settled in comfortably into her new home and took charge of the housekeeping, the laundry, the mending, and all the chores a married woman usually did. In three months time she told her husband that she was with child. Cajetan was excited about the news. Finally, he would have his own family. Wandal reminded him that it was her family as well.

Cajetan began to think seriously about and plan for his masterpiece. He wondered what it would be. Perhaps a buttress design that had not been done before. Perhaps a full scale model of a new cathedral that goes beyond the Gothic style. That was a thought. Perhaps even a rose window that outdoes other rose windows by its design and stained glass. All kinds of ideas were swimming in his head. He was going to talk about his masterpiece plans with Master Marquardt.

In six months time Wandal gave birth to a little girl, cute and cuddly with light hair, and a very fair complexion. There was a hint of reddish hues in her hair, and she smiled all the time. She was a happy baby. Wandal said that the baby was happy child because she was born on a Sunday, and a Sunday's child is a child full of grace, and sunshine, added Cajetan. It was the mother's privilege to name the first baby girl but she turned over this privilege to her husband because she knew in her heart that Cajetan would want to call the little girl Grisoulda, after his mother. He was overjoyed at the privilege passed on to him by Wandal, and so they had the baby baptized, Grisoulda.

Meanwhile at the construction site, things were moving fast. The lead sheets had been cast and now they were working on the gutters and drain pipes. The stone cutters and the sculptors carved the stone gutters and down spouts that were to be installed in the buttresses. These down spouts through which fell the water from the roof to the ground, were carved to look like weird creatures, almost frightening at times. The sculptors used their imagination to carve what were called gargoyles. When it rained, especially when it poured, these gargoyles appeared to be disgorging water onto the ground below. They were designed to convey water from the roof and away from the side of the cathedral thereby preventing rainwater from running down masonry walls and eroding the mortar between. The gargoyles were the product of, not only a vivid imagination, but were inspired by nightmarish stories that had filled the heads of many since childhood. They were considered to be an agent to ward off and protect from any evil or harmful spirits.

Master Sculptor Harand Millefois explained to Cajetan that the origins of the gargoyle came from the monster named *Gargouille*. *La Gargouille* was said to have been the typical dragon with bat like wings, a long neck, with the ability to breathe fire from its mouth. When it was slain, its head was cut off and mounted on the wall of a newly built church in Rouen, France to scare off evil spirits.

----I'm sure you have seen some at Notre-Dame de Paris and most probably in Amiens.

----Yes, but Master de Chaussoyes did not spend any time on them. We had too much to see.

----Some gargoyles are depicted as monks, or combinations of real people and animals, many of which are humorous.

----So they don't always scare people.

----Right. There's all kinds of gargoyles like there's all kinds of foliate heads.

----I've heard of them but I know very little about them.

----You have a lot to learn about cathedral sculptures then.

----I guess so.

----Talk to Master Marquardt about gargoyles and the monk, Bernard de Clairvaux. He'll tell you a thing or two about what the Church thought about them, or at least what some churchmen thought. Bernard de Clairvaux was famous for speaking out against gargoyles.

----I'll certainly do that.

The following morning bright and early Cajetan walked swiftly to Master Marquardt's workshop and began to ask him about gargoyles and Bernard de Clairvaux.

----Wait a minute, Cajetan. You haven't even greeted me yet and here you are questioning me about Bernard de Clairvaux. What's all this with that monk? Are you joining a monastery and becoming a monk?

----No, no. It's about gargoyles and this monk. Harand Millefois, the Master Sculptor told me to ask you about him and those monstrous figures.

----First of all, good day Cajetan and now I'll tell you about Bernard de Clairvaux. Bernard de Clairvaux was primarily a reformer. He reformed the Benedictine Order because it had become too liberal and that's the reason why he formed the Cistercian order, the order of white monks because they wore the white habit, not the black one. Bernard de Clairvaux wanted his monks to follow literally Saint Benedict's rule, and he reintroduced manual labor. He was involved with the Crusades, and Bernard played a leading role in the development of the cult of the Virgin Mary which is definitely one of the most important manifestations of popular piety of our century.

----Yes, I can see that. All of those cathedrals dedicated to her, what a manifestation of reverence and love for the Mother of God.

----Moreover, Cistercian architecture is considered to be of high quality and has gained many followers. Cistercian architecture avoids superfluous ornamentation so as not to distract from religious life. It is simple and utilitarian. It can be seen as a transition from the Romanesque and the Gothic. You look at the Abbey of Cîteaux, the Abbey of Saint-Jouin-de-Marnes and the Fontenay Abbey all splendid examples of Cistercian architecture.

----I guess that I will have to visit those abbeys some day and learn about Cistercian architecture. Now, what about the gargoyles?

----Bernard de Clairvaux was one of the most important figures in the Church, and he was highly respected for his intelligence and his deep faith conviction.

----Yes, but how about the gargoyles?

----I'm coming to that. Bernard de Clairvaux was not the only one to speak against gargoyles. Some members of the clergy did too. As a matter of fact, they considered gargoyles to be a form of idolatry.

----That's strong thinking.

----Yes, idolatry. It is said about Bernard de Clairvaux that he wrote something to the effect that these monstrous things did not belong in a church or a monastery. I remember the first lines of what he wrote on this account: "What are these fantastic monsters doing in the cloisters before the eyes of the brothers as they read? What is the meaning of these unclean monkeys, these strange savage lions, and monsters?" That always struck me and I've had that in my mind ever since I read the passage from Bernard de Clairvaux. Isn't that amazing?

----Sure is. Apparently the gargoyles survived the bad blood and rejection by some.

----I think you must not take gargoyles too seriously. Sure they scare some, and make others think about evil and hell, but overall they're funny and make people laugh. They entertain people while serving particular functions such as drain spouts. We'll have some in our cathedral. They look great. I'm all for them. And, we'll have foliate heads too.

----Oh, tell me about foliate heads, please. I neeed to know more than what I know now.

----Not now, Cajetan, later when we have time. Right now we have to assess the condition of the roof with the roofers and carpenters.

Cajetan and Master Marquardt went to the exterior of the building and looked at the buttresses being set into place. Several had already been completed and they revealed a thinness and lightness that Cajetan had not noticed before.

----Look at that, Cajetan. See how thin the buttresses are.

----Why?

----It's to lighten the architecture and make the cathedral appear more Gothic. Almost like lace. I know that buttresses are supposed to help with the thrust of the vaults, but they need not be heavy and thick. I've designed them that way. Besides, the Bishop likes them. He told me that the buttress structures help to save time and money, and he was glad about that.

----Will they truly support the walls and help with the outward thrust.

----What do you think, Cajetan?

----It's not what I think, Master, it's what you think.

Cajetan was really trying to be diplomatic here.

----I think that the entire program of buttresses will do the job. I have no reason to believe that any buttress in this building will not hold its share of the thrust.

----That's good, Master. That's all I wanted to hear. It's really a matter of trust, and I trust your word, Master Marquardt.

The gargoyles were installed on the buttresses and connected to the gutters. Then large vats of pitch were hoisted up to the roof and the timber was coated to prevent it from rotting. Finally, sheets of lead were nailed to the framework. Everything looked tight and secure ready for the construction of the vaulted ceiling and the foundation of the transept.

Cajetan knew something about the transept but he did not fully understand its construction and its value in architecture. He did know that it was a crossing, but how the craftsmen managed to craft it was somewhat a mystery to him.

----Master, exactly what is a transept, and how is it constructed and why?

----Cajetan, that's why you're my journeyman. I know you were an apprentice for six years and now a journeyman. You learned much about architecture in those thirteen years but in architecture there are mysteries to be unraveled and transepts with vaulting are one of them. That's why I'm a Master Architect because I have learned to unravel the mysteries of architecture when it comes to design and planning of a cathedral. Mathematics, geometry and especially the science of design must be mastered. Now, you're very good at mathematics and geometry, but you need to learn more about design.

----I know that I'm weak in design, and I really want to learn from you for it is said that you are an expert in design.

----Who says?

----People.

----What people?

----People in the know like my former master, Albert de Chaussoyes and Timon Chenovert, Master Sculptor in Reims, and even Bishop Artevelde speaks highly of you.

----I'm glad to hear that. I have made design my specialty. As a matter of fact, design was my masterpiece offered to the guild for my promotion to Master Architect.

----What was it about? What was your masterpiece?

----It was the design of a huge marketplace for the commerce of woolen cloth and other goods to be sold. I had designed it so that it would draw merchants from all over, and keep them here in Ghent for a while longer to barter, buy, visit and enjoy our city. There were galleries and stalls and ornate places for refreshment. The guild especially liked the blended quality of both Christian and Muslim, the ornate and the geometric values of architectural design. It evoked the importance of Ghent as a city on the rise receiving peoples from many areas and cultures. It was approved and I got the master's promotion.

----Can I see it?

----No, because I don't have it. The guild got to keep it.

----Oh, I didn't know that about masterpieces.

----Well, now, about transepts. The concept sprang from the need for more space in a cathedral. As the members of the clergy increased in number, there was need to increase the required space. It was also a way of allowing for a proper celebration of the services in a cathedral. Transepts extend beyond the walls of the nave. In a cross-shaped church like the one we are building, the design is organically developed from the structure itself. It's part of the overall design, you see. Do you get it, Cajetan?

----Yes, I do.

----To form the shape of the cross, you have three squares which in breadth and height correspond to that of the main nave. Beyond the central square, called the bay, and connected to it is a fourth square, the choir. Beyond and connected to the choir is the apse. That's the cross shape. Do you get it?

----Yes. What about the transept?

----I'm coming to it. The transept generally terminates towards the north and south in a straight line. Transepts are the arms of the cross, so-to-speak. Of course, you know that the choir and the nave form the long or tall part of that cross.

----Yes, I know.

----Gothic architecture also emphasizes the choir by giving it, in the large cathedrals, three aisles so that very beautiful vistas are produced.

----All right, I'm with you.

----Furthermore, there's the ambulatory and its radiating chapels. The ambulatory is behind the choir and the main altar. It's so designed for the people visiting the cathedral can circulate behind the main altar where services are being held. It's a way of preventing distractions.

----Why the radiating chapels?

----Because every priest must say one mass every day, and when there are many members of the clergy around, the radiating chapels accommodate them for each mass being offered. It also means that more than one mass can be said at a time.

----What about the construction of the transepts?

----That's a challenge like many parts of a cathedral. First, the masons must insure that the cut stones are ready, and that the masons themselves are ready to climb up above. They usually start with the south transept, then they will cross over to the north transept. Rather than explaining to you each and every step of the construction of a transept, we'll come right here tomorrow and watch the masons do it. It will seem complicated to you, but to the masons it's just another job of putting the stones together to form an elongated arm extending from the crossing that's right before the choir.

----That will be great. I like to watch the craftsmen work on their specialty.

Every day after that, Cajetan watched diligently the ongoing work of the masons on the transepts. Then came the vaulted ceiling, a work of mastery if there was one. The days went by and Cajetan stood there with his head held up high until his neck began to ache. Wandal told him repeatedly not to keep holding his head up because he would wind up having a crooked neck. He would skip a day or two to rest his neck but soon afterwards, he was right back watching the masons. Master Architect Marquardt would smile every time he would see Cajetan standing there close to the choir looking up for hours. For Cajetan, the construction of the vaulted ceiling was a beautiful burst of architectural splendor way up there in Gothic space. The formation of the arched stone ribs supported by the wooden centerings on the scaffolding was an amazing thing for Cajetan. Architecture comes alive, he said. The ribs carried the webbing which was the ceiling itself.

By 1272, the transept was complete. It had been a long and arduous process, but the masons kept repeating that it was part of their craft, and they enjoyed doing it. It seemed arduous for those who watched the process of constructing the full transept and the vaulted ceiling, but for those who constructed them, it was a delight and they were very happy with the result. So was the Bishop as well as the Master Architect. Cajetan celebrated with the masons and got tipsy again. When he came home that evening, Wandal knew that he was filled with the blissful joy of Gothic architecture that was an integral part of his dream. He was inebriated with the ale and with the wine of his dream. Cajetan did not want to step into the house before he had time to gaze at the stars so bright and wondrous they seemed to him. Wandal had to push him inside the house for she told him that his meal was on the table and the children were already in bed.

Cajetan did not feel well enough the following morning so he stayed in bed until noon. He got up, washed and drank some cool water. Wandal wanted to give him something to eat but he refused. She was worried.

He told her that there was nothing wrong. He simply wanted to rest. Cajetan played a while with little Philippon, and then decided to go out for a walk. The sun was high in the sky and the heat from the sun was burning his neck. He went to the grassy knoll next to the baker's outdoor ovens and lay down on the grass. It felt cool and soft to the touch. Cajetan looked up at the blue sky and wondered where Maureen was, and what was she doing. He had not thought about her for years. Why now? he asked himself. That thought brought back the shrill memory of Cardinal Archbishop Tintamarre. What a dastardly hypocritical man, he thought. The semblance of reverence mixed with the horror of carnal deviance, he said to himself. He quickly got up and brushed those thoughts away not wanting to wallow in them like a swine wallows in mire. There were good people in my life, thought Cajetan, but there were also some not so good ones. Rielbert, for instance. Cajetan's naiveté had, for too long, masked or even hidden the evil aspects in life. He realized that now. Wandal was a foil against the evil that he recognized in some people. Thank God for her, he said to himself. She and Marie Dieudonnée along with my mother are three good presences in my life, he thought. Three good women that I admire and love. They're the good graces in my life. That's why I want to call my cathedral Mary Mother of Good Graces and it will be dedicated, in my heart, to all good women who cast a meaningful and righteous influence in men's lives. Cajetan turned around and slowly walked away satisfied that he had put one more notch in the design of his cathedral.

Cajetan began to make plans for his masterpiece for he realized that it would take time to finalize his project. The work on his masterpiece would have to be done on Sundays only, for the rest of the week was dedicated to his work with Master Marquardt. That was the understanding of the guild and all its members. Wandal tried to encourage him by giving him some suggestions, but he told her that the idea had to come from him and not an outsider.

----But I'm not an outsider, Cajetan. I'm your wife.

----I know that, but you're an outsider as far as architecture is concerned.

From that day on Wandal stopped giving Cajetan suggestions about his work and especially about his masterpiece.

The cathedral was coming along nicely what with the masons busy at work finishing the ribs. One by one, the cut stones of the ribs, called *voussoirs,* were hoisted onto the centering and mortared into place by the masons. Cajetan stood down below in awe of the work being done. Finally, the keystone was lowered into place to lock the ribs together at the crown.

----What is the crown? asked Cajetan to Master Marquardt.

----The crown is the highest point of the arch.

----What's the keystone?

----It's the central locking stone at the top of the arch.

----Oh, I see. The finishing touch, you might say.

By late spring 1273, the vaulting was complete, and then it was time for the glaziers to continue their work until they were done. There would be the rose windows and the other large windows, some as high as sixty feet. The tracery for the rose window in front of the cathedral took time for it was demanding work. Slowly and carefully the glaziers, the stone cutters, the sculptors, the carpenters all worked as a team of craftsmen to bring the cathedral in the shape of the design as planned by the Master Architect. Then again, it was a question of time and that meant years since the work could not be done year round, not in the harsh winter months. One of the last stages would be the casting of the bells. They would be cast in bronze at the foundry. Cajetan told Master Marquardt that when the time came, he would like to see that process, but Master Marquardt told him that it might not be possible to go see it because it was a process that could be dangerous for those who tried to watch it. The heat would be almost intolerable.

----Besides, you're talking about more years, and you might not be here then. You have got to think of yourself and your family.

Master Marquardt was referring to an addition to Cajetan's family. Wandal had given birth to two more children, another girl and a boy that Cajetan adored. Melodia and Philippon.

----How about the spire? asked Cajetan.

----That's another project that will take much effort on the part of carpenters and roofers. The tall wooden frame structure has to be built and covered with sheets of lead. Besides, it's quite a feat to be working way up there in the sky, I might say. It takes very skilled craftsmen to do that work. It can be dangerous too, and that's why we often call on volunteers to do the work. Some men just cannot climb that high without feeling giddy or weak in the legs. Would you climb up that high, Cajetan?

----I don't know. Perhaps if I had to and I was trained to do it, I would attempt to climb up to the sky. At night, I would be able to practically reach the stars and even touch some of them.

----I don't think so, Cajetan. Furthermore, we don't work late in the evening when it's dark.

----I was just kidding, master.

----But you're not kidding about reaching the stars, Cajetan the Stargazer.

----No, I'm not.

----Besides, the whole process for the spire will take years to complete, and we're not even ready to begin the spire. It's all in the plans and design though, but it will take time, what the Bishop always talks about.

Early the following year, after a long and harsh winter, work on the cathedral stopped. The chapter had run out of money. The Bishop was in a quandary. He did not want to stop the work due to a time schedule he had adopted for himself. There was nothing he could do. Sources of funding had simply dried up. The merchants, the money lenders and members of high nobility, all had obligations to meet, the Bishop was told. He complained to Master Architect Marquardt in hopes that the craftsman would have his own sources of contacts for funding. The Master told the Bishop that he had no funding sources, that if he had, he would gladly share them with the Bishop. The Bishop then turned to the Archbishop of Ghent. Archbishop Thomas Glaftsherf told him that he must be mad to ask for funding when money was tight everywhere. Besides, he said, Bishop van Artevelde had overstepped his boundaries and that he, as Archbishop of Ghent, thought that the cathedral project in Zelzate was extravagant in design and execution. "You don't need a flamboyant piece of Gothic architecture in your diocese. It was bound to cost too much for your needs. A simple Gothic church would have sufficed. No need to copy Paris, Chartres and Amiens. It's a waste of money. Where are you going to find the necessary funding to complete it?" the Archbishop told sternly the Bishop of Zelzate.

Bishop Romuald van Artevelde had struck a blank and very hard wall. He spent many a sleepless night thinking about his cathedral and, of course, the delay in time. He had to come up with an idea to be able to resume work on his cathedral. But what? He finally came up with the idea of displaying a major relic for people who would come as pilgrims and donate money to view and venerate the relic. It had to be big enough and important enough to attract hundreds if not thousands of pilgrims to Zelzate. It might take a few years, but the Bishop was willing to wait that span of time to recover his cathedral. What more could he do? It was that or lose his cathedral. What can I do with half a cathedral, he asked himself almost with despair. And so Bishop van Artevelde began searching for a major relic. He needed contacts and someone willing to part with it, and that would indeed be very difficult. No one in his right mind would part with a major relic, unless he needed something like money (the Bishop was willing to split the profits) or find a better place to house the relic. The Bishop spent days, even nights, thinking about the right contact he needed. He came up with the idea of borrowing the much appreciated and much venerated relic of Sainte Foy of Conques in southern France. He had seen it a long time ago and remembered that it was a gold reliquary with jewels and was purported to hold the head of the little martyred saint. It was part of the Pilgrimage to Santiago de Compostela and everybody seemed to know about this precious relic. Would the Abbey part with it? Would the populace of Conques part with it? Even for a while? He did not think so. But, he had another idea. Could there be a second relic of the little saint? If he were to manufacture another reliquary for the little saint, say for her finger (if that existed at all), that would draw pilgrims en masse, he thought. Why not? He would only talk about his project with a very select group of people who would tend to agree with him. Two or three people. That's all. He would need a reliquary expert and a goldsmith to make the reliquary. He would also need a person who had contacts to publicize the relic once it was encased ready for exhibition, or rather veneration, he corrected himself. The Bishop was desperate. He thought of his close friend, Abbot Saint-Germain of the Val-de-Pas Abbey in nearby Zottegem. He would know. Abbot Saint-Germain was considered to be a very rich man in a wealthy abbey. He held the purse strings of a wealth of treasures and money brought in by wealthy postulants and members of the nobility who wanted to be in a cloister for a time, meditating on their past sins and failures, and making amends by fasting and praying in a sacred place such as the Abbey Val-de-Pas. If he could not get the Sainte Foy relic, then he was sure that his friend, the Abbot, would certainly have a major relic in his stores. Besides, the Abbot owed him a favor for saving the Abbot's' skin some time ago. It had been a question of perjury in a case dealing with a land deal that benefitted the Abbey. Bishop van Artevelde, then diocesan interpreter of *jus canonicum*, canon law, who enjoyed a very good reputation, had vouchsafed for the Abbot, and the Abbot was cleared of any and all charges set against him.

Well, what the Abbot offered to the bishop was a large relic of Saint Callixtus, a martyr Pope of Roman times. It was a long bone of the forearm that had been venerated by people with maladies of the back for centuries, for they sought his intercession for a miracle cure. With time, the relic was translated to Santa Maria Trastevere in the 9th Century. Somehow, the relic was stolen, no "taken" as some people said, and brought to Spain in the

11th Century where it was kept under lock and key. Somehow, and no one knew or no one was willing to testify to its transfer, the relic wound up at the Abbey Val-de-Pas, and had been there for over two hundred years. People seemed to have forgotten about it, and no mention was made by the Abbey and its clergy in order not to draw attention to itself. The Abbot told the Bishop that he would be only too glad to lend him the Saint Callixtus relic for a period of five years when it would then be returned to its rightful place at the Abbey. That would satisfy the debt the Abbot owed the Bishop.

Bishop van Artevelde made all the preparations for the official acceptance of the relic of Saint Callixtus in his diocese. The relic was to be placed in the choir of the new cathedral, of course guarded night and day by reputable men. When the relic arrived, two months after the bargain between the two prelates had been struck, it was received with pomp and pageantry. The Bishop wanted full recognition of the relic by the public so that news of it would travel fast, and pilgrims would start arriving the very month it had been placed in the new cathedral with an offering plate next to it. When Cajetan heard of the relic of Saint Callixtus being brought to the cathedral in the *chantier*, he thought that it was a very good omen since he remembered a statue of the saint in a trumeau at the cathedral in Reims where he had worked as an apprentice. Saint Callixtus is standing upright fully dressed in his pontifical robes including a pallium around his shoulders with a long lappet in the front. The chasuble has many folds in the front thus revealing the sculptor's skill and craftsmanship. Cajetan liked this sculpture the minute he had laid eyes on it in Reims. The Zelzate chapter thought that this was a wise and practical solution to the funding crisis, and it expected the maneuver to succeed. All that the Bishop and the chapter had to do was wait.

After almost nine years of being a journeyman, Cajetan was very serious about his masterpiece. He had to get started on it for it would take time in designing it and constructing whatever he would conceive. One Sunday afternoon, he began by laying out some ideas on paper. It had to make sense, architecturally speaking, and it had to show some mastery of mathematics and geometry along with the necessary skills of an architect. That's what the guild would be looking for, mastery. That's what Master Marquardt had told Cajetan, "Mastery, mastery of your craft which is architecture. Some of the finest architects in Flanders will be there judging you and your masterpiece."

Cajetan took Master Marquardt's words to heart and began in earnest choosing the one idea among many that best suited his penchant for architecture. He finally picked the one related to the guildhall. He knew that such a project would most probably please the guild members who, at that particular time, needed to restore the old one or build a new guildhall. The old one was not useful anymore, and it had weak architectural features. Cajetan had heard about these features and thought that he could make a contribution to the guild of architects and builders. That would be his pièce de résistance, his best piece of craftsmanship as a journeyman.

The weaknesses of the existing guildhall were the lack of architectural qualities such as, the plain, oblong feature that made the building so very plain and dreary that few people recognized it as the guildhall of the Master Architects. Then, there was the lack of space since the membership had grown in the last few years, and its members could hardly congregate in that building to discuss certain problems or advance any particular propositions. Every member of the guild talked about these weak features, but no one had yet to make any suggestions or bring forth ideas about a replacement.

First of all, Cajetan brought his idea for a new guildhall to Master Marquardt. He wanted to get some feedback from him. He also wanted to make sure that he was on the right track as far as a masterpiece was concerned. Cajetan did not want to advance an idea that would be rejected right away by the masters. Master Marquardt told Cajetan that he thought his idea for a masterpiece was excellent, and that it would certainly be accepted by all the masters of the guild to which he and journeyman Cajetan belonged.

Comforted by these words, Cajetan began immediately to put his ideas down on paper. From there, he would explore which ones would work and which would not do. He came up with several, but finally chose four: a building that would have character and style, probably in the modified Gothic style; a building large enough to accommodate its membership; a construction revealing the different skills of the stone cutter, the mason, the sculptor and the glazier, so that the building would feature the unity and harmony of craftsmanship; a cupola that would make this building unique and worthy of calling itself the latest in architectural style and design for a guildhall. Cajetan would present his concepts on paper with drawings and some kind of illuminations as seen in the large volumes in abbeys that he had seen in the Abbey of Saint-Sauveur. Then he would make a model of his plans and design in order to better concretize his concepts that would develop into his masterpiece.

Again, he presented these four concepts to Master Marquardt who told him that three of the concepts would be easily accepted but the other one, the one dealing with the harmony and melding of the other crafts like sculptures and glass would most probably be rejected.

----Why? asked Cajetan.

----Because guilds are territorial. They do not easily accept crafts outside their particular expertise into their so-called territory. I think it's a good idea, and it would show the unity among many craftsmen and their skills, but the politics of craftsmanship will not tolerate such an idea. You can try, but I don't think it will succeed.

Cajetan worked every Sunday for six months on his project. Others used to tell him that masterpieces took not only months but sometimes years to develop and actually realize. Cajetan would not accept that. He was determined to finish his masterpiece in record time, he told Wandal. She left him alone and took the children out somewhere when Cajetan was working on his project, so that he would not be distracted. That was her way of encouraging her husband in his efforts to succeed at crafting his masterpiece. Wandal knew that such a project was terribly important to their future.

At the end of six months Cajetan was almost done with the construction of the model when he noticed, one day, that the cupola was missing from the roof of his building model. Where could it be? he asked himself. How could it be missing when I've been careful to protect it from any danger of theft or destruction? he added with great discomfort. Come to find out, his son, little Philippon, had gotten up in the middle of the night and had grabbed the cupola off the roof of the model, and had hidden it in his toys. It was young Grisoulda who found it after much commotion and worries over it. Cajetan had reached his wits' end, so frazzled were his nerves. Wandal kept telling him not to worry that they would find it. Of course, he could have built another one, but he had spent countless hours on the original cupola to ensure that it had style and craftsmanship. He did not feel like starting all over again. Cajetan put the cupola back where it belonged without chiding little Philippon. Rather, he promised the boy that he would make him one, a cupola of his own. Finally, when the entire masterpiece project was done, Cajetan put on his best Sunday clothes and presented himself and his masterpiece to the cadre of Master Architects at the guildhall. They were all waiting for him since they had been alerted about his presentation that morning.

Cajetan was so proud of his masterpiece that had taken him six and a half months, a record time for the making of a masterpiece. He stood in front of the membership, and, after the one in charge welcomed him and said a few words, he was told to explain in detail his masterpiece. He told them why he had done it, and how it could be realized. He talked extensively about the reasons behind a new guildhall, and they all nodded their heads in silent agreement, except one old master with white hair and teary eyes who withheld his consent. He had not nodded approval but rather he had fallen asleep sitting there. Then Cajetan explained his four concepts making sure that he was giving sufficient time to each and everyone. The four concepts would make or break his masterpiece, he thought. However, when he came to the concept dealing with the integration of craft disciplines, the Masters gave him a hard time.

----Why do you want to go outside of the strict discipline of architecture? one master asked.

----Well, I wanted to break the old concept of territory that's been the rule ever since the guilds were founded, I believe.

----That concept was established because it made it easier for our guild to justify our own rules and regulations. Although all guilds operate under rules and regulations, some guilds see things differently than others, and regulate differently. This way we, in this guild, the Architects' Guild, can maintain integrity of standards.

----But I thought integrity of standards was the same in all guilds.

----It appears to be but it's not always adhered to by the membership of various guilds.

----You mean that standards vary that much?

----Our standards, the Architects' standards never vary. We remain faithful to our founders and their established standards. We like it that way.

----I don't want to make you change standards. That's not my intent.

----What exactly do you want, journeyman Cajetan?

----My intent is to make your guildhall reflect the harmony of crafts. That's all.

----We don't need harmony. We need independent integrity.

----Can't you have both?

----We already have harmony. Each guild works on its own and respects individual performances of craftsmanship. No interference, no disharmony.

----All I want to do is create a concrete manifestation of crafts interconnecting with one another.

----It's clear to us that you are an intelligent journeyman, and you are good at your craft, and that's architecture. You're not here to fuse all crafts together under one roof, one umbrella, are you?

----No, I'm not.

----Then let's look at your masterpiece project, and then, we the Masters, can decide if it will qualify you as one of us, the Masters of Architecture. What do you think, Master Marquardt?

----Well, I can vouch for Journeyman Cajetan, for his keen sense of knowledge, his intelligence, his drive to learn more than just his craft as an architect, his love for the planning and design of our craft, and his deep sense of loyalty to architecture. Cajetan has been working under me for over six years and I highly recommend him for acceptance in the ranks of Masters of Architecture.

----We appreciate your honesty and your fidelity to your craft, Master Marquardt, but we also recognize your partiality to Cajetan, and that's to be admired. However, we are here to judge this Journeyman Cajetan on the merits of his masterpiece and not his personality. Therefore, we ask you, Journeyman Cajetan, please leave the room while we Masters deliberate on your project.

Cajetan stepped outside for he also wanted some fresh air. He felt that the air and the ambience in the guildhall was close and somewhat stifling. He simply wanted to breathe fresh air and collect his thoughts. After some forty minutes, they called Cajetan back into the guildhall, and one of the masters addressed Cajetan with a tone of formality and authority.

----Journeyman Cajetan, we are prepared to accept your project for consideration as a masterpiece. However, we must hear from you on how much you adhere to your concept concerning the melding of crafts.

----I'm not recommending that all crafts be melded together.

----Let me finish. It is important to us that we hear from you if you are ready to abandon that particular aspect of your project or not. Please tell us for it is of utmost importance.

Cajetan thought for a while before answering, for he realized that his concept of harmony of crafts was a sensitive issue with the Masters, and he knew that it could put his candidacy at risk. He was practical enough not to make an ideological issue out of this.

----I am ready to delete from my project that very concept that you want me to renounce as part of my masterpiece. You, the Masters, know better than me what a masterpiece for designation of Master Architect should be, and I bow to your wisdom.

Cajetan was told that he would hear from the Masters in a few days about the acceptance or rejection of his project. He went home and told Wandal about his ordeal and the response of the Masters of Architecture. He was tired, a bit frustrated and somewhat disappointed but not discouraged. In two days' time, he was asked to appear before a representative of the guild. The man was cordial, sincere and honest with Cajetan. He apprised Cajetan of the deliberations of the guild, and that the guild was prepared to accept him and his modified masterpiece with the designation of Master of Architecture. Cajetan was relieved and joyous. His heart could not stop beating loudly in his ears so happy and proud was he. He had finally reached his dream of the final step before building his cathedral. He rushed home to tell Wandal but she was out with the children. When she came home, Cajetan was fast asleep with his arms around a big soft pillow. Wandal smiled and knew *qu'il avait gagné ses épaulettes*. He had earned his stripes, his designation as Master.

8

THE COLLAPSE OF A CATHEDRAL

Bishop van Artevelde's plan to raise funds for his cathedral was working well. He had received the relic of Saint Callixtus from his friend, Abbot Saint-Germain, and had placed it under the choir of the cathedral yet unfinished. It had been eight months since the relic had been placed in the cathedral, and pilgrims kept pouring in just as had been predicted. The offering plate had to be emptied every so often until the Bishop decided to replace it with a bigger receptacle, much like a large ciborium. The season of Lent had been particularly fruitful for the Bishop. Thousands of pilgrims came from England, France, Germany and even Spain to atone for their sins by making a pilgrimage to Zelzate and its cathedral. Expiation was a primary factor for those who needed it; it had been ingrained in them by countless preachings. Furthermore, news of a healing had traveled fast. People kept saying that through the intercession of Saint Callixtus, a woman from Germany had been healed of her back injury. She had been in pain for over a year until she came to Zelzate to be healed. The Bishop had accepted the healing as being miraculous which helped to lend faith-filled credibility to the merits of the relic.

At Easter, the pilgrims kept coming in droves to celebrate the most auspicious of Feast days in Christianity, the Resurrection of Christ from the dead. The Alleluias were sung and kept ringing out their peals of joy by the local church bells. There was a joyous feeling in the early April air. However, Master Marquardt was not as joyous as he ought to be. In mid-March after a severe winter, the harshest of winter months with thick ice, blustery snows and penetrating cold winds not seen in years, the Master Architect went to the foundation site where the walls of the foundation had not been totally covered with dirt, and he inspected closely all parts of the walls to see if his suspicions had been realized or not. The Master Architect had suspected all along that, come a severe winter when the frost penetrates deep, the chances for cracks in the foundation were real and quite possible. At one point at the far end of the northern portal, which was still wide open and not yet completed, he noticed small fissures in the wall of the foundation, right below the confluence of the cathedral wall and the foundation wall, a serious and inauspicious sign of deep penetrating frost. Ever since they had dug the foundation and then raised the thick walls, the Master had not liked the depth of the excavation as prescribed by the Bishop. Instead of the usual depth of twenty-five feet, the Bishop, in order to save time, had ordered a reduction of the depth thus putting the foundation in jeopardy, according to the Master Architect's best knowledge of walls and foundations. He had repeatedly told the Bishop about his concerns, but the Bishop had brushed them aside thinking that God would take care of that.

Master Architect did not know what to do. Should he tell the Bishop or just let it lie. The Bishop, he said to himself, would not want to hear about it since he had other cares what with the lack of funds and the stoppage of work on his cathedral. He knew he had to tell the Master Mason. Master Mason Hilaire Desautels reacted in a way that surprised Master Marquardt. He told him that he did not worry about the fissures, and that they probably were superficial. Anyway, what good was it to worry about something that had not happened, and most probably would never happen, the collapse of the walls of the building. "We, the masons, did a superb job on the thick walls of the foundation, and we have no reason to believe that small fissures will prove to be harmful to the entire structure," he told Master Marquardt. Was Master Marquardt conjuring useless fears? Was he too sensitive about possible faults in the foundation? All that Master Marquardt knew was the fact that he did not feel good about it. He decided to talk to Cajetan, now Master Architect himself.

----Cajetan, I've discovered some fissures in the foundation. Would you accompany me to take a look at them?

----Some fissures? Sure, I will look at them with you. Are you disturbed by them?

----I certainly am. But I'm not sure if I'm overreacting.

----Let's take a look.

They both went to the area where Master Marquardt had spotted the fissures.

----They're certainly there, Master Marquardt. I don't like the looks of them, if you ask me.

----I thought so.

----Are you going to tell the Bishop about them?

----He's only going to dismiss my concerns. He has so many other things on his mind. A few fissures in the foundation are not cause for worry to him.

----How about Master Mason Desautels?

----I've already talked to him about it, and he dismisses my worries as useless and products of my imagination.

----That's too bad. Then, what are you going to do about it?

----Nothing I can do, Cajetan.

----Do you really think that the fissures are a cause for worrying? About the stability of the foundation, I mean.

----I'm not so much concerned about the foundation as I am about the Gothic walls and the buttresses. Remember, I told you about the thin buttresses? I don't know if they will support the walls and the thrust if anything happens to weaken the foundation. The fissures are small but I don't know if below the surface the fissures are not major cracks. This year's winter months were harsh ones what with the deep frost and persisting frigid weather. One never knows, Cajetan.

----Can we go deeper close to the foundation and verify it the cracks are there?

----We would have to dig too deep, and that would endanger both the foundation and the walls on it. We just have to trust in the Lord and hope nothing major, no catastrophe, will happen.

----Is that what you're going to do, pray and hope?

----What more can I do?

----As an architect like me, you must be worried just the same.

----Sure I am. But, I may be just overly apprehensive, and that fills my mind with worries.

----I think that all architects worry, worry about the implementation of the plans and design of a cathedral.

----If we did not worry, then we would not be good architects.

Every day the Bishop would stand in front of the cathedral, at least what had already been done, and he would stare at it with a kind of daze, his eyes glossed over. Then he would go to the area of the choir, look into the large vessel where the coins had been dropped by the pilgrims, and walk away content. Each day was a step closer to the resumption of the work needed to complete his cathedral, he thought. Every coin was counted each evening, and the sum had now reached a sizeable amount, enough to resume the work in probably six months time. It had been three and a half years since the relic had been placed in the choir. Abbot Saint-Germain would be pleased indeed that his relic was accomplishing its miracle of funds.

Meanwhile, Cajetan had farmed his services out to the wider community because he needed to feed his family. Very little income was coming in since work on the cathedral had been stopped. He found work at a new abbey being constructed in nearby Kluizen, the Abbey of Saint-Clothorius. The Benedictine Abbot was looking for an architect who would be able to help design and plan his Abbey from the ground up. Abbot Wiegelstern was an able designer of abbeys since he had done so in many instances. but he was getting old, and his skills as an architect were diminishing. He wanted to supervise the planning and design, but not execute them. He was looking for new blood. The Abbot was pleased with Cajetan for he was impressed by his keen intelligence, his superior skills as an architect as well as his dedication to his work. But, he was most impressed by his dream to, one day, build a cathedral for that was Cajetan's dream. The Abbot was also deeply impressed by the fact that Cajetan loved to gaze at the stars which was, for him, an indication that God was speaking to Cajetan in the stars and guiding him spiritually and architecturally. Cajetan was pleased at that interpretation, for no one had said that to him before. Gazing at the stars, then, was not daydreaming or wasting time in foolishness and stupidity but dreaming constructively and with the oversight of God the Creator and Great Architect. That's how Cajetan saw it now, even though, right along, he didn't think he was simply daydreaming. He was dreaming of building a cathedral some day.

Wandal was delighted that Cajetan had found himself a job and that it really pleased him. The children were growing, and she wondered what they were going to do when they grew up. Most mothers think that way. She told Cajetan that she thought Philippon would become an architect like his father, and that Grisoulda would be a healer in a hospice and take after her aunt, Marie Dieudonnée. As for Melodia, well, she might become a musician and play an instrument at court somewhere. Or, she might even be a singer, in a church or cathedral or at court where they're always looking for good musicians and singers. Melodia, like her name, was very good with music, said her mother. Cajetan agreed with her. What if none of the three turned out the way their mother thought was their strength in talents. God dispenses talents to humans, and it was up to us human beings to make the best of them. To make them fructify, as Bishop van Artevelde had said once. Wandal didn't think she had too many talents except to be a wife and mother. She had very little schooling and few talents, she said. Cajetan kept reassuring her that she did have talent, and all she had to do was to make them emerge out of her deep down self. She told herself that her deep down self was silent and too deep to reveal anything worthwhile. Wandal was a humble person with a retiring soul.

She always placed herself behind others and did not think of herself as a superior being. She said that she followed Christ's teaching of whoever wanted to be first in the kingdom of God had to be last in this life.

The rest of the year went by fast, and Cajetan was still very happy with his project of the new Abbey. Every day he would come home and share with Wandal the pleasure of planning and design or when it was appropriate, the progress of the excavation. He would tell his wife that the depth of the excavation was the normal depth with no diminishing of the designed measurements. Time was not the main factor, he said. Quality of work and the integrity of the design in its execution were of the highest priority. Wandal told him that he was right in maintaining his own standards. He told her that they were not his own but the guild's standards. Who would want to deviate from such standards? she asked. Cajetan did not reply but he knew who would do such a thing, or rather who had done such a terrible thing, but he kept quiet.

After another winter of terrible cold, deep frost, and glacial winds, the population of Flanders appreciated the coming of spring and its mild weather. Cajetan checked the foundation of the new Abbey, and confirmed that it was sound and without any fissures. The mortar was holding well, and the walls were as straight and solid as they should be. Abbot Wiegelstern was very pleased with the results and that the harsh winter weather had not damaged the foundation.

In late spring, the pilgrims were still coming to see the relic of Saint Callixtus and pray to the saint for a healing or some favors they asked for. It was late April and the rains had come. They had lasted for days with dark clouds announcing more bad weather. Someone said that it was some kind of ill omen. Others pooh-poohed them. Nevertheless, the dark clouds persisted, and some people were worried that some catastrophe might occur. The good news was that sufficient funds had been raised for the work on the cathedral to resume. The craftsmen were ever so glad, the laborers very happy, and the Bishop was overjoyed. Master Marquardt was relieved. Even Cajetan was glad that work could now be resumed without any worries of failures. It had been a long and strenuous wait for all, what with no work to be found and no income for those who desperately needed wages. They had suffered the pains of deprivation long enough, many said.

The work on the last buttresses was coming to an end. The glaziers were ready to continue their work on the rose windows. They had already done some of the windows in the clerestory. The nave was yet to be done, awaiting the completion of the walls. Things were looking up, and the Bishop was satisfied with the pace of the work. Nevertheless, Master Marquardt was still concerned about the fissures in the foundation, especially since one bad winter on top of another had plagued this building.

One late afternoon on a Friday when the pilgrims had decreased in numbers and the workers were finishing some of their work, there was a very loud rumble throughout the unfinished cathedral followed by a shattering of glass, then the rib vault above the choir came crashing down as if someone had shaken it from its very foundation. C-R-A-S-H !!! C-R-A-S-H !!! Yells and loud cries from people down on the floor were heard throughout the village. Chaos reigned in the yet unfinished cathedral. THE COLLAPSE OF THE CATHEDRAL ! someone shouted in a loud voice. Everyone scattered in fright. Others were left behind. Some were pilgrims who had not left yet, and others were the craftsmen who were still working in the interior of the building. Painful cries, mournful cries of people in distress, desperate cries, all sounding the alarm that something had gone terribly wrong. Everyone involved was running in whatever direction, just to get out of the way of danger and harm. When the falling debris had stopped, bodies were seen on the floor, while others sat there holding a leg, an arm, or a wrenched neck, while still others just stood there in a complete daze. Here, there was an old woman moaning, there, a middle-age man was crying out to God for having forsaken him while here and there were people, old people, middle-age people and even young people who were crying and crying because they could not stand whatever pain had been inflicted on them by this horrible catastrophe. They all felt like victims, abandoned by God and stricken by His avenging justice for whatever sins they had committed. They felt not only disoriented but the shock of the calamity rendered them helpless, if not totally confused. Paralyzed by such an unexpected happening. The awkward silence that ensued covered the entire area and seemed to mollify, for the moment, the pain of adversity and complete lack of understanding of what had truly happened. It was too hard to make sense of what had occurred. The collapse seemed to have shattered every parcel of the dream of having a cathedral. It seemed that it had also shattered the notion that the safe and secure place that was so often called "sanctuary" had been taken away and had vanished in the confusion of the disaster.

Master Marquart, as well as Master Mason Desautels, came running completely shocked in silent amazement that such a calamity had occurred. How could it? whispered Master Desautels to himself. Master Marquardt said nothing but shook his head in disbelief while remembering that those fissures in the foundation had meant something. They were real and, without a doubt, had caused the collapse of walls and vaults. It only takes one weakness somewhere, but an important weakness, to bring down an entire building, or at least a whole section of a building like this unfinished cathedral, Master Marquardt told himself. What a catastrophe! What a loss! What an utter failure of weak architectural faults! All of that was running in Master Marquardt's mind. "What do we do now?" asked Master Desautels. "Take care of the hurt and those who are dead," said Master Marquardt. Everyone who came running to the site was on the floor amid the debris trying to take care of those hurt in the collapse of parts of the cathedral. Master Mason Desautels tried to tell them to be very careful that more debris could fall on their own heads, but very few would pay attention to him. They all wanted to lend a helping hand to those suffering. "Afterwards, we will take care of the dead," they said. There must have been two hundred pilgrims affected by the collapse and some sixty craftsmen, all in some kind of pain due to their injuries. At least thirty dead bodies lay there waiting for someone to lift them up and bring them to a nearby location.

Suddenly Bishop van Astevelde rushed in shouting, "My cathedral! My cathedral!" and ran to the place where the relic had been placed. The reliquary lay on the floor smashed to pieces, and the relic crushed beneath some fallen stones. He tried to pry whatever remained of the relic but had a hard time even to scrape a small piece of bone so shattered was the entire forearm. The Bishop found bone splinters here and there. "Oh my God! Oh my God" he kept shouting. "What will the Abbot say?" He became as pale as a white alb, and his tone of voice was delirious. Master Marquardt tried to tell him that what was most important right now were the dead, and would he give them conditional absolution of their sins as the Church prescribed. He would not listen to reason and kept ranting about the relic being destroyed. It is then that Master Marquardt left him alone and went to the people that were hurt, first the ones with the most serious injuries. Master Mason had other craftsmen looking after the injured while some others were picking up the dead bodies and carting them to a nearby dwelling until they could be placed in a more proper location.

Some of the injured were brought to the small hospital in Zelzate run by a community of nuns. Others were taken to the larger hospital in Ghent, the Holy Ghost Hospital, and still others were taken to the hospital for the poor in nearby Oozengard. It seemed that everyone in Zelzate was attempting to help out in whatever way they could. It became truly a mission of mercy. Wandal was there and she did her best to administer compassionate care to several women. Cajetan only heard of the collapse when he got home from the Abbey site. He rushed to the *chantier* and began to organize volunteers into groups to better bring order to the rushing around of those who were involved with the care of either the injured or the dead, so that there would not be any disorder in the process. Once the dead had been carted away and the injured placed in hospitals, Cajetan and Master Marquardt looked at one another and let out a big sigh of relief. At least, the people had been taken care of for now the best they could. As for the cathedral partially in ruin, the two Master Architects along with the craftsmen left on site looked at the big hole in the vault of the choir and part of the north wall and its buttresses laying there like cadavers, and they all wondered what had happened.

Master Architect was so disenchanted with Bishop Artevelde's behavior and myopic view of the Gothic cathedral, that he resigned his post the following week. So did the Master Mason and several of his men. Many of the other craftsmen followed suite. Very few, it seemed, wanted to be affiliated with a devastated cathedral project. As for Cajetan, he decided to devote all of his time and energy to the designing and the building of the Abbey of Saint-Clothorius. At least, he had a real good project he could hold on to and progress with care and integrity of pursuit. He truly liked and admired Abbot Wiegelstern. He had character and tenacity, and he knew what he was doing. As for Bishop Artevelde, he was transferred somewhere and no one knew where exactly. Some rumors had him in a lonely hospice for the confused out in the mountains. Abbot Saint-Germain of the Val-de-Pas Abbey never forgave the Bishop for having forced him to relinquish his prized relic.

Three days went by and Marie Dieudonnée suddenly appeared and told her brother and sister-in-law that she had come to bring comfort to the victims of the cathedral disaster. She had heard of the collapse from a neighbor who had returned from Zelzate. She worked night and day devoting herself to the much needed tasks of putting splints skillfully on fractured bones, she used her remedies of herbs and special concoctions to try and heal bad sores, cuts and bruises, and she worked tirelessly at bringing good cheer to each and every patient she met. Cajetan told her repeatedly to rest and take care of herself or else she would easily drop from fatigue. Everyone said that Marie Dieudonnée was a devoted, compassionate, highly knowledgeable and able care provider and healer.

She certainly made a name for herself by her extraordinary skills and knowledge of medicine, so many people said who saw her work with the sick and the injured. Her reputation as a healer was definitely established now that she had demonstrated her healing skills on a broader scale. Some started calling her Marie Dieudonnée, la Guérisseuse.

After six weeks in Zelzate, Marie Dieudonnée told Cajetan that it was time for her to leave and that she had accomplished her mission as a healer for the unfortunate.

----Cajetan, my brother, I have confirmed my true vocation here in Zelzate. Not that I did not have a sense of it before, but I know now that I belong in a monastery among the caregivers and the *hospitalières* . I want to go to Fontevraud where there is the finest cloister and the best of hospitals attached to the monastery. I have made some inquiries and that's where I want to spend the rest of my life. I want to heal others for the greater glory of God and His creation. That's my calling. A religious vocation with a facet of service to the unfortunate be they poor, injured or abandoned by society. I want to minister to the least of the least. That's gospel truth.

----My dear sister, I know that you have been searching for the right place and the right calling for yourself, and I'm very happy that you have found them. No better thing than one's right place on this earth. I know, I have found mine, and I would not trade places with anybody. My dream is to build a cathedral someday, and I'm aiming for the stars that will guide me and assure me that I'm on the right course in life.

----I know, and you're fortunate that the stars have always been favorable for you, Cajetan the Stargazer. May they be favorable to me also, but I pray especially to the Holy Ghost to keep inspiring me in my decision to answer the call of the Divine Savior. I know that I'm on the right path, my brother.

Just before Marie Dieudonnée left Zelzate, Cajetan slipped into her hands a small packet containing her dowry that she was to hand over at Fontevraud Abbey as was required by custom and rule.

After Marie Dieudonnée left, Cajetan, Wandal and the children settled in the surety of a home where one is always happy to have found comfort and peace. However, the collapse of the cathedral never left Cajetan's mind. He wondered if he could have done anything about it. Cajetan was a noble architect, one who kept his ideals strong and praiseworthy. The collapse of the cathedral had never been part of in his plans or design as an architect, for he had never even considered it possible. For him, the collapse of a cathedral was an omen of failure to adhere to standards of fidelity to the integrity of architecture itself. He told himself that structural weaknesses oftentimes reflect human weaknesses, and that human capacity can be easily thwarted by haughtiness and sometimes greed. .

9

ON THE ROAD TO FONTEVRAUD

The long distance between Cambrai and Fontevraud l'Abbaye near Chinon in Anjou gave Marie Dieudonnée time and leisure to enjoy the pleasures of travel. She left Cambrai with a letter of introduction from her parish priest, Father Honoré Langlois, who vouched for her upright character, her deep sense of spirituality and charitable soul as well as her ability to heal. She had few belongings. What she brought with her were the necessary things and the rest, she gave away to the poor. Marie Dieudonnée was not a woman who attached herself to things. Her only attachment were her fond memories of family and close friends. She had never attached herself to place and location either. She prided herself in being detached from earthly things that hold one down. Things were things, and she could easily live without many of them. So, the thought of living in religious poverty, chastity and obedience as well as permanence of site was not an impediment for her. Rather, it was a welcomed gift from God, she told herself. What truly mattered to her was the notion of selflessness and compassion toward others. She did not consider herself to be a saint nor a person of heroic virtue. She was a simple and ordinary person, she claimed. Hypocrisy was not her game neither was self-righteousness. Marie Dieudonnée was a woman of simplicity and integrity of conscience. She had a capacity for love and a tendency to share her love with many. She had thought of marriage and her own family, but she wanted more. She wanted a larger family, and a multitude of people around her. The idea of living in a community was appealing to her. So, she was on her way to the Fontevraud Abbey. She honestly and trruly felt that she belonged there.

Marie Dieudonnée stopped at various sites on the way to her destination. She slept in convents that welcomed her, at times at an inn where the food was simple but good, and she often took advantage of the good will of people who wanted to give her shelter for the night. She was a trusting soul and she managed quite well with whatever was offered to her. Along the way, she visited a few pilgrimage sites. She considered herself to be a pilgrim heading for a site of the sacred dwelling place of prayerful souls in search of salvation through good works. She felt that her calling was indeed a pilgrimage, a path trodden with mercy and selflessness. That's how she felt and it felt good.

Along the way, before she got to Laon, she met this older woman, dark complexion, deep dark penetrating eyes, black lustrous hair with streaks of grey, and with hands that fluttered like the wings of a bird. Marie Dieudonnée was captivated by her. This woman introduced herself as Marie-Ange Dolthérien, and claimed to be a descendant of a lost tribe of Israel. Her ancestors had arrived in southern France in the eighth century, and had gradually integrated themselves with the general population, although some bands remained disassociated with them and formed their own enclaves in the low southeastern part of France, specifically in the Camargue where beautiful white steeds, these noble and brave animals, could be seen. Marie Dieudonnée asked her where she was going, and she told her, "Anywhere my destiny brings me."

----What exactly is your destiny?

----I don't know. I just know that I have one and it will unfold at every step in life I take.

----But how do you know which step to take?

----I get up in the morning, look up at the sky, and read my destiny in the clouds. If there are none at that particular instant, then I wait until some clouds come rolling by.

----What is it you read in the clouds, and what kind of clouds tell you your destiny?

----I look at the big white puffy clouds and sometimes the long elongated ones with tinges of rose and mauve, and then I know what my destiny is for that day. I only know it from day to day.

----So it may change suddenly at every cloud formation you see in the morning sky.

----I suppose that's one way to put it. When I look up and see the clouds, I read in them my destiny for that day. That's one thing I know.

----But how do you know?

----I know through the deep resonance in my breast.

----Like a premonition of sorts?

----It's not a premonition. Not a warning either. It's an enlightenment of my awareness as a human being.

----How's that?

----It's difficult to explain it to you because I don't know how. All I know is that this morning I knew where I was to go. Which path to take. On that path, I met you. You're part of my destiny, you see.

----I am?

----Yes. You're going to Fontevraud and I will be your companion of the road.

----Are you an angel of some kind sent by the Lord to be messenger and guide?

----No, I'm not. I'm a Christian of Jewish ancestry. Not an angel. I'm real.

----But Jews believe in angels don't they? Take the Old Testament where we come across angels of the Lord delivering messages. Abraham for instance.

----Yes, Abraham. We all share his story, but the Jewish Covenant with God is different than the Christian covenant, I know. Yahweh made it directly with Moses while Christ fulfilled that Covenant and developed it into his own.

----I know that.

----I don't want to elaborate on covenants. All I know is that I am to be your companion, *votre compagne de route*. It has been decreed by the penetrating voice of the mystery in the clouds and it's my destiny. Do you consent to this, Marie Dieudonnée?

----Yes, of course. Why should I refuse a companion? I love people and I love having someone along the way. I still have a long way to go.

----Well then, let's get going. Do you have enough to eat for the journey?

----I say that the Lord will provide, although I do have some bread and fruit. I'll drink the water at the fountains or wells that we'll see along the way.

----I have food for both of us. I come prepared.

----How did you know you would need extra food?

----I knew.

Marie Dieudonnée and Marie-Ange Dolthérien started walking side by side until they came to a fork in the road.

----Which way do we take? asked Marie Dieudonnée.

----Why, we go to the left.

----Are you sure?

----Yes. Don't worry, I'm here to guide you.

Marie Dieudonnée did not know what to think about all of this. Was it genuine or not? Was it some kind of trick? Why should she trust this woman? These and other questions ran through her mind.

----I'll have to trust you because I don't know my way to Fontevraud. I was simply going to ask for information as I went along.

----Well, now, you have the information you need.

Their first stop of the day was at Laon. The commune was in a hilly district, and both women had a hard time climbing the hills to reach whatever attracted their interest. They stopped at the marketplace to buy some fresh bread and Laon's famous *pâtisserie, le petit four*. Marie Dieudonnée seldom spoiled herself by buying pastry but Marie-Ange urged her to try one, and the taunting odor of the delicacy was too strong for her resistance. Marie-Ange bought two and gave her companion one. Marie Dieudonnée bit into it and couldn't resist finishing it off immediately. Then, they went to the flower stall where they looked intently at the lovely flowers with their alluring scents and colors. The owner wanted them to buy some, at a very reasonable price, he told them, but they refused to buy any. "What are the flowers in the open fields for?" asked Marie Dieudonnée. "They're free to anyone who bothers to stoop down and pick them." The seller of flowers turned around and stopped talking to both women. He seemed miffed at their response.

Climbing another hill, they came face to face with the cathedral, Notre-Dame de Laon. They could see that there were some oxen sculptures on the two towers of the church, and they wondered what they were doing there. A young man standing next to them explained that these oxen were on the church because of some miracle that had happened during the construction of the cathedral. The laborers were struggling very hard to push their loads of stones and mortar up the hill when all of a sudden appeared some oxen that pulled the loads for them. The laborers were so dumbfounded that everyone heard about the miracle of the oxen, and the sculptors decided to honor those beasts of burden and place them on their cathedral. That's the miracle of the oxen of Laon. Marie Dieudonnée thanked the young man and gave him a b*être de Cambrai*, her own candy that she made.

The two companions spent the night at a small inn run by two ladies who were part of a local guild of innkeepers. They so pleased the visitors and the pilgrims with the comfort of the inn as well as their warm reception, *leur accueil chaleureux*, that they received an acclamation by all, such that the guild invited them to join their group. "See there are women who become members of guilds," Marie Dieudonnée told Marie-Ange. "I know, I know," said the other. The next morning after a light breakfast, the two travelers took to the road once again and headed for Soissons. That's the next town that Marie-Ange pointed out as their next destination. Marie Dieudonnée followed.

As they got to Soissons, they met a man who was begging at the huge portal of the commune. Marie-Ange gave him two small coins. He thanked her and told her that if she needed shelter she could find some for herself and her friend in a nearby *ruelle* called *Bout en cul*, a dead-end little street. He told her that the shelter belonged to a friend of his and that it was safe and secure for two women travelers. Marie-Ange and Marie Dieudonnée decided to seek this shelter before it got too late in the day. It was easy to find. The old woman who owned it told them that the man they first met was her brother. He was a beggar because he liked to meet people and earn some money. He was not poor, she said. The owner's name was Elphèse la Batouche. She liked to cook and to sew, she told them. Once they were settled in their small room upstairs, they went off to explore the commune. The old woman gave them some information about the locale, and told them that she had lived in Soissons all of her life. She also told them that Soissons was one of the most ancient towns in France. The great and mighty King of the Franks, Clovis I, won the Battle of Soissons and the territory became his to rule. "Oh, he was a great leader of the people", said Elphèse. "I learned that from my great grandfather who got it from an old book on the history of Soissons. In the book, was written the legend of "Le Vase de Soissons." It is said that the vase was the most precious possession of the church of Sainte Élodie, and it was made of precious metal. As a result of the Battle of Soissons, the vase became the booty of Clovis, but one of his soldiers took his battle-axe and crushed the vase. Remigius, Bishop of Reims, who was later to convert Clovis, sent messengers to plead with Clovis to spare the vase and remit it to the church, but it was too late, the vase had already been crushed. Clovis sent the broken vase to the Bishop. At first, Clovis said nothing but a year later he took the soldier's own battle-axe and split his skull saying, "Just as you did to the vase of Soissons!" That's a legend that is part of Soissons's history and most people here know of it."

After Soissons, the two women took to the road again and headed for Reims. Marie Dieudonnée had heard of Reims from her brother, Cajetan, and she was impressed by it's cathedral and especially its sculptures. Marie-Ange pointed out to her the angel with a smile. "That's a woman angel," she said.

----Yes, my brother told me about her.

----Did he have anything to do with her?

----No, but he knew the sculptor, and he explained the reason behind the smile of a woman angel. Men angels are more serious while the women

135

angels have a sense of humor. They smile. I wonder if God is as severe and stern as He is so often depicted.

----And angry-face.

----Full of anger and even revenge, the God of the Old Testament.

----You mean the Old Testament God of Sodom and Gomorrah.

----Yes. The great punisher, Adam and Eve, David, Solomon, not Job because he was being tested, but the people of Noah's time too.

----If heaven is a place of happiness where every saint is blessed with smiles and laughter, then the angels must also smile and laugh. Of course, all except those who were damned like Lucifer.

----Have you ever seen happy people with a frown on their faces?

----No. It would be ridiculous, not real, don't you think?

----I agree.

----What else is interesting in this cathedral, Marie-Ange?

----*La Sainte Ampoule*, the Holy Flask holding the sacred oil with which French kings were anointed. The last one was Philippe IV le Bel right here in this cathedral. I have an old uncle who was here for the *sacre*, the coronation rite. That was in 1286, not too long ago.

----Reims certainly has very interesting features, especially the cathedral.

Marie Dieudonnée and her companion left Reims before sunrise the day after. They wanted to be able to reach Troyes before sunset, the following day, if possible. They found the journey, so far, not too long and really uneventful. After half a day of walking, they decided to hitch a ride on a cart filled with broken pottery, some pieces of wood and a few earthen jars. They wondered what the driver of the cart was doing with all of this. He told them that he had been cleaning a loft in a house where a *trouvère* used to live. He had lived there over one hundred years ago, he told them, and the house had been empty for the last twelve years. Somebody had just bought it and wanted it cleaned. It was full of junk, he said.

----Isn't a *trouvère* a poet of some kind? asked Marie Dieudonnée.

----Why, yes, replied Marie-Ange. *Trouvères* and *troubadours* are poet singers, as far as I know. They still exist today, as a matter of fact. I know a few of them. But the greatest one was named Chrétien de Troyes. They didn't know his real name but they said that he had lived here once.

----I've heard of him, said Marie Dieudonnée.

----I know somebody in Troyes who is well versed in romances, and I want you to meet him.

----Really? You know quite a few people who know things, don't you?

----Yes, I've been around for a long time.

----I don't know too much about romances but I do know that they're stories about love and chivalrous tales.

----Yes, courtly love. Not about peasants and craftsmen and ordinary people. People at court have a different lifestyle and different ways of expressing themselves. Besides, they all have a lot of time on their hands. Ladies have to be entertained, and they have dreams about knights and the pursuits or adventures of love. It's all about an idealized love, I am told.

----Not in my own life. I'm too ordinary to go through that. I live from day to day and do not worry about what they call love.

----Yes, that's a very difficult subject and, besides, ordinary people do not worry about love. They worry about their children, their work and how to put food on their table.

----I guess people at court have their own problems. They get bored and so they have to think about something to keep them busy.

----Yes, like adventures about knights and demoiselles in distress.

----That's like dreaming all of the time. I mean, not having one's two feet in reality. I have a brother who's a dreamer but not that kind of dreamer. He dreams of building a cathedral, a real one. He's a Master Architect now.

----That's not the same thing, I agree. Well, I do hope he gets to build his cathedral someday.

----I think he will. He's determined to build one especially after the collapse of the last one he was working on.

----Where was that?

----In Flanders. Many people were injured besides the ones who died in that calamity. I went there to help out with the healing. I was there two months.

----Some people died?

----Yes, there were workers and pilgrims. The rib vault above the choir fell down.

----How could that happen?

----My brother told me that the foundation had fissures in it, and that made the entire structure weak to deep frosts and harsh winter months.

----Didn't they know about that?

----Well, the way it was explained to me, the Bishop did not want an excavation dug as deep as is customary, and so the foundation was susceptible to cracks.

----Why did the Bishop do that?

----Because, says my brother, the Bishop wanted to save time.

----Save time and lose a cathedral?

----I guess you could put it that way.

When Marie Dieudonnée and Marie-Ange arrived in Troyes, they first went to get lodging. They found some at a hospice called "L'Hospice de la Bonté du Seigneur."

----The goodness of the Lord, said Marie-Ange. That should be a good place for us.

----It looks like it.

----Let's go in.

----We'll get settled and then I'll bring you to my friend, Maître Sobricourt. He's a former teacher and a lover of books, especially romances. He's retired now and spends all of his time reading. What a life!

----I should think so. Is he married?

----He was but his wife died many years ago. He now leads a solitary life, like a monk.

----Oh, I see.

When they got to the house where the solitary man lived, Marie-Ange knocked at the door, but there was no answer.

----Let's go see in the garden. That's where he spends most of his time when the weather is nice.

They went around the small house and found an elderly man seated at a table reading.

----Maître Sobricourt, what are you reading now? asked Marie-Ange.

As the old man looked up, he saw Marie-Ange with a friend standing before him.

----Ah, Marie-Ange, *l'ange de la route*, the angel of the road. What are you doing here, my old friend.

----I may be an old friend to you but I'm not that old, Maître. I want you to meet my new friend of the road, Marie Dieudonnée. She comes from Cambrai and she's a healer.

----Pleased to meet you Marie Dieudonnée, a lovely name. Your mother made a privileged choice.

----Yes, I've been blessed by the Lord, replied Marie Dieudonnée.

----What are you reading now, Maître?

----I'm reading Chrétien de Troyes's **Yvain**. Have you read this romance?

----You know, Maître, that I don't read romances. They make your head spin. Besides, I'm not in love with anyone especially knights who wander off. Ah! wanderlust.

----Now, now, Marie-Ange. Romances are meant to entertain, not to make hearts and heads spin.

----From what I hear, they certainly make courtly ladies swoon over them.

----What do you expect from ladies who read day in and day out about love?

----You read all the time. Don't you get a bit off the track of reality?

----My dear, Marie-Ange, I'm too old to let romances affect me that way. I read them for pleasure. Besides, Chrétien de Troyes's writing is sheer delight for anyone who loves poetry.

----Maître, please tell us more about Chretien de Troyes. My friend here would like to hear about him.

----Well, Chrétien de Troyes was a gentleman of the court. Not that he was of nobility himself but he was often at court with the ladies. Besides, he was friends with Eleanor of Aquitaine and her two daughters, Marie and Alix. It was Marie, Marie de Champagne, who requested a romance from Chrétien de Troyes. He wrote for her and dedicated it to her as far as we know. Although he did not serve at the court of his patroness, Marie of France, Countess of Champagne, we do know that between 1160 and 1172 he had some kind of role at court. His works include "Yvain, the Knight of the Lion" and "Lancelot, the Knight of the Cart." In his last years, he was attached to the court of Philip, Count of Flanders. We know very little of his personal life. Most of what we know about him is about his romances. His great influence in writing subjects were the Arthurian legends. Are you familiar with the Arthurian legends?

----Not really. I've heard about them but know very little about the subject.

----Neither do I, said Marie Dieudonnée.

----Well, that's another matter that I will discuss with you at a later date. I'll tell you all there is to know about the Knights of the Round Table and their chivalric adventures and the quest for fame and glory. Right now, I'm hungry, and I invite both of you to share my meager meal of bread, fruit and some wine from the Champagne valley.

After the meal, Marie-Ange and Marie Dieudonnée exchanged conversation with the master until they detected that the old man was tired and ready for a nap. They left thanking him for the information about Chrétien de Troyes, both feeling enriched by the conversation about the poet and his works.

The two women were ready to go on the road again, but they figured they had traveled far enough so far as to merit some rest for, at least, a full day. They knew that they were going to Sens, a small commune near the Yonne River, and that its annual fair, "La Foire du Bon Temps", was coming up. There would be a surge in population for Sens attracted many visitors at that time. They both sat down on the grass at the edge of the woods, enjoying a respite from their walking. They talked, they ate and they reminisced about their journey so far. Marie Dieudonnée said that she enjoyed the time spent on the road with Marie-Ange, and the interesting information she shared with her. She told her that she was truly impressed by her knowledge and *savoir-faire*. Marie-Ange thanked her but told her that she wasn't that knowledgeable about things, and that she did not have any real education. It all came to her through experience, she said.

----What I'm pursuing is not *savoir-faire* but *savoir-vivre*. Knowing how to live is the principal thing in life, Marie Dieudonnée. Living the Christian way, the way Christ taught us. The way I've been following ever since I became a Christian and a member of Fontevraud Abbey.Do you know how old I am, Marie Dieudonnée?

----Well, I would say that you're around sixty years old.

----I'm eighty-three.

----No. No one lives that long nowadays.

----Well, according to some records my mother kept, I was born eighty-three years ago.

----I would have never known you were that old, not by your appearance. You look as young as I am.

----No, Marie Dieudonnée. You're still young. I'm old in age and experience.

----I hope I'm young enough to be accepted at Fontevraud Abbey. What I'm doing now is my pilgrimage toward my vocation. I have prayed long and hard, and I now truly believe that the cloister is my calling in my mature life.

----If you feel that way, then that's what it is.

----How do you know?

----Well, I know through intuition and voices within me.

----What voices?

----They're like silent voices that I hear, not through my ears, but through my soul. I hear them and I feel them. You know, when I first met you you probably thought that it was coincidence but it wasn't.

----What do you mean?

----I mean that I sensed that I needed to be there for you. That you were in search of something, something very important in your life.

----Yes, I was, no, I am, I mean.

----You also told me that you had a younger brother who was in the Carmelite Order but then came out, and that you were left with conflicting thoughts about the cloister.

----Yes, I was caught between the meaning of cloister life and its actual purpose, and the way it was being implemented. Especially with men who follow sternly and without any tolerance the strict letter of the Benedictine rule. Actually, I believe they change the rule to fit their own purpose.

----I think you will find that at Fontevraud things are not run that way.

----Have you been there?

----Yes, I have. I am a former Abbess of Fontevraud.

----What?

----I am a former Abbess of Fontevraud. I still am, in a way. I no longer am the active superior, but serve as roaming representative of our order. I have become the voice of the calling, you might say. I serve a very special ministry in that I was dispensed from the actual cloister life on site, but I still lead a life of a cloistered nun. My cloister is my soul. My interior life is my anchor. You see, I have become a pilgrim too, a pilgrim on the road to salvation for myself and for others who cross my path. You see, I am, in a way, a messenger and a guide.

----I knew that there was something special about you the minute I met you.

----So you see, I must follow through with our pilgrimage together. It's about two callings, one being called and the other, calling.

----That's extraordinary!

----Extraordinary for us but ordinary for the Lord and sweet Mother Mary, my patroness. My name Marie-Ange is a testimony to my Marian calling. My real name was Ruth Dolthérien, the Ruth of the Old Testament.

Once in Sens, the two women found shelter in a small inn where the owner told them to avoid a particular section of the commune during the fair because it was not safe. It attracted thieves and dangerous characters, she said. Notwithstanding this irregularity in the population at the time of the fair, Sens was a very old commune dating back to the time of the Celts. It also went back to the Roman times during the rule of Julius Caesar. Sens's current Archbishop along with others before him held the prestigious role of Primate of Gaul and Germany. The archdiocese of Sens, she told them, rules over the dioceses of Chartres, Auxerre, Meaux, Paris, Orléans, Nevers, and Troyes. The owner, Isabeth Lalimonde, also told them that starting from 1135, the cathedral of Sens, dedicated to

Saint Stephen, was rebuilt as one of the first Gothic cathedrals. Marie Dieudonnée was thinking, as the owner was saying these words, how interested her brother, Cajetan, would be in this fact. Isabeth Lalimonde continued by saying that it was here in Sens at the cathedral that Louis IX of France celebrated his wedding to Marguerite de Provence.

----So you can see that this commune is an important one full of history and events.

----Thank you for your information, said Marie Dieudonnée.

Marie-Ange then asked the proprietor of the inn where they could have something to eat, and she replied that they did not have to go too far since she herself offered some meals like breakfast and the noontime meal. Since it was a little past noon, Marie-Ange asked her if it was too late for the meal. She answered, no. After the meal, Marie-Ange and Marie Dieudonnée went to visit the cathedral. Late afternoon early evening, both women went to the square where the fair was being held. There were candles lighting brightly the areas with booths and open stands. They were selling all kinds of things, ribbons, candies, herbs for cooking, spices, medicinal herbs, toys for children, and a variety of foods. Marie-Ange went to the booth on the far side of the square where darkness began to overshadow the immediate area. However, it was lighted enough to be able to see what was going on in and around the booth. Marie Dieudonnée followed her.

While Marie-Ange was asking questions to the woman behind the counter in the booth, Marie Dieudonnée stayed a little behind her looking at some candies displayed there. She thought of her own *petites bêtises de Cambrai*. As she was examining a small package of candies, a big hand went over her mouth, the hand of a rough and burly man, who dragged her behind the booth. She wanted to scream but couldn't. All she could see was the shoulders of the man. He hit her and told her to keep quiet or else. She was so frightened that she could not scream, not even utter a single word. Her face went pale and her heart was pounding. The man dragged her even further behind some bushes. Marie Dieudonnée was so terrified that she lost consciousness for a few minutes. When she came back to herself, she saw the man had bared himself from the waist down and was showing an erection. She wanted to scream, yell or do something but couldn't. He then stuck his fingers up her very private parts and Marie Dieudonnée felt sick inside her. She felt something wet going down her leg. His fingers had created in her vagina such a burning sensation that it was almost unbearable. Oh, she thought, I do not want to lose my virginity to this ruffian of a man. No! No! No! she told herself. As he was preparing to enter her, she recovered her voice and managed let out such a scream that it must have gone over all of the booths and stands, and well over the entire commune so loud was it. People started to run in the direction of the scream including Marie-Ange since she had just noticed that Marie Dieudonnée had vanished. She told herself that she must have disappeared the instant she had turned her back to her. Two men jumped on the ruffian and held him back until they had him in their hold. Marie-Ange came running toward Marie Dieudonnée and tried to comfort her the best she could. Marie Dieudonnée could not stop weeping. It seemed that the tears were uncontrollable. They reflected the awesome fear that Marie Dieudonnée had inside her, and was now coming out as terrified feelings of anger and remorse. The culprit was taken away. After a while, Marie Dieudonnée was mollified and assuaged of her deep fears enough to be led to the inn.

Once inside a secure place, Marie-Ange asked the owner for hot water and some rags. She led Marie Dieudonnée up the stairs and started undressing her. She saw that there was blood down her right leg. She washed the blood and gently probed inside her vagina to check if there was anything wrong. No, thank God, the ruffian had not penetrated her and there was no damage done to her virtue, she told herself. However, Marie Dieudonnée explained to her friend that she felt violated and that she considered herself deflowered since she was convinced she had lost her virginity because blood had flowed. Marie-Ange tried to convince her that was not the case.

----But there was blood. Vaginal blood. I lost my virginity even though he did not go inside me. I know I lost it.

----No you did not. He did not deflower you.

----But I feel violated and what will the Prioress of the cloister at Fontevrault think? I will not be accepted into their order. I will be rejected like a spoiled fruit, I know.

----No, Marie Dieudonnée, I know the Prioress and the Prior, they will not reject you for you are pure of heart and chaste of body, still.

----But I feel dirty somehow. I need to offer some sacrifice or go through some sacramental cleansing in order to feel clean.

----It is not your fault. God has nothing to forgive you. You are clean. However, tomorrow morning I will conduct with you some prayer service and wash you with clean water and bless you with holy oils that I carry with me so that you may, once more, feel innocent and free of sin. But, Marie Dieudonnée you are not the sinner, he is.

----I know. I do need to go through some ritual of cleansing. That will confirm that I am whole again.

Marie Dieudonné slept that night with many interruptions in her restless sleep for it was furrowed with a horrific nightmare. In the meantime, Marie-Ange slept with an eye open for her companion. There wasn't much sleep that night. The following morning, Marie-Ange took her friend to a sheltered spot at the inn and accomplished the ritual she had promised Marie Dieudonnée, a ritual of pure water, oils and prayers uttered reverently over the abused victim. The ritual done, Marie Dieudonnée felt well enough to have breakfast and smile a bit with a few words of conversation. "Let's get away from here," she told her friend. And so they left immediately.

Auxerre was a relief to both women. It was inviting as it was beautiful, what with its wine cultivations and splendid vistas. Before getting a place to spend the night, the two women visited the cathedral of Saint-Étienne and remarked how fine the stained glass windows in the choir and apsidal chapel were. They were surprised to see some foliate heads in evidence. Some of the most remarkable to be seen.

----They're usually situated in some dark corner somewhere, remarked Marie-Ange. But these are part of the corbels.

----What are they doing in a cathedral? asked Marie Dieudonnée.

----A lot of people have asked that question.

----I wonder what they mean. Are they Christian, Celtic or of some other pagan source? I wonder.

----I don't really know. We don't have any in Fontevraud.

----Do you have gargoyles?

----Gargoyles, yes. They're useful and colorful as well as imaginative.

Both of them laughed.

On their way to Vézelay the two traveling companions remarked how gorgeous and enticing the countryside was. For Marie Dieudonnée it was a tonic that seemed to alleviate her bad experience in Sens. Marie-Ange told Marie Dieudonnée that she was glad that she was slowly leaving that experience behind her although she realized that a scar would remain.

----Only a woman would understand that, Marie Dieudonnée.

----Yes, you're absolutely right.

Marie-Ange brought Marie Dieudonnée to the cathedral of Sainte Marie Madeleine, the Penitent. She told her that she had often prayed to Mary Magdalene because she herself had been a penitent.

----You couldn't have. You're too good. You're a woman of God.

----I wasn't always. I sinned in my youth.

----And you became Abbess of Fontevraud?

----Yes, because God in His mercy chose me, a sinner. He often does that. We are the plums that He picks through the grace of the Holy Ghost. We have gone through the sun drying process and have come out wrinkled but whole and sweet. Through His grace, all is possible to God.

----Then, I will not be rejected.

----Of course not. You are a plum that is ripening.

----Yes, but I hope I will not rot before it's time to be plucked by the Lord.

----Stop thinking in the negative, Marie Dieudonnée. God is ever positive in His mercy and love.

----Thank you for your revelation and especially for your kind words. I needed soothing. You see, my mother died when I was young and I had to take care of my brothers. One was older than me and the other younger. Our father was a good man but he had to earn a living, and he worked hard. He also lived away from our home because he chose not to raise any concerns about impropriety what with our aunt raising us and living there. I loved her, but she wasn't my real mother. I could not confide to her some of my more delicate cares and concerns. I prayed a lot to Mother Mary, our Lord's Mother, and asked her to watch over me and my brothers. Especially over me since I had no mother. My brothers had a father, a man to talk with and listen to their cares and little problems. I had no one. I'm very close to my brother, Cajetan, and even my other brother, Abélard François, but they're not women. Do you understand?

----Perfectly well.

----A woman needs another woman to really and truly understand her, don't you think?

----Yes, certainly.

----Then, thank you for being that woman in my life.

----I'm like the Archangel Gabriel. I was sent by God to you, my dear and sweet friend.

----Perhaps Gabriel was a woman and not a man-angel. After all, he was sent as a messenger to announce the forthcoming pregnancy of the young Virgin Mary. He's, no, she's the one who carried Mary's *fiat* to the Father. Only a woman would know about those things. I mean virgin birth, pregnancy, birth of the Child and even the betrothal and marriage to a man who doesn't quite understand what is happening. Mary did, and so did Gabrielle. I'm calling her the feminine version of the name.

----You're so funny, Marie-Ange. You make me laugh.

----But it's true.

----I know.

Marie-Ange told her companion that she knew about the Benedictine abbey in Vézelay, and that it had been founded on land that used to be a Roman villa. It was looted early on and then burnt to the ground. But in the ninth century it was refounded and became an affiliate of the Benedictine Order of Cluny. And, as you may know, Vézelay stands at the beginning of the four major routes through France for pilgrims going to Santiago de Compostela in Galicia, said she. The site where they found the relics of Saint James, the Apostle.

----I know about that. It's very important as a pilgrimage site.

----Have you been there yet?

----No, unfortunately, I haven't. I'd love to someday.

----We could go but right now we don't have time. You have to be at Fontevraud by the next two weeks. And, I have to return to my northern France area. I have more "calling" work to do, if you know what I mean.

----I certainly do.

----Do you like doing that kind of work?

----Any work in the vineyard of the Lord is fulfilling and good for the soul. Yes, I like it.

----You're a good woman, Marie-Ange. Or, should I say, Mère Abbesse Marie-Ange.

----I am no longer an Abbess. I suppose you could call me Abbesse Émérite. *Passée.*

----You will always be *présente* for me.

There was one more stop before approaching Fontevraud that Marie-Ange wanted to show Marie Dieudonnée. It was Autun and its cathedral. The cathedral of Saint Lazarus.

----I want to show you a particular tympanum. It's special in its sculpture.

----Why is it special? What does it have that other tympanums don't have?

----A signature.

----A signature?

----Yes, a famous signature. The name of the Master Sculptor. As a matter of fact, the entire program of sculptures is by him. Come and see.

The two women walked over to the tympanum of the western portal, and Marie-Ange showed her companion the huge sculpture of the Last Judgment with Christ in Majesty, and his opened hands stretched out in mercy and in justice.

----But look here, read the inscription in the middle, right below the feet of Christ.

----*Gislebertus hoc fecit.* Gislebertus made this. Who is Gislebertus?

----He's the Master Sculptor. He put his name right on the tympanum of the main portal, right in front of the cathedral. I call that prominence. Other sculptors had signed their names before him but did not place it in such prominence. Gislebertus will be famous for that, wait and see.

----He certainly caught the horror of the monster devils clawing at people and hauling them away.

----That's part of the accepted way of portraying the Last Judgment with the struggle between the angel and the devil, salvation and damnation.

----It makes me shiver.

----As much as I like this tympanum, I prefer the sculpture of Eve on the lintel of the north doorway. Let's go there.

They went to the north portal to see what Marie-Ange was talking about.

----Actually there are two lintels, the one with Eve and the other block with Adam. The one I like is the sculpture of Eve with its true sense of sensuality, that of the virgin flesh. Look at her breast as round as the apple she's holding, so sensuous and so real. Nothing like we've seen so far. She is the mother of all creation, our earthly mother who fell from grace through temptation of the devilish serpent. It was through pride. Pride of being like God Himself in knowledge and wisdom. Now, look at Adam, he's stretching out his hand to take the apple from Eve. He's tempted by the woman created out his rib. Flesh of his flesh and bone of his bones. Ever since, poor Eve has been branded the evil temptress of poor weak man. As far as I'm concerned, he was weak and soft to temptation when it came to Eve's offering. Of course, that portrayal of Eve as the temptress with the apple eaten from the forbidden tree of knowledge, is just that an image from Genesis. It's to concretize the personalities and actions of the fall of the first created human beings. One made from the dust of the ground and the other from the rib of the created one. Genesis says fruit and not apple, you see. But, sculptors have adopted that image from the Church, and it became part of the total image of the cathedral as the Bible in stone. And, it works, works for ordinary people who do not read the Bible and do not understand words and ideas not concretized.

----I know that I don't understand everything in the Bible. I hear it from the priests at church when they are teaching us about the Bible but if it were not for the sculptures, I would not know too much about Adam and Eve, Abraham, Isaac, the flight from Egypt, Jonas in the whale, Noah and the ark and so many things in the Bible. That's besides the gospels of Christ and his parables. I still don't understand about all of the parables in the New Testament.

----Don't worry, you're not the only one. Even cloistered men and women don't understand everything about the parables. But, you'll learn once you're in the cloister. It takes a lifetime to learn everything in the Holy Book, and there are those who spend their entire life learning and sometimes teaching, and they still don't know everything. The Bible is a rich overflowing text like a fountain that has not given all of its waters yet. I'm still learning. I will never stop learning.

----Even at your age?

----Yes, even at my age.

----Does the pope know everything? The bishops and archbishops?

----Not even the cardinals. No, no human being knows everything about everything, including the Bible. That's why the Holy Ghost has to inspire us to learn.

Both Marie-Ange and Marie Dieudonnée left Autun filled with the awe of learning. Especially Marie Dieudonnée who was now fired up with the burning hunger of learning. She no longer felt spoiled and rejected but replenished. She had a future ahead of her, the bright future of the challenge of learning and of the giving of oneself to others. She was going to be part of an entire community of women who lived life to its fullest in the gospel way.

10

FONTEVRAUD L'ABBAYE

Fontevraud Abbey cast a very imposing impression on Marie Dieudonnée's mind as she approached the site from afar. It was as if her entire dream of belonging had come true. Here was the cloister that would offer her the comfort and assurance of being secure as a woman. Not that she had not experienced that security beforehand, but this was big, encompassing and fulfilling. She felt herself, woman that she was, heart, soul and flesh. She was herself now that she approached the entry to her maturing life physically, spiritually and within her psyche. She felt whole and wondrous. Why would she feel that way, she pondered. The answer came to her in the form of a prayer, "Be it done to me according to your word." Mary's words. Holy Mary Mother of God. Then, in the silence of her heart, Marie Dieudonnée began to sing, "My soul magnifies the Lord, and my spirit rejoices in God my Savior, for he has looked with favor on the lowliness of his servant." And she kept repeating, "I am blessed! I am blessed! Surely, I am blessed!"

Marie-Ange kept looking at her companion, and she could not help but seeing the bright look of sunlight in Marie Dieudonnée's eyes. She was coming home as was Marie-Ange. When the two companions reached the Abbey's huge oaken door that opened onto the cloister, before pulling on the long cord to ring the bell, Marie-Ange told Marie Dieudonnée that there were two cloisters, one for women, the nuns, and one for men, the monks.

The porter came to open the door and asked who was seeking asylum or care for the body. "We are here for the care of the soul," said Marie-Ange. The porter recognized her immediately as she spoke and bade her to enter with her companion.

----Welcome home, Mother, we've been expecting you.

----I'm delighted to be here once more. This is my companion, fruit of my calling, Marie Dieudonnée.

----Please feel welcomed, and may the Lord and his Blessed Mother Mary welcome you and make you feel at home. You are indeed blessed to be in the company of Mère Marie-Ange. She's a privileged person, a holy presence for all times.

----Stop exalting me, Brother Cajetan, I am not a saint nor a holy person. I'm a plain, ordinary individual who is on a pilgrimage, the pilgrimage of life and salvation.

----Aren't we all, Mother, aren't we all?

As they entered the Abbey and started to go down the many long polished hallways, Marie Dieudonnée whispered to her friend, "Another Cajetan." "Yes," said Marie-Ange, "another Cajetan and another reason to feel right at home." The porter led them to a small room, bare except for a statue of Mary on a pedestal and a crucifix on one wall. The room was very clean.

----I will leave you here, Mère, for you know the way to the nuns' cloister. I don't need to guide you. Mère Eulalie du Bon Secours is expecting you, I'm sure.

Marie-Ange told Marie Dieudonnée that Mère Eulalie du Bon Secours was the present Abbess. She had been her assistant for several years until Marie-Ange retired and became exclaustrated by obedience to the will of both the Abbot and the Abbess of Fontevraud. Hers was a very particular case that few people understood the reason behind it. Marie-Ange knew it, and did not feel she had to tell anyone, especially those not connected with Fontevraud.

The two women entered a large parlor with chairs and small tables scattered here and there, although there was no disorder in the room. Both of them sat down while waiting for whoever would come to greet them. Marie Dieudonnée had no idea who it would be, perhaps the Abbess. But, it was not the Abbess. It was Mère Françoise de Picardie, a very close friend of Marie-Ange. The latter introduced her to her companion, and rushed to tell her of the recent pilgrimage the two of them had undertaken, and how successful it was. Marie Dieudonnée was very pleased and relieved that Marie-Ange had not mentioned the unfortunate incident in Sens with that ruffian, the man who had tried to rape her. A twinge of horror marked her face slightly while a cold shiver went up her spine. She recovered quickly.

----Anything wrong, Marie Dieudonnée?

----No, Mère. I'm a bit tired from the walking and the dust of he road has dried my throat somewhat.

----Blessed Lord, here I am chattering away and I forgot my manners as one who receives. It's part of the hospitality of our founder, Saint Benedict. His rule is the same in every monastery and every cloister, receive guests as one who receives the Lord himself.

----Yes, said Marie-Ange, that's our golden rule. Would you have the kindness to offer Marie Dieudonnée some fresh water, and I could drink some myself.

The old nun got up, went through the doorway and into the hallway. One could barely hear her footsteps so in cadence with the rule of silence and modesty as prescribed by the code of proper behavior for a nun and a monk. Everything in moderation, everything in its proper place, everything done in the whispers of silence and everything kept absolutely clean. Above all, everything done for the greater glory of God.

Mère Françoise de Picardie came back carrying a pitcher of water and two cups, one for Marie Dieudonnée and one for Marie-Ange. None for her since it was not an appropriate time for her to enjoy refreshment, she said. Marie Dieudonnée knew that everything in a monastery was prescribed either by the rule, the code of conduct or by conscience. She would have to remember that and learn to adhere to all monastic prescriptions now that she was about ready to enter the cloister. She did not have a hard time with that nor did she feel she had to reject all previous ways of doing things. It would be definitely a transition. A transition that would allow her to be molded silently and carefully into a woman in consecrated life. There would be certainly some small hitches along the way, and perhaps some big ones too, but she was a survivor and a fighter of sorts, and she would manage as she always did. Don't go against the grain of things, but go with it and flow, she used to tell herself all the time. Well, she would not go against the grain and she would definitely flow with the tide of things, no matter what. She was a woman of strong will and strong determination but also a woman of tolerance and adaptability. Above all, she was a woman of strong spiritual insights and convictions. The spiritual part, she had; the religious part, she would learn. She would muster all the courage needed to persevere in this new life and free herself from all constraints be they the small caprices of daily life or the unfortunate reversals that come up now and then.

After having met Mère Françoise de Picardie, Marie-Ange brought Marie Dieudonnée to see the Abbess, Mère Eulalie du Bon Secours. She had been Abbess for eighteen years. She had succeeded Marie -Ange. Marie-Ange knew her well and they were on friendly terms. Although the rule forbade what was called *amitié particulière*, special friendship, the two nuns enjoyed a relationship that was friendly, reserved and not too close so as to be called *particulière*. Mère Eulalie du Bon Secours welcomed both woman and kissed Marie-Ange on both cheeks as a testimony of her spiritual love for a sister in Christ. She also welcomed warmly Marie Dieudonnée and told her that she had a lovely and precious name.

----Dieudonnée means not only God-given but loved by God, said the Abbess. Furthermore, you hold the name of Marie, the Mother of our Lord and our Order is dedicated to the Virgin Mary. Your name is very à propos, you see.

----Thank you, Mother, replied Marie Dieudonnée. My mother gave me that name after she was not able to give it to my older brother. He carries the name of my grandfather, the Stargazer.

----That's an interesting name, Stargazer.

----Yes, they call him Cajetan Stargazer. He's now a Master Architect and his dream is to build a cathedral.

----That's quite a dream. I trust he will be able to fulfill his dream. Where is he now?

----In Flanders working on an abbey.

----That must be the Abbey of Kluizen. You see, we in the monasteries know about most abbeys, existing as well as those being constructed. Especially if it's a Benedictine Abbey like the one in Kluizen.

----Cajetan is an intelligent and wise person with a lot of experience. I'm sure he will find his cathedral project some day.

----Well, now Marie Dieudonnée, you must rest for a while and then I will talk to you about your calling and our monastery. We will give you a cell for the night where you can gather yourself to pray and then sleep. You will not have to participate in the liturgy of the hours for now. That, you will learn.

Marie-Ange told Marie Dieudonnée that she would not be there in the morning since she had to leave very early to be on the road once more. She then told her companion of the road to take care of herself for she had a lot to learn and much to accomplish before becoming a cloistered nun.

----But, do not worry. Everything will come in steps and the Blessed Virgin Mary will guide your every step of the way. She's our official protectoress.

----I'm going to miss you, Marie-Ange, missionary of the "calling." You inspired me, you helped and you provided for me. Most of all, you helped me in my torment of the bad moment, the sinful moment in my life.

----Remember, Marie Dieudonnée, I'm the broken vase; you're only the scratched one.

Marie Dieudonnée smiled. They parted company and Marie-Ange told her as she was going through the door that would separate them for a long time, "Remember, do not break, bend only. You have the strength to do so and the gift of healing."

Marie Dieudonnée remembered how both women had talked for quite some time about healing, and Marie Dieudonnée's long experience with the healing process. She had told her about Geneviève la Guérisseuse and what her mother had learned from this well-known healer. How she herself became her disciple in healing, and how much she had learned from her, although some people mistrusted Geneviève and called her, at times, a sorceress. Marie-Ange had told her then not to take that bad-mouthing too seriously for people mistrust what they do not know, and refrain from knowing what they should know. "Ignorance, my dear, is the mother of prejudice," she had told Marie Dieudonnée.

The following morning, Marie Dieudonnée was woken by the deep silence that wafted through the cloister and seemed to impregnate the entire monastery. It was not the sound of footsteps nor the sound of bells, not even the sound of voices, but silence, monastic silence that woke her up. It was as if the earth stood still, and everything in it obeyed at the beck and call of the grand silence. Marie Dieudonnée washed her hands and her face then got dressed and waited for someone to come and get her. In the meantime, she said her morning prayers silently in a heart full of joy and contentment for having found her niche in life. She also thought of Cajetan and his family wondering if he was still in Flanders, and what would be his next step in architecture. She remembered that Marie-Ange had promised her to get in touch with Cajetan, and tell him where his sister was. However, she was going to tell him that he could not visit her until such time she was a professed nun with perpetual vows. Marie Dieudonnée then thought of Abélard François when he was part of the Carmelite Cloister, and how would Cajetan accept the fact that she was now part of an Order of cloistered nuns without the privilege of visiting her, not before several years. Her mind wandered and she began to ask herself if Abélard François was happy and where could he possibly be by now. All she knew was that he had told her that he was headed for England with a troupe of performers and musicians. She was hoping that her brother would finally reach his own goal of no longer being an "à part." Everyone must belong to someone or something, she thought to herself. And, she thought of Cambrai, her home for many years. But, that was over with. She would henceforth belong to Fontevraud.

Someone did come to get her and brought her to the chapel for morning mass. She relished that liturgy for she had been craving for the Eucharist one more time. To her, the Eucharist was part of the healing she needed. After mass, all members went to breakfast in the refectory. It was a very simple large room, bare in furniture and decorations, but sufficient for the needs of the nuns who ate their meal in silence. Marie Dieudonnée ate what was given to her. Everyone ate the same thing, dark, heavy bread, a small bowl of gruel and something hot to drink. She would have liked more bread, but she refrained from asking for some. A nun who was sitting next to her reached for the bread basket and offered Marie Dieudonnée some more bread. Marie Dieudonnée resisted the urge to take some but the nun insisted she eat some more bread by nudging her. For she knew that strangers to the monastery are often hungry after a monastic meal. After breakfast, someone came to get Marie Dieudonnée and brought her to the Sub-Prioress. She introduced herself and said that she was Mère Solange des Saintes Plaies.

----I am the Prioress's assistant. You are now a postulant and we are having this conversation because you are postulating your candidacy or demanding to be one of us. This is your first step. Then, after six months of probation, you will be accepted as a novice and take the habit of a novice with the white veil. After a full year as a novice, if you persevere, you will become a scholastic, that is, a dedicated member of our community with the vows of poverty, chastity, obedience and stability. Stability means staying in one monastery, and not moving around. After four years of temporary vows, you will pronounce your perpetual vows, and that means you will become a full member for life of our community. Afterwards, you will enjoy whatever the Abbess deigns to give you as an appointment. But, remember, first and foremost, you are a cloistered nun and your life will be centered on prayer and sacrifice. Mortification, fasting and self-denial will be the staples of your daily life. You are here for the salvation of your soul, and that's what we intend to do with you and for you. We, your sisters in Christ, want what is spiritually beneficial to you. Do you understand that?

----That's why I am here, Mère. I came here to respond to my calling as a woman dedicated to the service of God and to others in need.

----I'm glad you understand your path in this monastery. Besides being a cloister, the Order of Fontevraud was founded in 1099 and consists of a group of monasteries: the main Grand-Moutier cloister, Sainte Marie, houses the nuns, the virgin women. That's where we are right now. La Madeleine, for married or other non-virgin nuns, those considered to be social outcasts, *les femmes déchues*. There's also a hospice for the sick, Saint-Benoit, and a house for lepers and other afflicted persons, Saint-Lazare. Then Saint-Jean-de-L'Habit, outside the Abbey walls, for the monks. The monks are responsible for conducting the sacraments for the entire community. So you can see that the Order's ministry is quite varied and broad. Our founder declared that the leader of the Order should always be a woman, and appointed Petronille de Chemillé as first Abbess. You will learn more about our history during your novitiate.

----I'm very interested in the healing parts, especially Saint Lazare and Saint Benoit. I did not know that you had lepers here.

----Lepers are not a healing part, for as you know, there is no healing for them. They are condemned by their disease.

----But, they're human beings, and I would like to work with some of them, if that's possible. I've done some healing before.

----They're untouchables, my sister.

----I know that's what they are called, but even Christ touched them.

----We'll see later on. I see that you are *une guérisseuse*. That's interesting but of no use here. Now, you must proceed to vest yourself with the initial habit of the postulant.

Marie Dieudonnée found Mère Solange des Saintes Plaies intelligent and knowledgeable but a bit stilted in her approach to healing and compassion for the sick. She was one that she would not try to imitate, she told herself.

After six months at Fontevraud, Marie Dieudonnée was admitted to the novitiate. First, she was vested with the undyed woolen garment of the bride of Christ and given her while veil. They had shorn her hair and gotten rid of all her personal belongings which was not much. It was considered detachment, and Marie Dieudonnée accepted that. Besides, Marie Dieudonnée was never one to be attached to things. She was attached to family and now she belonged to a new family, a much larger one.

After the ceremony, Marie Dieudonnée was told that since she already had a sound Christian and monastic name, one that combined the virtues of dedication to God and the Virgin Mary, she would keep the name. It would be Soeur Marie Dieudonnée. The designation of Mère would come later after the profession of the perpetual vows. She then met the Mistress of novices. Her name was Mère Marie de la Visitation and she was an older nun with a twitch in her face that made her wince now and then when she was nervous or under the weather. She seemed nice enough but Marie Dieudonnée thought that this nun was too inquisitive and too personal in her questioning. That type of questioning was fine for younger women and especially for girls sent to the monastery by their parents to protect them from the vagaries of the outside world, but not for a mature woman like Marie Dieudonnée who had experienced life in the world out there, and knew the many ways of encountering the challenges of living outside the monastery walls.

One day, Mère Marie de la Visitation asked Marie Dieudonnée to meet with her privately. She wondered why the Mistress of novices wanted to see her alone. Probably for spiritual counseling, she thought. As soon as Marie Dieudonnée arrived in the room where the Mistress of novices was, she realized that the session was going to be one of inquiry. She felt it in her bones. Mère Marie de la Visitation was seated in a large stuffed chair with polished wooden arms in front of a table with some documents opened before her. She did not make Marie Dieudonnée sit down. The novice remained standing facing her inquisitor, so she thought.

----Soeur Marie Dieudonnée it has come to our attention that you may not be a virgin, and so you do not belong here at Sainte Marie.

----But I am a virgin. What makes you say that I'm not?

----That is not of your affairs.

----But it is my affairs. It's about me.

----Don't be impudent, Soeur.

----I'm not impudent, Mère, I simply want to know where you got that information.

----It's from a reliable source, and I have to investigate your condition as a non-virgin, if that is the case.

----But I swear that I am a virgin. Assuredly, it was not Mère Marie-Ange who told you that.

----Leave her out of this.

----But who?

----It does not matter who. What matters is whether you are a virgin or not.

----I am a virgin and I swear it by Our Holy Mother, the Virgin of Virgins.

----Do not swear with the name of Blessed Mary the Mother of God. Do not use her name in vain.

----But, I'm not using her name in vain. I'm using it to support my claim as a virgin.

Then swallowing her pride and pushing back her fears of intimidation and regret as well as intimations of remorse, she said to the nun:

----I have to admit that I have been defiled but not raped. I did not lose my virginity. I swear.

----Well, we shall see. We will pass an examination on you to verify if what you say is true or not. I am sending you to the infirmary so that the *infirmière* there can examine you and tell me if you are still a virgin. We, the virgin nuns at Sainte-Marie, cannot tolerate such a deviance from our rule. *La pureté, la sainte pureté, chère soeur dans le Christ*.

Of course, Marie Dieudonnée consented. What else could she do? Besides, she knew deep down that she was a virgin unpenetrated by the lustful desires and thrust of a man. If they wanted proof, then let them get it, she told herself. She was told by the Mistress of novices that if they found that she was not a virgin, she would immediately be sent to La Madeleine where she belonged. "We do not want to soil our dear virgin monastery," Mère Marie de la Visitation told her. After an hour or so, Marie Dieudonnée was sent back to the novitiate of Saint-Marie and back to the Mistress of novices. The latter looked a bit disgruntled but her haughtiness of superiority had not vanished from her face. Her facial expression was cold, distant and hard, her way of masking any disappointment or deceptions she might have had. Marie Dieudonnée could not help herself from smiling and feeling well justified. Marie Dieudonnée never reveled in any victory over another but she enjoyed the afterglow of having surpassed her own fears and the insecure fears of the other.

The nuns at Sainte-Marie discovered that they had a jewel of a woman in Marie Dieudonnée. Her face glowed with spiritual satisfaction and it showed. She was at peace with herself and with others living with her. But most of all, she was at peace with her God who had called her to Himself in the cloister. That spiritual fulfillment was joy to her soul. A joy sought by so many nuns and monks for months, and even for years. It did not come easy and had to be purchased with sacrifices and a multitude of prayers and long meditations in front of the Holy Eucharist. They also said of Marie Dieudonnée that she was a good nun, a nun of devotion to her God and to others in need. Of course, she had not yet had the chance to prove herself in the service of others since she was just now finishing her novitiate after a full year of prayers, spiritual readings, and the study of *la sainte règle,*the Benedictine rule, so that, she was told, if the rule ever was lost, all one had to do was to follow and imitate an old nun who had internalized the rule. So, the leaders of the monastery reported to the Abbess that Marie Dieudonée showed great promise, and that she would, one day, become one of their best in both the monastic and service facets of the cloister.

The morning Marie Dieudonnée took her vows in front of the Abbess was a most memorable one. The Abbess had on a black habit with scapular down to her feet, a long rosary hung down her waist and she wore a cross on her breast, the cross of the Abbess to denote her authority and the dignity of the office she served and represented. Marie Dieudonnée smiled at the Abbess dressed in her formal habit with long cape. She went up in front of the altar where Mère Eulalie du Bon Secours, the Abbess, was seated. The Abbess smiled back. It was a warm smile. Kneeling on a large pillow and with a lighted tall taper in her right hand, Marie Dieudonnée recited the formula for vows, pledging fervent allegiance to God and the Order and pronouncing vows of poverty, chastity, obedience and stability for one year. She then rose and went to sign the register of profession. She was now officially a professed member of the community of Benedictine nuns in the Abbey of Fontevraud. As she knelt down on the polished wooden floor, she silently prayed and held both Cajetan and Abélard François in her heart for they were still her family and she did not want ever to forget them. She prayed that they would both find happiness in what they endeavored and peace in their own hearts. Head held high and hands hidden in the sleeves of her habit, Marie Dieudonnée processed back to the refectory where a special meal was being served in honor of the day of profession. That morning, she ate two pieces of barley bread and a large portion of thick porridge, some cheese with fruit from the Order's own garden.

As a scholastic, Soeur Marie Dieudonnée progressed well in her studies assigned to her. She read every day, books on the lives of saints, books on the history of the Church, books on Saint Benedict and his rule, did some spiritual exercises, she read parts of the Bible in groups, wrote in her spiritual diary and recited the Divine Office as prescribed by the rule. All of the members of the Order did it religiously: Matins and Lauds, before sunrise; Prime, Tierce, Sext and None; Vespers at dusk followed by Compline to end the day. She went to bed early and got up very early to recite Matins followed by Lauds as all the nuns did. The Divine Office gave each one of them a rhythm, a flow of time that regulated the cadence of the day. Time by hours and minutes was not kept, rather the hours of the Divine Office substituted for the telling of time each day. The nobility, the clergy, the craftsmen and even the peasants regulated their lives by the hours of the Divine Office. *Le pas sacré des heures bat son plein et le peuple de Dieu s'incline à sa cadence*, said the Abbess of Fontevraud to her flock. Yes, the sacred pace of the Holy Hours leads everyone according to its cadence.

The pace of life for Marie Dieudonnée never seemed to change, for every day was like the previous one, the waking, the prayers, the meditations, the chores and the sparse meals. Except when an incident like the one that happened the second day of the third month after her profession that came to interrupt her day. Such was the incident of the unexpected illness of the Abbess. Mère Eulalie du Bon Secours woke up one morning in a cold sweat trembling and disoriented. She was transported to the infirmary. After two days with no change in the Abbess's condition, the Sub-Prioress, the Mistress of scholastics, the Mistress of novices as well as the nuns of the Abbess's council, became distressed at the news that their leader was losing ground, and her condition, grave. She seemed to be in some kind of a coma, unresponsive and cold at the touch. They sent for the Prior of the Saint-Jean-L'Habit monastery so that the Abbess might receive the last rites. He came, blessed her, applied the holy oils on her five senses as well as her feet that had followed in the footsteps of the Lord, and gave her conditional absolution. Someone mentioned Marie Dieudonnée's name, for somehow it had gotten around that she had healing capabilities. After all, she had healed her brother from a mysterious illness and helped to heal the many injured pilgrims of the collapsed cathedral. It must have been when she was asked to reveal part of her life and service to others after the *culpa* this confessional exercise. Somehow the benefices of her healing had circulated like a rumor that no one could stop. All of her community seemed to be aware of Marie Dieudonnée's gift of healing, but had, so far, never asked her to use it.

It was Mère Solange des Cinq Plaies who had recommended the healing powers of Marie Dieudonnée. Even though the Sub-Prioress had told Marie Dieudonnée that her healing was of no consequence at Fontevraud Abbey, she now recognized the possibility of a healing through the capable hands of an experienced healer. Something had to be done for the Abbess, no matter if it pained the Sub-Prioress to admit that she was wrong. She never admitted to that. It was not part of her psychological makeup. Marie Dieudonnée came to the infirmary and looked at the Abbess lying on a bed covered only with a thin white sheet. They had not removed her habit nor her veil. Marie Dieudonnée asked that the habit of the Abbess as well as her veil be taken off. They all looked at her hesitatingly but did what she reverently requested. She then examined the Abbess, ashen, hardly breathing, cold to the touch with the white of her eyes turning yellowish.

Marie Dieudonnée took her leather pouch that she had always carried with her but was taken away by the Sub-Prioress and now returned to her. She opened it and found some herbs, unguents and other healing medicines. She asked for some hot water and a small basin. She then took some of the herbs and put them in the water and then asked that the mixture be held over a flame until the brew was complete. All those in attendance watched Marie Dieudonnée with awe and incredulity. While the mixture was brewing, Marie Dieudonnée intoned, in a very low voice, some incantations. The others were wondering if this was part pagan part Christian. Was Marie Dieudonnée's healing part of witchcraft or not? Then, the healer started to recite intercessory prayers for the sick and dying. The nuns all looked up and joined Marie Dieudonnée in prayer.

Marie Dieudonnée repeated her healing ritual for three days and nights constantly keeping vigil with the sick Abbess. The other nuns were impressed with the dedication, seriousness and spiritual depth with which Marie Dieudonnée brought to her healing. On the fourth day, the Abbess opened her eyes and asked for something to drink. All were overjoyed at the sign of life displayed by the Abbess. Marie Dieudonnée was greatly relieved, not only at the recovery but at her own power of healing. She knew that she was capable of it but always had some doubt deep inside her as to whether her knowledge and strength would come to bear. For her, healing was a mysterious ritual and happening. It was empowered by faith in God, faith in oneself to heal and faith in the powers of nature in providing the necessary herbs and substances. Marie Dieudonnée had, once more, held that power in her hands, and was able to deliver it to the one in need. She had done it before with Cajetan, Abélard François and now Mère Eulalie du Bon Secours. Of course, she had done healing rituals before that too, but these three were difficult cases, and she had triumphed. Marie Dieudonnée recognized fully how she was empowered by God to heal people, and she wanted, more so now, to be in the service of the sick and the dying. The present healing would convince her community that she was able to do it and would provide an immeasurable service to the Order by so doing. The Lord had answered her prayers for he too was, first and foremost, a healer.

Marie Dieudonnée was appointed temporarily to the Saint-Lazare infirmary by the Abbess who recognized, with gratitude, her gift of healing. The Abbess told her that she would not be able to take care of the lepers because that was too dangerous, and that she was not prepared yet, if ever, to handle such cases. However, when she did take her perpetual vows, the matter would be reconsidered, the Abbess told her.

After the required four years of temporary vows, Marie was accepted as a professed nun, and was ready to take her perpetual vows. The date had been set for the second Sunday in August. The year was 1282 and she had been away from Cambrai for six years. She had not seen either brother. She missed them and so wanted to see them again. However, she knew that it would be almost impossible for her to contact them, and she would not attempt to do so. It was part of her total commitment and dedication to her vows and the rule of her Order.

The day came for her final profession of vows and Marie Dieudonnée was prepared for it. She had spent twenty-one days in closed retreat redoubling her efforts to pray, meditate, fast, and deepen her spiritual life. She was ready. The day was bright and filled with the newness of things. New day, new beginnings, new life. Marie Dieudonnée joined the other nuns who were to pronounce their perpetual vows also, and they were processed into the chapel where the Abbess was waiting for them. As she was walking down the aisle, Marie Dieudonnée caught sight of Marie-Ange sitting on one of the chairs. Sitting next to her were Cajetan and Abélard François. Marie Dieudonnée was so struck with surprise and delight that she felt weak at the knees with a sensation of losing her full consciousness, but she recovered quickly and gave a big smile at all three of them.

The profession of final vows was a solemn moment for Marie Dieudonnée and the other professed nuns. It was solemn, soul-refreshing and at the same time heartwarming for them. They now belonged in perpetuity to the Order. It was indeed a great feeling to belong to a community of dedicated and consecrated lives. Perpetual vows sealed the prefigurative years given to the exercise of the sacred rule. Now, the rule was theirs and they would spend the rest of their lives living it day after day until they died.

After the profession of vows, Marie Dieudonnée went to the refectory where she was able to meet her two brothers and Marie-Ange. Her friend told her that the Order, rather, the Abbess herself, had dispensed them from the rule, and was allowing them to eat with her and spend some time with their sister. *Deo gratias!* shouted Marie Dieudonnée after she apologized for the loudness of her gratitude to God. She did not want to show her affection openly, so she greeted them with the warm kiss of religious greeting, kissing on both cheeks. Cajetan took a hold of her and hugged her for a long time. Abélard François did the same. Marie Dieudonnée who was usually given to the spontaneity of affection looked somewhat embarrassed.

----Don't be embarrassed, Marie Dieudonnée, said Marie-Ange, it's family.

----I don't know what to say right now, replied Marie Dieudonnée, I'm totally struck by your presence here to a point that I do not know what to say or do.

Cajetan looked at her lovingly and told her the reason both he and Abélard François were there.

----We're here because Marie-Ange, or should I say Mère Marie-Ange, invited us. She knew that you were taking your final vows and she told us that she would like us to accompany her to Fontevraud for the profession. How she found both of us is still a mystery to me.

----I found you first because I knew you were still at the Abbey of Kluizen. As for Abélard François, I saw a large poster of the troupe he was playing with and it said "Grand Théâtre de Valenciennes---mardi soir---le 2 septembre", so I rushed to go see the troupe and met Abélard François there. That was last year in the fall. It took me all this time to organize our trip here to Fontevraud. And, here we are.

Marie Dieudonnée had so many questions swimming in her head that she did not know which one to ask of either brother.

----Tell me, Cajetan how is Wandal and how are the children?

----They're all fine. Wandal sends you her love. She often thinks of you and your pilgrimage in life, as you call it. Grisoulda is now ten years old. Melodia is eight and loves music that one. Philippon is six and a half. And we have a new one, Emmanuel who was born Christmas day three years ago.

----Your family is really growing, Cajetan.

----Yes, and that's what I've always wanted, a family.

----How about you, Abélard François?

----Well, I'm not married. Not yet, anyway. I'm too busy traveling and performing.

----Where have you been with your troupe?

----It's not my troupe. It belongs to Master Fulgence and Master Athanasius. The first one comes from Paris and the second one from London. They have formed a troupe of various players from France and England. We are now adding people from Flanders and Germany. It's really a varied troupe of players. I so enjoy meeting performers from different areas.

----My, you're really not *un à part* any longer, said Marie Dieudonnée.

----And you, Marie-Ange, what have you been doing? On the road?

----Yes, that's my calling, as you know. I have six new postulants waiting to enter Fontevraud. I'm slowing down because last year I had twelve. I'm getting old, Marie Dieudonnée.

----You'll never be too old to be with people and convince them of their own calling. Have you been reading romances, Marie-Ange?

----No. I'm too busy preparing my own pilgrimage to the Holy City, the New Jerusalem with the Lord. One has to prepare one's death. I'm not afraid of it. I'm just not quite ready. How does one get ready for the greatest transition in human life? That's the way I see it, Marie Dieudonnée. It's not an ending but a new beginning. However, I know very well that the Lord can come like a thief in the night, suddenly, surreptitiously and without warning. We have to be ready.

----Well, I'm sure that you've been ready right along. You are bringing with you baskets and baskets full of good works. And, I may add, love. You have the capacity and the outpouring of love as I have never known anyone to have.

----There are others who have much more than I have. Besides, I am a sinner. The Lord knows it, and I'm waiting to expiate them here on earth while I still have time.

----But remember, Marie-Ange, love covers a multitude of sins, as the disciple says.

Cajetan cut in the conversation saying,

----Stop it you two. This is not a theological encounter, I hope.

They all laughed.

----When are you going to start building your cathedral, Cajetan? asked Marie Dieudonnée.

----We're finishing the Abbey at Kluizen, and then I want to investigate possibilities either in France or England. Although, I have been asked to assess the possibility of constructing one in Germany next to Bamberg.

----That's where the foliate head is. The one on the console. I've seen it, Cajetan, said Marie-Ange.

----Oh, you have to see the ones in Auxerre, Cajetan, replied Marie Dieudonnée. They're outstanding. Ask Marie- Ange.

----I want to travel and try to see as many of them as possible although they're not essential to my cathedral, but they're part of so many cathedrals. It's an intriguing sculpture this foliate head.

----Do you plan to put some in your cathedral?

----Yes, I do. I'll have to find a sculptor who can and who wants to do it. It's a curious blend of Christian and pagan symbolism this foliate head, I think. I'm fascinated with it.

Abélard François added,

----They have them in England, not only in churches but in pubs and inns. They even have festivals of the Man of Nature. Of course, the clergy is not too happy with this, but they cannot stop people from creating green men and the merriment attached to it.

----I'm not opposed to the foliate head, said Marie Dieudonnée, but I just don't want it to overshadow the meaning of a cathedral. It is, after all, the house of he Lord, and we do not want to paganize it or desacralize it with pagan symbolism and rituals.

----I don't see it that way, said Cajetan. I prefer to see it as the melding together of the sacred from both beliefs, pagan and Christian. We often build cathedrals right on pagan sites no longer in use. Speaking of Auxerre, that cathedral was built on a pagan Roman site.

All four of them continued to talk about various topics until it was time to depart from the Abbey, for Cajetan and Abélard had to return home, while Marie-Ange had work to do with the Abbess. They had talked, laughed and commiserated at will. Marie Dieudonnée thought how Grisoulda, their mother, would have enjoyed this get together. She was such a people person, my mother, she thought. She loved people and especially her family. Too bad she died so young. She would be so very happy that I have made something of my life as well as her two boys. Life is meant to be accomplished in some way, thought Marie Dieudonnée, because a life without the reward of something done and accomplished is a wasted life. Life is meant to be lived and lived in the fullness of human expression. That is, the fullness of the Lord as he accomplished his own human life in the divine mode, thought Marie Dieudonnée. Salvation is accomplished by giving of oneself fully as Christ did, and I mean to do precisely that. There is no other way than *caritas*, the burning flame of love. It may sound like a platitude but it's the very basis of Christ's message of simplicity in his gospels, she mused. He made it very simple. No rules, no complicated ordinances, just love. That's so easy, so easy that people just lose the sense of it. Look at me, mused Marie Dieudonnée, I may be talking gibberish but one thing I know, love is the core of things and people. It may not always be easy to love in a community like ours, so many people, so many characters, so many personalities. I may not like some of them, God, they're so un-likeable at times, but I love the potential love that's in them. What I try to do is wean it out of them. I'm sure that Christ did not like some people he met. That's just being human. But he loved the potential in them, the possibility of love that's in all human beings. Why, he created us that way. We humans just don't get it sometimes. I pray, thought Marie Dieudonnée, that I be given more and more the capacity to love…like Mary, Our Mother, the Mother of God. What a loving capacity she had. The bell rang and Marie Dieudonnée obeyed its call immediately. Her interior conversation was over for now.

As she walked down the long corridor to the chapel, Marie Dieudonnée felt the pangs of departure for she did not know if she would ever get to see them again especially her two brothers. She realized that she had her own family now, her Order, but her brothers remained her family of the heart. Cajetan and Abélard François left the following morning having spent the night at the hospice house of the monks. The Benedictine rule emphasized the importance of giving pilgrims lodging for at least one night. It was the code of hospitality. As for Marie-Ange, she stayed on for three days, said her farewell to Marie Dieudonnée and left. There was a trace of loneliness in Marie Dieudonnée's heart but she told herself that she had to overcome that since it was all part of detachment under the rule. Detachment from things is easy, said Marie Dieudonnée to herself, but detachment from family and close friends is much harder.

As the days went by, the months accumulated and then the years flew by. In was the year 1288 and Marie Dieudonnée had been at Fontevraud twelve years. She had learned a lot about the Abbey and its history, a very rich history indeed. First of all, she learned that the Abbey had been founded in 1100 and became a double monastery with both the monks and the nuns. That was a breakthrough. It all started when Philippa of Toulouse persuaded her husband, William IX, Duke of Aquitaine, to grant Robert Abrissel land on Northern Poitou to establish a religious community. This Robert Abrissel, the wise one as he was known, declared that the leader of the order should always be a woman, and he appointed Petronille Chemillé as the first Abbess. She was succeeded by Matilda of Anjou, the aunt of Henry II of England. She was called "aunt" by Eleanor of Aquitaine, Henry's wife and Queen of England. That was the start of a function that attracted many noble Abbesses over the years.

In the early years of the Abbey, the Angevin monarchy was a great benefactor of the Abbey. Henry II's widow, Eleanor of Aquitaine eventually found solace there towards the end of her life, after her son, Richard Coeur de Lion, died at the age of forty-one. Marie Dieudonnée also learned that Eleanor of Aquitaine was imprisoned for fifteen years by her husband, and she fought him every step of the way. Then she fled England and was involved in many a hassle until she got to a point that she felt tired, enough to withdraw from the world and enter a monastery, Fontevraud, where the cloister benefitted her and her need to find solace in the Lord for her salvation. She was the Eleanor of Aquitaine who favored poets such as, Chrétien de Troyes and the Poitevin troubadour, Cercamon, as well as Bernard de Ventadour, famous for his sensuous lyrics that sang the praises of Eleanor. Eleanor also accompanied her husband King Louis VII on the Second Crusade and dealt with her children who often fought among themselves, and resisted the efforts of her husband, Henry II, whom she considered a tyrant. She exerted a tremendous influence in Poitiers when she lived there with her husband Henry II and favored the construction of its cathedral. Eleanor of Aquitaine was a woman of considerable strength of character and played an important role in the historical development of France and England. Although Marie Dieudonnée admired the courage and determination of Eleanor of Aquitaine, she did not like her complicated life and struggles at court. Nobility, for Marie Dieudonée, was simply a way of life that seemed to trap people into the conspiracy of birth and heirs, not to mention the many wars and battles over the conquest of lands and domains. She was so glad that she had been born an ordinary person, a commoner. She did not want those privileges that mire the conditions of living, and allow for no real freedom to be who you really are. I suppose that Eleanor of Aquitaine was finally at peace with herself and the world when she entered the monastery, mused Marie Dieudonnée. Although it was much later, at the age of eighty, that she took the humble habit and the veil of a nun and thus followed the Benedictine rule. Above all, Eleanor of Aquitaine, at the end of her life, was getting ready to meet her Creator and true Lord. She had abandoned the quest for power and *renommée*. That fame that led to difficulties in marriage, child bearing, territorial struggles and feminine independence. *À la fin, elle est devenue une des brebis du cloître,* she had become one of the flock of simple nuns although her heritage and renown would never be erased. Marie Dieudonnée, now a professed cloistered nun herself, often pondered the history of Fontevraud Abbey and meditated on the ineluctability of God's will in all matters whether it be accepted by human beings of all ranks or stages in life, or not.

When she had time and wanted to meditate on the vanities of life, Marie Dieudonnée would walk through the large rooms where the graves of some of the nobles were. There was, of course, Eleanor of Aquitaine, Henry II and Richard Coeur de Lion, the favorite son of Eleanor, a courageous fighter and hero of the crusade until he was captured and put in prison in Germany, and kept there because his brother John of Lackland did not want to pay his ransom. John wanted to keep him captive so that he could get the crown of England. It was later on that his mother, Eleanor of Aquitaine, was able to make arrangements to pay the ransom for her beloved son, and bring him back home. What turmoil, what treachery, what pain and trouble, thought Marie Dieudonnée. Indeed, the Abbey at Fontevraud has a very rich history, she said to herself, and I'm a small part of it.

One day in June, the Abbess called Marie Dieudonnée to her office. It was a simple office with no fancy furniture or faiences. It had that Benedictine look of austerity and simplicity. She bowed to the Abbess and sat down at the invitation of her leader.

----*Benedicite*, Marie Dieudonnée.

----*Deo gratias,* Reverend Mother Abbess

----I have something to offer you. You may refuse if you feel you cannot accept it.

----What is it, Mother?

----You know that we buried Mother Matilda de Poitou, our Prioress, three weeks ago. Since then, the Sub-Prioress, Mother Solange des Cinq Plaies has been replacing her. I would like you to become the Prioress of Fontevraud.

----Why me, Reverend Mother?

----Because you qualify in great measure. You are a loving person, generous with your time, knowledgeable, and you have integrity that I greatly admire. You are a mature person and get along well with everyone. You are ever alert to the needs of others, and you are a woman of experience. Evermore, you are a healer. Above all, you are humble of heart, and you carry within you our rule which is the touchstone of our monastery. You are everything that I want in a Prioress, Marie Dieudonnée.

----But what about Mother Solange?

----She will remain Sub-Prioress. She may feel a bit humiliated by being passed over but she has to learn the full exigencies of obedience and accept reversals in her life. Besides, she will accept you more as Prioress than anybody else I might choose. She admires you, Marie Dieudonnée.

Marie Dieudonnée was totally stunned by this declaration. She told the Abbess that if it was God's will and the will of the Abbess who represented the Abbey, then she could not refuse the offer which was, of course, in her mind, an obedience. Marie Dieudonnée was to become Prioress of Fontevraud, the function she never thought she would ever get. God operates in mysterious ways, she mused, as the bell for Tierce rang.

11

THE FOLIATE HEAD/LA TÊTE FEUILLUE

Cajetan sat there captivated by what he was staring at. It was the Foliate Head of the Bamberg cathedral. It was part of the console on which sat horseback the Bamberg Rider. Here he was this human head of leaves, right below the horse's right front hoof, eyes peering through acanthus leaves, the eyes of a savage-like being, aloof and mysterious. The Germans called it a *Blatte Maske*. It did look like a mask of leaves hiding a face unknown and daring. Daring to glance at the world with a mysteriousness that intrigued Cajetan. Who was that man behind the mask? asked Cajetan to himself. Was he a man or not? Perhaps a beast of some kind? Was it the sculptor himself? Nobody seemed to know. Nobody seemed to know who the rider was either. A king? A prince? He's wearing a crown. Was he a real nobleman or just a symbol of chivalry?

Cajetan loved the Bamberg foliate head, and kept it in his creative memory to be part of an entire list of foliate head possibilities for his cathedral. Some of his architect friends and sculptors told Cajetan that he was going about it the wrong way. You don't plan and design a cathedral by starting with an ornamental sculpture, they told him. But, the foliate head is not an ornament, he told them, its an active part of the myth of the cathedral. They replied really with consternation by telling him that the construction of a cathedral was not a myth. It's a reality, a concrete reality, they told him.

----I'm not talking about a non-reality. I'm not talking about an untruth. I'm talking about a cultural truth, a myth, said Cajetan.

----A myth is a lie. It does not exist in reality, Cajetan, said Thomas Cranavache, a sculptor friend of his who did not recognize the esthetic nor religious value of the foliate head.

----Yes, it does. The way that people see things and live and breathe and spend their lives dreaming about their future is all part of the phenomenon of what is called myth.

----Now, you're talking like a philosopher, and we do not follow you.

----Follow me or not, the foliate head is a myth in creation itself, and it is linked to our beliefs, in our own selves, in our world, in our possibilities and our achievements as makers and doers. The foliate head is a creative myth. It helps one to link our sacred trust in the Creator and the sacredness of our living breathing environment.

----Now, you're talking nonsense, Cajetan. You mean to tell us that everything is sacred?

----In a way, yes. Everything is interconnected as we are interconnected in our own lives, bodies, souls, minds. We are one even though we are formed with parts.

----You're crazy, Cajetan. You're just plain dumb.

----I may be, but I strongly believe that the foliate head is an example of the creative self in seeing our Christian belief and the sacredness of all living things coming together in a tangible, concrete symbol. I live to be creative. I want it in my cathedral as a testimony of human creativity and of the imagination at work making connections with living and thriving things.

----Watch out for the bishop who will sponsor you and the clergy who will serve in your cathedral. Many are against such symbols, symbols of the devil, they say.

----They can say what they want but I'm going to have my own foliate heads. They mean something to me. They become part of my creative outlet. They will be part of the program of sculptures.

----Leave the sculptures to the sculptors, the masonry to the masons, the carpentry to the carpenters, the roofing to the roofers and the stone cutting to the stone cutters. You gaze much too much at the stars, my friend. You've become star-struck.

They all stood there and laughed and laughed. Cajetan did not refute their statements but he still believed in the creative magic of the imagination to furnish him with new ideas and thoughts about what it means to be human and creative. He believed in myths.

Cajetan left Bamberg thinking about the cathedral he had just visited. He remembered that it was built in stages. The first one dated back to 1012. Then it was partially destroyed by fire in 1081. It was consecrated thirty years later, and received it's present form in the thirteenth century. Not too long ago, thought Cajetan. Master Architect Cajetan noticed that the Bamberg Cathedral was not Gothic but late-Romanesque. However, there are parts of the cathedral that are Gothic. There are really three styles to this cathedral, said Cajetan to himself, first, the Romanesque, second the Gothic and then there's the Transitional. The Transitional is characteristic of the nave. A strange melding of style over the years, thought Cajetan.

When I build my cathedral, it will be totally Gothic. Unless, something or someone changes my mind, but I don't think so, he mused.

From Germany, Cajetan then went on to Flanders to see his family, and draw a list of cathedrals that had worthwhile foliate heads, *les têtes feuillues* as they were known in France and Flanders. He did not only want to view them but try to find what was behind these sculptures. So far, he had not been able to get any important information about their meaning and symbolism. Furthermore, what were they doing in a cathedral? a question asked by many members of the clergy and even laymen who were not only intrigued by foliate heads but also bewildered as to its place in a Christian space of cult and devotion. Cajetan knew that his endeavors into inquiry to satisfy himself about the foliate head would take time, and delay the construction of his cathedral, as he liked to call it. But, he was still young and the wait would put more maturity into his project, he told himself. Time for reflection was never wasted time, he said to many who questioned him about his plans. As he grew older and did not have to worry about his own identity and the safety of his family, he became more and more reflexive and prone to meditating on his spiritual life. He had been struck by his sister's accomplishment in her own spiritual life, and influenced by his mother's too. He did not want to forget his father's spiritual inclinations and his work as a cathedral stone cutter, "For the glory of God the Creator," he would say. Cathedral building was a vocation to both Philippon and Cajetan, a calling from above beyond the stars, although the stars themselves were heavenly inspirators to both of them.

Wandal was safe and secure in her stance as wife, mother and consort to a Master Architect. She had inherited money from her father's estate. He did profitable business as a bourgeois businessman buying and selling woolen goods. Her brothers had gotten the business but she had received money, enough money to live on comfortably. That allowed her husband not to worry about providing for herself and helping out the children when they needed it. Besides, they weren't babies anymore. Cajetan did not want to live on his wife's inheritance but she convinced him that he was not taking advantage of her and her money. She wanted him to become the best Master Architect around, and make a name for himself. That someday the name of Cajetan, the Master Architect and Stargazer would be known throughout the land and possibly throughout the world. Wandal had high dreams for her husband. Wandal decided to stay in Flanders while her husband traveled, for she had an established home there and she did not want to leave it. Wandal had grown a little fat with the years but she still maintained a lovely face and an endearing smile. She was loved by everyone especially her four children, Grisoulda, Philppon, Melodia and Emmanuel. People said of her that she had grown to be *une bonne bourgeoise*.

Cajetan started to draw a list of all the cathedrals he knew that had foliate heads. First there was Auxerre, of course, then Poitiers with its choir stalls, Sens, Dijon perhaps, and Moissac for its Abbey, as well as others. But first, thought Cajetan with deep conviction, I must make a pilgrimage before I build a cathedral. I need a sacred journey within and a journey without, so the two can meld together and bring me peace and inspiration. I need a sacred place and a sacred destination. That for Cajetan, as for some other pilgrims, was Santiago de Compostela. He had heard about it through his sister, Marie Dieudonnée, Sir Knight Évrard de Châteauloup who had died in battle not long after he had departed for the Eighth Crusade under King Louis IX, and from Master Architect Kurt Marquardt who was now retired from his trade as Architect, and enjoying the countryside at his small estate in Flanders. He had also heard about it from Abbot Wiegelstern of the Kluizen Abbey. The Abbot had spoken highly of the sacred place known as Santiago de Compostela, and the relics of Saint James. First, Cajetan told himself that he had to go to Fontevraud and meet with Marie Dieudonnée and get her spiritual advice. He also wanted to know how she was doing since he had not heard from her since her profession of perpetual vows.

Cajetan left for Fontevraud on a Monday morning when the May sky shone with bright translucence, a radiance from the sun that he had not ever noticed before. He wondered if this was a sign of blessedness, an omen of light overcoming the shadowy streaks of his doubts if not his fears of undertaking a journey such as a pilgrimage to a far land. It was not the Crusade of kings and knights, but it was, for him, a bold adventure into the unknown to bolster his Christian faith in God the Savior. Cajetan was not a man of broad education, having studied when he was quite young under the tutelage of the Masters of theology and human knowledge, but he had read much and had been able to penetrate inside the word of the Lord and the teachings of the Church as well as many intricacies of cathedral building. However, Cajetan realized that architecture was not a study or a learning process in a vacuum. It was attached to several other disciplines of knowledge such as theology, astrology, geography, mysticism and symbolism. The greatest source of knowledge, of course, was the Bible, for how many times had he heard that the cathedral was the Bible in stone. "I don't know much," thought Cajetan, "but I will not let my lack of knowledge hold me down, for I have a thirst for knowledge however it may come my way. I am an open book. Let God and his creation write in it what I truly need to live and be saved. Let Cajetan become your instrument, Lord, let me become part of your grand design as I mature and master my craft and my life as a simple voice among many. For I want to shout, God, my Creator, let me be the best that I can be and let me build you the finest of cathedrals, Gothic of course, for the Gothic reaches to the heavens, and I will be content to continue living my life as a Stargazer." This and much more did Cajetan express into thoughts and silent, hushed words that express more than can be said out loud.

When Cajetan reached Fontevraud, he immediately rang the bell to the monastery and the porter, a young monk, came to open the huge oaken door that opened on the vast space that was reserved for the Monastery of Sainte-Marie, and that of the monks, Saint-Jean-de-L'Habit. Cajetan asked for Marie Dieudonnée and told the young man that she was his sister. The Porter told him that Mère la Prieure, was preoccupied but if he wanted to see someone else, he would try and get permission to do so. Cajetan was surprised that his sister had gone up in rank and that she certainly exerted some influence at Fontevraud at the present time.

----Then may I see Mère Marie-Ange, said Cajetan.

The Porter hesitated then said,

----Mère Marie-Ange died last year. She is buried here in our monastery cemetery. Would you like to see the gravesite?

----No. I did not know she had passed away. I need to see my sister, if you please.

----You cannot see whomever you please without permission.

----Then get permission.

The Porter looked somewhat miffed at Cajetan's insistence. However, knowing that he was facing the Prioress's brother, he hesitated, at first, but told Cajetan to wait in the garden until he reached someone who would give him permission to let this stranger enter the monastery walls. He came back after an hour a bit downcast for he had been mildly scolded by the Sub-Prioress for having made the Prioress's brother wait so long to be able to see his own sister. The Porter then excused himself in front of Cajetan and then told Cajetan to follow him. They went through some long cloister arcades, then went inside through long hallways until they reached a small room where the Sub-Prioress was. She introduced herself as Mère Mérilda de la Passion, and made Cajetan sit down on a straight back wooden chair. She told him that his sister was very busy and that, if he chose to wait, she would get in touch with the Prioress and see if she would be open to a meeting with him.

----You see, I cannot make promises for my superior.

----I understand. I'll wait.

----It may take some time. You see Mother is with the Abbess, and the Abbess is quite ill. We do not expect her to live too long.

----Oh, I'm sorry.

----Well, she has lived a long and productive life, Mère Eulalie du Bon Secours.

----Who is going to replace her?

----That, no one knows. It's part of God's plans in His mercy and wisdom.

----Surely, someone must know something. Don't you nuns plan for such an event? You don't pull an Abbess out of the air, do you?

----Well, of course not. But we deliberate on it, and sometimes for a long time. A very long time, weeks even. It's a very important decision that must be accepted by the community, and those in the leadership of the Order.

----Who is next in line then, the Prioress?

Cajetan was thinking of his sister as Abbess. She surely was qualified, as far as he was concerned. But, how those living in monasteries do plan and decide those things, he wondered.

----The Prioress may be in line, as you say, but no one is sure about the nomination and election. All that we know is that it has to be a woman. It was so from the very beginning with Mère de Chemillé, and will continue to be so until the end of time.

----Do you think that Fontevraud will last that long?

----I do not know that, but I certainly hope it will. This is the foretaste of the New Jerusalem.

----You certainly have great hopes for Fontevraud, the immediate step towards the Kingdom of God.

Someone came to tell the Sub-Prioress that Mère Marie Dieudonnée would meet with her brother in the small chapter room.

Cajetan was led to the specified room, and there he met with Marie Dieudonnée who was all excited about seeing her brother again.

----Please sit down, Cajetan. You look so full of health and full of life. Have you started on your cathedral plans yet?

----No. I'm not at that point yet. I'm here to see you, and to get your advice, your spiritual advice.

----Oh, I see. But first, how is the family? Wandal and the children?

----Wandal is fine and fat around the haunches, and the children are growing fast.

----They must be leading the good life then.

----Yes, they are, Marie Dieudonnée. How are you doing? They tell me that you're the Prioress of this vast monastery. I didn't know that.

----Yes, I was appointed by the present Abbess three years ago.

----That must be an important position.

----Well it has its responsibilities. I'm responsible for the management and organization of the entire monastery. I answer to the Abbess alone. The position is important and worthy of the dignity of the position, but the person herself is not. I am not a person of importance, Cajetan. I'm still the Marie Dieudonnée I used to be.

----But you are an important person by the simple fact that you are an important leader here.

----A leader leads by the voice of her flock. That's the way I operate and the way I see it. I'm not a person seeking power or control. Far from it.

----You are a humble person, Marie Dieudonnée. You sure are.

----Humility is being who you are and how you value people. It's neither the superior nor the inferior layer of one's role in a given community. It's just plain being true to oneself. Being untrue to oneself is sheer hypocrisy, and Christ hated hypocrisy above all else.

----Well they can't call you a hypocrite.

They both laughed.

----Tell me Marie Dieudonnée are you in line to be the next Abbess?

----I don't know and I really do not desire it. There are many other nuns who are worthier than me, Cajetan. More knowledgeable and capable too.

----That's what you think, but, I'm sure they don't all think that way.

----Be it as it may, I'm not wasting time worrying about who's going to be the next Abbess. I leave that in the hands of God. I just hope He looks the other way when He casts His eyes on us poor nuns and sees me in my unworthiness.

----You always told me to accept whatever talents I had and not to hide them under a bushel basket. Well, do what you preach, my sister.

----Let's not waste time on something that may or may not be. Let's talk about you, Cajetan and your reason for coming to see me. You said that you wanted my spiritual advice. How may I help you?

----I'm contemplating a pilgrimage to Santiago de Compostela and I want your advice on it.

----That's good, Cajetan, very good. First you must decide if you want this to be a journey of adventure and terrestrial delight or do you want it to become a true pilgrimage, a journey of the soul in meditation and prayer. A pilgrimage is a sacred venture, Cajetan. It's a calling from the Lord to examine your soul and see if you have accomplished what you set out to be. You will be under the guidance of the Holy Ghost, the Inspirer and Holy Dispenser of the gifts to the soul, wisdom being a very important one.

----I want this pilgrimage to be what you say it must be, a sacred journey of my soul to reclaim the things that I might have lost along the way such as wisdom and fortitude in the Lord. I have wandered and sometimes wandered far in my deliberations about myself and my craft as Architect. I wonder if I have let myself wander too far with thoughts of success, and perhaps envy and pride.

----Have you talked with some priest about this?

----No. I don't always trust priests, especially bishops.

----Why not?

----Because of the incidents I have witnessed and gotten to know about them. I wish that Brother Abélard Marie were still alive. He might have been able to help me in that direction.

----Well, he's not with us anymore. We must move on, Cajetan. We must not let our lives be focused on only one person, nor distrust those who are in a position to help us.

----But I do not trust priests.

----There are some good ones, Cajetan, those who have earned our trust. You must try to find them. There are some right here at our monastery. I'll introduce you to them. Before starting out on your pilgrimage, you will need to confess your sins and obtain absolution, then you'll have to receive the Eucharist in order to begin anew, spiritually, I mean. A sacred journey must begin in a sacred way, Cajetan. It's not unlike a knight in the service of his lord who must get prepared for his adventure by following a spiritual exercise before his wanderings into the forest of Brocéliande. I don't know too much about knights and their adventurous journeys but I do know a bit about the spiritual end of it. Take for instance the tale of Sir Galahad and the quest for the sacred cup.

----What sacred cup?

----The cup of the Lord at the Last Supper. The Holy Grail, as it is often named.

----Did he ever find it?

----I don't think so. I do not read romances. All I know is that Sir Galahad was on a quest for the sacred cup and he had to prepare himself physically and spiritually to be worthy of his quest.

----I'll have to read about it someday. That would be a great subject for a stained glass window or a sculpture on a trumeau.

----This pilgrimage of yours is truly not unlike a knight who sets out on a long journey to claim his calling and prove his chivalry. It's veritably a sacred journey since sacredness is linked to the Creator. It's an uplifting of the soul towards His Kingdom.

----I understand, but…

----But what? You cannot continue to live in doubt and fear of advancing spiritually. You need the anchor of the sacraments and the ballast of good strong moral values to which you can cling and hold on for a proper journey deep inside of the soul.

----What are your spiritual values, Marie Dieudonnée?

----What you see is what you get when you look at me, Cajetan. I believe that I mirror the spiritual values that I practice. Humility, obedience to God and the sacred rule, poverty in detachment, chastity in my God-created body, patience, prayer as a value, and above all, love. Love, Cajetan is the greatest of my spiritual values. That's when one tends to bend towards the other and meet her needs. I live by that value every day. You must read Saint Paul's epistle to the Corinthians, chapter thirteen, 'If I speak in tongues of mortals and of angels, but do not have love, I am a noisy gong or a clanging cymbal. And if I have prophetic powers, and understand all mysteries and all knowledge, and if I have all faith, so as to move mountains, but do not have love, I am nothing.' Nothing, Cajetan. 'Love is patient; love is kind; love is not envious or boastful or arrogant or rude. It does not insist on its own way; it is not irritable or resentful it does not rejoice in wrongdoing, but rejoices in truth. Love never ends.' Never ends, Cajetan. 'Pursue love and strive for the spiritual gifts.' That's part of Saint Paul's letter to his friends in Corinth. Do you have a Bible?

----I think I have one at home in Flanders.

----What's it doing there. You should have it with you. I will give you one.

----Thank you.

----So you see, what I have been quoting to you from the great Apostle of the Gentiles, is precisely what my own spiritual values are. There's nothing new. These values have always been there for us to adopt and nurture.

----You must know the entire letter by heart for you didn't stop reciting it to me.

----That's not the entire epistle. I read Corinthian 13 every day.

----So that's why you know it so well.

----Yes. When are you beginning your pilgrimage, Cajetan?

----I was planning to begin as soon as I met with you.

----Why don't you spend some time with us and take a few days for a retreat prior to your departure for the pilgrimage to Santiago de Compostela. You know that you must start at Vézelay, don't you? That's the usual departure point in France. We, the followers of Saint Benedict's rule, offer hospitality to people like you. You will stay with the monks here in St-Jean-de-L'Habit. Please say yes, Cajetan. It will give me time to take care of Mother Abbess and visit with you when I can make time. Mother is very ill and we do not expect her to live long. I cannot heal her of her illness. She's very old, and has resigned herself to the path that will lead her to her eternal joy. She barely utters a few words, and her lips offer prayers for perseverance in faith and love in Christ and his Holy Mother. I can see it as I watch over her. Her journey on earth is almost over. I must go and see her now. Will you be all right with the monks, Cajetan?

As she was saying these words to her brother, someone interrupted her and whispered something in her ear. Mother Abbess had just died. The chapel bells were tolling the death knell.

Cajetan stayed with the monks for six days since his sister, now interim Abbess, had asked him to join the members of the Order in grieving for the Abbess, followed by funeral services and her internment in the hall of past Abbesses. Cajetan acceded to his sister's request for he was thrilled to be invited to such an occasion, if not a once-in-a-lifetime event. As they were preparing the funeral ceremonies while the Order was officially in mourning, Cajetan was on his spiritual retreat with guidance from the Sub-Prior of the monks' monastery. Cajetan found him to be affable and kind in his advice to him. Cajetan thought that he was easy to talk to and related well to him and his spiritual counseling.

The grieving time was to be one month and no one even talked about the possibility of who was to be the new Abbess. That would come after the grieving period. Monastic propriety demanded it. However, there was no question that the whole issue was on the mind of each and every member of the community, at whatever degree of thought. It was only human.

On the fourth day, the body of the Abbess was carried into the chapel for the funeral mass. The "Dies irae" was sung reverently on a mournful tone by both the nuns and the monks. The mass started and every rule of decorum and respect towards a deceased Abbess was observed. She lay there in full view of the Order dressed in her official habit as Abbess with the cross of authority and honor on her breast. She looked so peaceful and serene even though the mask of death had covered her face and eyes, and taken away every sign of vitality. She truly had passed on. Cajetan was sitting in the back of the chapel and observed every motion and every act of ritual offered for the repose of the soul of the Abbess. He was impressed by what he saw, if not charmed by it. For him, it was myth in motion. Years of solemn tradition was in that ritual of the dead. It would keep repeating itself, be it for an ordinary person to the highest placed of mortals. Cajetan kept repeating in his head the words he always heard on Ash Wednesday, "Memento homo pulvis es et pulvem reverteris." Dust unto dust. Creative myth, myth of tradition, mythic conception of humans, and gods and goddesses who hunger for re-creation.

They processed the body of the Abbess, Mère Eulalie du Bon Secours, née Marie Eugénie LaTourette, into the great hall of the dead where the deceased Abbesses were placed under a marble slab with inscriptions. The hall of passed Abbesses stood next to the great hall of nobles who lay there in state with a marble effigy to mark their place in history. Then, in the great monastic silence when one of its members had been laid to rest, the entire community returned to their individual tasks working as hard as they were wont to. Cajetan was told by the Sub-Prioress that Marie Dieudonnée was in chapter with the members of the chapter, and would be there for the rest of the day deliberating. Cajetan went back to the monks' monastery and read the better part of the afternoon. When the bell rang for Vespers, he returned to the nuns' monastery to meet one last time with his sister. It had already been arranged. As he walked silently in the long hall that led to the Abbess's domain, he saw Marie Dieudonnée walking his way pensive and solemn. As she approached him from a distance, Cajetan could see something hanging from her neck. He caught sight of it, and the closer she got to him the better he could see that it was the cross of the Abbess.

12

THE PILGRIMAGE

There was no moon in the dark sky and the leaves in the trees were very still. It was mid-July and Cajetan was now in Vézelay. He was trying to look at the sky to see if he could spot a star, any star, but none were visible to the naked eye. He spent some time thinking about what Marie Dieudonnée had told him, and about her rise to the position of Abbess of one of the largest monasteries in all of Christendom. He was proud of her and her accomplishments. She deserves to be the top leader at Fontevraud, he told himself, for through her flowed the richest graces that God could impart to a human being. Of course, he was biased; she was his sister. Grisoulda and Philippon had done well, he thought. After some time outdoor under a dark and cloudy sky, Cajetan decided to go indoor and get to bed. He was starting a long journey tomorrow, and he needed his sleep.

To his great surprise, Cajetan found a large poster on one of the walls of the inn where he was staying announcing the presence of a troupe of players called, *La Troupe du Paradis* featuring Ernst Zumberger, Harry Trotwell and Abélard François. They were to present a play by John Treblain of London, called "Morte d'Arthur" the following evening. They were on tour for several weeks, and they expected to have, as one of their guests, none other than Sir Knight Lancelot de Beaucours and his Lady, Lady Fortunata of the House of Poitiers. Her mother was a distinguished noblewoman from the Val de Noto in the domain of Sicily. Pretty important guests, thought Cajetan. He was glad that Abélard François was doing well in his craft. Performing was indeed a craft since one had to put in so much creative energy into it, and work hard at perfecting his skills as an actor-performer. He knew himself he could not possibly do it, and respected those who could and were good at it. If he was a Master Architect, then there had to be master performers in the trade of performing in public, he thought. I wonder what level my brother has reached, he mused. Had he mastered his craft? Cajetan looked forward to seeing his brother perform. It might delay his pilgrimage but it was worthwhile. He missed his brother.

The following evening Cajetan attended the performance without letting his brother know. He wanted to surprise him and, at the same time, be able to give Abélard François's his reactions to the play and the performance of each of the three actors. The play was of English origins. Harry Trotwell and Ernst Zumberger were featured in the play about the mythic king, Arthur. Cajetan thought that the play was not too entertaining but the actors were good. As for Abélard François, he did a performance of Adam de la Halle's play, **The Play of the Greenwood**. It was a truly creative performance what with faeries and other supernatural occurrences in the play. Cajetan truly enjoyed this performance, not because his brother had done it, but he appreciated the imaginary and creative elements of the dramatic offering . Both performances were held on two pageant wagons in the middle of the street. The first play was held on one while the other play was set up on the other. It was quite a feat, thought Cajetan.

After the performances, Cajetan went up to his brother to congratulate him. Abélard François was totally surprised to see Cajetan there. He showed his pleasure by embracing his brother who was not accustomed to that gesture by another man.

----Welcome to my craft, Cajetan. Did you like the performances?

----Yes, I did, especially yours. What spirit, what creativity! How did you manage to learn your lines and deliver a very lively performance? Did you have to train a long time to get those results?

----Yes and no. I have been doing this so long that, after a while, it gets to be second nature. I love it, Cajetan. I really love it. Did you like the staging? We have to use pageant wagons because we have to pull them aside after each performance, and haul them to the nearest town where we will then perform again. We have workers helping us. Some don't like pageant wagons because there isn't too much room for broad gestures and moving around, but we manage quite well, I think.

----You certainly did. What about the play you did. Where did it come from?

----It comes from the genius of a man from Arras in France. His name is Adam de la Halle, and he's truly gifted. He's a *trouvère* and a poet-writer. He has a marvelous singing voice too. I met him last year when he was giving a performance of this play about green fields, faeries and other wild stuff. I so loved it that I asked him if I could use it as my vehicle for performing, and he said, yes. He's a generous fellow.

----I would say he is.

----I started out with mystery plays but turned to secular plays because there was more variety in them. More fun too! Adam de la Halle has written many plays. Most of them are musicals such as the well-known "Le Jeu de Robin and Marion", followed by "Jeu de la Fueillee in Arras". Arras is a town known for its playwrights. Perhaps you might know Jean Bodel and his "Jeu de saint Nicolas"?

----No, I'm afraid I don't. You're truly well versed in theater aren't you?

----Of course, Cajetan. It's my craft, my trade. I live for it, I dream of it and I would die for it. That's my passion, Cajetan.

----It's good to have a passion for something or someone. Do you have a passion for a particular woman?

----No, I don't. My passion is for the theater and for certain performers.

----But they're all men.

----Exactly.

Cajetan did not wish to elaborate on this. He met with Abélard François the following morning and told him about his pilgrimage and his great joy of having met, once again, Marie Dieudonnée at Fontevraud . He seemed radiant when he announced to his brother that their sister was now Abbess.

----Good for her. She deserves such acclamation and belonging. I know I did not belong in the monastery I went to. Remember?

----Yes, Abélard François, I do remember and I want to forget it.

----Me too, Cajetan. Please keep me in your prayerful pilgrimage for I need prayers. I need the comfort of my family praying for me and still remembering me.

----We will never forget you, dear brother, the performer. The artist-craftsman. Never stop being creative, Abélard François, because that's the lifeblood of any good craftsman.

The two of them left each other, and Cajetan walked toward the cathedral. As he was slowly walking, he wondered who his brother's passion was, and whether he was happy with whomever. He was not going to judge his brother for his tendencies and his choices in life, but he thought it strange how things develop in the heart of a human being. He would indeed keep Abélard François in his thoughts and in his prayers, and, furthermore, he would make him part of the pilgrimage itself. He would dedicate his pilgrimage to him as a votive offering to Saint James and our Holy Mother, he said to himself.

Two days after his encounter with his brother, Cajetan set out for the first leg of his pilgrimage from Vézelay to Moissac. He wore his best tunic, a long woolen cloak, thick and soft to guard himself against cold nights. It would also serve as his bed when he slept under the stars. He carried a large pouch over his right shoulder in which he had put his belongings for the journey, and he carried a tall staff made of good solid oak, the staff of the pilgrim. He made sure he had the sheaf of Bible excerpts his sister had given him. Since he wanted to travel as a pilgrim and not as a man of means, he had very little money on him, for he would go without rather than feast on some rich food and wine. Besides, people had told him to be careful about thieves along the way, those *routiers,* road robbers. Not that he was a penitent but he wanted to follow the path of abstinence and prayer as many of the monks that he had met at Fontevraud did. He was ready. This would be his adventure into the realm of introspection, meditation, prayer and star gazing that would deepen his sense of spirituality. He thought of this pilgrimage as his retreat from the hustle and bustle of daily life when all he had to do was seek serenity and peace as well as the comfort of freedom from all cares.

As he went along, he met all kinds of people on the pilgrimage to Santiago de Compostela. There was an entire family with three children chatting as they walked, an old man with a younger man guiding him for he was a retired knight, and as for the young man, he called him his squire. There were three women wrapped in layers of cloth, a blind man with a guide following the motion of the pilgrims, four monks with white flowing tunics and scapulars who recited the rosary every four hours, and several others that made up the cadre of pilgrims. But there was one special pilgrim, a woman in her early forties or so, who carried a heavy burden on her shoulders, a cross made of lead with which she struggled trying to keep it from falling. It wasn't a large cross but a heavy one. Each time someone tried to help her, she told them, no. Her steps were as heavy as her cross of lead, and she told anyone who wanted to hear her story that she was doing penance for the sins of those who cheated and humiliated the poor. Herself in particular. She would stop now and then to rest a while and continue with her story. Cajetan found her story sad, filled with pain and suffering, but fascinating for its lack of self-deprecation. She knew who she was and what she had done and not done. She was not fatalistic about her plight, simply realistic and bold in her attempt to right the wrong in her life. Apparently it had been a life of reversals. Cajetan decided to stop and listen to what she had to say because it sounded so pitiful and at the same time inspiring. She told him that, at one time, she was well off and spoiled by her father who was a rich merchant. She had the finest of embroidered silken gowns, the best of brushed woolen copes with tassels made of gold threads. She also had exquisite gold and silver jewelry that she wore with pride to a point of haughtiness. She lacked nothing and gave nothing to no one especially the poor, for she lacked mercy for them. She did not even pity them. She considered them less than human and worse than groveling animals. She could not stand them and their sorry state of affairs. Why should she even care for them if they did not want to help themselves, she said. Get rid of them and society in general will be much better off. Good riddance! She became an angry and spiteful woman who spat out her bile against everyone and everything especially the poor and miserable creatures that they were. She even spat on the image of Christ to the horror of those who watched her do it. She could not stand him, this lover of the poor and downtrodden, this man-God who preached that misery and poverty were not only to be pitied but embraced, and those in that miserable state should be cared for and even loved. What hypocrisy! she maintained with vehemence. How can anyone who calls himself God be so stupid! she cried out. Until one day, she met this woman who was with child and who was begging for her food out in the streets. She recognized her as her very good friend, Madeleine, who had shared the delights of her childhood growing up. Why had this creature become this beggar woman? She could not possibly be her old and dear friend, she thought. But she was. Why was she in such a dire state? Why should she even care for her now that she had become an abhorrent beggar? Why indeed? Her friend Madeleine told her that she was homeless and had been raped by a *routier* and that she was carrying his bastard child. What was she to do?

The woman, whose name was Véronique Ypres, continued with her story even though there was only Cajetan who was listening to her. She said that for once in her life she felt a hint of compassion for this woman beggar because she remembered how Madeleine had always been her friend and had never abandoned her even when she, Véronique, had turned ugly and mean. Véronique had turned that way after she lost both of her parents in a terrible fire and started to blame God for her loss. She began hating the poor when she saw that so many of them multiplied and had so many children, and lived on the charity of others, while she felt so terribly alone, if not abandoned totally and irretrievably so. She complained so much to the authorities about the wasted lives of so many poor people she met on the streets, that she branded them *vauriens*, useless, and hounded the authoritites until many of these beggars were thrown into jail for vagrancy and being a public nuisance. She even paid some of the local authorities to put these people away. How she vilified the poor bastards, as she called them. It was their fault if they found themselves that way, she proclaimed with fury in her voice. They were all stangers to her and she wanted to keep it that way. Absolutely no commiseration, no mercy on her part. They all deserved to die or, at least, be driven away. Until the day she had a vision of a man in a dream who cried out to her, "Woman, why are you persecuting me? I died on a cross for all, even the very poor." She woke up, her nerves shattered. Night after night she could not sleep and the vision haunted her. When she saw Madeleine with child out in the streets, she recognized her own fault and offered to help her. Her fault of cold heartedness and hatred for the helpless poor. It seemed to her that she had lost the power to love. Love had become a ghost, a phantom of her former capacities. The human being that she once was had turned to stone. She would attempt to turn her life around and not harden her heart any longer. She would try and help her dear friend. However, Madeleine had become a sickly woman filled with despair and fright until, one day, she threw herself into the river and drowned. Véronique regretted not having done enough for her childhood friend. She could have saved two lives, she told herself. She herself fell into despair and rather than throw herself into the river, she threw herself at the foot of the cross begging for mercy and forgiveness. She did not know why she had done that all of a sudden, like an impulse that drove her there, but she knew that someone, something had made her do it. When she looked up and saw the cross with the Lord crucified on it, she saw an inscription at the base of the cross that read,"My grace suffices." Later, when she heard about the pilgrimage to Santiago de Compostela, she resolved to follow the steps of those pilgrims who went on the pilgrimage to expiate their sins and make amends for all their shortcomings and hatreds in life. Since she had found salvation at the foot of the cross, she had a blacksmith make her a cross forged of lead for her to carry on her shoulders while walking the pilgrim's way to Santiago. She detached herself from all of her richly possessions and gave them to the poor whom she saw begging at the doors of churches and monasteries. She told Cajetan that ever since she had started her pilgrimage, she was able to sleep at night. But before she went to sleep she stopped to gaze at the stars at night for they comforted her. They gave her hope, the hope that someday she would be at peace with herself and with others. Cajetan just smiled at her and wished her well on her journey, thanking her for her inspiring story. He offered Véronique to help her carry the lead cross but she refused saying that she had to carry it all the way to Santiago by herself. Only she could make amends for her sins. It was her responsibility and no one else's. "No one can expiate my sins except me and I mean to do it through sacrifice and prayer while throwing myself on the mercy of the Lord." she told Cajetan. "I spat on him and he graciously smiled on me in return." Cajetan thought that was so true and he tried not to judge her but to feel for her and her misery that had plagued her soul for so long a time. The memory of Véronique, the penitent, stayed with Cajetan for a very long time.

Every day, it seemed that one or two people would come and join the group. Cajetan enjoyed the walking, the joyful and carefree air of the great outdoors and the vistas of green grasses and hills, fields of golden grain and tall trees that cast long shadows to shelter him from the heat of the noonday sun. He would occasionally fall into brief conversations with one of the pilgrims, and they would talk about the weather, their plans for the day, and some banal topic just to be friendly. Once in a great while, Cajetan would find one who would be of genuine interest to him, and they would talk at length about some important matters such as, cathedrals, some philosophical questions or the creativity of certain craftsmen. Cajetan had, as of late, become interested in ideas, ideas like the role and existence of the Creator God, the role of reason in a person's life or the eternal question of what is the earth made of.

Cajetan decided to take advantage of a short stop in Moissac before entering Spain, and follow the Camino Francés. He had heard much about the Abbaye Saint-Pierre de Moissac and its Romanesque architecture, and he ardently wanted to visit it while he was in the southwestern area. He especially wanted to see the sculpture program at Moissac. He had heard great things about it. Cajetan joined a small group of pilgrims and followed the man with a purple cloak who was their guide. "Unfortunately, the Abbey church roof collapsed and later fire destroyed practically everything that was left of Moissac's Abbey," said the guide. Then the guide related how the Great Abbey of Cluny came to the help of Moissac, and sent one of their most experienced monks, Durand de Bredons, who became Moissac's Abbot. Fifteen years later in 1063, a new Abbey church was consecrated.

What Cajetan was most interested in was the architecture and the sculptures. He wandered off the guide's path and settled for his own tour. First, he went to the portal in the southwest corner where there was a creatively carved tympanum with an elaborate statue of the prophet Jeremiah on the east side of the trumeau. With his gaze cast askance and his long hair, mustache and beard flowing like small streams of water, the Old Testament Prophet is holding on to a long scroll with both hands. His elongated body is graceful and majestic, thought Cajetan, a real piece of artistic creativity. Then he saw on the other side of the trumeau, a statue of Saint Paul with his hand uplifted, so one could see the palm of his right hand. He is carved with the same elongated body that elevates the trumeau to new heights of artistry.

Cajetan then went to the west left side wall where some bas-reliefs were, and caught his eye. Many dealt with various sins but the one that fascinated Cajetan was the one depicting the poor man, Lazarus and the rich man, the well-fed and thoughtless man who is cast into hell while on the left side, there is the bosom of Abraham where is beatifically sheltered Lazarus like a tiny child, the representation of a soul that is saved. Amazing how this parable is often seen in cathedrals, thought Cajetan. Then he went to look at the capitals much reputed for their intricate sculptures. He saw some with delicate foliage, animal and human figures, Biblical scenes and legends of saints such as, Abraham's obedience to Yahweh, Daniel in the Lion's Den, the martyrdom of Saint Lawrence, the legend of the tumbler and the Virgin Mary and many others. What truly fascinated Cajetan were all of the capitals showing the acanthus leaves and palm leaves. He also saw various animal figures such as the lion, the eagle, the griffin, the lamb, and the goat, besides the many wild birds. Leaves were truly an important part of church sculpture design, mused Cajetan. He was most fascinated by foliate heads on the outer jambs of the south porch. One of them was huge with two large branches coming out of both sides of its mouth. As Cajetan was looking at this particular foliate head, the guide happened to come by and started telling him about the strong influences from Moorish Spain. "It is known," he said, "that many Muslim craftsmen and architects worked in Christian Europe. The change in the standards of cutting masonry stone which began around 1100 has been attributed to the influence of these craftsmen with their superior techniques. I need not tell you that it has certainly embellished our Abbey and church here in Moissac." Cajetan recognized the knowledge of and the insights into architecture of this particular guide, and he thanked him abundantly. His short stop in Moissac was truly worthwhile, so thought Cajetan as he left the Moissac area, and got back to following the pilgrimage route.

Romanesque architecture has it's worthy place in the history of building abbeys and churches, Cajetan mused. "I had put the Romanesque style out of my mind and supplanted it with the majesty of the Gothic, and even swore that I would only do Gothic as far as my cathedral was concerned, but now I have changed my mind of sorts. I see now the great influence of the Romanesque and its contribution to creative artistry, and I want some of that creativity in my church. My church may be Gothic but I'll find a way to make room for Romanesque art. It seems that we borrow from one age to another, from one style to another without fully realizing it. We are indeed craftsmen on the shoulders of past masters." Those were the thoughts running through Cajetan's mind after Moissac.

The second night on the road, Cajetan did not go to the prescribed inn in the guidebook of the Calixtine Codex, Book V. This book was attributed to Pope Callixtus II but most probably was the work of the pilgrim Aymeric Picaud. Most pilgrims relied on this guidebook for references and suggested stops. It included what relics to venerate, sanctuaries to visit and inns where to spend the night. Cajetan did not have a copy of this guidebook but he was able to borrow one from a man het met along the route. His name was Gilbert de Rumanie and he came from Dijon. He started the pilgrimage from Vézelay also. He told Cajetan that his trade was that of artist-painter. He painted small icons and his specialty was the Trinitarian icon with three young men representing the three persons in God, the Trinity. He explained to Cajetan that he did not represent the Trinity as God the Father , the old Man with white hair and beard, then the son and then the Holy Ghost as a dove, but that his icon was based on the Orthodox concept of the unchangeable youthful presence of all three persons. Cajetan liked that idea. He might place it in his cathedral somehow, he thought.

Gilbert showed him the different routes to take once at the border in France beginning with Saint-Jean-Pied-de-Port on the French side of the Pyrenees. This led to Roncesvalles on the other side of the border with Espagna. This was called the Camino Francès. It was fed by the Voie de Tours, Voie de Vézelay and the Voie du Puy. They had taken the Vézelay route and were now close to the border. Cajetan was glad to meet Gilbert not only because he was knowledgeable but he also seemed to be a kind and generous man who cherished creativity. Cajetan anticipated having long conversations with the artist-painter.

Gilbert de Rumanie explained to Cajetan the legend behind the story of Saint James in Galicia. According to tradition, said Gilbert, Saint James decided to return to the Holy Land that he knew best after preaching in Galicia. There he was beheaded, but his own disciples managed to get his body to Jaffa, where they found a marvelous stone ship which miraculously conducted the Apostle's body and the disciples to Iria Flavia and back to Galicia. There the disciples asked for permission to lay to rest in the Galician soil the body of Saint James. The local pagan queen, Lupa was annoyed with the newcomers and decided to deceive them, sending them to pick a pair of oxen she allegedly had by the Pico Sacro, a sacred mountain where a dragon dwelt, hoping that the dragon would kill the Christians. However, at the sign of the cross, the dragon exploded. Then the disciples went to pick the oxen which were really raging bulls that the queen used to punish those she did not like. Again at the sign of the cross the bulls calmed down and subjected themselves to a yoke so that the disciple's body was led to Compostela where it was buried.

Gilbert went on to say that later on, the relics of Saint James were rediscovered by a hermit named Pelagius who, after observing strange lights in a local forest, went to the Bishop for help. The Bishop was then guided to the spot by a star. Compostela thus means "Field of Stars" said Gilbert.

----I like the legend, said Cajetan, and I especially like the meaning of "Field of Stars." This is my place under the stars.

----You'll have plenty of time to sleep under your stars and meditate on your proposed cathedral, Cajetan.

Cajetan had already told Gilbert that he was planning to build a cathedral.

----Now let me tell you about the symbol of the scallop shell as related to the pilgrimage. It's often found on the shores in Galicia, and it has long been the symbol of the Camino de Santiago. If I may say based on my capacity to create and use symbols in my work, I think that the scallop shell in reference to the pilgrimage to Compostela has become a myth. Not an untruth but a cultural truth, if you know what I mean.

----Yes, oh, yes. I agree. Myths are never a lie. They mean something and live in the memory of people using them.

----Well, two versions of the myth exist. After the death of Saint James who was killed in Jerusalem, version one says that his disciples shipped his body aboard a ship, and that the ship was hit by a heavy storm and the body was lost at sea. However, later on, the body washed ashore undamaged and covered with scallops. The second version deals with a wedding taking place on shore, and the groom being on horseback saw the ship carrying the body of Saint James and the horse spooked and both horse and rider plunged into the sea. Through miraculous intervention, the horse and rider emerged from the water covered in seashells. I prefer the first version.

----I do too.

----The scallop shell also acts as a metaphor. I live with metaphors, my friend the Architect. I breathe them and devour them, for metaphors are images of the creative imagination merging the idea or ideal with concrete reality. It causes the thinker to see, taste, smell and hear what goes on in his mind. I just like it.

---I do also, Gilbert.

----Well the metaphor of the scallop shell goes like this: the grooves in the shell which come together to a single point represent the various pilgrimage routes traveled, and eventually arriving at a single destination, the tomb of Saint James. Pilgrims, as you know, need souvenirs of their journey to bring home with them and keep them as a reminder of God's grace of the pilgrimage they did. Well, here in Galicia scallop shells can be found on the seashore and are easily available to pilgrims. Many wear them on their cloaks or tunics as a sign that they have persevered in doing the Santiago de Compostela Pilgrimage from beginning to end. Did you ever see somewhere on the façade of a cathedral a statue of a man wearing a scallop shell and holding a staff? Well, that's the pilgrim of Santiago de Compostela.

----Yes, I did and I always wondered what it meant. Now, I know.

----Besides, the scallop shell is useful and practical. It can be used to gather water to drink or for eating as a makeshift bowl.

----How do you know all these things?

----I studied a lot and I have done this pilgrimage fourteen times.

----Fourteen times?

----Yes, fourteen times as a penance for a crime of passion, as they called it.

----Who were they?

----The authorities.

----Where was that?

----In Paris.

----Did you live in Paris? I thought you said you were from Dijon.

----I am now, but I was born in Paris and lived there. I was forced by my parents to enter the seminary of Saint Sulpice. They wanted a priest in their family. I could not refuse them, so I went.

----How long did you stay?

----Three years until they wanted to make me a deacon. I did very well in my theological and philosophical studies. As a matter of fact, I loved those disciplines.

----What happened then?

----Well, I left. My parents were completely crushed by my decision. My father threw me out of the house. So, I had to find a place to stay. I went to my friend's house on rue Bellechasse. He was a close friend of mine. My parents never liked him because he was "un vagabond" as they called him. He liked to displace himself from time to time. His parents died when he was very young, and he was brought up by an aunt that he never liked. She was a nasty woman, always angry and never kind to anyone. She was a spinster who was jilted by a lover when she was young, and she never got over it. She hated men, she said, and never wanted to see one again. She lived a very sheltered life.

----Did your friend like living with her?

----He had no choice. He hated it. She was always after him. Poor aunt Edwige, poor her, such a miserable life.

----What happened to her?

----I don't really know. Jean-Claude, that was my friend's name, left his aunt's house when he was sixteen. He never said goodbye to her. He just took off.

----Where did he go?

----He didn't know where to go, and he felt so alone. He hung around wherever they would have him. Later on, we met at a tavern one evening. We got to be good friends. We were both seventeen, and we craved for adventure. He tried to find work but without a trade or an education, all he could find was menial work as a laborer. He worked for a while for a carpenter but did not like carpentry. Then he tried to become a stone cutter, but without a patron he could not find a way to get in the guild or even contact the membership. I tell you he was truly alone and isolated.

----What did he do?

----He went into prostitution, and even though he did not like it, it gave him money to survive.

----I didn't know there was such a thing as male prostitution. I must be naïve. You see I too lived a sheltered life.

----Yes, there is such a thing. A sad thing for young men seeking a life of their own. That's when he met Angélique.

----Who's Angélique?

----She was a young prostitute who walked the streets of Paris and was well paid for her services. She was good at it, people said, and older men with money asked for her, and even fought over her. Oh, she was a coy, daring, teasing girl. She was both beautiful and full of life. And, I may add very desirable. She was like a rare fruit that you need to taste, that you must taste or die.

----Your friend liked her?

----No, he loved her. "*Assez pour en mourir*" he told me once, to die for.

----How did you get involved with her, or didn't you?

----At first, I wanted nothing of her. But then, she played with my emotions and taunted me. She took me like a puppeteer who holds on to the puppet strings and makes the puppet dance the way he wants. That's how my passion started. I fell deeply, voraciously, madly in love with her. I could not sleep at night, and I prowled the streets of Paris thinking how I would win her over. You see, Jean-Claude was also in love with her, and he was jealous of anyone who would dare take her away from him. She knew it and she played both sides, him and me, and sometimes she did it deliberately, I mean, she would taunt him and rile him about me and what she called our affair.

----Was it truly an affair?

----No. I loved her but she would have nothing to do with me. At least not as a lover. She would let me kiss her savagely and with deep passion until my heart was up in flames. Then she would laugh and pout like a naughty girl until she knew that she had inflamed my passion for her.

----Why didn't you leave her and your friend, and just go away?

----I couldn't. I just couldn't. *C'était plus fort que moi*, it was more than I could endure. I simply could not fight it. If you've never been madly in love with someone as insanely desirable as I was for Angélique, then you don't know how it was. How miserable I felt, and not only miserable but I was going insane with this love affair that was not truly a love affair. It was a one-sided affair. *J'étais fou d'elle*, I was crazy in love with her.

----So what happened?

----One night, I saw her with my friend in a tavern, and she was drooling all over him. When she saw me, she looked at me with contempt and began to throw herself daringly at any man who would have her for the night. I got mad, enraged at the sight of her flaunting herself that way, and looking at me with scorn and dastardly disdain. She knew she was hurting me. She knew that I was getting angrier and angrier. My passion for her turned to jealousy and hatred. I lunged at her and started strangling her with my bare hands. There was so much strength gathered there in those two hands of mine that they became dangerous. Really dangerous. She tried to scream but could not. She turned blue with her eyes bulging out of her head. I squeezed so hard that my hands hurt from the force

I exerted to kill her. Before anyone could intervene, I had killed her so strong was my physical strength at that peak moment of jealousy and desperation.

----You killed her? Did you want to do that, really do that? Kill her?

----I could not think straight, Cajetan. At that very moment of my unleashed desires and boiling hatred and jealousy, I just acted out my passion, my unfulfilled passion of love. I did not know what I was doing and I did not care.

----That's terrible, Gilbert.

----Yes, terrible and shattering for the soul.

----What happened next?

----The authorities were called in, and they took me away. I never fought it and never struggled with them. I knew that I had done wrong but I felt that it was not me who had done that, it was my passion and its drive, that terrible drive to snuff out jealous feelings. Jealousy can be a horrible thing, Cajetan, a horrible and devastating thing. Like a nightmare, my life was taken over by jealousy and hurtful pride. The authorities called my sin a crime of passion and they had mercy on me for they only sent me away to prison for seven years. There, I learned to control my desires and live with myself as a man who casts away all sinful drives that destroy the heart and the soul. I started to pray the Virgin Most Pure and begged her to please change the person that I had become and allow me to do penance for my sin. When I got out of prison, I learned about the pilgrimage to Santiago de Compostela and that gave me the notion of satisfying my penance in a way that was pleasing to me and to God, our Savior and His Mother, the Sorrowful One at the foot of the Cross. That was fourteen years ago, and now I'm on my fifteenth pilgrimage, this sacred journey to the next point of my salvation, I call it.

----Don't you feel that you have satisfied your penance already?

----Not yet, Cajetan, not yet. I have to feel deep inside me that I have finally been absolved of my sin, and have made full restitution. I must make restitution for taking the life of Angélique. Restitution will be complete only when I have given back what I have taken from God. A life. You know how important a life is, Cajetan? What it's worth in the sight of Almighty God? A soul that he's created and redeemed by the blood of his Son is worth more than gold or any precious earthly thing. I cannot put a price on a human life, and therefore I must continue to do penance through the mercy of this sacred pilgrimage. Lord, I trust and hope that I will be able to satisfy you and your justice before I die.

----Throw yourself on His mercy, Gilbert. Isn't that the only way?

----What else can I do. But, I must, I must, I must do penance. I must. If I don't my soul will wither and shrivel like a dry weary fig tree. As Christ says in his gospel, cut it and throw it in the fire. There's nothing good left. Nothing.

That night Cajetan slept under the stars weary but not too tired to gaze at the blackened sky where a myriad of stars looked down on him in the quiet exercise of creature looking up at the created firmament of light and darkness. He lay there on his cloak, his two arms held high and folded under his head. There was a serenity in the air that he welcomed this moonlit night. He luxuriated in it, for he felt good about his surroundings. He could even feel within himself a certain sensuousness that pervaded his body, even his very soul. He didn't have to worry about anything, not even the planning and design of his cathedral. He lulled himself into sleep.

Cajetan woke up suddenly when he heard footsteps at some distance. Then they stopped. He wondered whose they were. Probably Gilbert's. Then everything was still. He looked up and saw that the dark sky was full of stars, and they seemed brighter than when he first saw them when he was looking up before falling asleep. He could not help gazing at the milky way, this broad brushstroke of stars. His eyes were captivated by it, and stared until he felt that he was being hypnotized by the stars in his gaze. The heavens seemed that much closer to him now that he was facing it and gazing as if it were an imaginary dream come true. Is this the way my grandfather saw the stars? he wondered. Hubert the Stargazer. What did it mean to gaze at the stars? To be so captivated by them that everything else seems to disappear. It was as if the earth was no more, and the heavens had completely taken over all of creation. There was a hushed brilliance all over the dark sky that made it shine like thousands and thousands of candles lit all at once. Cajetan could not get his gaze off of them. He was mesmerized by this brilliance until he saw, if only in his creative mind, a cathedral, a Gothic cathedral perched on a small incline with stones of pearls, sculptures of smiling angels, solemn Prophets, quiet saints, regal kings and queens, *le Beau Dieu*, and suddenly the Virgin Queen with a diadem of a myriad of stars illuminating the entire heavens. Cajetan woke up suddenly and said, "That's it, I'm going to name my cathedral *Mary Queen of Heaven and the Stars.*" *Sainte Marie de la Belle Étoile.* I've changed my mind about the name of my cathedral. He fell back to sleep until early morning.

Gilbert and Cajetan set out on the road again in the direction of the French route with Pamplona as its first stop. As they got near the region, they were told that they should visit the Monastery of San Salvador of Leyre and its church with the relics of two young martyred saints. People could easily see that both Cajetan and Gilbert were pilgrims on their way to Santiago de Compostela. They both carried staffs, and they wore broad brim hats to guard them from the burning afternoon sun. Once they got precise directions for the monastery, they did not hesitate to follow those, and they reached their destination in no time. It was a large monastery and housed about one hundred monks of the Order of Saint Benedict, they were told. They wanted to know if the relics of Nunilo and Alodia were still kept in the church, and they were told, yes, they were. They went to the large wooden door at the monastery and knocked to gain entrance. When the porter saw that they were pilgrims, he made them enter and told them to be respectful of the monastery and its rule. Cajetan and Gilbert knew that part of the rule was hospitality to strangers. Then, the porter got another monk, a young man, no more than twenty years old, and he directed him to show them the church. When they got to the church, the two pilgrims asked to see the Porta Speciosa, and their guide knew immediately that they wanted to see the carving of Nunilo and Alidia, and most probably their relics. Standing in front of the portal, Brother Aloysius, for that was the young monk's name, explained the history behind the two child martyrs. He told them that they had died in the ninth century, and that they were from Huesca. Born of a mixed marriage, they eschewed the Islam of their father in favor of their mother's Christianity. They were executed by the Muslim authorities in accordance with the *sharia* law as apostates. The two girls refused to disavow their faith, and then were placed in a brothel and later beheaded. Their relics were translated from Huesca to Leyre where they remain as of this day, said the young monk.

----Would you like to see them?

----Yes, replied Cajetan. We have come from far away, and this is our first stop to revere relics and gain indulgences, for we are both pilgrims on our way to Santiago de Compostela.

----I know, said the monk, I could tell right away.

They went inside the church and knelt in front of the relics of the two young saints. They were in a gold reliquary with a glass to show the pieces of bones of the martyrs. "Can you imagine children being killed by adults for not disavowing their faith? The Muslims are most severe about that. No one, absolutely no one, must renounce Islam," Gilbert whispered in Cajetan's ear. After the veneration of the relics, both pilgrims went back to the Porta Speciosa to look more closely at the wide carving of the two martyrs. Then Cajetan stepped back to get a better view of the church.

----Definitely Romanesque, said Cajetan. It's a heavier style with thick walls and narrow windows. But this one is remarkable for its design and execution. I like it.

----Do you like the Romanesque style?

----Yes, I like it but I prefer…

----The Gothic.

They both laughed while the young monk smiled rather naively.

Cajetan and Gilbert spent the night at the Monastery of Leyre and were graciously received by the community. After Matins, they left with precise directions for their next stop in Logroño. They were to take the Corridor of Berdún and Jaca that led directly to Santiago while remaining on the Camino Francès.

Logroño was a good size community with its cathedral, Concatedral de Santa Maria de la Redonda. That's a different title for Blessed Mary, thought Cajetan, Holy Mary of the District. They looked at the huge concave front portal with its carvings, and then, looking up to the sky, they examined the two bell towers. Cajetan thought that these towers added style to this rather plain cathedral. No important relics there, they were told. The two of them went to a small restaurant where they ordered *pinchos* and *tapas*, the specialty of the area. They had not eaten since breakfast at the monastery and they were hungry. They did not usually indulge in restaurant food for they did not want to spend their money carelessly. But, this time, it was a feast for them, a respite from bread, water and occasionally a piece of fruit. Cajetan had to persuade Gilbert to indulge a bit since Gilbert was following the dictates of his self-imposed regimen of penance, fasting, abstinence, prayers and meditation. All of this was fine with Cajetan as long as he wasn't dragged into the severity of the penance. He told himself that he was going to Santiago in the spirit of the pilgrimage which was spiritual development of the soul, but he wasn't doing it out of a need to do penance. It was a joyful journey for him, not a penitential exercise.

That night they spent it at a small inn that had been indicated by their first guide who was following the Codex instructions. They found the inn to be quite rudimentary in its appearance but clean inside. The owner was a woman in her late fifties, and although polite and cautiously reserved, she did not talk much. She answered questions by a "yes" or a "no". When she could not answer with these two words, she simply shrugged her shoulders. There was no breakfast served at the inn the following morning. So, the two pilgrims set out on their way on an empty stomach that, once in a while, growled with hunger pains. Come noontime, since they had neither food or drink in their sacks, they decided to stop at a local market to get some provisions for the next couple of days while assuaging their empty stomachs. They bought some bread, dark and very crusty, some small oranges and two plums that they ate right away. They also purchased some kind of tarts made with local vegetables that they thought would be delicious once on the road. Gilbert also bought two very small fish in observance of the required abstinence. The fish looked scrawny and not too fresh, but he got them anyway for they were cheap, said Gilbert. And, they would get water at the fountain in the middle of the square. That's where they met a very lively couple, a man in his forties and his wife who was not much more than twenty-two.

Maria and José were native of Burgos, the next stop on Cajetan's and Gilbert's itinerary. Burgos was a lively town with very lively people. It also had a fine abbey, the Abbey of Santa Maria la Real de Las Huelgas. It was a monastery of Cistercian nuns. That fact reminded Cajetan of Fontevraud. Maria and José told the two pilgrims that they would bring them to the Abbey and show them the town in the process. They seemed to be very open with their talent for making people feel at ease. Cajetan liked them from the start. Gilbert had some reservations about them. His first impression, he said, was one of concern. He didn't like the way they kept asking personal questions, and the way Maria kept prying, he said.

----What do you mean prying? Gilbert.

----Prying, Cajetan. Always peering into things, and ever touching things like my large pouch where I keep my belongings.

----I don't think she means any harm by that. She's young and vivacious, that's all.

----Still, I do not trust her. Too friendly, I think, overly so. She's looking for something, I tell you.

----Don't be so mistrustful, Gilbert. It's nothing, you'll see.

----Still, beware of her every move, Cajetan.

All four of them talked the greater part of the afternoon, and José offered them some wine to drink. Cajetan took some while Gilbert refused to drink for personal reasons, he said. José and Maria dragged Cajetan to watch a puppet show not too far from where they were sitting. Gilbert did not want to join them. They called him a fun breaker and off they went. About an hour later Cajetan came back his tunic torn and his cloak full of dust. He looked miserable.

----Where is your staff and your large pouch?

----I don't know, Gilbert. I don't know. I feel so drowsy and I feel lost.

----Where are your two friends, José and Maria?

----They took off without my noticing it. Here I was watching the puppet show and fell to the ground. Someone helped me up but it wasn't either one of the two friends.

----Some friends they are. I'll bet you they put something in the wine they gave you. They drugged you and stole from you. I told you about thievery along this journey, for so many thieves are on the lookout for pilgrims like you, gullible and naïve persons. That's precisely what the guide told us before we started the pilgrimage at Vézelay.

----Where's my pouch?

----That's what I asked you, Cajetan.

----They took it then. Everything I had was in that pouch. My food, my rosary, my medals and the sheaf with my Bible readings.

----How about your money?

----That too, but I had very little of it. That's not the important part.

----Let's go back to where you were and we might be able to find something they left behind.

----You think so?

----I know so. Thieves are not interested in Bible sheaves or medals unless they're made of gold.

They went back to the exact spot where Cajetan had been watching the puppet show. They looked around and found nothing in the vicinity. Then a young boy walked up to Cajetan and handed him his pouch. Cajetan was so surprised that he couldn't say anything. The boy told him that he had found it on the small path where he lived, and that his mother told him to bring it back to its owner. He told Cajetan that he remembered seeing him at the puppet show with exactly the same pouch, and that he recognized him immediately because he was the one who had fallen to the ground and had been picked up by Arturo Tambien, a neighbor. Cajetan thanked him and reached in his pouch to find a coin to give the boy but all the money was gone. "See there are still honest people around," he told his friend. "Yes, but a lot of thieves too," replied Gilbert.

Cajetan and Gilbert got to the Abbey of Santa Maria la Real de Las Huelgas the next morning when the sky was covered with clouds and the threat of rain was imminent. They learned that the Abbey was founded by Alfonso VIII of Castile at the behest of his wife Eleanor of England, daughter of Henry II of England and Eleanor of Aquitaine. This queen

Eleanor spread her influence almost everywhere, thought Cajetan. They also learned that the monastery became the burial place of the royal family. Alfonso and his wife created the Royal Hospital with all its dependencies subject to the Abbess. Pretty powerful women these Abbesses, said Cajetan to himself. Later, a community of lay brothers was gradually developing to help the nuns in their care of the hospital patients.

Cajetan and Gilbert were fascinated by the power invested in the Abbess of this monastery. She had royal prerogatives and exercised an unlimited secular authority over more than fifty villages. Some said that she had the same religious power as any bishop did. She was privileged to confirm the Abbesses of other monasteries, to impose censures, and convoke synods. I wonder if she had a hand in the confirmation of Marie Dieudonnée as an Abbess, thought Cajetan when he heard that. Both pilgrims were given permission to visit the royal tombs and the monastery church. A nun by the name of Madre Anna Sueltoro was their guide, and told them about the history of the monastery. At Vespers, they were allowed to walk through the cloister arcade and enjoy some cool drink that the nuns made with citrus fruit. In learning that Cajetan's sister was the Abbess of Fontevraud, the guide told him that the Abbess of Santa Maria la Real might be interested in meeting with him, and that she would talk to the Prioress about it. In the meantime, they were both offered hospitality, not in the monastery, but in the hospital for the night. They both accepted. Early in the morning while having breakfast, Cajetan was informed that the Abbess wanted to see him for a brief encounter. Monastic contacts are very important in getting certain privileges, said Cajetan to Gilbert, and he smiled teasingly.

Cajetan was admitted to the cabinet of the Abbess, and he bowed before her thanking her for the tête-à-tête. She asked several questions about Marie Dieudonnée, and then told him that she had met her once at a synod in Trent. She considered her to be quite intelligent and wise, and that she was truly impressed by her qualities as an Abbess. Cajetan thanked her for the compliments for he admired his sister and above all, he truly loved his sister for her warmth and compassion for people. Before leaving the Abbess, she handed him a small leather pouch, and told him that he might be able to make use of its contents since she had heard that he had been robbed a few days before. He thanked her profusely. He wondered how the Abbess had gotten to know about his being robbed, then it hit him. Me and my big mouth, he said to himself, I remember telling our guide, Madre Anna, about it never thinking she would tell the Abbess about it. Cajetan returned to the cloister where Gilbert was waiting for him, and before he reached the arcade, he opened the pouch and found some gold coins and, to his pleasant surprise, a medal of Saint James. As they were leaving the monastery, Cajetan met this old man outside who handed him a staff with a hook at the top. "The Abbess told me to give you this," he said. "For your sacred journey to Santiago de Compostela."

The next stop for our two pilgrims was León. Cajetan was ecstatic upon hearing that a new cathedral was being built in León. He ran toward the cathedral site and asked to speak to the Master Architect. By chance, the Master Architect was French by the name of Fernand Belfondoro. His mother was French while his father was Spanish. He was born in Paris and studied there until the family moved to Reims. After his journeyman stage, he managed to study under one of the finest, Master Architect, Albert de Chaussoyes. His masterpiece for the title of master was the design of the façade of Saint-Firmin church in lower Flanders under the guidance of Master Architect de Chaussoyes. Cajetan had seen this façade and had admired it greatly. Cajetan was surprised at hearing that Fernand had studied under the same Master Architect that he did. After chatting for quite some time, Fernand Belfondoro gave Cajetan and Gilbert the history of the site, and the plans for this new cathedral which the Bishop, Martin Fernandez de Suenen, had designated as la Catedral de Santa Maria de Regla de León. It was to be in the Flamboyant Gothic style patterned after the Reims cathedral and Notre-Dame d'Amiens, said the Master Architect. The Master Builder by the name of Simón Bonvillar, wanted it that way and this was also the wish of the Bishop who was raising the necessary funds, said Fernand.

----This site is the ancient site of the ruins of Roman baths. It's perfect for the cathedral site.

----Why, Fernand?

----Because we did not have to excavate too deep since much of the excavation was already done. All we had to do was clear the ruins.

----So many cathedrals are built on ancient Roman sites aren't they?

----I know of seven or eight right here in Spain.

----Is the Bishop having a hard time finding the funds?

----No, since the funds come from King Alfonso the Wise himself. He's a great admirer of the Gothic style.

----You are indeed fortunate to have such a generous patron. Nobility helps especially if it happens to be the king.

Fernand explained that there would be two giant towers, one on the right and the other on the left of the cathedral, and that the flying buttresses would be between the main building and the towers, not on the outside where they're usually placed.

----The west façade, as you can see, is made of pale yellow stone. The quarry for the stones is right here in León, and we are very fortunate in having such a beautiful stone. It's our pride and joy. As you can see, we also have a large rose window on this façade. The south transept has three carved portals with a rose window.

----I want to see that.

----Do I see a cloister there? asked Gilbert.

----Why, yes indeed. The cloister adjoins the north transept. I will show you all of this later.

All three of them entered the main building which was in the stages of completion. It had not taken years and years to build it since funds kept flowing in without interruption. The King was indeed generous, remarked Fernand. As they stepped inside, Cajetan was awed by the splendor of light that streamed through the many stained glass windows. There must have been over sixty of them.

----Light is our most precious endeavor in capturing the light of heaven, according to Abbot Suger, said Fernand.

----I agree, said Cajetan. That's the essence of the Gothic.

----In fact, these cathedral windows illuminate a harmonious interior. The cathedral has three aisles, a short transept, a five-bay choir, and an ambulatory with radiating chapels, all bathing in the soft and, I might say, spiritual light that favors harmony of style and sacredness of tone.

----I see that you have ably worked in the architecture the ambience of Gothic splendor.

----As a matter of fact, the pale stone outside in harmony with the dazzling rays of sunlight filtering through the windows inside give the cathedral an amazing brightness, to a point that some call it the House of Light.

----How about the choir stalls?

----We plan to have some carved out of walnut. We're looking for a Master Wood Carver probably French of Flemish. I am told that Flemish wood carvers are truly masters of their trade.

----Don't forget the foliate heads, or don't you believe in them?

----I certainly do, but I'm not sure Bishop Martin Fernandez de Suenen would approve of them in his cathedral. We'll see. But I'll show you one later on. Not well known but a well carved head. Let me show you the side chapel where the statue of our Lady stands.

----Which Lady?

----Our Lady of Expectation, Virgen de la Esperanza. I'll show you.

They went to that side altar off the choir where the statue was, and Fernand explained that it was Our Lady of Expectation since it's about the Virgin expecting the Child Jesus. Many expectant mothers come here to pray, Fernand told them.

----That's an interesting concept, said Gilbert.

Then the three of them went to view the reliquary in yet another side chapel where the relics of Saint Froilán were kept. He was the patron saint of León, explained Fernand. Finally they stepped outdoor in full sunlight and Fernand bid them farewell telling them they should now visit the basilica.

----What basilica, asked Cajetan.

----The Basilica of San Isidoro. Ask for Madre Sancha Gonzales. She's a Benedictine nun, and she'll show you around and explain to you the history of the Basilica and the monastery. She's a good friend of mine.

Cajetan and Gilbert thanked Fernand and walked away. When they arrived at the site of the basilica, they noticed that it was rectangular with a rather flat façade, unlike the churches they had seen before, churches with tall bell towers. They went to the convent and rang the bell. The portress opened the sliding panel in the door and asked who was there, and what they wanted. They asked for Madre Sancha Gonzales at he behest of Fernand Belfondoro. She hesitated at first but then she opened the door and let them in. She asked them to wait, and went to get the nun they had asked for. Within fifteen minutes, a portly woman in her mid-fifties, wearing a black habit and veil, came prancing towards them like a mare who is excited about something, so bouncing was her walk.

----So you are friends with Fernand?

----Well, we just met him, and he showed us around the new cathedral. He's a kind and knowledgeable man, and we made friends with him. He's the one who instructed us to come and meet you, for you're the expert on the basilica.

----I'm no expert but I know something about it.

----How long have you been here in León?

----I was born here. It's a lovely place to be.

----It looks like it would attract people who enjoy life and good food. We've seen many restaurants and inns around town.

----That's because we're on the Pilgrim's Way to Santiago de Compostela. Are you pilgrims?

----Yes, we are, my friend Gilbert and I are indeed pilgrims. My name is Cajetan.

----Yes, Cajetan the Stargazer and builder of cathedrals, added Gilbert.

----Really? Have you built many cathedrals? You're so young. Are you a Master Architect?

----Yes, I am a Master Architect and I haven't built my cathedral yet but I have helped to build four of them, two in France, one in England and one in Flanders.

----My, you are indeed a busy man for your age. You must have earned your station in the trade at an early age.

----Yes, I did.

----And what's this with the Stargazer?

----Like my grandfather on my mother's side, I like to gaze at the stars. I'm a dreamer.

----Well, there's nothing wrong with that. I'm a dreamer too but I dream of strawberry filled tarts as well as delightful and scrumptious *tapas*.

They started to laugh.

----Please tell us about the history of the basilica. It truly interests me as well as my friend, I'm sure.

----The Basilica de San Isidoro is located on the site of an ancient temple dedicated to the Roman god, Mercury. The original church was built in the pre-Arab period over the ruins of the temple. In the 10th century, the kings of León established a community of Benedictine nuns on the site. Following the conquest of the area by Al-Mansur Ibn Aamir , the first church was destroyed and the area devastated. León was repopulated and a new church and monastery established by AlfonsoV of León. The nuns of the original convent had fled and sought refuge in the north where Islam was not as well established. The new church has benefited from its position on the pilgrimage route to Santiago de Compostela. Sculptors, stonemasons and artists from across Europe came here to work on the monastery. I've been here twenty–three years.

----Are you the Abbess?

----God no, I'm too lazy and boisterous to be an abbess.

----What is your role here then?

----I'm the archivist and I sometimes work at the hospital near the cathedral when I'm needed.

----What about Saint Isidoro? asked Gilbert.

----Good question. In 1063, the basilica was rededicated to Saint Isidoro of Seville. Isidoro was Archbishop of Seville, and the most celebrated academic and theologian of Visigoth Spain in the period preceding the Arab invasion. That was a terrible time, I was told. Then, with the agreement of Abbad II al-Mu'tadid, the Muslim ruler of Seville, Isidoro's relics were brought to León where they could be interred on Christian soil. The tomb of the saint draws many pilgrims.

----What about the basilica itself,? asked Cajetan.

----It's built mostly in the Romanesque style, as you can see. You're the Master Architect, I don't need to tell you that. The basilica has had major additions including some Gothic renovations. The arches on the crossing of the transept go back to Islamic art. However, I am told that over all, it's a harmonious whole.

They then proceeded to walk toward the basilica and stood facing the central tympanum.

----This is the carved tympanum of the Puerta del Cordero, and it's one of the basilica's most notable features, I am told.

----It's a Romanesque tympanum. What are the carvings about?

----It depicts the sacrifice of Abraham.

----Oh, I see now.

They then entered the basilica, and surveyed all of its interior features. Madre Sancha Gonzales brought them to the funeral chapel where the kings of León were buried.

----Look at those columns! shouted Cajetan.

----These columns are crowned with rare Visigothic capitals with floral or historic designs. You know that the Muslim did not depict in art any gods or human figures. They had no gods like the Romans, only one, Allah, never illustrated or sculpted. You must look at the painted murals. They consist of an ensemble of New Testament subjects.

----Why, yes, said Gilbert. Here's Jesus with Peter and another showing the Transfiguration.

When the tour was completed, Madre Sancha left them at the door of the basilica, and told them to enjoy the rest of their journey. Before they left her, she cautioned them about thieves along the pilgrim's route. Cajetan told her that he knew that since he had been robbed. She asked them if they had food for the rest of the journey, and they did not want to express their lack of food. They just stood there silent. She realized that they were in need of provisions. She asked the portress to go and fetch some food, and gave it to the two pilgrims. They thanked her and Cajetan wanted to give her one of his coins, but she refused. "For the glory of God and Saint Benedict," she told them.

As they were stepping out onto the square where the cobblestones were not as level as they ought to be, Gilbert tripped on one of them and fell to the ground with cries of pain coming out of him. Cajetan rushed to his aid and tried to help him, but the pain was so intense that Gilbert did not want Cajetan to touch him.

----But I have to try and help you, Gilbert.

----It's my arm. It hurts so much. I think I may have broken it.

----I'll try to find a hospital for you. I remember Fernand mentioning one near the cathedral with Hospitalers of Saint Benedict serving the sick.

Cajetan ran as fast as he could while onlookers were asking if they could help. Gilbert just lay there in pain. About a half hour later, Cajetan came back with two men who helped Gilbert on to a canvas stretched by two horizontal poles at either end. They did so with agility so that they did not worsen Gilbert's pain in his right arm. Already his arm was swollen and turning blue. They carried him as fast as they could with Cajetan at their heels huffing and puffing. When they arrived at the hospital, they brought Gilbert to a large room where someone dressed in a long white tunic was waiting for him. He told Gilbert that he was an Hospitaler and that he had much experience in broken bones since it was all too clear that Gilbert's arm was indeed broken. The Hospitaler looked at a chart hanging on the wall and located the arm and pointed to the humerus where the break was. He slowly touched the arm and rotated it until he could feel the break, and held it tightly in his two hands. He said that he now had the break together and that the two pieces of bones were back to where they belonged. He then bandaged tightly the break so that it could not move, and told Gilbert that it was a simple fracture and not a compound one, or else he would have had to go inside his flesh to put the bones together. For that, Gilbert was so grateful. The Hospitaler then put the right arm in a cloth sling around Gilbert's neck, and told him to keep it in the sling for several weeks until he did not feel the pain anymore. Of course, it could take months too. It depended on the mending of the bones and how responsive was Gilbert's system to injury. He then told Gilbert that the pain would not subside fast, and that he would spend several nights in pain, but that he would give him something for it.

----I have studied with the grandson of a Muslim physician who followed Avicenna's theories of medicine, and I have learned a lot from him. Christians, as a whole, do not necessarily have faith in Avicenna's theories. They think that he's not of our theology of caring and healing. But I trust in him and follow his way of treating illness and pain. I'm going to give you some herbs that he prescribed. Put some in boiling water tonight and drink some of it. It will lessen the pain. Continue to do so for several days. Eat some eggs and drink milk, if you can. Stay healthy, and do not overdo it on your pilgrimage. Say some prayers for your healing. That helps too.

Gilbert got up and tended to favor his broken arm. Cajetan helped him. Before leaving, Cajetan took a coin that the Abbess had given him and gave it to the Hospitaler. The Hospitaler told him that he had done it out of charity and that it cost nothing. "Take it anyway. Do some good with it," said Cajetan.

Both Gilbert and Cajetan were invited to stay for at least one night at the monastery near the hospital. They did so with relief, for they had no place to go. There were inns in the vicinity but rooms at the inns were expensive, especially when it came to welcoming pilgrims. Both men stayed two more nights at the monastery since Gilbert was still suffering pain in his right arm, and could barely move it. On the fourth day, they were able to leave León and be on their way to Astorga, their next stop before reaching Santiago de Compostela.

It seemed that every day, Gilbert gained strength in his right arm although he kept it in his sling. He was careful walking, especially on cobblestones. That's when Cajetan supported him in order to make sure he did not fall again. They stopped for a break along the way, and had some nourishment and water from a local fountain where they found that the water was called "Agua della Madre." Someone told them that it had miraculous qualities for whoever used it or drank it for they would receive favors form the Mother of God who had herself blessed this water while travelling through the small village. "But why was she traveling through here?" asked Gilbert less credulous than his companion. The reply, "No one knows why but we do know that the water is miraculous." Gilbert told Cajetan that many superstitions were fabricated around the Virgin Mary and her intercession by poor peasant folk. "They need some small miracles in their hardships and toil since they are drenched in what I would call, faith-filled gullibility." Before leaving the fountain, Gilbert took off his sling and placed his right arm in the water for a few moments. Then he put on his sling and walked off telling Cajetan, "Just in case."

Astorga was a village with a Celtic background, the two pilgrims found out. Then it became a Roman stronghold, and the bath ruins were still visible to this day, they were told. Although Christian now, the village had no cathedral. It had one relic, that of Saint Turibius, Bishop of Astorga in the fifth century. "There's nothing much to this village," said Gilbert to Cajetan. So they set off toward their final destination filled with anxious moments of joy and anticipation. That evening, as they were sitting down at the brow of a small forest right outside of Astorga, Cajetan told Gilbert that it was time to recite the **Benedicite**. He took out his retrieved sheaf and started reading reverently: *Benedicite, omnia opera Domini, laudate et superexaltate eum in saecula/* Bless the Lord all you works of the Lord; sing his praise and exalt him forever. "I'm going to recite one part every night until I've done them all. Will you join me, Gilbert?"

The following morning, the two pilgrims had their breakfast on the grass as they watched the sunrise. The rays of the sun filtered through the branches of the trees, and the rustle of the leaves seemed to whisper soft melodic strains that Gilbert said reminded him of Saint Sulpice.

----How long were you there, Gilbert?

----Three years.

----Was it a good experience for you?

----Yes and no. I learned a lot but I could not stand the rector. He was so imperious and demanding. Never a kind word from him. He said that he was of the nobility but he could not prove his claim. He was a constant liar, that's what I think. I can't stand lies and hypocrisy. I'm a bit like Christ of the gospels. How he disliked those Scribes and Pharisees.

----You're a good person, Gilbert, a good soul.

----No yet, Cajetan. I have not been purified yet. My penance endures.

----Will it not end some day?

----I do not know, my friend. I do not know.

With that both men resumed their journey, a long time in silence.

Cajetan and Gilbert stopped after three hours of walking for the sun was reaching its apogee in the milky sky. When they got to about half way to Santiago, Cajetan exclaimed, "How great are Thou, God of mercy and might. How great is your creation. Please give me the light that I need on this pilgrimage to see more clearly your gifts and talents that you have bestowed upon me. Please Lord, show me the way to the plans and design of my cathedral, for without your wisdom and strength, I am nothing, see nothing and can conceive of nothing. I am nothing but clay. Helpless in the night of my searching mind." Gilbert stood there motionless for he was stunned at Cajetan's sudden exclamation of prayer.

----I've failed, Gilbert. I am a failure. I don't have any well-thought out designs or plans in my mind for my cathedral. Even my imagination has become sterile. I thought I had it all stored in my mind but there's nothing there. Not anymore. For the first time in my life, I'm a failure as an architect. I've failed. God help me, I've failed.

Cajetan looked sullen and defeated.

----You're not a failure, Cajetan. You are going to build that cathedral, for it is your magnificent obsession. It grew out of your passion to create, and it will not die. Believe me. You need to go back at star gazing and find your plans and design that you so crave for. Dreamer of dreams do not stop dreaming. That's why you came on this pilgrimage, isn't it? To find yourself and your dream that someday you will build a cathedral.

----I suppose so.

----You suppose so? I know so.

----Thank you for believing in me, Gilbert.

It was a very long trek from Astorga to Santiago de Compostela. The two pilgrims met several other pilgrims heading that way. Everyone seemed exhausted but they all appeared to be determined to reach their goal, the Cathedral of Saint James and its relics of the saint. The evening just before reaching their destination, Cajetan and Gilbert slept under the stars. It was a dark sky but one full of stars as if the heavens had opened it's gates to let all of the stars shine with fervor, including those not very often seen. Cajetan lay there not thinking but dreaming his usual self. Star gazing seemed to be so natural for him, inherited perhaps. Just gazing at myriads of stars gave him the courage to dream, dream of his mother, his father, and others who had preceded him into the great beyond of the stars. Designs started jumping in his head, and his imagination began to embroider them like lace on a white cloth. He wanted to hold on to them and never let go. After the design came the plans, he told himself. Thank God he had started dreaming again, the way he had always done before he hit a dry spell. The curse of losing confidence in himself and his talent as an architect seemed to be over and done with. Totally dissipated like brush in the wind. All he needed, he told himself, was to come face to face with the Cathedral of Saint James, and he would know. He would know what design he would cling to. All architecture is a borrowing, he said to himself. We all borrow from our predecessors somehow. Nothing is perfectly new in all of creation. Man creates from templates already there. He does his creative work by building upon those templates. Enlarging them, reworking them and putting ideas together that come out as a new way of seeing things. We all stand on the shoulders of giants, he told himself. I've seen that in one of the windows of Chartres Cathedral, he mused. Then Cajetan fell asleep, a deep and restful sleep. Gilbert was already snoring.

Early the next morning, Cajetan awoke and reached for his sheaf, The **Benedicite** : *Benedicite, caeli, Domino, benedicite, angeli Domini, Domino/* Blessed the Lord you heavens, bless the Lord you angels of the Lord. After a very brief breakfast, the two pilgrims set out to encounter the much acclaimed cathedral at the end of their journey.

As they entered the great square in front of the imposing Cathedral of Saint James, Cajetan and Gilbert were amazed at the majesty of the cathedral standing there tall and glorious singing the praises of the Lord in its jubilation of Romanesque architecture, the finest that Cajetan had ever seen. He had studied its history, and Cajetan knew that the construction of the cathedral was started in 1075 under the reign of Alfonso VI of Castile, and the patronage of Bishop Diego Piláez. It was built according to the same plan as the monastic brick church of Saint Sernin in Toulouse, probably the greatest Romanesque edifice in France then. Cajetan had seen it, and agreed that it was splendid in the imitation of its model. The cathedral was consecrated in 1128 in the presence of king Alfonso IX of León. What interested most Cajetan were the names of the architects according to the *Codex Calixtinus* that he had seen: Bernard the elder, his assistant Robertus Galperinus, later possibly Esteban, Master of the cathedral works. Bernard the younger was the one who finished the building. Cajetan had heard of one of them, Bernard the elder, a wonderful master according to Master de Chaussoyes.

Cajetan explained to Gilbert that at the northern façade there ends the Way of Saint James, coming from France, as they did, ending at the Francigena or the Gate of Paradise, the Romanesque portal built by Bernard, treasurer of he church. Going to the southern façade, they encountered a guide who told them that this square was confined on two sides by the cathedral and a monastery. The *Porta das Prateirias* is the portal that leads to the south transept, he told them. The two-arched portal shows us the fine works of sculptors who came from Conques in the French Pyrenees, Toulouse, Moissac, Losarre and Jaca resulting in a harmonious whole, said the guide. A happy joyous synthesis of their artistic traditions, he added.

Then the guide took Cajetan and Gilbert along with some other pilgrims inside the cathedral. "Notice the barrel-vaulted cruciform Romanesque design here." Cajetan knew exactly what the guide was talking about. "It may give an impression of austerity but, overall, the church is a splendid example of strength, endurance and durability," stated the guide with authority. "Just what I need," mumbled Gilbert. Then the guide took them along with other pilgrims to the portico behind the western façade.

----Perhaps the main beauty of the cathedral, is the *Portico da Gloria* that you see right here. It's a masterpiece of Romanesque sculpture by Master Mateo, a great artist. The central tympanum gives us an image of Christ in Majesty as Judge and Redeemer, you will notice.The column statues represent the Apostles with their attributes, along with Prophets and Old Testament figures. Noteworthy is the faint smile of the Prophet Daniel looking at the angel of Reims.

Just then Cajetan had a large smile on his face in consonance with the Prophet and the Angel of the Smile that he had seen several years ago while working on the Reims cathedral.

----What are you smiling for? asked Gilbert.

----I'll tell you later.

----The middle pier, continued the guide, represents Saint James in all serenity. It is customary for pilgrims like you to touch the left foot of the statue signifying they have reached their destination. Would you like to do it now?

They all rushed to comply with the tradition.

----Behind the portico stands the statue of Maestro Mateo, Master Architect and Sculptor in charge of the cathedral building program. It is said that whoever butts his head three times against the statue will be given a portion of Mateo's genius, and perhaps enhanced memory. I did it four times, and I'm just as dumb as ever.

Cajetan stepped up to the statue and butted his head saying, "Please give me the genius necessary to build my cathedral," followed by Gilbert who whispered to Cajetan,"I'm a hopeless cause, but I'll try anything."

The guide showed them the nave then the choir with three bays surrounded with an ambulatory with five radiating chapels. Then Gilbert asked the guide, "Where are the relics of Saint James?" "Under the main altar," replied the guide. "I'll show you." They all followed the guide, and standing in front of the large altar, the guide told them that the relics were so precious that they had to be placed somewhere secure. "Besides," he told them, "the main altar is the site of burial for the Apostle Saint." They both thanked the guide for his instructions. "Wait," said the guide, "there's more. It is said that the remains of Duke William X are also buried here before the high altar and next to the shrine of Saint James. He was the father of Eleanor of Aquitaine. It is said that he died here in the cathedral of Compostela after receiving communion. He had undertaken a pilgrimage to Santiago de Compostela to seek forgiveness of his sins and to pray for God's help against his enemies."

Cajetan and Gilbert found this revelation by the guide to be most interesting. Eleanor of Aquitaine had become a well-known figure in the history of France and England and to know that her father had died in this cathedral was truly revealing as far as history goes. Mortality deals her blow to everyone, rich or poor, king or peasant, thought Cajetan as he stood in front of the main altar and then kneeled to venerate the sacred relics of Saint James. He uttered several prayers, one for the repose of the souls of his parents, one for his sister, Marie Dieudonnée and another for his brother Abélard François wherever he may be, and one for his own family, wife and children. Finally, he said one, a long prayer, for himself without mentioning the cathedral. He was hoping that Saint James would not overlook his dream, Cajetan's dream, the Stargazer. Then he got up and followed Gilbert out of the western portal, and onto the main square.

Once outside, the two of them went to a small open market to get some food. They bought garnacha grapes, Cadanera oranges and figs from Seville. Also, some cheese and small loaves of hearty bread. Cajetan wanted something exquisite for himself, and so he purchased some local wine that tasted like smooth fermented oranges. Then the two of them took the northern route, el Camino del Norte, because the porter at the monastery where they spent their last night advised them to take the northern route. Fewer Muslims and fewer chances of getting robbed, he told them. "There are fewer pilgrims on that route, and so the prices at the inns along the way are more reasonable," he told them. He also advised them to spend some time on the bay called *El Mar del los Vascos* or, at least, on its shore where fresh breezes alleviate the heat of the sun. "Most of all," he told them, "the route is not crowded, and the pace much more relaxed. You won't be so tired when you get home," he added. "Besides," he told them, "this is early December, and you will not have to be in the gloom of June when the large fog triangle fills the southwestern half of the bay." They listened to him and took the northern route. They were told that there were far fewer villages along that route, and that provisions had to be bought well in advance. That's the reason why they stopped at the Market of Plenty, El Mercado della Abundancia, to buy extra provisions for the road.

The first night, they stopped at a very small village where there were but some twenty people living there, all fishermen. They looked like hardy, tenacious men with leathery skin for having spent so much time in the sun out at sea. Their wives were also bronzed and had the skin of some lizard, and they wore bright colored bandanas around their necks to add color to their appearance. One of the fishermen's wives hailed the two pilgrims and offered them shelter for the night in her small granary where they stored some grain and hay for their two horses. The fisherman and his wife liked to prance along the shore of the bay and even do some racing with the horses. Quite often, they were told, the wife would win the race. Thus, Cajetan and Gilbert spent the night in the granary with the horses. They slept on the hay and found it quite comfortable. They were so tired that they did not mind the sometimes neighing of the horses. In the morning, the wife served them grilled fish, very dark bread and some sour wine. They paid her and took off once more on the road. It was a little later that Cajetan noticed that his cloak had been cut. Someone had cut a large piece of cloth from his cloak without his noticing it. It must have been the fisherman's wife, he thought. But why? "Oh, well," he said to Gilbert, "it's warm and I don't need a cloak. I only use it to sleep on. Come to think of it, I left it on the stool where I was sitting last night and I did not see the loss when I retrieved it this morning until now. Well, I'll be!"

When they got to Santander, they were both very tired. It had been a long distance and they had not stopped but twice on the road going to sleep early in the evening and rising very early in the morning. Cajetan and Gilbert did not find Santander very interesting and, besides, they were in a hurry to return home. Gilbert told Cajetan that he felt that his penance was now accomplished nearing the end of the pilgrimage. His prayers to Saint James had been answered, he told him. Cajetan was very happy for his companion, and he told him so. On the other hand, Cajetan revealed to his friend and companion of the road that he was ready to take on the challenge of the building of his cathedral since he had found both at the León Cathedral and at the Saint James Cathedral the building blocks for his Gothic building. These two Romanesque cathedrals would be the giant shoulders on which his cathedral would stand. He could build on the past while being creative. All he had to do was to take the leap of light, as Abbot Suger had done. He insisted on light, that glorious light that permeates every aisle, every radiating chapel and every inch of a Gothic cathedral. He told Gilbert that he too was grateful to the Lord for his mercy and inspiration.

That evening, while standing on the shore in a small village near San Sebastian, Cajetan recited yet other parts of the **Benedicite**: *Benedicite, sol et luna, Domino, benedicite, stellae caeli, Domino; Benedicite, lux et tenebrae, Domino, benedicite, fulgura et nubes, Domino*/Bless the Lord sun and moon; bless the Lord you stars of heaven; Bless the Lord light and darkness, sing his praise and exalt him forever.

Now they were both ready to face a new dawn, a new challenge that would reenergize them and give them the courage to face head on their calling, one as architect and the other as artist. One as star gazer and the other as catcher of stars. When they crossed the border into France, they were indeed ready, and if there was a miracle that happened on their pilgrimage, it was the miracle of readiness, that readiness that draws its power from inner strength found anew in the furrows of oneself.

13

REVISITING THE FOLIATE HEAD

Cajetan had promised himself that he would not let the foliate head escape him, but that he would pursue it in every cathedral where this phenomenon had been placed. Cajetan called it a phenomenon because it had no real name nor did it have a *raison d'être*. It just was. Who had put it there? Which sculptor had the audacity to place it in a Christian sacred place? Or was it Christian in substance but not in appearance? Was it a symbol of synchronization, as Master Sculptor Harand Millefois had said? What exactly was it all about? Such questions swam in Cajetan's head and never left him. He had to find some answers since he was determined to put foliate heads in his cathedral. But, of course, he had to find the right sculptor too.

After Cajetan left Gilbert in Vézelay, he went back to Flanders to tell Wandal about his pilgrimage and how he had found, at last, the creative strength and energy to conceive the design and plans for his cathedral. Now, he had to find a site, and above all, a sponsor-bishop or better an archbishop. But, first of all, he had to finish his project of locating and assessing the foliate head. It had become an obsession with him. He didn't know why, but he had to. It was now flowing in his veins like a torrent of lava. It was a burning issue for Cajetan. Besides, he had had long conversations about the foliate head with Wandal, and she encouraged him to satisfy this want, this need within him. She knew that he would not be able to seriously concentrate on the design and plans of his cathedral without first fulfilling this craving that haunted him. Like a worm that gnaws on one's mind, the foliate head was ever gnawing inside his imagination, churning and churning things around until he could visualize all kinds of sculptures that represented the head of leaves with eyes peering through the apertures. He had seen some but now he wanted to explore the entire field of foliate heads. "Satisfy your craving, my husband, and we'll see what comes of it. Maybe you'll discover some never seen before by others. They crop up almost everywhere, you know." "I know," said Cajetan, "but will I come up empty with just the few that I have already seen?" "You might be greatly surprised." " I know that my cathedral project is not based on foliate heads, and some may think that I'm dreaming again, but that's part of my being creative and I must satisfy this need that's in me." "That's why people call you Cajetan the Stargazer."

After six weeks at home with his family, Cajetan said goodbye once more, and departed for his next location, Chartres. He knew where the foliate heads were placed at Chartres. He had seen them but had not really examined them. Now, he was going to spend some time studying these sculptures that seemed strange at first but, at the same time, appealing to the eye, and especially to the imagination. Cajetan liked that. On his way there, he took out his sheaf and said another part of the **Benedicite**. His heart was filled with gratitude that morning, gratitude for being able to explore the many niches of, not only his craft, but of his thriving imagination. *Benedicite, omnis imber et ros, Domino, benedicite, venti, Domino/* Bless the Lord all winds that blow; bless the Lord you fire and heat. It was late January and the winds from the north were blowing wildly that day.

Cajetan reached his destination in France five days after he set forth from Zelzate. It was now mid-February and the sky was of the deepest blue with puffy clouds here and there. Cajetan could not help looking upwards and compare the vast blueness of the heavens with Gothic space that he had experienced before, especially in the Amiens cathedral. He wanted to recapture that feeling of floating in space by simply closing his eyes and pretending he was walking from the western portal of the cathedral all the way down the nave up and through the choir facing the apse, but not with his eyes shut but wide open, and with his head held high while staring at the vast vaulted ceiling. It was indeed a feeling of floating on air. It made the head spin and the eyes dilated much like star gazing. When he got to the cathedral in Chartres, he immediately went to the south transept portal where he found the three foliate heads he remembered seeing when he was there years before.

They were so evident and so well defined. It was a threesome type of sculpture. The one on the left had the branches, leaves and clusters of grapes of the vine, while the one on the right disgorged on either side of its mouth sturdy oak branches with acorns. In the middle stood a large face with broad forehead and wide open eyes with closed mouth, and the entire head issuing the acanthus leaf, especially coming down its cheeks like large lilting leaves hanging down. Three foliate heads as a triptych of human figures enmeshed in the vegetation of the local area of Chartres. What a marvelous idea to mark this cathedral with the sign of generative impulses of God's creation, thought Cajetan as he stood there mesmerized by what he was looking at.

Cajetan must have stayed there for close to an hour when someone tugged at his sleeve. It was an old woman with her outstretched arm and opened right hand begging for coins. He looked at her, then looked at her wrinkled face and teary eyes before he dug deep into his pouch and, at that very moment, he thought of his mother, Grisoulda asking for food. Cajetan immediately put two coins in the woman's hand and told her to spend it wisely on food for herself. She replied, "It's not for me, it's for my two grandchildren who are starving. I'm just trying to come to their assistance so that they can have a piece of bread in their stomachs. At least for today; tomorrow will bring its own cares and worries. All my life I struggled and fought the pains of going hungry. My husband left me when I was still young. He left me with three children, and later two of them died. The other one left and went somewhere, I don't know where. I was left with two grandchildren because their mother abandoned them. Gone away. So you see, I'm a desperate but caring woman. Unlike Job, I did not regain any family nor riches. I am a poor woman, and that's why I have to beg. Believe me, it's not a sin to beg although I am often ashamed of myself like pangs of remorse that stab at the heart."

----No, no, woman, there's nothing to be ashamed of. I admire you for what you must do.

He put his hand into his pouch again and drew out two more coins and gave them to her. She kissed his hand, turned around and asked him,

----Why are you looking up at those faces?

----They're foliate heads.

----They may be heads with leaves for you but they're devils for me.

----Why?

----That's what our priest says.

----Do you believe everything your priest says?

----Yes, don't you? If I didn't trust him I'd be damned. Don't you know that?

----That's a strong statement, woman.

----I'm an ignorant peasant woman, and I trust those in charge and those who tell us how to attain salvation as the Good Lord promised us.

----Don't you think that you've already reached that by your suffering and good deeds with your family?

----No, for our pilgrimage here on earth never ends, you know. We must continually fight the devil so that he must not win and pull souls into hell. Didn't you see that on the cathedral? It's right there in stone.

215

----But there are good souls and those deserving of hell. You're one of the good souls.

----What makes you say that?

----Because I sense you are a good soul and you have good thoughts.

----What makes you think I'm not lying to you and that I'll spend your money on myself, and that I have no grandchildren?

----Because I trust you on the soul of my own mother who was a good soul herself.

----What was her name?

----Honest Grisoulda.

----That's a nice name. Just the same don't trust anyone these days. You never know.

----I trust you and I trust your two grandchildren will eat tonight.

----You must be a dreamer.

----Yes, I am.

----What do you do in life?

----I am an architect. I build cathedrals.

----That's a big job. Do you build them or plan them?

----I design and plan them. The other craftsmen actually do the work.

----And the laborers? The ordinary people, don't they do the work too?

----Yes, indeed but without the craftsmen, like the stone masons, the sculptors, the stone cutters, the carpenters and the roofers, there would not be any cathedrals.

----I know, but without the common, ordinary workers, nothing would be done since they put in a lot of themselves into their work, don't they? They help the craftsmen deliver what these people create, don't they?

----I suppose so.

----You suppose so?

----You're right, without them, I as an architect would be lost. I can create, I can plan, I can design and all of the craftsmen can do what they're good at, but without the workers and laborers, nothing would get done.

----Remember that when you build your cathedral. One more thing. Are you going to put some of those faces with leaves on your cathedral? Like those up there?

She pointed to the three foliate heads of the south portal.

----Yes, of course. They're beautiful. They represent art and creativity.

----I don't know too much about that. I told you, I'm just an ignorant peasant woman. What is beautiful for me is when I'm not sad or hungry, and when my grandchildren are not starving because I no longer have food to give them. That's beautiful for me. Not those devils up here.

----They're not devils. Don't you see the vine branches with the clusters of grapes? That's part of the natural beauty with which we interact every day. That's part of us. We get wine from grapes. And the oak leaves and the acorns, that's part of our daily lives too. That's our natural surroundings. That's where we live and breathe, work and play. Don't you see that?

----You like to talk a lot don't you? You see what you see and I see what I see. I see devils in those faces with leaves.

----Are there many people who think like you?

----I know of some. I'm the only one who dares talk about it though. *Je n'ai pas la langue dans ma poche*, she told him, I don't keep my tongue in my pocket. There are many poor people like me. There are even some in the stories in the stone sculptures that I've seen. Look around you. Look at the churches that have the stone sculptures, and you'll see poor people of olden times. We've always existed. Take for instance, the story of Lazarus and the rich man. Not the Lazarus who died and was brought back to life, but the beggar, the poor Lazarus who died of starvation and went to the bosom of our beloved Abraham. He's one of us. That's one you should put on your cathedral, not just kings, queens, knights and those crazy faces of devils with leaves sprouting everywhere.

----How about angels?

----Angels are fine. I like angels. They bring me comfort when I feel lonely. I look at them and I feel I can fly on their wings.

----I like angels too. You know your Bible quite well.

----I don't read books and what is written down. I can't read. But I do read the Bible stories of the stone sculptures on cathedrals once they're explained to me. I'm poor but I'm not dumb.

----What's your favorite story?

----I have several but the one I really like is the story of David and Goliath. You know, the little boy with his sling and he kills the giant monster Goliath with a pebble. Can you imagine that! A small stone right in the middle of his two eyes. It's about time that little people defeat big people like Goliath. We're always at the mercy of big people, you know.

----Are you at the mercy of big people?

----I sure am. The village master is a big man, and he takes whatever he wants from poor people like me just because he has power. The power to crush the poor.

----Don't you have someone to defend you?

----No one. Since we're not nobility, we have no knights to fight our battles. We struggle and we lose all the time. We have to be satisfied with what we have. Some have good fortune and some, bad fortune. The wheel goes round and round, and we don't know where it will stop, good or bad. I always seem to have the bad stops.

----Surely there are times you have some good fortune.

----I guess I'm just a lost sheep. I'm still waiting for the Good Shepherd to find me.

----Don't lose hope, woman. There may be devils out there but remember there are also angels.

----Yes, angels like you, kind man, dreamer of dreams.

When the old woman left Cajetan standing under the triptych of foliate heads, he wondered why things were the way they were. Why couldn't the Good Lord arrange things better? he asked himself. "Oh, well, I can't change things, and He has too many things to fix like the poor in this land," mused Cajetan. "Lord, where will my new cathedral be? I need a site and a bishop. Who's going to give me that? God or good Fortune?" he said out loud. " Probably a little of each."

The next cathedral that Cajetan visited was Saint-Étienne of Auxerre. He remembered that the foliate heads were above head high in the ambulatory, and that one of them had angry eyes and pouting lips. At least, that's what they appeared to be, as much as he could remember. He went through one of the three doorways and walked inside where some people were standing looking up at the vaulted ceiling. He went down the ambulatory and there it was, the *feuillu* with big clusters of leaves entirely covering its face and head with only the eyes and the lips as recognizable human features. The big bulging eyes stare at you while the pouting lips seem to express disdain or, in the least, dissatisfaction of sorts. Cajetan looked up at this head of leaves and examined its structure. Bushy leaves jutting from the head covering it like a headful of hair with three fronds of threefold stems, one jutting up from the bridge of its nose and the other two sprouting from either side of the nose. Cajetan noticed that this was a leaf mask and not a disgorger of vegetation. Nothing coming out of its mouth, its eyes, its nose. Beautifully crafted foliate head, thought Cajetan.

Next came another foliate head, this time a smaller head with the same large eyes but with closed lips indicating no feelings of dissatisfaction or disdain. Huge thrusts of leaves emanate from its forehead and chin, jutting on either side with a leafy mustache going up on both sides of the face. A good complement to the other foliate head, mused Cajetan. One particular sculpted head that interested Cajetan was that of the king's head, or some member of the nobility wearing a crown made of what appeared to be large clover leaves. What truly fascinated him was the long mustache made up of flowing leaves on either side of his mouth. The mustache grows out of the middle part of his lips and forms a heart-shape downward curve while the rest of it juts out towards the ears. Very impressive, thought Cajetan, and very noble looking. It's a majestic head. Why, he told himself, there are leaves, grapes and fruits from trees all over these corbels that hold the heads. A very leafy borrowing from nature, he thought.

Cajetan went from head to head, and there were many in the ambulatory, Prophets with their cone-shape hats, sibyls, those prophetesses sort of fortunetellers, and lovely ladies of the court whose heads had been sculpted by a very creative craftsman. He was exploring every nook and cranny to uncover whatever the Master Sculptor might have done but hidden somewhere. He craned and stretched his neck, he stooped, he crawled and he even did contortions to get at whatever was there. Suddenly, he looked under one of the heads, and crouching down, he noticed that there were not only leaves but the presence of what looked like a large button there. He could not distinguish any features from the front but, as he turned, he slowly realized that there was something there. He took a candle out of his pouch, lit it to better see what was underneath the head of the lady sculpted and there, he saw what seemed to be another head. When he turned around, he could now see clearly the bold face of a man surrounded by leaves. He was not disgorging any but he had what seemed like two big teeth on either side of his open mouth. It almost looked like a death mask. What was that doing under there? Was it something to make fun of people or play a game of foliate heads? What was it? There were many questions that Cajetan was left with that afternoon in Auxerre.

From Auxerre Cajetan went to Dijon. He had heard of the foliate head in the vaulting boss in Dijon, and he wanted to take a look at it. He did not want to leave any stone unturned when it came to foliate heads. What he saw was a large foliate head as a vault boss at the Chapelle de Bauffremont attached to the Abbey Saint-Bénigne. What he stared at was a round circle of vine leaves with grapes surrounding the face of a man with eyes softly staring directly at the one who views him. He has a closed mouth. From the lower lip stemmed two branches on either side of the mouth from which sprung the golden leaves. It was as if the sun or the moon was encircled with leaves, and looking down on the earth. Cajetan thought it was worth the trip to Dijon just to see this masterpiece. There was a wooden staging right under the ceiling that Cajetan climbed to get a better view of the ceiling boss where the foliate head had been placed. They were apparently repairing some stone work. The face he was looking at was a serene face, nothing devilish or monstrous about that face, he told himself. This foliate head is in full harmony with its surroundings of vines and vineyards, he mused. So, the foliate head can be harmonious and pleasing to the eye as a work of sculptural beauty, he muttered.

Bourges and its cathedral was Cajetan's next stop. He had stopped at a local inn to get a bed for the night, and had eaten some supper. He planned to go to the cathedral the following morning. That evening, wanting to relax a bit, he went to the local tavern and drank some hearty ale in large tankards. There he met several men who were having a good time telling stories and laughing. One of the men, Paupistord, was his name, told Cajetan that what was going around were peasant tales called *fabliaux*. Just to make people laugh at themselves, he told him. They're down-to-earth tales, and sometimes a bit *piquantes* or *grivoises*, he said, but people love them for their salty flavor . The one that was going around was the tale of a cleric who was sleeping with the cooper's wife thus making the naïve and stupid husband a cuckold.

----Do you know such tales, Cajetan? asked Paupistord.

----No. I've heard some before but I don't remember them.

----Don't you ever have fun, mon ami? What do you do for a living?

Cajetan hesitated at first and then he said,

----I build cathedrals.

----You build cathedrals? Alone , all by yourself?

The other men started laughing.

----Of course not. I'm a Master Architect and I design and do the planning for cathedrals.

----You're not here to build a cathedral in Dijon, are you? They're in the process of finishing one where Saint-Benigne was. Big fire, terrible fire destroyed the Abbey chapel.

----No, I'm here looking at foliate heads here and in other parts of the land.

----Are you finding any?

----Yes, I have an entire itinerary of foliate heads that I'm pursuing.

----That's all you do, running after heads of leaves?

Laughter again on the part of all in the tavern.

----What are they laughing at? Foliate heads are masterpieces of sculpture. They're intricate and fascinating.

----Intri... what?

----Intricate. They're made very well and with care.

----Whatever you say, Master Architect. You use intracost, intricost, whatever, complicated words, and you must be an educated man.

----Somewhat.

----What do you mean somewhat?

----I mean that I did not study very long in a monastery school, What I learned, I learned through experience with other masters of the trades.

----Experience is good, my friend. Experience at work, experience at the market and experience in bed.

Laughter again, this time very loud and even boisterous.

----I know what you mean and I enjoy your laughter. I'm not that stupid.

----Aren't you a bit stupid running around for foliate heads? They're grotesque, at least the ones that I saw. I did not see them on cathedrals but outside on public buildings or even in parks. I guess they're everywhere. Strange things they are. I suppose they'll start naming taverns Foliate Head Taverns some day. That would be quite the thing.

----I'm only looking for those in churches or abbeys. As for being stupid about them, well, I leave that to you. You can call me a dreamer for I dream of building a cathedral, and I will include some foliate heads in it since I think they're really works of creativity.

----Works of what, Master? And Paupistord bowed to Cajetan.

----C-r-e-a-t-i-v-i-t-y, Paupistord, but I suppose you would not know what that means.

----It means doing things out of your imagination, hollered one man sitting at a table with three other men.

----Shut up, Tammarin, what do you know about imagination?

----Well, *fabliaux* for instance, that's imagination.

----Yes, imagination based on everyday real life, added Cajetan.

Everyone in the tavern laughed but this time with a gentleness that had not been there before.

Cajetan went to the cathedral anticipating looking at a foliate head that was intricate and fascinating, and he saw one on the southernmost portal of the west front of the cathedral. It was a smaller version of the foliate head but it had all of the splendor of one. It was a kinder, younger and less leafy foliate head. It had full lips with a branch sprouting from the bridge of its nose to the forehead in a fan of leaves covering the entire top of the head. The other two branches descended down on both sides of the face to cover the lower part of the cheeks. Then from the chin there was a long beard-like growth of long pointed leaves descending and covering the throat. There were other leaves coming up to the chin from the cornice that added to the ambience of the foliate head. It's a simple and youthful foliate head, like an elf, mused Cajetan as he thought of his children back home in Zelzate.

Cajetan stepped back to get a better look of the main entrance of the cathedral freshly completed. He marveled at the five entrance portals that gave a truly majestic broad view to this cathedral. He said, "What a unique idea, these five portals like giant mouths letting in the people." Then he went closer to look at the upper corner of a small arch where he saw the sculpture of the naked Eve holding a fruit in her left hand while a long creature, half lizard, half dog lies at her feet. The entire scene is covered with leaves. Eve in the garden of Eden, thought Cajetan, the domain of the foliate head. Afterward, Cajetan went inside the cathedral and was simply amazed at the interior with its tall vaulted ceiling, its long nave and its brightness stemming from the stained glass windows. As he approached one of the windows, he saw, as part of the scene, a corner of stained glass where was depicted Poor Lazarus with spots all over his body, holding a crutch on his left side while two arms reach out to him from below in an opened red door. Here it is again, said Cajetan to himself, the poor man Lazarus begging for his food. The old lady in Chartres was right, he's everywhere if you look for him. The poor are everywhere, mused Cajetan.

That night Cajetan had his evening meal at the local inn where he was staying, and ate what the menu called *Taine aux carrot's*. He enjoyed it since it was far different from simple bread and water with sometimes a piece of fruit. Not that he was without money to be able to afford a better fare but Cajetan had now ingrained in himself the conviction of the pilgrimage that called for leaner and more stringent table food. It wasn't the monastic fasting experience but one that was similar to it, as it was rooted in the same gospel invitation to fast and do penance for one's sins. Cajetan had thus gotten in the habit of doing without, either in food or daily luxuries, and he felt comfortable with it as long as he wasn't "fasting" on Gothic architecture. For that, he was a gourmand.

From Bourges, Cajetan headed west toward Poitiers. Although he had heard of the wonders of Poitiers, its history, culture and, of course, its cathedral, Cajetan had not spent too much time on Poitiers. Now, he was going to indulge in the culture of this city, the former residence of Eleanor of Aquitaine and her husband, Henry II. He was going to truly investigate the cathedral, its architecture, its sculptures, its stained glass and its wood carvings reputed to be some of the best. Poitiers's history was also fascinating since it was the scene of the great military Battle of Tours under Charles Martel and the Franks when they routed the Muslims. But Cajetan wasn't so much interested in the history of the area as much as the culture in which it was immersed.

First, there was the influence of the Dukes of Aquitaine and their cultural contribution to Poitiers as well as the benefits of the court of Eleanor of Aquitaine as a cultural center where refinement was sought and attained. What truly interested Cajetan was the Cathedral Saint-Pierre. This church was a mixture of the Romanesque and Gothic, Cajetan remarked. The front west portal was flanked by two huge mismatched towers, it seemed. Except for the portals themselves, the front of the cathedral was genuinely Romanesque, flat and rigid, although pierced with a rose window. When Cajetan went to the north door, la Porte Saint-Michel, he found sculptures from the transitional period between Romanesque and Gothic.

Once he had penetrated inside the cathedral, Cajetan noticed the brightness due to the lofty Gothic vault. Gothic space exists here, mused Cajetan. That's the great virtue of Gothic architecture, he added. Glancing at the corbel tables on the wall, he saw a variety of carved human heads that was interesting to him. Then, looking at the choir stalls he discovered excellent wood carvings on the misericords and the spandrels, one of which was a magnificent foliate head in the shape of a large V. This one was indeed a work of artistic creativity, thought Cajetan. The quality of the lustrous wood brings out the beauty of the leaves with the eyes and nose clearly carved. The branches of leaves spring out of the corners of the mouth of the foliate head and shoot upward and sideward so that the entire face is swathed in the luxuriousness of leaves carved out of aged wood. Truly an enticing work, thought Cajetan. Furthermore, it was fascinating for Cajetan to notice that the foliate heads were not in stone here, but in wood.

Then he stepped outside to look again at the entrance and examining carefully the tympanum, he saw right below it on the corners where the capitals joined the tympanum were some foliate heads. They were not large carvings in stone but delicate ones with leaves sprouting around their faces, adorning their foreheads, mustaches and chins. These were certainly not grotesque, thought Cajetan. Nothing devilish about them.

Once he had seen what he wanted to see, Cajetan thought of returning to Zelzate and reunite with his family. The thought came to him to revisit

Reims and Amiens on his way back which is what he did. At Reims, he visited with cherished memories the cathedral where he had worked with Maître Albert de Chaussoyes. He went inside and looked around. When he was about to exit, walking slowly and in deep thought, he happened to glance upward at the inner façade of the West front, and there he saw again the Old Testament figures but also what he had not noticed carefully before, the vegetation surrounding the figures. There were rectangles of different kinds of leaves on top of the figures and below them. He stood there admiring the creative work of the sculptor. What admirable work, he said to himself, and then went outside where the sun was shining brightly.

From Reims, Cajetan went to Amiens. There he stood outside in front of the cathedral and stared at it for a long period of time. He marveled at the majesty of the architecture and the solemnity of its presence there next to the river. Surely, it's one of the very finest of Gothic expression, he thought. He then remembered the joyous feeling of Gothic space inside the church. He stepped into the interior and looked upward ever experiencing that Gothic space as if he were inebriated with it. He just happened to drop his eyes a bit and caught the garland of vegetation streaming all around the upper part of the arcade right below the triforium. He had not examined that natural ornamentation before. It certainly added some measure of local plant life to a place of worship much admired by its people. Cajetan now recognized fully the importance of vegetation in the construction and decoration of Gothic cathedrals, and he resolved, with extra confidence, that his cathedral would have vegetation, be it in the shape of foliate heads, foliate friezes like the one in Amiens, or of other forms. That, he was certain of. Everything in his mind was being sifted through his imagination and creativity to a point where he envisioned very concretely the cathedral he was going to build. Cajetan then went straight home to Zelzate to tell Wandal all about his cathedral. He had the design and the plans all figured out. All he had to do was to put them down on his drawing board. He was ready. Ready as he ever would be.

14

CAJETAN'S CATHEDRAL :
the planning

When Cajetan arrived home, he took off his cloak and tunic and he asked his wife to help him wash the road dust off his skin, and then wash it off his clothes. He seemed to feel the readiness of getting the old skin off and the new one on. He was ready to start fresh and anew. Wandal scrubbed and scrubbed the dirt off his body making sure she was not rubbing too hard so that the skin would turn red, but she knew what she was doing since she had done the scrubbing many times on the children and on her husband, that is, when he was around. It was good to see her husband again, revitalized, enthused about his architectural project and excited like a baby who discovers all of his fingers and toes for the first time.

After Wandal and Cajetan had eaten, Wandal started playing with her cat, Popoussin. Cajetan sat down and invited his wife to sit next to him for he was going to tell her about his plans for his cathedral. He called it his cathedral for he had done so for such a long time that he could not help himself from calling it his. His cathedral, not the Bishop's cathedral nor the chapter's cathedral. HIS. Of course, he did not know yet who the Bishop was going to be nor in what diocese it was going to be situated. All he knew was that his cathedral was finally being realized by sheer power of his will and determination to finally concretize his dream. He had waited all his life practically to build a cathedral, and now his dream was coming to fruition, like a ripe pear that has been hanging on the tree for a long time when the green skin turns a pale yellow and then bright yellow with small brown spots on it, ready for the picking, and succulent when you put your teeth into it. Oh, the first bite! His dream had ripened and plans and design were now in order.

----It's going to be Gothic, Wandal.

----Yes, I knew that. You've been saying that for years, Cajetan.

----Gothic with probably a touch of the Romanesque.

----What exactly is Romanesque?

----It's a style that's sturdier, heavier, with thick walls, no flying buttresses, and small windows that let in very little light. It gives the cathedral an obscure ambience. However, there are Romanesque churches that are very lovely like the Léon Cathedral in Spain. Oh, I wish you could have seen it, Wandal, such a beautiful sight, resplendent in its creative beauty.

----But I thought you only considered Gothic as resplendent in its beauty, Cajetan.

----I know, I know but now I've reconsidered the marriage of both styles. I'm not as fixated as I used to be, Wandal.

----You have mellowed, my husband. You now realize that ideas can and do change.

----I suppose so, wife.

----You suppose so? I know so.

----I have to agree with you, Wandal. However, Gothic is still my preference.

----Abbot Suger first created the Gothic style, didn't he?

----I don't think he actually created it but he certainly promoted it.

----Which cathedral do you like the most in the Gothic style?

----That's not an easy question to answer, Wandal. If I had to chose, well, I really like Notre-Dame de Paris and Reims cathedral but when I get right down to it, I favor Amiens cathedral.

----Why?

----Because it's a jewel of a cathedral with its Gothic space, its rayonnant rose windows, especially the front one on the western side, and sculptures like *Le Beau Dieu*. And, I must not forget the foliate frieze that marks the division between the main arcade and the triforium in the nave. It goes all around the nave like a triumphant garland of well-sculpted vegetation, so well done that you would think that every inch of it is real. Sheer beauty that you could touch with your hand raised up high. It's true, you can almost touch every leaf, every branch. It's absolutely stunning as sculpture goes. Didn't I tell you about that?

----No, you must have forgotten it when you were spilling out your words of wonderment about the cathedrals and their foliate heads. Cajetan, my dreamer husband, the Stargazer, you are so amazing with your ease of wonderment that you fall into the raving delight of dreams.

----It's not my fault, I think that way, I see that way and I live that way, Wandal.

----Don't you think I know that? All it takes is a foliate head and there you go raving.

----Yes, foliate heads, I can't forget that either.

----Are you going to put some in your cathedral? I know that's a question many people ask you but are you really going to put some in your cathedral? I mean, is the foliate head really part of your plans and design?

----You're absolutely right. Everyone asks that question of me. I'm certainly going to pressure our Master Sculptor to include some. I met this old woman in Chartres who thought that foliate heads were like devils, simply because her priest had told her that.

----Why would he tell her that?

----Because he's prejudiced and tainted with negative thoughts about the imagination.

----Why would he think that way?

----Because some of the clergy have biases against whatever is secular. Everything in God's creation is sacred to me, Wandal. Everything. Devils belong to the domain of hell and damnation, not the domain of beauty and creativity. The beauty of creation exists because it's part of or the continuation of the overall Grand Creation of God the Creator. That's my way of thinking.

----Mine too.

----Let's talk about something else, let's talk about the name of my cathedral.

----What are you going to name it? Notre-Dame like so many?

----Notre-Dame, no, but I will dedicate it to the Virgin Mary. I'm going to name it "Sainte-Marie de la Belle Étoile." Isn't that beautiful and appropriate?

----Appropriate for you, Cajetan but not appropriate for everyone. Will the Church and any bishop recognize that name as a sacred name, a name designating the sacredness of Mary, Queen of Heaven and Earth? And besides, "Marie de la Belle Étoile," what does that mean. Mary is not the mother of a star. She's the Mother of Jesus, Our Savior.

----But the stars are sacred, Wandal. They're in Genesis and God the Creator made them. So Mary, Mother of Jesus is also Mother of all the stars. Besides, they're also in the Psalms, the songs-poetry of King David. Take Psalm 147, for instance: *Praise the Lord!...He determines the number of the stars; he gives to all of them their names.* Isn't that sacred, as sacred as it gets because the stars are given names by the Lord and, to me, that means they're sacred.

----I know but...

----But what?

----But will the Church and its leaders approve of it?

----They'll approve because I'll prove to them that the sacredness of a beautiful Gothic cathedral relies not only on a name but on its architecture and design. It all goes together in harmony of style and reliance on the truth of a name that incorporates the virtues and the intercessory power of Blessed Mary, Most Virgin, Most Pure and Most Beloved. A Star named by God. Mary is the Star of all stars.

----You should have become a monk, my husband, or an abbot like your sister. You head spins in the realm of theology.

----Well, theology is the study of God and we're all part of that study one way or another.

----How?

----God is the beginning of everything. At least, that's what I was taught.

----The beginning and the end, am I not right?

----Yes, of course. That's part of salvation as we are told.

----And our paths in life directs us toward that goal, right?

----Yes. I chose to become an architect because that's what I was meant to be, I know that. It's been there in the deepest of my soul ever since I was born. I'm not making it up, Wandal. That's my calling, my dream, like Joseph's dream in the Bible. And I'm a Star Gazer because that binds me with the stars, the domain of dreams. An architect builds upon dreams.

----Yes, the dreams of a seeker and provider of imaginary journeys into the spirit of what is truly creative.

----You're right, Wandal. I wish that every craftsman and worker would follow my lead into creativity, into imaginative creativity.

----Many do, Cajetan, but not all have your power of the imagination. But, one must leave the imagination behind at one point and face reality.

----You mean that imagination is not real?

----That's not what I mean. I mean that if everyone were to live in the land of the imagination all the time, then nothing would be accomplished.

----But, in order to accomplish things, great things, one must use his imagination to be able then to create. The two go hand in hand, don't you see?

----Yes, I see, but how long must one dwell in the domain of the imagination before doing something great?

----I would say, always. You cannot separate creativity with imagination. They coexist.

----We're just going round and round here, Cajetan. You stick with your thoughts on creativity and the imagination and I'll stay with my thoughts of concrete reality and creativity.

----But you can do both, Wandal. Once the step of creativity has been accomplished through the imagination, then one steps into the domain of concrete reality. That's what I'm doing, don't you see? I'm now ready to build concretely my cathedral. It's real and it's going to be grounded in the concreteness of plans, design and stone.

----It seems to me that it took you a very long time to do so.

----Well, I had to learn first, learn from the masters. Then I had to progress slowly according to the rules of the guild in order to get my certification as Master Architect. And, now, I have to find a site and a sponsor. I admit that I went through some circuitous route what with my own studies, my travels to Fontevraud, and the pilgrimage to Santiago de Compostela, but that was for my spiritual benefit. One does not build a cathedral without a strengthened spirituality. Building a cathedral is a sacred trust, Wandal.

----What about the search for the foliate heads?

----Well, I must admit that was more for my imagination, but it was an artistic imagination on my part and on the part of the sculptors who imagined them and executed them. For me, foliate heads are the sparks of creative genesis in nature.

---- There you go again. I have yet to fully understand that you are a dreamer and a stargazer, Cajetan. You were born with it, I know. You are above all of us who have their two feet on the ground; we don't have our heads in the stars.

----You wait when I have done building my cathedral, you'll understand what I'm all about. Just you wait, woman of hard work, child bearer, woman of doubt, you just wait. You may have a penetrating mind but you don't fully understand me.

It was getting late and both Cajetan and Wandal were tired, and had talked a long time. They went to bed and made love that night, a night of fulfillment and delight. The next morning, Wandal let Cajetan sleep late. When he woke up, he chided her for letting him sleep so late. She told him that he needed rest in order to create clearly and imaginatively. "You must not exhaust yourself, Cajetan," she told him "or else you'll burn out. You are now forty-three years old, *mon ami*. You're not young anymore, Cajetan," she told him. "No, I'm not old, I'm in my full maturity when things come to a head." Cajetan got up, got dressed and after a light breakfast, he was on his way to talk to other craftsmen, contacts that he had made in the past. "That's how things work," he told himself, "contacts lead to actual opportunities."

First, he recited a verse from the **Benedicite** : *Benedicite, Anania, Azaria, Misael, Domino, laudate et superexaltate eum in saecula*/ Bless the Lord Ananias, Azarias, Misael, bless ye the Lord, praise him and magnify him forever. Cajetan chose to recite this verse because he had convinced himself that he was going to use Biblical scenes from the Old as well as the New Testaments in his cathedral, and one of those scenes would definitely be the one from the Prophet Daniel where the three young men who abide by Yahweh's law defy King Nebuchadnezzar's order to eat royal portions of food and drink since they, along with Daniel, did not want to defile themselves. And later, the three young men, refusing to worship the golden statue, are put in a blazing furnace where Yahweh delivers them from certain death. Cajetan would assuredly talk to his Master Sculptor about this creation in stone as well as others he wanted, such as the Legend of Theophilus.

The first person Cajetan contacted was Master Architect Albert de Chaussoyes, his old master in Reims. Cajetan had learned that he was still alive and living in Reims. He would certainly be in a position to know where the new *chantiers* were, and who the patron bishops were. Then there would be Sigismond de Longchamp, Master Architect in England, but the latest news was that he had succumbed to a heart attack after a brutal accident somewhere outside of Devonshire. Then there was Kurt Marquardt of the Saint-Amand site in Flanders, but after the collapse of the cathedral in Zelzate, it would be useless and even grievous to contact him. Cajetan thought that he was most probably retired some place away from Flanders. There was, of course, Abbot Wieglestern of the Kluzien Abbey and that was a good contact, a very good idea indeed, mused Cajetan. As a last resort, he thought of the guide, Mathieu Delamarre. The jolly guide most certainly knew many people and had traveled extensively. He was a wise and even cunning bird, by now an old bird, a very knowledgeable one.

Cajetan now realized that he could bank on the years of experience he had accumulated over time, and that the intellectual learning experience, as well as the actual work experience, collaborated with his insights into architecture and the appreciation of creative arts. That, with his many travels, enhanced his vision, his dream of accomplishing his calling, his vocation, as his sister called it. Yes, he was called by the Master Architect, God the Father Creator who had molded him from clay to actual being. He sometimes thought that he was being too impulsive in his way of thinking, even pretentious, but he was convinced deep in his soul that inspiration came from above, and that he was the vessel that had opened up to graces given abundantly and freely without the asking. What he had to do was to humbly accept them as gifts, and develop them with the talents provided. Cajetan never thought he was special, not at all, but he did not reject nor deny the talents with which he had been endowed. "I do not hide my talents under a bushel basket," mused Cajetan. Presumption had never taken hold of Cajetan, only a sense of *fierté* in having the measure to accomplish his goals in life.

When he got to the Kluzien Abbey, Cajetan realized that the Abbot might not be the same as when he worked there as an architect. Maybe Abbot Wiegelstern had died or grown too old to govern anymore. Perhaps he was sick or, even worse, incapacitated with a severe illness. All of these questions ran through his head as he stood in front of the cloister that he himself had designed. Cajetan had not heard a word from the Abbot ever since he had left Kluzien to visit Fontevraud at Marie Dieudonnée's profession of final vows. After that, he traveled in search of the foliate heads, and then, of course, there was the pilgrimage to Santiago de Compostela. That was nine years ago. A long time to lose touch with a dear friend, the Abbot.

Cajetan rang the bell outside the huge oaken door, and the porter asked who was there. "It's me, Master Architect Cajetan," he said. The porter recognized the voice and the name and immediately opened the door.

----Master Cajetan, I'm so glad to see you again. It's been a long time.

Standing there in front of Cajetan was an elderly monk with white hair and clear blue eyes whose voice trembled a bit after each and every word.

----Brother Elsteneer, what a joy to see you again. I remember the days when you brought me a little bit of wine from your cellars just to have me taste it, so that you would be sure of its quality when you served it to guests. You knew that I was not a connoisseur of wines but you wanted me to enjoy having some wine after a hard day's work just to soothe my tired head from all of the calculations and plans that I was working on. I knew that you did that just to relieve my stressed mind. I will always remember that.

----Remember the talks we used to have in the garden? We would talk about your work and your dreams, and whatever filled your mind and your imagination. I was your sounding board and I just listened. I was patient with you, Cajetan. You were, to me, a man of ideas and good moral values, and I respected that. You would have been a good candidate for the monastery.

They both started to laugh.

----Listen, Brother, is Abbot Wiegelstern still here at this monastery?

----Why yes, where else would he be?

----I don't know. I imagined perhaps that he might have been relieved of his leadership due to ill health or other conditions in his advanced age.

----No, he's well and strong. He may be old but he's still filled with vitality. He hasn't changed much since you left.

----Good, I'm glad to hear that. Do you think I could talk to him?

----He's at a chapter meeting right now and may not finish for a couple of hours. Do you mind waiting?

----No, I have all the time in the world. Maybe you and I can talk a bit as we used to.

----You know how I enjoy talking, Cajetan, especially before the grand silence. Here at Kluzien we work, we pray, we eat and we talk when we're given time to do so. Being the porter, I have many occasions to talk to people. It suits me fine. Let's go to the garden where I can hear the bell if it rings.

Cajetan and Brother Elsteneer walked over to the pleasant garden still in bloom with roses and the lavender. "Smell the lovely roses, Cajetan, They're my favorites." They both sat down on a stone bench and started to chat. The monk asked Cajetan about his family, his travels and other occurrences in his life since his departure from Kluzien. Cajetan talked about Wandal and the children, and told him about his sister at Fontevraud, his pilgrimage to Spain and his adventure with foliate heads, as he called it. After a while the chimes of Tierce were heard and Brother Elsteneer excused himself. He then turned to Cajetan and asked him if would like to join the community in saying the Divine Office in the chapel. "We'll be in the choir, but you can sit in the nave," he told him. Cajetan agreed and followed the monk into the Abbey chapel.

After the prayers, the Abbot sent word to Cajetan that he would see him in an hour's time, and sent his regrets for not being able to be with him sooner. Brother and Cajetan went back outside to sit on the bench and continue their talk.

----Cajetan, tell me about your adventure with the foliate head. That interests me.

----Well, I went to several cathedrals and one of the most fascinating sites for the foliate head is in the cathedral in Auxerre. There, you find several outstanding foliate heads, in my estimation. Others are found in Chartres and Poitiers. The Cathedral of Poitiers is notable for its foliate heads carved out of the wood of the choir stalls. There is one that is outstanding, in my estimation. Others are found at the entrance to the cathedral. They appear in almost every Gothic cathedral I've seen. I'm sure there are more. If I were to travel extensively to every Gothic cathedral be it in France, England, Germany or Spain, I'm positive I would find them. This phenomenon, I call it an artistic phenomenon, seems to have emerged in the last two centuries or so. I'm not an expert on this subject, so I cannot give you more detailed information. I don't know about abbeys and abbey churches. All I know is that Bernard de Clairvaux was dead set against foliate heads. He thought they were grotesque, if not devilish, and did not belong in sacred spaces such as cathedrals and certainly not his Cistercian abbeys.

----Bernard de Clairvaux was against excesses, and he was a reformer, a holy man, and had a great devotion to Our Lady. He would certainly have seen the foliate head as an intruder in holy places. He was for the simple gospel life and the simple, if not stripped down, décor of any abbey or church. He took the vows of poverty, chastity and obedience quite literally. Total detachment from worldly goods, denial of bodily appetites and their entanglements, and obedience to authority, especially divine and ecclesiastical authority that lead all of us to salvation. I may add that I agree that the temper of the times, especially the trend of monastic abuse of earthly goods, was getting to a point where those vows were just a farce of monasticism. Wealth corrupts, Cajetan, wealth corrupts and is insidious and leads to the abuse of monastic privileges. However, I find that Bernard de Clairvaux's opinion on creative expression was a bit excessive. So, I'm not surprised about his distress over unholy heads with leaves coming out of their mouths, ears, noses and every facial aperture it seems. But I personally am not against them.

----You're not?

----No, not at all. Do you know the history of the foliate head? Who made them and for whatever reason?

----I've always wondered about that.

----I don't have all the details but I do know one thing, the influence of non-Christian artisans. Before I joined the monastery, I travelled a bit and I saw several cathedrals being built. You see, I was very interested in art and sculpture. As a matter of fact, I wanted to be an artist but my father refused to acknowledge my talent as a creative person. He was dead set against it. He thought that it was foolish for a young man to waste his time and effort pursuing worthless things like art. My father saw things in a most practical way. For him, artists were useless to society. They contributed nothing to it, he said. That was far from my way of thinking, I tell you. He wanted me to become a craftsman or a person selling things.

I, a merchant of wares and things. Not me. His main concern was money; mine was not. Well, I left home I was seventeen and wandered here and there. I did a few jobs for people just enough to earn a small living. I felt that I did not belong anywhere and to no one. I really felt that my father had disinherited me by not allowing me to be who I truly was. One day, I met a group of non-Christians who were kind to me and let me live with them. They were from various parts of Europe. Some came from the northern plains, others from parts of the world I had never heard of. They all were seeking work. They were very creative people, and they wanted to do sculpture. That's what they had been trained for. However, most of the sculptures done here in Europe were done in churches or abbeys or some Christian establishment. They knew that they would not be well-received by Christians on account of their beliefs. Their beliefs were considered pagan. Not that they worshipped false idols, but they believed in nature gods and professed faith in earthy healing with herbs and incantations, fire and incense, and the like. I found it very interesting. Of course, I wasn't too involved with my own religious faith. I had fallen by the wayside of my Christian faith, you might say. Well, I found out through them that many of the so-called pagan artisans were forced to convert to Christianity for that was the only way they could become sculptors in cathedrals and churches. It didn't mean they renounced their beliefs totally. No, while they professed renouncing their old beliefs publicly they remained tied to what they knew best, their beliefs in the nature gods, and that's what they used as a source of inspiration for the many foliate heads that started to appear in our churches in the guise of Christianized nature symbols. Some Christians even went as far as seeing a transition from pagan nature to Christianized nature, and the image of the Resurrection of Christ as a blossoming of a new beginning. From death to new life. Of course, they never did take credit for all of those foliate heads. They were simply delighted they could exercise their craft and be content that they were allowed to do their creative work. I don't think that all foliate heads were done by converted Christians, but many were.

----That's very interesting, Brother. But how and when did you decide to become a monk?

----I really felt alone in the world with no one to turn to. I learned that my father had died and that he left me nothing. Everything went to my younger brother. I didn't want to fight him and try to get my share of the inheritance, so I left him to his own devices.

----How did you survive?

----The same way I had been doing. One day, I met a young man who was a loner like me, and he introduced me to the life of the abbey. Like him, I became a guest for one night in the Kluzien Abbey. I met people, and with time, I decided to join the Benedictine monastery at Kluzien in part because I had grown to admire Abbot Wieglestern for his straightforwardness, his honesty and genuine Christian beliefs and values. He lived the gospel simplicity, that's what I thought of him. You might say that I answered the call in a round-about way. When I met you, I knew that I was indeed in the right place because you allowed me in your creative world of imagination and dreams. That's my world. I'm a common, ordinary monk, a regular person without much formal education, but I live my faith through dedication and works of charity. That's what Saint Benedict wanted of his followers.

----That's admirable.

----So you see, I look at things as God sees them, that everything created by Him is sacred in some way. I tell people just read Genesis.

----You think the way I do, Brother.

----I know I'm not the only one but there are some who want to separate totally what is profane, as they call it, and what is sacred. Life is sacred, Cajetan, living things are sacred, creativity is a sacred trust.

----Thank you. You say it better than I do.

----Well, let's go and see if the Abbot is ready to see you. I hope you don't mind my asking, but what is it all about?

----My cathedral, Brother.

----Oh, your cathedral that you've dreamed of building for a very long time.

----Yes, for too long. I must get to the reality of constructing a cathedral. By that, I mean site and patron.

----Yes, very important first steps. I'm sure the Abbot will be able to help you in some way. If I ever can be of service to you, Cajetan, please don't hesitate to call on me. *Benedicite, frater Cajetan.*

----*Deo gratias* .

When Cajetan finally got to sit down with Abbot Wiegelstern, they began with small talk but then the conversation turned into more serious things like the need to finish the south portal that Cajetan had designed and left to the masons and sculptors to complete. Cajetan promised the Abbot that he would stay a while to go over the designs and help the craftsmen finalize their work on the portal. Perhaps with a little help from the Architect, they might finally get it done, he told the Abbot.

----Cajetan, I'm so grateful for your help. I want to see things through once and for all. There are other things I must attend to as leader and spiritual father of sixty-seven monks.

----I'll be only too happy to help you out in whatever way I can but I need to talk to you and get your advice on something that I must resolve, if you can grant me some of your precious time like an hour or two.

----No problem, Cajetan. I'll find the time.

Cajetan stayed at the monastery four days, long enough to work with the craftsmen of the south portal and get his time with the Abbot. Abbot Wiegelstern told Cajetan that he did not know of any specific new *chantier* being opened but that he would try to find out if any Bishop or Archbishop that he knew were planning to build a cathedral. He left Cajetan with the assurance that he would do his best to find out any information that could help him as architect and builder of cathedrals. Cajetan was somewhat disappointed but glad that he had spoken to the Abbot and especially to Brother Elsteneer.

Cajetan's next encounter was with his former Master Architect Albert de Chaussoyes of Reims. When he got to Reims, Cajetan went directly to the cathedral to take a good look at what he had helped to build. It was truly an amazing work of Gothic architecture, he told himself, one that would last with the ages. He felt good about being an architect himself. As he was standing facing the cathedral, someone tapped him on the shoulder and he turned around to see this old man, hair white as bleached cloth with a long mustache, piercing dark eyes smiling at him.

----Don't you remember me, Cajetan?

----I'm sorry but I don't. Who are you?

----How can you forget Maniple Chrétien, clerk of the works here at Reims?

----Maniple, how you've changed.

----Well, it's been thirty-one years. I'm seventy-three now.

----You look fine. What have you been doing?

----After my position was abolished and they needed me no more, I had a hard time finding another job. I tried to move around and find another *chantier* but I just did not succeed. So, I took a job as a clerk of bottles and wares, selling them and trying to market them for this owner/buyer who was just as stingy as they come. I eked out a living and now I'm penniless and living the best I can. I go where I can find bits and pieces of work but they tell me that I'm just an old man, worthless. I come here once in a while just to remind myself of what I used to do, and how proud I was of my work and collaboration with Master Architect Albert de Chaussoyes.

----Is he still alive? Do you get to see him sometimes? Where does he live? Can I go see him?

----Wait, just one question at a time, Cajetan.

----Yes, he's still living. He's here in Reims. However, he's not well. He was sick for a very long time. He stopped being a working architect some twenty years ago after his wife died. His children moved on and sort of abandoned him. Now he's alone and waiting to die, I guess. Life has no more meaning for him, he tells me.

----So, you do see him.

----Yes, I see him now and then. I try to console him but what can I contribute to his welfare. I'm down and out myself. But thank God I can walk and see people.

----Can I see him? Where does he live?

----He lives up the street from the cathedral. It's not far. He lives in a modest home that he acquired when he was Master Architect for Notre-Dame of Reims. Thank God for that benefit. Neighbors take care of him, bring him food and do his errands. They remember the time when he did the same for them. He lives at 14 ruelle de la Belle Aurore, up that way.

Maniple pointed the way to Cajetan.

----What a marvelous coincidence….*la Belle Aurore*.

----You're still the dreamer, Cajetan, I can see that.

----Will you come with me? I'll buy a small bottle of champagne of the area and we'll partake of it as in the good old days.

Maniple and Cajetan walked up the road and crossed it until they came to a very small street that went up winding and filled with houses all crammed together like a beehive. Maniple knew which one was Master de Chaussoyes', a small red house with dark green shutters tucked in among many others, Number 14. Maniple went up to the door and knocked. The neighbor came out and told him that Master de Chaussoyes was in prayer at the shrine. "What shrine?" asked Cajetan. "Why, it's a shrine to our Lady of Succor. Master de Chaussoyes goes there often since he has all this time on his hands, and knows that earning one's salvation takes prayers especially to Our Lady, our hope and intercessor. Come follow me."

They arrived at a modest shrine made of carved wood on top of a slope where someone had placed the statue of Mary inside the wooden shrine for all to see. "This is the shrine of the poor," said Maniple to Cajetan. "But why a shrine here when there are many in the churches all around?" asked Cajetan. "Because here it belongs to the neighborhood and people need it as a sign of belonging." Just then Cajetan spotted Master de Chaussoyes sitting on the sides contemplating the sky and closing his eyes when the light got too bright for him. Cajetan went over and touched his shoulder. Master de Chaussoyes turned around and saw Cajetan right beside him.

----Cajetan, what a pleasant surprise. How did you find me?

----I came with Maniple. He's right there.

----Oh, poor Maniple, seems lost all of the time, but a good fellow.

----Master, I'd like to talk to you privately, if I may.

----Certainly. Let's go to my humble dwelling. I'll give Maniple an errand to do so that we can be alone.

They both started to walk but Cajetan saw that his Master was not very steady on his legs, so he held him by his right arm and led him home. Once there, both of them sat down and Cajetan began to question him on possible sites and patrons for his cathedral.

----You know that I've been dreaming of building my own cathedral since I'm now a Master Architect myself.

----Yes, I know that, Cajetan. When and where do you propose to build this cathedral?

----That's the reason I'm here to ask your advice.

----You mean you have no clue as to where you're going to build a cathedral?

----I have some general idea but, no, I have no idea where.

----That takes a long time to finalize plans for the building of such a project. A cathedral is not a house, Cajetan. First, you have to decide on a site, then get a patron or the other way round, find a patron bishop or archbishop who already has a site in mind, get the chapter to approve the project, no slight task, I tell you, then raise the funds, get the crew of craftsmen to build it, and obtain the necessary materials. That's a whole lot of planning and getting what you need, Cajetan. And you have not started yet?

----I know I'm late but everything is in my mind and in my imagination.

----That's good but it's not enough, my friend. You must have things clearly planned and a design all figured out in black and white. Dreams are dreams, Cajetan, but dreams do not actually build cathedrals. If you want to build a cathedral, stop dreaming about it and get started now. How old are you?

----I'm forty-four.

----You're in the prime of your life but a bit old to start building a cathedral from scratch. I was thirty-two when I started. It takes about thirty to forty years to build a cathedral if everything works out well, and that means you'll be at least seventy-four years old by the time it's finished, if you live that long.

----Are you discouraging me, Master?

----No, I'm just being realistic about it. I don't want you to be deceived by your grand dreams. That's all.

----Well, cathedrals begin with grand dreams and they end that way too. Without a dream, a cathedral would just be a building that's all. I'm sure you had a dream at one time.

----Yes, I did but I made it happen when I was still young. Besides, I was fortunate to have a good sponsor who could raise funds and convince the chapter to undertake such a vast project.

----I'm not giving up on my dream, Master de Chaussoyes. I'm not.

----I'm not asking you to. All I'm asking you is to decide right here and now if you are willing to put in the time and effort to even begin the plans and the design. If so, put everything down in black and white. Get going now.

----I'm here to see if you would have some idea about a *chantier* somewhere, and a patron bishop who is looking for a master architect. You have contacts, I know.

----Cajetan, I've been out of that business for a very long time and I rarely see my friends, the craftsmen and master architects. I wouldn't know where to start. I'm old, Cajetan, and I'm almost disabled as far as my weak body is concerned.

Maniple happened to come in at the very minute.

----What are you two talking about?

----We're discussing Cajetan's project of building a cathedral.

----You mean you haven't started yet, Cajetan?

----No, I need a site and a patron bishop.

----I know of two possible sites, one in Nevers and the other in Évreux. I've heard people talking about it.

----What people? asked Master de Chaussoyes.

----You know people talk. They hear things and sometimes they turn out to be true. I go around and I hear things.

----What do you know about Nevers and Évreux? asked Cajetan.

----Not much except I can give you the name of a sculptor who might give you some information. His name is André Cassegrain.

----Where can I find him?

That night Cajetan was at an inn in Paris talking to a man, a sculptor by the name of Cassegrain. Cajetan had decided not to lose any more time and get going on his cathedral. The sculptor told him that he had heard that a certain Bishop Ambroise Villepigne near Nevers was planning to build a cathedral in Nevers, and that he was searching for a master architect to direct the project. However, word was that he had few funds to get started. On the other hand, the possibility of a cathedral in Évreux was real and Master Sculptor Cassegrain was himself looking into getting work on the proposed cathedral of Évreux. He did not know who the master architect would be but he was doing his best to get all the information necessary to achieve his goal. Cajetan took it upon himself to solicit the help of Cassegrain and accompany him on his next trip to Évreux. It was a done deal.

The following week Cajetan and André Cassegrain were off to Évreux to explore the possibility of a cathedral in that area. Fortunately, the sculptor had a friend in Évreux who was on best terms with the Bishop's secretary, Monseigneur Arthur DeLally. Cajetan had had it with running around to get information here and there, and he was going to trust this sculptor and his contact. What was he going to lose by putting his faith in another craftsman, a member of the guild? Well, it turns out that Bishop Antoine de Champigny was indeed contemplating the construction of a cathedral on the outskirts of Évreux, on an ancient site where Roman baths had been built, and now stood in ruins. And, the Bishop had already raised a considerable amount of funds to get started as soon as he found the right architect and the right team of craftsmen to build it. He had already put out feelers in the surrounding communities, but had gotten nothing back.

Cajetan and André were standing in the hall adjacent to Monseigneur's office when a cleric came to greet them to tell them that Monseigneur DeLally would meet them in his office. They were escorted there, and soon a tall and dignified man dressed in a black cassock with purple sash, black hair, high cheek bones and light brown eyes greeted both of them with a smile. They talked for half an hour, and Cajetan was reassured that the Bishop would meet with him the following morning. André thanked the secretary for his time and walked out feeling comforted by the fact that the meeting had gone well for both himself and the Master Architect, Cajetan.

The following morning Cajetan rose early, had breakfast and felt excitement in anticipation of his meeting with the Bishop. Things looked good. André was still sleeping. He had had a boisterous night at a local tavern, and did not mind not going with Cajetan to meet with the Bishop. When Cajetan arrived at the Bishop's residence, he was told that Bishop de Champigny was waiting for him. Cajetan could feel his heart pounding.

The Bishop greeted him with a broad smile and told him to sit down. The Bishop looked stately, a man of high intelligence, it seemed, and evidently well-mannered, and expressed himself with dignity and confidence. Cajetan was impressed. The Bishop informed Cajetan that he was indeed looking for an able and mature architect for a cathedral that he wanted built on his *chantier Saint-Odelard*. He did not want a grandiose church nor one that would be plain and sober-looking. He wanted a well-designed and awe-inspiring cathedral where people could worship and be inspired by what he considered the "Bible in stone." He wanted a Gothic building with a lot of light, as he had seen in other Gothic cathedrals. Above all, he did not want to compete with the grand matrons of cathedrals such as, Notre-Dame de Paris, Notre-Dame de Reims and Notre-Dame d'Amiens. They were the queens of Gothic architecture, he said. He wanted a princess. Cajetan told him that he understood what he wanted, and would do his best to satisfy his wishes. Cajetan told the Bishop about his experience in the field of architecture and how he had worked with some of the best in his field. That he was idealistic but also practical and realistic when it came time to be real and down-to-earth. (He rememberd Wandal's words to him about being idealistic but practical too). Above all, he believed in a strong spirituality that strengthens the bond of sacredness with a cathedral, a place of worship, a building where God, the Creator and God, the Redeemer were in evidence. Cajetan also told him about his contacts in the guilds, and that he was in good standing with all of them. They all knew him for his honesty and integrity. He told the Bishop about his sister, the Abbess of Fontevraud, about his Pilgrimage to Santiago de Compostela and about his family. He came across as being frank and open, gifted and especially qualified. The Bishop told him that he had to consult with his chapter, and that he would look into it as soon as he could. What was to be the name? asked Cajetan. Notre-Dame Reine des Cieux. Cajetan did not dare mention his own personal choice of name for his cathedral. Not now, he told himself. After all, it was to be Bishop Antoine de Champigny's cathedral, not his personally. However, he would be satisfied being its architect.

Cajetan returned to the Bishop's residence two days after he had first seen him. Bishop de Champigny told him that he was planning to recommend him as Master Architect to the chapter, for he was delighted to do so since he considered Cajetan a worthy architect and a convinced Christian to build his cathedral. He liked what he had heard from him and others that he had consulted.

----You have a good reputation in the field as well as friends that know you well. Monseigneur DeLally has done some investigation for me and I assure you he has many contacts. What's going to happen now is that I will require you to submit, within two weeks time, your plans and design for the cathedral. I cannot go to the chapter without that, you understand. Now, I know that you will need shelter. May I suggest that you seek it at the Franciscan Monastery in Évreux. I will alert them that you will be coming. The Abbot is a very good friend of mine. They will give you a room adjacent to the scriptorium to draw your plans and do your design work. You'll have all the comfort that you will need. It will be frugal as far as food and shelter, but I know you understand the rule of the monastery. May God be with you and bless your work, Cajetan.

----Thank you Excellency. You will not regret your recommendation of me for I will work very hard to accomplish my task as a Master Architect. I only hope the chapter will receive it favorably.

----The members of the chapter usually accept all of my recommendations since they trust me and my judgment. I do not fail them and they never fail me. *Benedicite*, Cajetan.

----*Deo gratias*.

With that Cajetan departed with his heart full of joy, that he had finally clinched the architect's dream of building a cathedral. It wasn't final yet, but he nursed the hope that things would come to full fruition in his favor. He could feel it in his bones.

Within less than two weeks, twelve days as a matter of fact, the Bishop sent for Cajetan and asked him how he was progressing on his design and plans. Cajetan told him that he had been working on them practically night and day, so enthused about the project was he, and besides, his mind, memory and imagination were all in harmony, enough for him to be able to put down in writing and drawings this dream of his that he had been nurturing for years, the dream of his own cathedral, designed and planned by himself as Master Architect. He was confident that the Bishop and the chapter would recognize his talent, his experience as an architect, his creative energy and his willingness to serve them and the Bishop in their own plans and vision for a cathedral designed just for them and the people they served. Cajetan was indeed ready. This was to be the test of his talent and skills that he very much welcomed. He submitted all that he had worked on for twelve days, and was now waiting for the chapter's response.

In the meantime, he got to know the Abbot of the Franciscan Monastery, Saint Anthony's Monastery of Évreux, Abbot Michel Sansoucis, o.f.m.,and he reassured Cajetan that Bishop de Champigny already had the funds necessary to build his cathedral. The Bishop was of the low nobility and he had many contacts at the court of Philip IV named the "Fair." The king had gotten married in 1284 and was indebted to his wife Jeanne de Navarre since her inheritance in Champagne and Brie, which was adjacent to the royal *desmene* in Île-de-France, became effectively united to the king's own lands forming an expansive area. Queen Jeanne was a very good friend of Bishop de Champigny since he had served as a foil to the thorn in the King's side as well as the Queen's, Bishop Saisset who had called the King "a useless owl." Queen Jeanne had used her influence on her husband to endow the proposed cathedral of Bishop de Champigny of Évreux, and he had received a generous gift, so generous that people who found out about it called it extravagant. In his own way of treating the matter at hand , a matter that interested seriously the Architect Cajetan, the Franciscan Abbot informed Cajetan about all of the virtues of having important contacts and influence when building a cathedral. Cajetan told him that he knew that all too well.

When Cajetan appeared before the chapter, they asked him many questions about he proposed cathedral, praised him for his plans and expert design, and asked him if he was ready to start the work soon. He told the members that first he had to get the necessary craftsmen to do the work, the stone cutters, the masons, the glaziers, the carpenters, the roofers and whoever else was needed, but that he himself was willing and ready. As a matter of fact, he had been ready all of his life practically. One member of the chapter, an old stodgy and grim-figured individual, started making comments on the design of the cathedral, that although the design was Gothic, it lacked of something Romanesque which he considered worthy of incorporation into any design, since he admired its solid and well-admired virtues. Cajetan responded by saying that he too admired the Romanesque, and that he had seen examples of its splendor in cathedrals such as, Léon in Spain, Moissac, and several others that he outlined for the elderly man. "Besides," he said, "I plan to incorporate some of the great features of the Romanesque in your cathedral here in Évreux. I want to show how admirable the two fit in harmoniously." This individual was so impressed with Cajetan's knowledge and perspicacity that he was now urging the others to give Cajetan a contract immediately. The Bishop interjected by saying that some formalities needed to be done before such a gesture was accomplished. After the meeting, and after Cajetan had waited patiently for a response, sitting in an adjacent room, the Bishop met privately with Cajetan and told him that the position of Master Architect was his, that he himself admired the plans and the design, and that Cajetan should go home and discuss with his wife the possibility, no the necessisty,of moving to Évreux close to the *chantier Saint Odelard* . Cajetan lost no time in returning home to Zelzate and announcing to his family that they were moving to Évreux.

15

CAJETAN'S CATHEDRAL :
organization and foundation

Wandal was all excited about the move to Évreux although she was somewhat wary about going to a location she knew very little of, but she assured Cajetan that his family was behind him altogether, since this was the realization of his dream. Cajetan the Stargazer had finally plucked his dream from the tree of plenty, she told him beaming with pleasure and satisfaction. Wandal was not a woman of many desires and whims. She was a humble but assertive woman and wife. She did not lean too much on her husband, while she often led him to believe that she relied on him for most decisions, although she had already decided on what to do in this or that circumstance. She knew that Cajetan was much more interested in his craft as architect than in petty household preoccupations, the price of meat and fowl, the expense of buying other provisions and, most of all, the bartering at the local market. She wasn't educated as some ladies at court were, reading romances, learning other languages, and practicing the latest dances and ways of behaving at court. Everything a bored or carefree woman did. Wandal was always busy what with her own everyday work, such as washing, mending, cooking, taking care of the children, teaching them how to read and write, and many other tasks that she had learned to do on her own. Above all, Wandal was an independent woman, not always relying on others to tell her what to do and how to do it. She was creative in her own way, imaginative when it took imagination, and inventive when she needed to resolve a problem. She relied on God and the Creator relied on her to bring her children to salvation. She never appeared to falter or even be unreasonable . She was a very secure woman, and she was proud of that. Cajetan realized what her qualities were but he did not pay too much heed to them. He knew that they existed and that they benefitted his family, and that was sufficient for him. No need to vaunt one's virtues and make a woman too proud for her worth, he used to say. Wandal was strong, reliable, intelligent, and no match for those bumbling, dilly-dallying, insecure few. She rose above all pettiness, especially the fatuous dishonesty to self and others. People knew that as well as they knew she was Honest Grisoulda's daughter-in-law.

Within two weeks, Cajetan and his family were on their way to Évreux. Their belongings were few, for neither Cajetan nor Wandal were scroungers, and kept very few things outside of the necessary dishes, pots and pans and clothing that they wore most of the time. Three of the children were all grown up except Emmanuel who was still young enough to be at home. He was now twelve. Grisoulda was nineteen and married to a carpenter, and she lived in Valenciennes with her husband's family. Melodia was seventeen and still living at home hoping someday to find a niche for herself in music. Philippon was fifteen and he had accepted an apprenticeship with a mason called Master Rondosius the previous year. He was at present working as apprentice mason in a *chantier* in northern Flanders where they were building a monastery for an order of cloistered nuns. So, Melodia and Emmanuel were the two accompanying their parents to Évreux.

It was an uneventful trip but a joyful one and they were there in less than two weeks. After Cajetan met with the Bishop's secretary and signed his contract, he was led to the *chantier Saint Odelard* where the cathedral was to be built. He was shown the small house where he was to stay with his family. They found it much too small for four people, so Melodia was offered a place in a nearby convent where she could study music and have privacy to do whatever she pleased with a minimum of supervision. Her mother told her she was old enough to live by herself in a convent with security, and that Wandal would visit her every week just to make sure everything was going well. Emmanuel slept on a makeshift bed in a corner of the kitchen, and prayed for the day the family could afford better housing. Wandal tried to tell him that this would be temporary and that she would do her best to make things less unbearable, although, in her heart, she truly missed the more spacious home in Zelzate. Wandal was not the type to complain, and Cajetan accepted things as they came. All he wanted to do was to be able to work with the dedication of an architect to his craft, and be satisfied with the least comfort, if necessary.

When Cajetan met next with Bishop de Champigny, they discussed the hiring of the other craftsmen necessary for the beginning of the work, as well as the continuation for the years to come. Cajetan wanted the best men available, and money was not a problem, he was told. The first craftsman he hired was André Cassegrain, the sculptor who had led him to the Évreux project. Cajetan trusted him and believed in his vision as

Master Sculptor. The two of them thought alike and liked the same things when it came to stone sculptures. Then, there was the Master Carpenter that he got from Reims, Joseph Mandaloup, one of the finest of his trade, he was told. Then, Master Mason, Robert Corneville, a most able man with the fingers of sweet harmony when it came to masonry, it was said of him as a mason. As for the Master Stone Cutter, Cajetan wanted the best available, Jeremiah Zelfester from Flanders. He had gotten to know him through Master Kurt Marquardt, and Cajetan knew that there would be no other that he would bring in to his cathedral site. He sent word to Jeremiah through André Cassegrain, and he was told that Jeremiah wanted to meet in person the Master Architect himself. So, Cajetan went to Flanders to plead with this stone cutter and offer him the job with more money than he had ever gotten before. When Cajetan returned to Évreux he had Jeremiah Zelfester with him. For Master of the Works, Cajetan got a mature and experienced friend called Isabeau DellaCarta who was originally from Provence. A good manager of things and men as well as a man of knowledge and high dintelligence, and recognized industriousness. He would be reliable in whatever capacity Cajetan the Master Architect would put him in since he trusted him and besides, Master Isabeau came with great recommendations. In no time, several boys, all about thirteen or fourteen came to see Cajetan and begged for an apprenticeship under him. He told them that first they had to submit references and produce proof of good character from someone who would vouch for them, and then he would decide.

Out of five candidates selected, three never returned. Cajetan chose a boy of thirteen, a tall youngster with red hair and dark brown eyes whose facial features reminded Cajetan of himself when he was thirteen. He specifically chose this boy whose name was Gilbert Tendrétoile because he admitted to Cajetan that he loved what he called "*la musique des étoiles*," and that his father's friends said of him that he was not only a dreamer but a good worker. How could Cajetan not take him as an apprentice?

There were laborers to be hired and other workers, but Cajetan was leaving that to the other masters and the Master of the Works. As for the Master Roofer, Cajetan would wait until he found one who qualified for the task. Besides, they were not at the point of roofing anyway. The excavation came first, then the walls of the foundation. When the hiring was done, Cajetan went to see the Bishop to report to him about the men he now had on site who would build the cathedral under his supervision. Cajetan told Bishop de Champigny that he recognized the line of authority, and that the Bishop was first in line, and that meant that all important decisions were to be made by him or, at least, approved by him. The Bishop acknowledged this order of things in making decisions, and told Cajetan that he was pleased with his choices of craftsmen, and added that his office would handle the finances, and the treasurer would be in charge. Cajetan did not like the financial end of building a cathedral anyway. The Bishop then told Cajetan that he truly liked his plans and design for they were what he wanted and trusted Cajetan in adhering to them faithfully. "Any deviation will be reported to me, and if necessary, approved by me," he insisted. He told Cajetan that the reason he liked the design was that it had simplicity of style while not disdainfully sober, nor too overly Romanesque. It had just the right touch of the Romanesque so that it blended well with the Gothic, and did not flare out with the flamboyant. Cajetan told him that he wanted something appropriate for the site, and at the same time not too tall nor too overly decorated with far reaching spires, but it would have the quality of the best of Gothic architecture with the color splendor of filtering light through beautiful stained glass windows. "We will have one large rose window in the western portal, as you can see, Excellency, plenty of stone sculptures to make this another Bible in stone," Cajetan told the Bishop. "When will you get started?" asked the Bishop. "Next week, if everything falls into place, Excellency. The masters have to finish getting organized, but I'm ready as I ever will be."

Excavation started the week after Cajetan met with the Bishop. It was May 1292, as noted in Cajetan's diary. Cajetan had insisted that the depth of the excavation be at least twenty-seven feet and not any less, for he did not want the episode of the *chantier* Saint-Amand with Bishop van Arevelde repeated. "You cannot cut corners in matters of building a cathedral," he told the Bishop. "Not to save time. That does not work." The Bishop fully agreed with Cajetan, and Cajetan felt he was in complete control of the destiny of the construction of the proposed cathedral, as far as architecture was concerned.

It was a beautiful morning and the air was filled with the soft fragrance of apple blossoms, and the waters of the River Iton flowed clear and sparkling in the morning sun. The laborers started digging very early right after daybreak, and everyone seemed happy to be part of a new cathedral project, for it provided work for so many who needed to work in order to earn a living and feed a family. The cathedral was not only a dispenser of grace but a provider for the people who needed work. It became also a gathering place for all of the craftsmen and their families who lived on or near the *chantier*.

By mid-June with the digging done, the first stone was ready to be laid onto the bed of small stones covering the clay at the bottom. Bishop de Champigny was there to bless the first stone as it was lowered into the large excavation hole. He was dressed in a long purple habit, and he wore his pectoral cross and Episcopal ring. He looked official and regal. He stood straight and tall as he blessed the stone: *"In nomine Patris, et Filio et Spiritui Sancto…*he began. After the blessing, he took Cajetan aside and told him to come and see him that afternoon. Cajetan shook his head in assent.

Cajetan had already met with the Master Quarryman, Carolus Quintal, to plan for the quarrying of stones, and the supervision of fifty stone cutters as well as some three hundred laborers needed to accomplish the task of cutting stones in the quarry. The laborers helped the stone cutters lift large pieces of stone out of the quarry. Then the stone was cut, chiseled, and hammered by the stone cutters, so it would match the patterns or templates supplied by the Master Mason. Every stone was marked three times, once to show its future location in the cathedral, here it was the §, once to show which quarry it came from, the ¶, and once to show which stone cutter had actually cut the stone so that he would be paid, ő, or some other applicable sign. Each stone then carried the signs of §, ¶, ő, or of whoever was the stone cutter.

The Master Mason checked with his mortar men to see that they were ready to exact mixtures of sand, lime and water. Laborers carried the mortar down the ladders to the masons who placed each stone, one on top of the other. With their trowels, the masons put a layer of mortar between each stone making sure the layers were well fitted. When it was dry, the mortar would be permanently fixed binding the stones together. Master Mason Robert Corneville, came to inspect regularly the stones to make sure they were perfectly horizontal. Then he used his plumb line to verify that the wall was perfectly vertical. These were thick walls and the slightest mistake in the foundation could endanger the wall that was to be built on top of it. Everything mattered in construction; no fault was to be tolerated for any reason. In the meantime, Cajetan met with his Master Carpenter, Joseph Mandaloup, to verify that he had already sent sufficient laborers with apprentices to the forest of Gauciel to select trees for timber. Master Mandaloup told Cajetan that he had already sent one hundred and seventy-five laborers and five apprentices to the forest, and that he himself was supervising the cutting of timber for the construction of scaffolding and the necessary workshops.

When Cajetan was satisfied that everything was in place, he went to see the Bishop and reported to him that he had all of the craftsmen he needed to complete the cathedral, except the Master Glazier. Here is the list he gave the Bishop: Master Quarryman, Carolus Quintal; Master Stone Cutter, Jeremiah Zelfester; Master Sculptor, André Cassegrain; Master Mortar Maker, Daniel Rouferlain; Master Mason, Robert Corneville; Master Carpenter, Joseph Mandaloup; Master Blacksmith, Athanase Primortain; Master Roofer, Abraham Steinhousen. As for the Master Glazier, Cajetan had someone in mind but had not been able to reach him or contact him. He knew that the well-reputed glass maker was on site in the Laon area. The Bishop congratulated Cajetan for his excellent choice of craftsmen, and thanked him for all the time and energy he put into the project so far. He told him that he knew that many an architect supplemented their income by working at more than one *chantier* or project, and that they were not always on site to make themselves available to both craftsmen and patron of the project. Cajetan reassured him that he was a one-man project architect, and that he was totally dedicated to this particular cathedral construction, and would not think of farming out his services just for more money. "After all, Excellency, this is my cathedral, the cathedral of my dreams," he told Bishop de Champigny.

----I admire your integrity and your dedication, Cajetan, and I will see to it that you are properly rewarded for your steadfast work with us. Listen, I hear that they call you Cajetan the Stargazer. Is that true?

Cajetan smiled.

----Yes, Excellency, I'm the Stargazer, as they call me. You could say that I've been gazing at stars ever since I was a young boy. I'm a creature of the imagination and creativity, and I dream. I dream of being the best architect and the best creator of the Gothic. I know I cannot reinvent the Gothic, and I do not intend to do so, but I want to give it the splendor it deserves for the greater glory of God the Creator. So money is not my main interest.

----I admire your sense of idealism and your sense of duty. I was that way once until I realized I had to be more practical with earthly matters.

----I'm practical too but in a more liberal sense. My craft is so important in my life that I cast aside petty worries and cares. What I enjoy is the reputation of being a creative person who creates important works such as the cathedral. If I attain any fame in life, it will not be me but my cathedral that will last for ages and testify to my craft as an architect. That's all I want, Excellency.

----That's an admirable goal, Cajetan, an admirable and worthwhile goal. You truly work in the gospel vineyard of the Lord. I wish I were as focused and dedicated as you are.

----But you are, Excellency. You have shown me that you truly are. Just do not deviate from the goal you have given yourself, to build this cathedral, especially do not deviate from my design, please.

For the construction of the roof, Cajetan let the Master Roofer determine for himself what needed to be done. As Master Architect he trusted wholeheartedly his master craftsmen to do what was professionally right. Large pieces of wood, some fifty feet long, had to be ordered from the northern countries. Soon the wood would follow the same path as the stones had, when they floated down the river from the quarry to arrive at the port in Évreux. It would be hoisted out of the boats with derricks and windlasses built by the carpenters, and put into waiting carts that carried them through the town to the *chantier Saint Obelard*.

By late October, the foundation was completed and Cajetan was assured that the mortar was perfectly dry, ready to accept the walls to be built on it. Solid as a rock, said the Master Mason. Cajetan did not know if the stone masons and stone cutters should start work on the walls of the nave or not, since they were getting close to November. November harkens the bad weather, the cold and rainy weather, and Cajetan was wondering if he should not postpone the work on the walls until spring of the following year. He was just being cautious, he thought. However, some of his craftsmen like the stone cutters and the sculptors told him that he was getting to be overly cautious, and that they needed the work to continue until mid to late December in order to survive until then. After all, this was not Flanders where the north winds and the snows come early, earlier than the valley of Évreux. Cajetan decided to extend the period of work to mid or late November. That meant that work on setting up the walls of the nave could get started right now. He thought he would consult with his Master Craftsmen, Corneville and Rouferlain, mason and mortar man, to see if the move was a wise one. They told him that he was a little too cautious with the weather, and that November in Évreux was bound to be rather mild. For precautionary measures, Cajetan went to see the Bishop and asked him about the weather patterns in Évreux during the months of November and December. He told Cajetan that ordinarily the weather is not too severe, but that, once in a while, terrible blasts of the north wind and their bursts of snow come earlier than expected. It had happened before. It happened in 1277, he told Cajetan. One never really knows, he told him. Cajetan thought about it, and thought until he was tired of thinking about the weather, and decided not to risk having an entire side of the nave wall fall after the craftsmen had worked on it before they left for the winter break. He was very cautious about the possibility of a collapse. He had seen it happen in Flanders and did not want it repeated. Not on his watch. He knew that some of his men would not be happy with his decision but they had to accept it since it flowed from the wisdom of the architect who took the necessary precautions to protect the men and their work. He was right. Some of the men, especially those who had to travel far, and had a large enough family to support, did not appear to understand Cajetan's decision. They were even angry, some of them. Why be so cautious and fearful? they asked. Once the mortar is dry, the wall will be solid enough to withstand the small ravages of winds and snow. We're in the mild area of the land, they maintained. But Cajetan would not change his mind. He told Wandal about it, and she did not see why the winds and the snows would come so early here in Évreux. She did admit, however, that this was her first year in Évreux, and that she could not advise Cajetan about the weather. Cajetan slept over his decision, and in the morning he resolved to mitigate the harm of certain difficulties his decision would have on those who would suffer some hardship without work and sufficient income during the extended winter months. He would offer them the surplus of his wages that the Bishop had granted him recently for his work and dedication. No one thought ill of him then, for they all thought he was being generous with them. Those who normally leave for the winter months to rejoin their families such as, the masons and the mortar men, since mortar work cannot be done in cold weather, they left in mid-November. Those who normally stayed, like stone cutters and sculptors who could no longer work outside, they sought shelter on site as they normally did. There, they cut stones and tracery, carved capitals and sculptures in preparation for the return of the masons and mortar men in the spring.

The snows came early and the north winds blasted with feisty force so that November, December and January were fierce and frigid months. People said that they had not experienced such a severe winter in ages. The Bishop brought heavy woolen blankets to Cajetan and gave him a warm cloak so that he could withstand the frigid weather. Wandal had her own woolen cloak and tunic while Emmanuel stayed inside most of the time learning the rudiments of the trade of the architect from his father. He wanted to become an apprentice. As for Gilbert Tendrétoile, the apprentice architect,

Wandal took a liking to him and often invited him for supper. He liked that. He was fond of Wandal and told her his story about being the fifth son of a large family that was often destitute, and could not afford to send him to school. Wandal knew that the boy was very intelligent and learned fast. She was glad that Cajetan had agreed to get Gilbert as an apprentice even though he had no patron. Cajetan told Wandal that he remembered when he was young and wanted so badly to become an apprentice. Besides, Gilbert had a sonorous and meaningful family name, Tendrétoile, he said. It was a sign, a good omen, he added. Of course, he was partial to anything that was linked to stars, Wandal told him.

Cajetan visited the craftsmen on site, now and then, to see how they were doing. He especially wanted time with Master Sculptor André to discuss the sculpture program for the cathedral. He had ideas about it and wanted to share them with the sculptor. First, Cajetan wanted certain specific sculptures for the tympanum of the western porch. Then he wanted other sculptures on the south portal, and a few more on the north portal. He also wanted to see certain ones inside the cathedral. He had many ideas of his own about sculptures. However, he did not want to infringe on the expertise of the Master Sculptor. Simply said, he did not want to impose his own authority on any master craftsman. Master André told Cajetan that he respected his ideas, and that he was glad to accept advice from someone he admired and trusted. He knew he had to please the Bishop first, then the Architect and then himself as craftsman. He had many years of experience as a sculptor, but he was open to new ways of seeing things. New and probably different legends and Biblical stories also to represent in stone. He told Cajetan that he was happy when he was allowed to be creative. He also respected his imagination as well as that of others. "Imagination does not mean monstrous creations or even non-traditional sculptures," he told Cajetan. "To imagine is to create, and to create is the impulse of the Spirit." Cajetan totally agreed with him and told him that he would return soon with a list of what he thought some of the sculptures should be. "I will only act as inspiration, André, and not as dictator. One who commands rather than suggests." Wandal told Cajetan later that, yes, he liked to suggest but that he also liked to have his way with certain things. "I like to have certain things my way, as you say, because I strongly believe in and am convinced of the worth of those things. Experience and travel have taught me much, Wandal." "And I suppose your dreams, Cajetan, your haunting dreams." And, they both smiled at each other.

December came and Christmas was celebrated with solemnity but with cautious expectations that the weather would change hopefully. The Bishop's mass was well attended, and both Cajetan and Wandal enjoyed the festivities of the holy day of Christ's birth. On the Feast of the Epiphany, they invited some of the craftsmen to join them in the celebration of the feast day, and shared the traditional pastry, the *galette des rois,* with their guests. The three who found the three beans in the cakes had the privilege of setting up a mock court as they became king, queen and jester for the day.

After January came February, and the weather changed dramatically from frigid to milder days. People said that this was due to heavenly intervention, making up for the fierce weather that had been sent during the past three months. Everyone believed in the intervention of God even in the weather patterns. Come the end of February, most of the craftsmen, who had left in November, returned to the cathedral site ready to work on the nave wall. By March first, all of them had returned. They were ready to resume their work on the cathedral that was officially the Bishop's and the chapter's cathedral, but known by all craftsmen as Cajetan's cathedral. They all deferred to his dream and to his continued determination to build on it. How can one not admit to dream visions?

16

CAJETAN'S CATHEDRAL :
the execution of plans and design----
une étoile s'éteint/ a star burns out

T he straw and the dung that had been placed on the finished stonework in the foundation to prevent the frost from cracking the mortar were removed. The site was cleaned up and the winter debris taken away. It was time to build the walls of the cathedral, and everyone was willing and ready for they had had a long winter. How good it is to be back in the cycle of work and social and religious activity, they said. No one complained about work. No one except those who did not like work and shunned it as much as they could, but craftsmen embraced work since they had been trained for it and they seemed to blossom by it. That's because they had all kinds of opportunities to display their craft creativity as well as their ability to accomplish assigned tasks. That was always a good feeling for them. That's why craftsmen working on a cathedral project relished their work and their accomplishments because they knew that a cathedral would last years and years, even centuries, and their contribution made it what it was. It's always good to be part of a grand project that has succeeded, thought Cajetan, and that's why I'm an integral part of the cathedral project along with the craftsmen who work on it. We are one whole creative unit. We are, in a sense, the Gothic, he mused.

Work on the walls began right after everything was checked and proven to be ready for the great work accomplishment that would rise up into the vaulting heights of a Gothic building. The walls of a Gothic cathedral consist of piers or columns that support the vaults and the roof. Cajetan wanted to make sure that the walls going up would be on solid foundation, and having talked to Master Mason, Robert Corneville, about it, he told him to get going on the walls as soon as he could. The masons, the mortar men and the stone cutters all went to work. Everyone knew what to do since they all had valuable experience in their trade. Cajetan had already shared his design with them and they comprehended the task at had.

255

The piers of the choir were to be one hundred and forty-four feet high and five to seven feet thick. They were to be constructed with hundreds of pieces of cut stones. That's why these stones had to be prepared ahead of time, ready for the masons and the mortar men. The whole operation did not tolerate well any delays. Everything had to be synchronized with care and diligence. Cajetan demanded that of his men. They all respected his determination and leadership. The tracery---the stone framework of the windows---all of which was cut from templates, was to be cemented into place along with iron reinforcing bars as the piers were being built. The templates had been ready for a week, and the iron bars lay on the ground next to the foundation. All was ready as the craftsmen began their individual trade work. Things ran smoothly when the Bishop came to see the progress of the construction, three days later. The appearance of the walls growing in height gave the Bishop confidence in his project as one that was not only attainable but realizable. He told Cajetan that he was genuinely pleased with the work. Cajetan told him that the name of the cathedral had to be resolved soon for he didn't want to continue calling it "the cathedral." He wanted a name. The Bishop told him that he thought he had made it clear that he cathedral's name was "Notre-Dame Reine des Cieux." Queen of Heaven was to be its name. Cajetan was a bit disappointed since he had long thought, after many changes, that the name of his cathedral would be Sainte Marie de la Belle Étoile. Of course, he realized that this cathedral was not his personally. It was the cathedral of Évreux and belonged to the Bishop and his chapter. But still, he hated to relinquish the name he had come up with, Holy Mary of the Beautiful Star. Cajetan and the Bishop must have deliberated on a name on several occasions, but when all was said and done, it remained as "Notre-Dame Reine des Cieux" and that's what it was going to be. The Bishop was in control on this point and not the architect. However, when Cajetan mentioned his dream name for a cathedral, Bishop de Champigny realized that Cajetan had given much time to a choice name of his, and it was a name to be considered since it was a worthy name for the Queen of Heaven. In order to lessen the blow to the refusal of Cajetan's dream name, the Bishop thought of a compromise. He would allow Cajetan to place a statue or some sculpture of Mary Queen of the Stars, in the south porch, if Cajetan wanted. How could he refuse such an offer? He was delighted that, at least, part of his dream would be realized in some form or shape whatever location on the cathedral he was building.

When Master Sculptor, André Cassegrain, heard of the news about the official cathedral's name, he told Cajetan, in a soothing manner, not to worry because he would hone the sculpture of the Queen of Heaven while incorporating the beautiful star that Cajetan wanted so badly.

----When I do the tympanum and its program of sculpture, I will give the Bishop his "Notre-Dame des Cieux." If in the heavens shine the stars, I cannot resist putting stars in Blessed Mary's crown as queen, and perhaps stars on her lovely gown of purity as well as any other places that will deserve a star. This will be perfectly in line with what the Bishop wants. As a matter of fact, it will be in perfect harmony with the name of the cathedral and the wishes of the chapter and the Bishop. Furthermore, I will make you a sculpture of your Holy Mary of the Beautiful Star. Wait and see what I have in mind. Both the western portal and the south portal will be in complete harmony with the name of the cathedral. How's that, my friend?

----You've read my mind and my heart, André. Thank you so much. I'm so anxious to see both tympanums.

----I'm going to discuss it with my craftsmen and apprentices, and I'll get back to you. Anyway, we're far from the sculpture program on the cathedral, at least a year away, I would say.

----It's never too early to plan, André.

That evening Cajetan told Wandal all about the Master Sculptor's plan for the sculptures of both the Queen of Heaven surrounded with stars and the one that Cajetan wanted, "Sainte Marie de la Belle Étoile."

----You see, my dear husband, everything is working out. And, Cajetan, you do get your way, somehow.

----Yes, I do, don't I? That's because I have some good and dedicated craftsmen working for me. Not only that, but most of them are very creative in their field and their work. I don't have to push them, nor do I have to tell them every single thing they have to do. They do it and without any recrimination or disdain. This cathedral will not only be done in the traditional time it takes to complete, but ahead of that time frame, I'm sure. Things are going so very well, Wandal.

----That's because the funds are there and none of you have to worry about delays on account of money. That's a big factor, Cajetan.

----I know, I know.

----Have you thought of some time for rest and diversion, my husband?

----I never think of that, Wandal.

----Well, I do.

----You do?

----Yes, I do. Because you don't want to burn yourself out, Cajetan. Then you would be no good to your work, to yourself and to others. Think about that.

----But my life is here with my cathedral. I would be totally lost without my architectural project. It's my very soul, Wandal.

----Stop being so dramatic, Cajetan. It's a building, that's all. A sacred building, yes, but fundamentally a building of stone and mortar.

----It's more than just a building, Wandal. You don't understand.

----Yes, I understand. You're the one who doesn't understand the reality of things, you stargazer, you dreamer with your head in the stars. It might as well be in the sand like an fabled bird.

Cajetan looked a bit hurt by that remark from Wandal.

----We live on different reality zones, my wife. I understand where you're coming from but I must insist that my whole life is sworn to the construction of a cathedral. I cannot help that. However, I will say, that you're right about time off, and I promise you that I will take sufficient time away from my work as soon as I can. That means that the two of us will go away and rest. I trust my craftsmen and my Master of the Works enough to leave the project in their capable hands. I know that the entire construction doesn't depend solely on me, Cajetan, the Architect. I know that used bodies and minds cannot function properly, if not given sufficient rest. I know.

----Then, do it.

As the walls grew higher, wooden scaffolding became a necessity. Cajetan knew that. So, he ordered the carpenters to build scaffolding made of poles lashed together with rope. The carpenters knew how. Hoists were attached to it so that the stones and mortar could be lifted. The scaffolding also held work platforms made of mats of woven twigs, so as to allow the masons to work at ease. These mats or hurdles, as they were called, could easily be moved.

Also, since long pieces of wood were not easily found, and were very expensive, the scaffolding for the walls above the arcade did not reach to the ground. It was hung from the walls and lifted as construction progressed. The men did not need ladders to reach it for several permanent spiral staircases were built into the wall itself. Everything had been learned through the experience of building cathedrals over time, and passed on from apprentice to journeymen to master craftsmen. Things were progressing well, thought Cajetan.

It was about that time that Emmanuel told his father that he had decided to become an apprentice architect. He had been following his father and other craftsmen in their work, and Cajetan had been suspecting that Emmanuel was nurturing a keen interest in architecture, but he did not want to push his son into something he might not like as a profession. Cajetan wanted it to come from the boy himself. Of course, he was very happy when Emmanuel announced his intentions. He would certainly accept him, and he would see to it that he got the best training possible. As of that day, Emmanuel became an apprentice architect and joined the ranks of the apprentices at the *chantier Saint-Odelard*. Emmanuel got along very well with the apprentice Gilbert Tendrétoile and so things were working well between the two. They even exchanged ideas about things and shared many a dream of their own. It seemed that with Cajetan as the Master Architect, dream sharing was contagious.

By mid-September, Cajetan was contemplating the work done and the coming of the winter months. He was hoping that the coming winter would not start as early as the previous year, and that winter would not be as severe either. Nothing to be done about the elements, thought Cajetan. You just have to accept what the Good Lord sends us, he mused.

Come November the craftsmen, apprentices, and the laborers all got ready to cover the foundation and the walls with straw as best they could. "It's hard to put straw way up there," said journeyman stone cutter, Daniel Courtemanche, to Cajetan. "We'll do the best we can, young man, and leave the rest to God." Cajetan parceled out his surplus income again to those in need before settling in for the winter months. Several of them left later than usual, and more stayed around the cathedral site. As for Emmanuel, he was now staying with apprentice friends and enjoying the newly found freedom that a fourteen year old discovers. Gilbert was going to visit an aunt and uncle he had not seen in years. They lived in le Poitou.

Cajetan told Wandal that he was now ready to go away for a rest, somewhere down south, probably in Provence. "Did you keep enough surplus money for our rest period?" "Never mind that, wife, God will provide." "Yes, God provides but how much?" The two of them left on a cloudy Monday morning in early December. The weather was good and the cold winds had not arrived yet. There was a light frost on the open fields but not enough to freeze everything. With sufficient warm clothing, Cajetan and Wandal were ready to take the road to Provence. They had never been to that part of the world. The closer they got to Provence, the warmer it got, and Wandal was delighted with this kind of weather in December. They stopped at several towns and got local foods to eat. They stayed at inns that provided comfort and cleanliness. After a week of traveling and staying only one night in one place, they decided to stay three nights in Avignon.

Avignon was a busy city right on the trade route between Italy and Spain. It was a merchants' city where almost anything could be purchased from herbs, spices, flowers, to different kinds of fish, fresh figs, big olives as big as a man's thumb, olive oil, silken and golden in the light of day. There were small garlic cloves that the natives called *aiet*, tarts made with delicious fruits and so many other wonders to the senses that it sent Wandal into a tailspin so caught up was she in all of the delightful offerings to be had. Everywhere they went, Wandal became ecstatic over the flowers and their perfume such as, the mimosa, the irises, the lavender, entire fields of them, and she marveled at the jasmine, this highly fragrant flower that she thought divine. Cajetan found out that there were guilds established for the craftsmen as well as the tradesmen. Trade was truly a bustling, busy and lively economic factor in Provence. Wandal and Cajetan also discovered that people down south said *"oc"* for, yes, instead of the northern *"oïl."* So, they started saying *"oc"* like the Provençaux did.

While in Avignon, they spent time walking around the river and saw the unfinished bridge, Le Pont Saint Benezet, and they wondered when it would be finished. Someone told them that construction had started in1185 and here it was 1293, eight years later, and it still wasn't complete. No one could cross over the river, he said. Also, it was in Avignon that Cajetan and Wandal met a Jewish individual by the name of Abraham Amar who introduced himself and told them that, as visitors, they should pay a visit to the Jewish crafts and trades center in the *carriere Isaac-Jacob*.

----I know that you're interested in our products here in Provence because I heard you talking about them with a delight that only visitors can conjure up and express.

----Well, thank you, said Wandal.

----Yes, we are grateful to you for such information, said Cajetan.

----I'll take you there if you so wish. But first, I must tell you a little bit about our history here in Avignon, I mean the Jewish people. The first Israelites to arrive here along the Mediterranean were a mixed assortment of refugees, traders and even slaves. The gateway was, of course, Marseille. You must visit Marseille before you leave Provence. Where was I? Yes, the Jewish population was well integrated then, enough to feel very comfortable and welcomed. But, with time and with some people, Christians I must say, the feeling deteriorated. But, we had our champions such as your monk, Bernard de Clairvaux who declared, and it was reported to us, that "He who touches a Jew is as guilty as if he had set to the eye of Jesus himself, for the Jews are his flesh and blood." Comforting thought, don't you think? At least for us, Jews.

----I did not know that, said Cajetan.

----Well, we are an important factor here in Avignon as well as in Provence. We work in the trades and crafts such as masonry, tailoring, dyeing, and bookbinding. Some of us are surgeons and doctors, very good ones, I might add. Those of us who practice medicine are very well respected.

----Are you a physician? What exactly is your trade, asked Cajetan.

----No, I'm not a physician nor a tradesman. I'm a rabbi and a healer of sorts, I might add. After I bring you to the trades center, I'll take you to Carpentras where half of our Jewish population in Avignon lives. It's here where we have our synagogue.

----You are indeed blessed by Yahweh and Abraham, said Wandal.

----And by Blessed Moses, let us not forget. However, we are somewhat signaled out since we, Jews, must wear the *rouelle* , the wheel, a special badge of identification on our outer garments, just like I'm wearing. We belong but we are separate.

----I see, said Cajetan.

----You said you came from Évreux, up north. Are you familiar with the Jewish learning center in Évreux? Its scholars are quoted in the Talmud called the Tosafot.

----The Tosafot? said Wandal.

----Yes, the Tosafot. The Tosafot are commentaries on the Talmud. They take the form of critical and explanatory glosses on the outer margins opposite Rashi's notes. He is very well known in our literature. We all read these commentaries and enjoy their enlightenment. Some of the best scholars in Évreux are Rabbi Samuel ben Schneor and Moses of Évreux.

----I'm afraid we are not familiar with them and their work, said Cajetan half apologetic and half contrite for not having studied them right there in Évreux.

----Well, that's all right. Someday you might have a chance to look into the Jewish Talmud and its history. Let me take you to the trade center and then I'll bring you to the neighborhood of Carpentras.

Both Cajetan and Wandal enjoyed the tour of the trades center and Carpentras. Cajetan was fascinated with the trades center and asked many questions about how they ran it, and how much trade they did. Wandal wanted to know how she could get some of the products, and several tradesmen gave her samples of lavender, herbs, spices, soaps, flowers, and a variety of herbal medicines. She especially liked the recipes for tomatoes with garlic and they gave her some. The two of them left the Jewish center enlightened, as they said, and thrilled with the fact that they had had a new and rewarding experience in their lives.

After Avignon, Wandal and Cajetan went to Arles, an ancient town where there was a truly ancient Roman cemetery in the section of the Alyscamps Saint Honorat where the remains of a very popular saint, Saint Trophime, were buried until they were transferred to the church named after him in the center of Arles. Cajetan was wondering if Bishop de Champigny could not inquire into the possibility that parts of those remains be acquired for the Évreux cathedral as relics, so that La Cathédrale Notre-Dame Reine des Cieux, could eventually become a pilgrimage site. Cajetan was going to talk to the Bishop about that, he told Wandal.

While in Arles, Cajetan and Wandal explored the colosseum in the heart of town. It was a Roman ruin but in good condition. Cajetan wondered how many could be seated in this colosseum. He had heard that the one in Rome seated some fifty thousand in its heyday. It was all done in the name of pleasure and entertainment, "bread and circus." He also wondered why men such as Emperor Nero and Emperor Diocletian could order the deaths of so many Christian martyrs just because they would not renounce their faith in Jesus Christ. Just for fun and pleasure?

When they left Arles, Cajetan and Wandal wanted to go to a small town further east, the town of Flayosc where they had a silk industry. Wandal was very much interested in that. However, someone told them that it might be dangerous to go there since it had been reported that there was a strange illness there, probably some kind of a plague that was affecting many people, and several had already died from it. Cajetan and Wandal decided to go home.

When they got home, the weather was mild and the trees and flowers were already budding. It was mid-February 1294 as noted in Cajetan's trusted diary. All of the craftsmen and laborers had returned to the cathedral site, and all were eager to get going. First, there was the general cleanup and then the removal of the straw and dung from the foundation and the stone work. "It's not easy climbing up there on the wall to get rid of the straw and the animal shit," said one of the apprentices. "It has to get done, my son, it has to get done, and I'm not going to do it," replied the Master Mason. The cleaning of the wall was soon done and without further comments from apprentices, journeymen or laborers.

Master Mason Corneville and Mortar Man Rouferlain got together to make sure they and their men were ready to continue the nave wall that had been started the year before. They were. The masons climbed up to the scaffolding and on to their mats, and started layering and troweling the cut stones with mortar that was being lifted up the scaffolding by the helpers. Not before too long, there was a block of wall on top of what had been done before, and things were running smoothly. Since the scaffolding for the walls above the arcade did not reach to the ground, it was hung from the walls and lifted as construction progressed. And progress it did.

Cajetan was now pondering the buttresses that had to be built to relieve the pressure that the vault would place on the piers. These buttresses erected on foundations next to the piers would later be connected to the piers themselves by stone arches called *arcs-boutants*. In Gothic architecture main piers had to remain thin and not heavy in proportion to their height allowing more space for the windows between them. Larger windows allowed more light from the outside to come in and thus a clearer brighter interior was had with the added feature of colors filtering through the stained glass. The virtue of the Gothic was precisely that, more light, higher vaults and an uplifting ambience of the sacred and the divine to glorify God and His Saints. And not to forget the Gothic space in the true Gothic cathedral that allows one to float in the air like a bird wafting on a stream of uncluttered air. That's how Cajetan understood it.

To build the flying buttresses it was first necessary to construct temporary wooden frames called centerings. This supported the weight of the stones and maintained the shape of the arch until the mortar was dry. These centerings were first built on the ground by the carpenters. Then, they were hoisted into place and fastened to the pier at one end to buttress at the other end. They acted as temporary flying buttresses until the stone arch was complete. Cajetan, along with the Master Stone Cutter, the Master Mason and carpenters understood that, and all would be put into motion like a symphony of crafts being executed flawlessly.

Now and then Cajetan gave advice and a few words of encouragement to Emmanuel, but he tried to treat all apprentices and journeymen alike. Except that, once in a great while, he would call his son and explain to him what he was doing and why. Cajetan knew that Emmanuel would eventually share that knowledge with his friends and other apprentices. He was teaching him how to teach.

Cajetan spoke to Bishop de Champigny about the Saint Trophime relics and how popular the saint was in Provence. He had seen the relics in the local church as well as some other relics, Saint Martha and Saint Alysope for instance, and he thought that having Saint Trophime's relics in the cathedral "Notre-Dame Reine des Cieux" of Évreux would serve as a pilgrimage link with Provence as well as other parts of the country, and perhaps other countries once the word was out. The Bishop told him that he did not know if that would work since Saint Trophime was not well known outside of Arles and probably Avignon. Why risk having relics of a saint that would not attract the wider populace, like those of Saint James in Compostela or the Veil of the Blessed Virgin Mary in Chartres? he asked. Cajetan did not know what to say and muttered under his breath, "I was only trying to help." To allay some of the fears Cajetan might have had as well as some frustration in not getting the answer he would have wanted, the Bishop told Cajetan that he was already looking into acquiring relics, important relics. But he did not tell him which ones. Cajetan also realized that there was a whole market for relics these days since every church and every cathedral was bargaining for them, and even going underground to try and find some of them. Favorite relics such as the forearm bone of Saint Agnes, the thumb of Saint Benedict, the heart of Saint Hubert de Bellecourt as well as the grill on which Saint Lawrence had been burned were all highly prized and greatly valued relics. .

The walls were going up swiftly thanks to the dexterity and swiftness of hand of the masons and the mortar men, as well as the laborers who climbed with nimble feet the permanent spiral staircases that led to the scaffolding. The flying buttresses were put in place as soon as the walls were declared safe since the mortar had dried. Cajetan noted in his diary that the year 1295 was the year of the buttresses. Cajetan was very pleased with the execution of his design for the buttresses. They were conceived with not too much flourish, as in the flamboyant mode, and had the reserve of good solid buttresses while maintaining the Gothic flair. He and Bishop de Champigny stood outside contemplating the walls with their buttresses, and the Bishop declared the finished work a marvel of design and a pleasant accomplishment in record time. Although Cajetan and his craftsmen did not aim to save time and hurry the construction beyond measure, they were most pleased with the results. Wandal kept reminding Cajetan that such results were due to the availability of funds, and that "Notre-Dame Reine des Cieux" was most fortunate in not having lacked funds due to the great generosity of the Queen and some of the peers. Who would have thought that the construction of a cathedral would go so well and so swiftly, people said with wonderment. Cajetan thanked his lucky stars and the good fortune of having recruited some of the very best artisans. At the end of the working year 1295, with the special donations from the Bishop and the surplus money he got every year, Cajetan was able to organize a huge outdoor fair for all those who worked on the cathedral. He wanted to show his appreciation for the progress on the construction, and announce that his son, Emmanuel, was now a journeyman architect.

The fair was a huge success for everyone. Cajetan had invited merchants and tradesmen to join him in the celebration, and their fees and contributions helped out with the expenses. There were jugglers, mimes, troubadours who sang songs, musicians with violas, lutes, mandores, sackbuts, flutes and drums. It was buoyant and cheery music with crescendos that the people wanted, and they got what they wanted and what they liked. It was merry-making at its best with acrobats, jesters, story-tellers, minstrels and even archery tournaments. The people who sold their wares and foods were absolutely delighted, and the buyers and eaters were especially satiated with the variety offered them. Someone suggested to Cajetan and the Bishop that the fair should become an annual event, The Évreux Fair. The Bishop told Cajetan that this was a good idea since it would perpetuate the delight of the people in going to an annual fair while drawing them to enjoy the Lord's bounty. It would not only stimulate the economy but stimulate souls to come together to pray in the cathedral, and make their donation and eventually become part of a pilgrimage to the cathedral. That's when Cajetan asked the Bishop if he had a relic in mind that would attract people. He told him that he was in the process of finding one. but had not been able to put his finger on one that would draw the crowds of people to the cathedral. Besides, he told Cajetan, the cathedral is far from completion, and that he was going to wait until the cathedral was near completion to get the major relic in place. Cajetan reminded him that he had told him before that he thought the completion date would be sooner than expected. At that rate, he told Bishop de Champigny, it should be done by the year 1312, twenty years from the starting date of 1292. That was Cajetan's estimate, that is, if everything went well and there were no serious problems including the funding. The Bishop reassured him that the funds would be there until the completion date.

With the success of he fair and the near completion of the walls of the nave, another work year was coming to an end. The next spring came and then summer and fall went by very fast. Even the years went by without Cajetan noticing the speed with which the months had gone one by one, year by year. By fall 1296, the walls were completed and the buttresses put into place. Cajetan announced to the Bishop that the walls of the nave and their buttresses were solid, and their architecture well done, and now the rest of the cathedral would begin. The craftsmen were now contemplating the construction of the choir with its piers and buttresses, and later the chapels in the apse.

The following spring, the work on the choir was started. There would be three stages, first the arcade of piers that would rise to seventy feet from the foundation, second, would be the triforium, a row of arches that would go up another fifteen feet in front of a narrow passageway. The last stage would be the clerestory, which consisted of fifty-foot windows that would reach right up to the roof. The cathedral was really unfolding in front of Cajetan's eyes, getting into shape, as he called it. Once the first part of the choir was done with the arcade of piers, it would truly look like a cathedral, Cajetan told himself. The choir and the nave were the very heart of any church, mused Cajetan, and the apse is the halo of a cathedral.

The arcade of piers in the choir went up very well with no hitches. Everything went according to plan and the design made by the Architect Cajetan. He was so pleased with himself and the craftsmen. The stone cutters worked extraordinarily fast, the masons troweled layers of mortar with speed and agility, while the mortar men climbed up and down like acrobats on a pole. The walls of the choir and aisle were completed in a little less than three years. In the meantime, the carpenters and roofers were getting ready for the mounting of the roof. Cajetan could not wait to see the next step for the interior of the cathedral, the vaults and the transepts.

The roof was made up of a series of triangular frames or trusses. The carpenters first assembled each individual truss on the ground. Master Carpenter, Joseph Mandaloup, supervised each step of the way. His carpenters kept watching him smile when things went well and growl when they did not. But the trusses were assembled one by one as they were supposed to be, to the liking of the Master. The timbers were fastened together by the mortice-and-tenon method. After test assembling, every part the truss was dismantled and hoisted, piece by piece, to the top of the walls. There, it was reassembled and the entire frame was locked together with oak pegs. The procedure was repeated until all of the trusses needed were up there ready to mount the roof. The first few beams were hoisted to the tops of the walls using pulleys hung from the scaffolding. Once the beams were in place, a windlass was set on top of them to hoist the rest of the timber and help in setting up the trusses. Apprentice Gilbert Tendrétoile watched every step of the way as the carpenters made the trusses and then hoisted them up to the roof. He was filled with amazement at the skill and agility of these tradesmen. Gilbert was fast learning his own trade as journeyman architect as he observed Cajetan's design being implemented step by step.

Meanwhile, on the ground, the roofers were casting lead sheets that would cover the wooden frame protecting it and the vaults from bad weather. They also cast the drainpipes and the gutters. Cajetan made sure that these roofers were following the design that he had made. Master Roofer, Abraham Shenhauser, reassured Cajetan that he indeed was following the established design, and his men were working hard at creating a system of drains and gutters that would work most effectively. The stone cutters and sculptors carved the stone gutters and downspouts that were to be installed in the buttresses. These downspouts, through which the water from the roof fell to the ground, were carved to look like all kinds of creatures, some benevolent some frightening. They were called gargoyles, and when it rained they would appear to be spitting water onto the ground below. When it poured it looked like streams of water rushing out of their mouths and splattering the pavement below. The stone cutters and sculptors enjoyed watching these creatures they had created, draining the water from the roof and disgorging it down below. Almost everyone enjoyed these gargoyles except the children who were frightened by the monstrous ones on account of their parents telling them that they were grotesque creatures from hell, and if they did not behave, they would go down into hell on a stream of water right into the fiery furnace of damnation. There is nothing like the imagination of a child fired by the fierce images conjured up in the mind and instilled there by a chiding parent to cast fear in the hearts of children.

Once the roof was completed and the gargoyles were installed on the buttresses and connected to the gutters at the base of the roof by a channel along the top of the flying buttresses, large vats of pitch were hoisted up to the roof and the timber was coated to prevent rotting. The sheets of lead were then nailed to the framework. The roof was done. Cajetan wrote in his diary that the roof was finally completed on August 14, 1301. Next came the construction of the vaulted ceiling and the foundation of the transept in the choir.

Emmanuel asked his father how the stones and the concrete were to be lifted up so high to the roof for the construction of the vaults. Cajetan replied that two devices were going to be used. One was the windlass and the second was the great wheel.

----The great wheel?

----Yes, Emmanuel. You have yet to see a great wheel. Well, you'll see one now. The carpenters are in the process of finishing the great wheel. It's a marvel of engineering necessity. It was designed and created to alleviate the burden of lifting up the heavy loads of stones and mortar needed to built the vaults. The windlass will raise it to where it will be used. It's big enough for two men to stand inside it.

----Then what?

----A long axle runs through its center to which the hoisting rope will be fastened. As the men walk forward, both the wheel and the axle turn winding up the rope. So, as you will be able to see, this method will enable them to lift very heavy loads.

----Oh, I see.

----Once the wheel is in place right below the timbers of the roof, the men can start working on the vaults.

In order to construct the vaulted ceiling, a wooden scaffold was erected connecting the two walls of the choir one hundred and fifteen feet above ground. Wooden centerings were installed to support the arched stone ribs until the mortar dried, at which time the ribs could support themselves.

----The ribs carry the webbing which is the ceiling itself, Cajetan told his son, the journeyman.

----I can see that the vaults are being constructed one bay at a time, said Emmanuel.

----Yes, they are, that's the area between four piers. It won't be long before the flying buttresses of the choir are completed and then the centering will be readied for the first stones of the vault. You're going to see quite a feat, Emmanuel, a feat of precision and craftsmanship. The rib vault is the mainstay of the Gothic interior. It's like huge hands in prayer reaching up to the heavens.

A year and a half later, the cut stones of the ribs called *voussoirs* had been hoisted onto the centering and mortared into place by the masons. Then the keystone was lowered into place to lock the ribs together at the crown, the highest point of the arch. The keystone is the mark of accomplishment of putting together all the pieces to produce a vaulted ceiling. If the cornerstone is the beginning of the construction of the walls, the keystone is the end of the building of the arched ceiling.

By June of 1306, the transept and most of its vaulting was complete. Cajetan explained to Emmanuel and Gilbert that the transept was the section that crosses the nave separating it from the choir. It's like the arms of a cross. At either end there is a portal, one is the southern portal and the other the northern portal. Cajetan noted in his diary that it was now time to talk to the Master Sculptor about the sculpture program for the cathedral. That would be a most fascinating project, he told himself. One that would complete his joy of the Gothic.

In the meantime, Cajetan was able to get a hold of the Master Glazier, Gabriel Vauglouse, and ask him about his intention of joining the craftsmen at *le chantier Saint Odelard* at Évreux. It took about three weeks for the Master Glazier to get back to him. He told Cajetan that he was completing his task at the Abbey where he was working, and that in two to four weeks he would be able to join him in Évreux. Besides, he told Cajetan, that he was bringing his men with him. You cannot separate a team of glaziers, he told Cajetan. That simply delighted Cajetan since he no longer had to worry about glaziers and the stained glass at "Notre-Dame Reine de Cieux." He told the Bishop about it, and the Bishop did not have any comments nor remarks on the craftsmanship of these men. He trusted his Architect completely. Besides, the Bishop had other things on his mind. He had recently been notified by the Vatican that he was to be made an archbishop, the Archbishop of Évreux and its surrounding area. This was in recognition of the work he had accomplished, especially on the cathedral and, of course, the management of the growth of his diocese. He told Cajetan that once he was fully installed as Archbishop, he would look into procuring relics directly from the Vatican. Cajetan told him that the choir was ready to receive the precious relics, so that pilgrims could come and venerate them and give their donations, even though the entire construction was not fully complete.

After a long and very cold winter, spring arrived once more and enticed the craftsmen back to work. Cajetan told himself that it was high time to continue discussing the sculpture program for the cathedral with Master André Cassegrain. There was one hitch. The fact that Master Cassegrain had not totally completed his masterpiece, or rather the guild had not certified him for the master stage, the guild warned the Bishop that so-called Master Cassegrain could not, in all honesty and integrity call himself master, and thus certify his work as a master. Should the Bishop have any questions about this, he was to report to the Presider of the Sculptors' Guild. Well, the Bishop was quite upset about that difficulty, like a fly in his soup. He had trusted his Master Architect to make sure that every craftsman was certified by their own guild. Cajetan told the Bishop that he knew about the difficulty, but that the sculptor craftsmen never once refused to work under Master Cassegrain since they admired his leadership and especially his superior knowledge of sculpture. Cajetan did not like to be in this quandary but had learned to live with it since he truly liked the work of Master Cassegrain. However, Cajetan had to look formally into this since the Bishop wanted this difficulty resolved once and for all. Cajetan was told by the Sculptor's Guild that the reason André Cassegrain had not been certified as master was that his masterpiece had not been accepted. Cajetan also found out by talking to several members of the guild that the reason the masterpiece had not been accepted was that it missed by a single vote, out of seven votes one vote had been cast against it. It was Master Tournedos who had, as they said, "*une dent contre lui*," a grudge against André Cassegrain. It turned out that this Tournedos fellow was angry with Cassegrain because he had lured the girl Tournedos was to marry away from him. Having talked to Cassegrain's wife about it, she told Cajetan that she did not care for Tournedos at all, and that it was her father who was forcing her to marry a man she did not care for at all. So she left him and married André since he had asked her to be his wife. Then the whole mess started. The father was angry, the mother was in tears and Tournedos was mad and blamed Cassegrain, and promised revenge. He got it by voting against the Cassegrain masterpiece even though most members of the jury considered the masterpiece a true work of artful craftsmanship. How was Cajetan to resolve the problem? Cajetan went to speak to the Presider of the Sculptors Guild and the Presider agreed that an injustice had been wrought, but at the time there was nothing he could do. He had to follow the rules of the guild. However, there was a clause in their rules that allowed for a review of certain decisions and a reevaluation of a masterpiece. And, since Tournedos was dead(he had died of a heart attack after a bout of drinking and binging, they said), the Presider could now easily reopen the case and ask the jury to vote on the merits of the masterpiece. Besides, André Cassegrain's reputation as a "master" sculptor was such that the Presider thought that André Cassegrain had already earned his master's certification. It was simply a matter of official approval. When things were finally resolved and André Cassegrain, the sculptor, became Master Sculptor officially and permanently, the Bishop was pleased and relieved. Cajetan felt honored to have resolved the problem, and Anré Cassegrain overjoyed at the results. He thanked Cajetan profusely and told him that he would sculpt for him the finest of Virgins of the Beautiful Star ever. Cajetan smiled with tears in his eyes trying to hide his feelings of pure delight.

Work had already been started on the radiating chapels in the apse, this semicircular part at the eastern end of the cathedral where individual chapels are built to offer visiting priests a place to say mass. Cajetan had planned to have five chapels, and having consulted with the now Archbishop, there would be one dedicated to Saint Peter with his keys to the Kingdom, one to Saint Hubert, the patron of hunters, one to Saint Martin of Tours with his link to Amiens, one to Saint Thomas Beckett who had been recently declared a saint by Pope Alexander III in 1173, and one to Sainte Geneviève who saved Paris from Attila the Hun's onslaught. Later on, when all of the five chapels were finished, the pilgrims would be able to walk through the ambulatory and visit each of the five chapels, and perhaps say a prayer to the saint to whom that particular chapel was dedicated. That was the understanding.

Master Sculptor Cassegrain sat down with Cajetan and they talked about what they had already discussed concerning the program of sculptures for the cathedral, specifically for the tympanums. First of all, Cajetan insisted on the statue for the southern portal that had been approved by the then Bishop de Champiny, that of the "Sainte Marie de la Belle Étoile." The Master Sculptor and he looked at some drawings that had been done. One showed the Virgin Mary with a star on her forehead, another with a radiating star on the lower part of her flowing gown, another with a star on top of her head, and yet another with stars on her feet standing on a huge tree trunk to symbolize the tree of Jesse, as André explained to Cajetan. Cajetan did not like any of them. After much deliberation, André came up with the idea of putting a large five-pointed star in the proffering hands of the Virgin with her eyes lifted up to heaven.

----Why didn't I think of this before?" asked André.

----That's it. That's the sculpture I want. That's the "Sainte Marie de la Belle Étoile," said Cajetan. She's holding the Star of the Heavens in her hands and offering it to the world. The star is both Jesus the Christ born in Bethlehem where the bright and virginal star in the heavens guided the Magi. It can also be the Virgin Mary herself offering her purity and brightness of soul and body to all the world for its salvation. I like it, André, I like it because it conjures up so much and at many levels of meaning. Now, what else were you planning to do, André?

----I want a sculpture of the Christ in majesty, *le Beau Dieu* as we see in other cathedrals but mine will really be in resplendent majesty. I also want the two Lazaruses, the one who is raised by Jesus from the dead, with Martha and Mary by his side, and the other Lazarus, the poor beggarman who was spurned by the rich man. I will show Lazarus in the bosom of Abraham while the rich man in hell where he suffers the pains of fire and thirst.

----How about Mary in her glory with the angels and archangels, Cherubims and Seraphims, Mary as Queen of Heaven in all of her glory crowned by her son, the Christ the Savior?

----And how about the various layers or stages of heaven itself with God the Father Creator, God the Savior Son, and God the Holy Ghost at the very top capturing in essence the Most Holy Trinity? Then underneath, Mary with Saint Joseph and the apostles. Under that layer, the saints that we choose to put there like Saint James, Saint Benedict, Sainte Anne, Saint Augustine...

----But Saint James will already be there with the apostle, André.

----Oh, yes. But, let's not think about all of the saints we're going to put in the cathedral. We must have room for more at a later date.

----I'd like to have some reflecting the Old Testament like the Prophets and other personages of the Bible.

----You're right. We'll discuss all of that at a later date, Cajetan.

----One thing we have not talked about...the foliate head.

----Ah, yes, the foliate head. That's an entirely different matter. We'll have to talk about it but sometimes later. I have some ideas on it and I have just the right man for the foliate head, his real name is Rachid Mommar-el-Shir. He's known around here as Roger Montmajeur. That's to disguise his true identity.

----Why, André?

----I'll tell you all about it later. Right now I have to go over the full design of sculptures with my men.

The following week, the Master Glazier arrived at the *chantier* with fifteen of his glass makers. They were supposed to be the cream of the crop, well experienced and creative with color. Cajetan was anticipating that they would give the cathedral some luster and great coloration that would make "Notre-Dame Reine des Cieux d'Évreux" the jewel of cathedrals when it came to stained glass windows, probably even surpassing Chartres and even Notre-Dame de Paris. "After all, that's what Gothic is all about, color and light in the uplifting ambience of a cathedral," he said. The other craftsmen told Cajetan that he had unreasonable expectations and that he would certainly be deceived. He told them to wait and see what these men will do for this cathedral. "You wait and see. They're superb glaziers under the leadership of one of the finest, if not the best, glaziers in all of Europe," he told them.

The glass makers arrived as a perfectly coordinated team of glaziers under the leadership of the Master Glazier, Gabriel Vauglouse. They had the reputation of being the most accomplished of all glaziers in most *chantiers* and their reputation had preceded them. Expectations ran high and Cajetan was full of hope that the stained glass windows at "Notre-Dame Reine des Cieux" would surpass all of the windows he had ever seen. However, the other craftsmen told him that this time he was truly dreaming and that his daydreams would be just that daydreams. They would indeed be far from reality. He told all of them that he wasn't just imagining but that he knew that Master Vauglouse and his team would deliver the very finest of stained glass windows. "Just you wait," he told them. "Glaziers are a special lot," he said, "and although I would put them in the same category as other craftsmen, I would elevate them to an even higher status, that of artists." Some of the other craftsmen thought that they were artists too, but not elevated to a point of haughtiness that Cajetan seemed to be lending those glaziers. The Bishop heard about the high esteem that Cajetan held for the glaziers and he told himself that he was proud that his cathedral would have some of the finest stained glass windows in the land. That truly made his day.

The glaziers made the glass from a mixture of beech wood ash and washed sand that was melted at high temperatures. After, different kinds of metal were added to the molten mixture for color. Then, the glass makers scooped up a ball of molten glass on the end of a hollow pipe and blew it up like a balloon. By cutting the end off the balloon of glass and spinning the pipe quickly, the glass opened up into a flat circular shape. That was the first step. The second step was to remove the flat shape from the pipe and let it cool. Once cooled, the glass was then cut into squares to fit the right shape and size for each window. Then came the patterns. The pattern for a particular window had been drawn on a whitewashed bench so that the glass could be cut to the exact size and shape simply by laying it over the pattern. Each window glass was made that way, step by step. It was intricate work and meticulous in its demands as patterns go.

Since Cajetan had already discussed patterns with Master Vauglouse, it was agreed that certain windows would follow the content design offered by the Master Architect, some by the Archbishop and the rest by the imaginative creativity of the glaziers themselves. Cajetan liked to allow craftsmen to use their own creative powers when it could be done and did not deviate from the initial design as set by the architect. Cajetan was not exacting in his view of things; all he demanded was an artistic sensitivity be brought to all work done by craftsmen. That, he firmly believed in. After all, crafsmen are craftsmen because they are trained to do fine tasks and nost just slipshod work that no one really wants or cares for.

Cajetan had chosen the legend of Theophilus as one subject for sculptures, but Master Cassegrain convinced him to have the legend in glass instead of stone since Notre-Dame de Paris already had that in one of its tympanums. So, Cajetan agreed that the Theophilus legend should be in stained glass with light striking through it, thus making the legend come alive for those who gazed at it.

Theophilus was basically the story of a man who sells his soul to the devil and runs to Blessed Mary to redeem it, Cajetan explained to Emmanuel and Gilbert.

----But how did Theophilus happen to sell his soul to the devil? asked Gilbert.

----Well, the story goes that Theophilus was a cleric and he wanted to maintain his position in a diocese in Sicily. For that, he made a pact with the devil and signed a contract in his own blood. After many years, he became fearful thinking about death. Touched by grace, he repented and asked Our Lady to rescue him from the pact.

----Did she do it?

----Of course, she did since she's the Mother of us all, and she hates the devil for what he does. So despite Theophilus's horrible sin, Our Lady appeared to him and promised to intercede for him with God. She stood before the devil and threatening him with a sword, took the contract from his hands and liberated the cleric. The story spread and more and more people found out about Theophilus, and now the legend has been immortalized. The main theme here is the unlimited mercy of Our Lady toward her children. She listens to all requests for mercy down to the smallest of one. Nothing goes unanswered.

----And that fits in very well with the name of the cathedral, "Notre-Dame Reine des Cieux," said Emmanuel.

----Yes. Theophilus's story establishes in all of our minds and hearts that even in the worst and most miserable situation, we will always find help and a solution if we pray to Our Lady Queen of Heaven. That's because of who she is, we can turn to her for a resolution for even the most desperate situations. That's why so many, in our times, have recourse to her and honor her with cathedrals such as ours. Saint Bernard strongly affirms this truth in the *Memorare*. Remember that prayer, Emmanuel?

----Yes aunt Marie Dieudonnée used to recite it every day, she said. She had learned it from grandmother Grisoulda.

----Yes, dear sweet mother and her daily devotions. Let's see if I can still remember it. 'Remember, O most gracious Virgin Mary, that never was it known that anyone who fled to thy protection, implored thy help, or sought thy intercession, was left unaided.'

----That's it. I will need to recite it every day so that I can finish my masterpiece, and for it to be approved by the Council of Architects.

----How are you doing with that, Emmanuel?

----Well, not too well, father. I talked to you about it a while ago and I really need your advice now. It seems that I cannot do it on my own.

----What's the problem?

----Remember I told you that I conceived of a project based on a tympanum with an entire program of sculptures including the trumeaus. I've been working at it and even consulted with Master Sculptor Cassegrain, but he kept asking me what I wanted, and I could not come up with it. At least, not with new and unique ideas. I'm afraid if I repeat the same old ideas in sculpture, the Council will not approve my masterpiece. It will be tied to old ideas with a different style spin. That's all.

----That sounds like a real dilemma, said Gilbert.

----I'll tell you what, Emmanuel. I will give you some ideas myself, but you must choose on your own and be creative about it. It must be your project, not mine.

----I know, I know.

Cajetan and Emmanuel sat down together one evening and discussed the sculpture program for his tympanum and trumeau masterpiece. Cajetan told him about the cathedral at Moissac especially about the trumeau with the elongated sculpture of the Prophet Jeremiah and of Saint Paul on the other side. "They're masterpieces in my estimation, Emmanuel, great works of artistry. You don't have to select the same Prophet and saint but this may be an interesting idea for you. As for the sculpture of the tympanum, study some possibilities, and come back and we'll discuss them. Be creative, my son. Think with your imagination and skill."

Emmanuel worked hard on his project. He worked at it for several months until he came up with a design that would rival any other masterpiece, he figured. Was he right though? he asked himself. "Let's see what father, the great Master Architect, will have to say about it. If he approves, then how can the Council reject it? He's so well known in the guild and highly respected by all." And off he went in a hurry to see his father who was glancing at some designs for a window.

Emmanuel's design for the tympanum was a semicircular program of sculptures figuring the Resurrection of Christ in all majesty and glory with the eleven apostles next to him looking upward at the heavens as he rises up to the Father. One level above another all well designed to reveal one complete cycle of Resurrection and Ascension. Below that plan was the Dormition of the Virgin Mary on one side and her glorious reign in heaven on the other. Angels with stars in their hands hover around and about.

----You see what I'm trying to do here, father?

----Yes, a marvelous concept and creative too, Emmanuel. The idea of Christ's Resurrection and Ascension to heaven along with the Mary's Dormition and Reign as Queen of Heaven fit very well together as one whole program. Here you blend creativity with the gospels and even reveal the heavenly quality of the stars. You knew I would like that.

Emmanuel smiled broadly with a light shining in his eyes.

----I'm going to verify with Master Sculptor Cassegrain what he can do with that. Just how he will conceive of the sculptures I propose. I'm sure he'll come up with a style unique and appealing to the eye.

----I'm sure he will. Now, how about the trumeau?

----Here it is. I propose a trumeau with the Prophet Isaiah, my favorite, on one side with Saint John with his concept of "the Word made flesh," on the other. I want some animals representing the four evangelists on the other two sides.

----With leaves and vegetation and maybe a foliate head or two. Not big ones, just small heads hidden in the foliage, perhaps?

----I'll see about that. You still insist on foliate heads, don't you?

----If you want to be creative, yes. I'll have them on my cathedral. On the Archbishop's cathedral I meant to say.

----No, it really is your cathedral, father, Master Architect.

They both laughed as Emmanuel was preparing to go and see the Master Sculptor in his workshop.

In the meantime, Cajetan was pondering the addition of yet another Biblical story for a window that would catch the brightest of light from the sun and that, he figured, would be on the eastern side where the sun would rise in the morning and stay there for a while. He was thinking about one of his favorite episodes from the Prophet Daniel with the three Israelites, Hananiah, Azariah and Misael sent to the fiery furnace to die because they refused to fall down and worship the golden statue set up by King Nebuchadnezzar. Cajetan wanted them singing in the furnace and praising the one true God, Yahweh, the Lord of the Old Testament Covenant. When he presented his plans to Master Vauglouse, the latter was excited about it, and he told Cajetan that he would have a marvelous time bringing out the fire of the furnace surrounding the three young men, but not consuming them. "I'm going to make that window burn with ardent flames and watch the sun light up that fire when it hits the stained glass," he told Cajetan. Cajetan was pleased with himself and pleased that Master Vauglouse wanted to create that window. It would be called Hananiah, Azariah and Misael blessing the Lord and singing in the flames of the fiery furnace. People of the diocese as well as pilgrims, especially children, would not only enjoy the story but stand there admiring the stained glass window that brought to life an Old Testament story in full splendor. That's what Gothic is all about, brilliant light and sacred uplifting grandeur and space, mused Cajetan.

The Archbishop wanted a window with the Virgin Mary in Heaven interceding for mortals who pray to her. He thought that would greatly please the worshippers who would come to the cathedral almost every day to pray to her to ask her some favor hidden in their hearts. He also wanted one with the genealogy of Jesus, just like at Chartres, he told Cajetan. Cajetan was pleased that he could satisfy the Archbishop's request, and at the same time beautify the cathedral with some outstanding stained glass windows. All of this was truly promising in Cajetan's creative plans, since the windows along with the sculptures would help round out the Gothic achievement.

When the stained glass was cut into pieces, these pieces were joined by strips of lead into sections. These sections were then inserted between stone mullions and the reinforcing bars so that windows as high as fifty or sixty feet could be created as were seen fit. First, the window with the legend of Theophilus was put into place, then the Archbishop's window of the Blessed Virgin Mary interceding in heaven. The third one was the window with the fiery furnace and the three Israelites. Next, the Archbishop's wish to have the genealogy of Christ. This one was done in soft hues of mauve and rose so as not to copy the blue of Chartres. After that, Master Vauglouse had his own choice of the four evangelists put in.

Afterward, there came the other tall windows with many subjects taken from either the Old Testament or the New Testament as well as portions of the lives of saints, saints who were revered by the people such as Saint Agnes and Saint Cecilia with her harp. Finally, there was one of Saint Tarcisius, a young acolyte of twelve, who died as a martyr during Roman persecutions holding the "Holy Mysteries" in his breast, protecting them from the gang who beat him up. He was bringing the sacred hosts to those Christians in prison awaiting death. One of the glaziers, a devout man in his fifties, thought that this was a very good subject linking it to Christ and the Eucharist. Besides, he said, this would be a good example for children growing up respecting the Sacred Mysteries.

Now, the glaziers were ready for the rose windows. Cajetan was waiting for that. He thought that huge rose windows were the epitome of Gothic design and architecture along with the vaults and buttressses. They were not only the seeing eye of God in the cathedral, but the beaming radiance of God's presence in the Gothic sacred space, he said. While the windows were being installed, plasterers covered the underside of the vault so that it looked finished and well accomplished. Then the stone cutters and sculptors finished the moldings and capitals while masons lay the stone slabs that made up the floor. They created a labyrinth pattern in the floor. After all, Chartres had one, why not Évreux?. Finding one's way to the center of the maze was considered as worthy of the Lord's blessing as making a long pilgrimage through the countryside that so many had to make in order to worship in a cathedral such a "Notre-Dame Reine des Cieux." The labyrinth fascinated not only the masons and their apprentices but many craftsmen who wanted to follow the paths that led to the center of the maze. It was a game of sorts, a challenge and one's pilgrimage to the center of God's graces in miniature. Even Cajetan attempted the maze after the craftsmen were done their work for the day. He even told Wandal about it. Gradually but surely the cathedral was closer to completion. It might take another five to six years, but the pace of the work overall had been good, very good. The Archbishop thought that the cathedral was looking great what with the windows in place and the bells being on order. The chapter had decided it was time for the planning for the bells before the spires go up and the towers are in place, they said. The foundry in Évreux was alerted.

To the great delight of the Archbishop, he called it his humble delight, the Archbishop had just been named a cardinal by His Holiness Clement VI, and was told that the consistory had been held in Bordeaux and not in Rome since the Pope was now in residence in Bordeaux. Archbishop de

Champigny was to be given his cardinal's red galero and other paraphernalia at a later date. Before he even got his red hat, the Archbishop received news that the Pope had moved residence to Poitiers, and that he was to go to Poitiers to be invested with the title and accouterments of a cardinal. Quite a shuffle there, thought the Archbishop. When he returned to Évreux the now Albert Cardinal de Champigny went to his chapter and told the members that he was planning to reward his Master Architect, Cajetan with a medal that he had gotten while at the papal court. He also informed them that he was able to get relics for the cathedral. First, relics for the main altar stone and second, special relics for the veneration by pilgrims who would come in droves, he told them. The special relics were those of Saint John the Baptist, a part of his skull that had been retrieved somehow. That would really put a damper on Chartres who claimed to have the only relic of the saint. The Cardinal told his chapter that people would truly flock to "Notre-Dame Reine des Cieux" to see and venerate this sacred relic. And that would put money in their coffers. Then the Cardinal informed Cajetan about the relics and also told him that he was giving him a medal signifying he was a Knight of Saint Thomas, the patron saint of architects. At first, Cajetan refused the honor claiming that he was not worthy of it, and that the other craftsmen deserved it much more than he did. But the Cardinal insisted and thus convinced him to accept it since it was for an architect and not for any other craftsman, and that he wanted Cajetan to have it. A special ceremony was planned at the cathedral for Cajetan to receive his medal. It was to be given in the choir under the vault with the keystone. Wandal was all excited about the medal and was so very proud of her husband architect. Emmanuel was very pleased, even emotional about it. Gilbert congratulated Cajetan and told him that he was ever so proud to be under him as an apprentice and journeyman. They informed Melodia and Philippon, but they could not come. They sent their best regards. Marie Dieudonnée sent a representative, for she could not come personally, she told the Cardinal in a letter. The day arrived. It was June 1308, the same year that Emmanuel was certified as a Master Architect. He was now 28 years old. The ceremony was held with all the pomp and pageantry that the Cardinal could come up with, for he was also displaying his pride in being a cardinal. Dressed in the red cardinal colors of his station and with the galero on his head, midway through the ceremony he had to hand it over to an acolyte because the large round hat kept falling off his head, the Cardinal blessed Cajetan then blessed the medal and pinned the medal on Cajetan's chest and proclaimed that henceforth he was a Knight of Saint Thomas and worthy of being called Sir, for he was indeed a knight. There was a large celebration after the ceremony, and everyone manifested their joy and pride over the knighting of their Master Architect by drinking beer and singing songs loud and clear so that the entire *chantier* rang with mirth and merriment.

At the foundry in Évreux, three large bells were cast in bronze. First a model of the bell was made of clay and plaster of Paris. It was covered with a coat of wax and then the inscriptions were carved on the wax. This was then covered with a layer of clay and plaster compound. When the entire construction was heated, the wax melted and ran out, leaving a cavity between the outer shell and the core. This became the mold into which molten bronze was poured. When the metal cooled, the mold was destroyed and the bell was prepared for shipment to the cathedral. This process was repeated for the other two bells. That's how bells were done as explained to the Master Architect. Cajetan was pleased with the way the cathedral was advancing, and it was nearing its final stages in the year 1310 faithfully recorded in Cajetan's diary of the Architect.

While the spires and the towers were being built, tracery for the rose window west, at the front of the cathedral, was being carefully cut according to plans. Voussoirs were carved to form the arched gables over each of the three front doors, and a tympanum was carved to go over each of the doors. Master Cassegrain told Cajetan that he was planning to place on the tympanum over the middle door a large and tall stone carving in bold relief of the Queen of Heaven with a crown of stars on her head, uplifted arms and hands, and angels around her like cherubims with youthful heads and wings only. On each of the further ends of the tympanum, he would put other carvings, on the right, people with raised arms pleading with the Blessed Virgin as if to ask for entrance to the Heavenly Kingdom. On the left, recognizable saints in their glory such as, Saint Benedict, Saint Paul, Saint John the Evangelist, Saint Mark and Saints Timothy and Titus, Saint Hilary of Poitiers, Saint Mathias, Saint Mathilda and Saint Scholastica, sister of Saint Benedict. Master Cassegrain also had plans for the other two tympanums. The one over the door on the right was going to have the Last Judgment as its main theme, and the one over the door on the left, Prophets and Judges from the Old Testament. All three trumeaus would be decorated with vegetation and fruits that were seen in the locality of Évreux.

Cajetan had sat down with Master Cassegrain and they had discussed the inclusion of foliate heads amid the sculpture program, not too evident, of course, but there if one bothered to look for them. Master

Cassegrain had explained to Cajetan that the placement of foliate heads was difficult and challenging for some people did not like them at all while some others tolerated them if they were not monstrous, he said. Certain clerics, priests and bishops did not want them inside or outside their churches and cathedrals. They considered them wild creatures taken from the forests or some untamed places where pagan creatures lived. The eternal question was, what are these creatures doing in a sacred place like a church? Of course, Cajetan had answers to that question but would they listen to him? Finally, Master Cassegrain told Cajetan that the Master of foliate heads was none other than his special assistant, Rachid who was known as Roger Montmajeur by the rest of the craftsmen and laborers. All of them knew that he was of mixed Arabic and Celtic background and had had different religious convictions before he was converted and baptized a Christian. Master Cassegrain also explained to Cajetan that in order to find work for a non-Christian that person had to convert first and then apply for a job. The same thing occurred for would-be craftsmen. These people could not even consider becoming craftsmen in a guild if they were not baptized believers in the Christian faith. No pagan need apply, was the word of the day.

People like Rachid brought with them their own beliefs, some about nature and its wild life, other beliefs in other gods and goddesses and still other beliefs in spirits that permeate earthly existence. Some of those beliefs went into the creation of foliate heads, explained Master Cassegrain. Foliate heads are the result of syncretic beliefs, he said. "If you want some foliate heads then talk to Rachid, I mean Roger," said the Master Sculptor to Cajetan.

Cajetan did talk to Rachid, known as Roger, and the two of them decided on some foliate heads for the cathedral. Cajetan did not bother to tell the Cardinal about it since he said that the less he knew the less he would complain about foliate heads in his cathedral. Rachid/Roger worked discreetly and often under cover sculpting foliate heads. He made one with acanthus leaves much like the one in the Bamberg Cathedral in Germany. As a matter of fact, he admitted to Cajetan that his relative, a great uncle of his was the one who had done the foliate head on the Console of the Rider and nobody knew about it since the architect had died and the bishop was gone and everything had been so secretive that the Foliate Head of Bamberg was attributed to some unknown German sculptor named Albrecht. Another foliate head that was placed on one of the capitals was the one peering through vine leaves with a long mustache of vine tendrils with young grapes. Still another that Cajetan liked very much was the foliate head with a long band of oak leaves winding around its head and down to the neck. It was placed in a far upper corner of one of the radiating chapels, and one had to crane his neck to really see it, but it was truly beautiful. Very artistic and created with imagination and subtle thinking, he mused. All in all, Cajetan was very happy with his foliate heads, and was eager to show them to Wandal when he told her about these creatures and the vegetation.

By 1312, the carpenters and roofers had completed work on the spire which rose above the crossing of the nave and transept. The spire was a wood frame structure covered with sheets of lead and decorated with sculptures and ornaments. Some of the sculptures were of angels with trumpets, doves and cranes seemingly in flight, as well as monks who were scribes with eyeglasses on their noses.

Meanwhile, the carpenters were busy working on the doors in their workshop. The center door alone was almost twenty feet high made with heavy planks of wood and joined with cross-ribs. All the metal parts like nails, bolts, hinges and locks were being done by the blacksmith and the Master Metal Worker. Work was also being done on the tower. That's where the three bells would be lodged. A heavy timber framework was being constructed in the south tower. It had been under construction for some eight months. The bells were to arrive in two to three months, and the carpenters wanted to make sure the tower would be almost done by then so the bells could be hoisted and fastened into place.

The latest news was that Cardinal de Champigny was retiring after forty years as Bishop, Archbishop and then Cardinal in Évreux. He was now seventy-six years old and had grown weak in the last two years, and had trouble with his eyes. He had told Cajetan about his condition and his plans to retire before he announced it publicly. He would remain in Évreux as Cardinal Emeritus and serve as an honorary master of the cathedral works, thus not completely leaving the project and his Architect Cajetan in a lurch. Cajetan loved the man for his courage in standing firm with his decisions and creative enough to understand Cajetan's plans and design for the cathedral. He never once argued with his Architect and never opposed him in his plans. He had the foresight to admit newness and imagination in his thoughts and actions, said Cajetan to his craftsmen. Of course, the Cardinal trusted Cajetan implicitly, and Cajetan never proved him wrong. What truly relieved Cajetan from any major worries was the fact that he did not have to struggle with funding. The money had always been there thanks to the efficient and trustworthy role of the Bishop/

Archbishop/Cardinal who always soothed his chapter with words of wisdom and assurance like an emollient on a stiff and sometimes resistant surface. The Cardinal was being replaced by Bishop Moisan Chalumeau, a younger prelate who proved to be efficient and tolerant of new ideas in his present diocese of Lyons as Adjutant Bishop. Cajetan just hoped that this new Bishop would tolerate his own ideas about the Gothic. Anyway, the cathedral was almost done and what was left were the rose windows, some pieces of sculpture and the finishing of the bell tower.

Wandal was worried about Cajetan's health. He had been complaining of pains in his stomach, then in his legs lately. Wandal told him to take it easy and to get more rest, but Cajetan was too much the driven architect to slow down. He was like a wound up mechanical device that keeps running and running constantly without reprieve. His age started to show. He was now sixty-six years old. He had come to the realization that he did not have the energy he once had, and that he was indeed getting old. He avoided the thought of leaving his work to retire somewhere in the countryside and do nothing but gardening and rest. That was not his solution to his final years on earth. He had to see the completion of his cathedral. It was truly his, even though it belonged to the diocese of Évreux under the trust of the new Bishop and, of course, the Cardinal Emeritus. Cajetan was so glad that the Cardinal was still part of the cathedral project, and he ever so often sat down with him to discuss the project that was so dear to his heart and to the Cardinal's heart. They had put so much creative energy, time and genuine concern in this project that it was no wonder that both of them could not let go completely. When one has invested so much of himself into a creative project like the construction of a cathedral, especially a Gothic cathedral, one cannot simply walk away and forget about it. It is not done or doable, thought Cajetan.

Cajetan continued his daily tasks as the Master Architect, and things rolled along as he had planned from the beginning. He wasn't as sharp with ideas and execution of certain plans, but he allowed himself the luxury of scaling back as far as projected plans for the future were concerned. He was more involved with the immediate plans like the completion of the spire and the south tower and, of course, the rose window over the front portal. He was anxious to see all of the different colored pieces of glass put into place to form the entire design of the rose window. Master Vauglouse had told him that he, Cajetan, would be very surprised at the finished product. Cajetan couldn't wait.

The masons put together the pieces of the rose window and installed the tympanums and voussoirs over the doors. The doors looked splendid in sturdy wood and metal cross-ribs. The trumeaus had just been carved and the central one showed the creative genius of Master Cassegrain. He had carved the Visitation in stone with the Blessed Virgin and Elizabeth on two sides with elongated bodies that showed the maternity of Mary and that of her cousin, Elizabeth. It was done with sacred discretion and modesty. On the other two sides were vines, grape leaves and small eyes peering through the leaves while baby angels seemed to hover nearby. People who gazed closely at the trumeaus said that they thought they saw very small foliate heads but they could be mistaken, they added. Master Cassegrain had been very discreet about those seemingly small foliate heads. Rachid known as Roger had helped him to execute the trumeaus. Master Cassegrain told Cajetan that he wanted the entire program of the three portals with tympanums to display the story of Mary, the Mother of God, the Savior. He added that the story was also one of salvation because salvation was made with the intercession of Blessed Mary and her *Fiat*. In the center tympanum the Master Sculptor, along with his craftsmen, had placed the Queen of the Heavens sculpture and all of the sculptures that had been explained to Cajetan before. In the Final Judgment scene of the right side tympanum, one could see the presence of the Virgin Mary opening up the heavens through her intercession. On the left tympanum, at the center with the Old Testament Prophets stood Mary the Mother of God pointing toward Isaiah and Ezekiel. On one side were the representations of artisans celebrating the Wisdom of Sirach from Ecclesiasticus as seen in these words from the Old Testament: "They maintain the fabric of the world and their concern is for the exercise of their trade." Cajetan smiled when he saw that. On the other side, the Peaceful Kingdom as proclaimed by Isaiah with a wolf and a lamb carved in stone next to the Holy Innocents and the words of Jeremiah about the lamentations of Ramah. Below all of that was the 'In Praise of Wisdom' words by the Prophet Baruch: "The stars shone in their watches and were glad." "Perfect," said Cajetan. Master Cassegrain told Cajetan that all he had left to do were some last pieces of sculpture that belonged in their niches. Then he would be done. "No more foliate heads?" asked Cajetan.

The window makers came and filled the front central rose window's twenty-seven-foot diameter with hundreds of pieces of colored glass that had been prepared by the glaziers. Many craftsmen, some laborers and other people stood on the ground gazing upward at the rose window's transformation from tracery to lead hollows to stained glass telling it's own story. The glaziers had put together the story of the Ancient Covenant leading to the New Covenant, starting with Abraham and his son Isaac. It was told from left to right in elongated lozenges. Then came Joseph and his brothers in Egypt, followed by the crossing of the Red Sea with Moses and Aaron, then the reigns of David and of Solomon and the building of the great temple in Jerusalem. Toward the right started the New Testament story with the Annunciation followed by the birth of Jesus, then the Finding of Jesus in the Temple, Jesus' public ministry and the naming of the twelve apostles ending with his Passion and Resurrection. Right in the center was Mary the Queen of Heaven seated next to her Son in full majesty and glory, and above them the Father and the Holy Ghost. All three radiant in the bright light of the sun penetrating the stained glass with colors of mauve, rose, cerulean blue with a touch of cardinal red. When the Cardinal saw that, he was practically in tears since he recognized the links to the name of the Cathedral and the carving of Blessed Mary as Queen of Heaven as well as the radiant masterpiece of the rose window and Blessed Mary's Heavenly Queenship. As for Cajetan, he discerned some stars in the cerulean blue of some lozenges and he was pleased. Ecstatically pleased, one might say. Cajetan went back home and noted in his diary that the great rose window was completed in May of 1314. Wandal told him to go and lie down for his complexion was ashen and he had bags under his eyes. For once, he listened to her.

By mid-summer, the tower was finished and the bells installed ready to be rung. The carpenters and the roofers wanted to ring the bells but Cajetan told them to wait until the Bishop and the Cardinal were present. Cajetan did not much like the Bishop because he was always glum and never seemed to smile at anyone, not even the Cardinal who tried to put the new Bishop at ease in Évreux. One would have supposed that the reason the Bishop was so glum and possibly irritated was because he had not been made an archbishop yet. Cajetan did not need the Bishop much except to sign and approve some documents that had to be made for the release of some information about the Cathedral. It was all a formality that higher ecclesiastics demanded as a way of protecting their positions in the Church and the archdiocese.

The following day, early in the morning as the cocks crowed and the birds sang, a clattering of bells was heard in all of Évreux. People got up and flung open their shutters to see what was happening. Someone had climbed the tower and had started to ring the bells with the hammers clanging in every which way since that someone did not know how to ring bells. It did not matter to people since it was proof that the bells could ring and that the Cathedral was nearing its completion. At last! They caught the culprit who did not try to get away. It was one of the apprentices who had little too much to drink the night before, and wanted to celebrate in the very early hours of the morning. They called him after that, Jacques the Bell Ringer. He was proud of his new name. Very proud. Except the Bishop who complained to Cajetan about the noise being rather vain and not in deference to the sacredness of the site and its Cathedral. Cajetan half apologized and turned around with the outline of a smirk on his face.

Once the rest of the sculptures were placed in their niches, the cathedral was declared finished, although not yet thoroughly complete. There were still some minor details to address. On August 27 in the year of Our Lord 1314 after twenty-two years of work and toil "Notre-Dame Reine des Cieux" was there for everyone to see in its glory and daring execution of Cajetan's plans and design as a Gothic cathedral in full display of its architectural achievement. Cajetan the Stargazer had his dream. Finally!

Seven days later on a Saturday morning, the Cardinal, the Bishop and the chapter led a grand procession through the narrow streets of Évreux and ending at the Western portals of the brand new cathedral, The Cathedral of "Notre-Dame Reine des Cieux." The entire population of the city was there to participate in the celebratory service of thanksgiving. Huge colored banners had been hung from the triforium, and all the candles on the piers were lit bright and dazzling with fire that resembled vibrating stars. Cajetan was there with Wandal as were all craftsmen, apprentices and journeymen as well as most laborers. Cajetan was wearing his medal, and most people saluted his as Sir Knight at which he turned a bit red. Emmanuel was there with his new wife, Sarah. Philippon was not able to be there due to some trade business that kept him away. His father understood. As for Melodia, she was there and prepared to sing in the choir. Reverend Abbess Dieudonnée sent her best regards for a happy and satisfying conclusion to a worthwhile and sacred Gothic project. They were not able to reach Abélard François and they figured that someday he would show up in their midst. As for Gilbert Tendrétoile, he was now working on his masterpiece. He stood in the aisle next to the choir completely enjoying the celebration. The bells were ringing loudly throughout Évreux and their joyous sound was like the peals of laughter from high above. As the choir intoned the "Te Deum" the building filled with beautiful sounds from the people singing, and these people, most of them children and grandchildren of the men who had laid the foundation, were filled with a tremendous awe and great joy that the Good Lord and the Queen of Heaven had indeed blessed them. It was a splendid celebration what with the painted stone carvings brightly glowing with light upon them, the stained glass dazzling in the morning light of the brightest of sun rays and the glow of interior light, airy and luminescent so that one would have thought that celestial radiance had come down from heaven to acclaim the wondrous work of all of the craftsmen who had accomplished such a marvelous task, this Gothic cathedral. That's what Abbot Suger promoted, whispered Cajetan to Wandal, the triumph of light and majestic ambience. Oh, the majesty of light! said Wandal. The majesty of the dream. There was enough wonderment that day to fill the hearts and minds of all citizens of Évreux as well as visitors who had come from afar to join in the celebration of a new cathedral. One who thoroughly enjoyed this wonderment was Véronique Ypres who had learned about Cajetan's accomplishment and had walked miles to be there. When Cajetan found out about her being there, he rushed to embrace her and wish her well. She told him that she no longer carried her cross made of lead, and was happy with the House for the Poor and Destitute that she had established back in her village of Voyanges.

The following day, as Cajetan was walking down the nave glancing at the ceiling and feeling that Gothic space, he happened to lower his eyes and saw that on one of the capitals was carved a pilgrim with a scallop shell on his cloak. He stopped to look at it and felt a twinge of nostalgia in his breast. He was so appreciative of this gesture by Master Cassegrain that he went over to his workshop to thank him for his generosity of remembrance and sacred indulgence into the past. Cajetan had his foliate heads, his Santiago pilgrim and his "Vierge Marie la Belle Étoile." What more could he ask for, he asked himself. The Master Architect had truly earned his medal and his title as Knight of Saint Thomas, Knight of Gothic architecture. He was in his brightest moment of achievement and appreciation of the Queen of Heaven's stellar embrace.

The following winter months were harsh and difficult months for Cajetan. The cold was severe and bone chilling. Cajetan was sick for a full month with the grippe so that he could hardly move, so bad were the aches and pains in his joints. Wandal tried to help him walking and getting some food in his stomach but he refused both. She called in a woman who knew her medicinal herbs and concoctions and her skills as a healer. Cajetan told Wandal that he wished that his sister were there to take care of him. She told him that Marie Dieudonnée had her own worries and possibly her own aches and pain. Weeks went by and Cajetan did not feel much better. Wandal asked him if he wanted to see a local doctor, and he said, yes. It did not take too long before she wrapped Cajetan in warm clothing with a woolen blanket thrown over his shoulders, and off they went to see the physician.

After much probing and testing with instruments that Cajetan had never seen before, the doctor declared that Cajetan was suffering from exhaustion and possibly pneumonia. He prescribed some remedies from the apothecary. The remedies did not work too well. Wandal was not only concerned but truly worried. She put on her winter cloak and went to see the Cardinal. He immediately told his clerk to let her in. He was sitting in a large stuffed chair near the fire and was reading his breviary.

----I'm sorry to bother you, Eminence, but Cajetan is really sick and I don't know what to do anymore. I took him to the doctor, he examined him and told him he was exhausted and possibly suffering from pneumonia. He then prescribed some remedies from the apothecary but they did not help his condition. What am I do do, Eminence? What am I to do? I'm at my wit's end.

----Now calm yourself down. Your husband needs a lot of rest. After the completion of the cathedral and the great celebration that we had, Cajetan felt a let down. His project was over and done with. He no longer was needed as an Architect and he felt that. It affected his mind and his body. That's quite a shock to the system when something like that happens. It means that you are no longer the hub of the wheel so-to-speak. The wheel spins and spins but nothing happens. You know how much Cajetan loves his craft and the creativity that comes with it.

----Yes, I know it all too well, Eminence.

----So, Cajetan has come to the end of his rope as far as being an Architect. He knows that no one will need his services as a Master Architect, and that hurts him and his pride. We're all human beings. I had a hard time adjusting to the fact that I was no longer Cardinal Archbishop of this diocese, and my expertise on this Gothic cathedral as far as organization and fund raising was not needed any more. I was put out to pasture like a lame horse. Not needed anymore, that's hard to swallow, Wandal.

----But you're Cardinal Emeritus and still in charge of the cathedral project. Everyone respects you and your work.

----Cardinal Emeritus is just an honorary title to set me aside. As far as the Cathedral is concerned, I'm no longer needed for all the funds have been raised and spent without a single coin of debt.

----You should be proud of that.

----I am. But what is my destiny now? Do I shut myself up in a cloister? Do I travel and see the countryside and its marvels of nature? Am I not too old to do that? What am I good for at my old age? Tell me, Wandal.

----You can consult with people, with dignitaries or other persons of quality. How about going to the Vatican in Rome and meet other cardinals who may have the same thoughts as you about being retired and not worthy of creative work?

----I'm afraid that Rome is still reeling from the politics of hierarchy.

----Then why not offer your advice and consolation to people who really need it like those who suffer the loss of religious support in small communities without monasteries, convents and even parishes?

----That's a good idea, Wandal. I'll think about it. Now, about Cajetan's health problems, what can we do to help him? Well I know of one healer who might be able to render some help. He has a considerable amount of knowledge about illnesses and healing. His name is Master Isidore Valvuchon. He's from Flanders.

----That's where we lived for so many years.

----I could try to contact to him and I'm sure that if I asked him he would come to see what's wrong with Cajetan, and most probably heal him from his malady.

----Oh, that would be great, Eminence. Thank you so very much.

----Cajetan deserves all of my care and concern, Wandal.

The following week Master Valvuchon arrived at Cajetan's door and asked to see the sick person recommended by Cardinal de Champigny for a cure. Wandal let the healer in, and quickly brought him to Cajetan who was sitting or rather lying prone on a large couch. The healer examined him and probed him. Then he tapped his chest with his fingers after which he made him open his mouth to collect a specimen of saliva that he then mixed with some chemicals he had with him. After several moments, the healer took Wandal aside and told her that Cajetan was much more sick than what he and Wandal thought. Cajetan had the beginning of the plague that had started devastating the southern part of France and the northern part of Italy. Cajetan had to be quarantined immediately, he told Wandal. "He has what is called the Great Plague or the Great Pestilence," he told Wandal. "You yourself should be quarantined separately. It's dangerous and spreads very fast. I shouldn't even be here. Don't tell anyone for fear of starting a panic, and people will do anything in desperation, even kill."

Wandal did not know what to do. She could not put her husband away without medication and care. Who would give them to him? She was the only one. So she decided to keep Cajetan home without letting anybody see him or come in contact with him. She would do her best to let the children know, if possible. She didn't even want the Cardinal to know. She gathered all of her strength, at least what she had left, and proceeded to boil water and make compresses that she would apply to the swellings on Cajetan's neck and shoulders. She left Cajetan only to get provisions and then was right back home. She locked the door all the time even when she was inside the house. She prayed a lot to the Virgin Mary so that the Mother of God would intercede with her Son for Cajetan's healing. Every day she recited the *Memorare* with Cajetan mumbling the words. There was no response from Heaven for the silence of the Lord and the Virgin Mother was felt with abnegation and pain without despair.

A week passed and Cajetan showed the slightest of progress and then he would fall back into his doldrums and periods of high fever. The Cardinal sent an envoy, his clerk, to find out how Cajetan was doing. Wandal told him that he was coming along but that it would take much time to heal. She did not even make him come into the house so frightened was she of people finding out about the malady Cajetan had. She did not want to call it the Plague or the Pestilence for fear that it would spread without her knowing it. She thought that a miracle would happen if she continually prayed to the Virgin Mary and offered her sacrifices for the repentance of her sins and those of Cajetan, even though she could not think of any on her conscience. She started to fast since the priest had claimed that fasting was a good way of obtaining graces and favors from Heaven. Fasting, prayers and sacrifices were the path of salvation and the way of obtaining what you prayed for, she told herself. She thought of Marie Dieudonnée and how she wished she were here with her and Cajetan. Then she put it out of her mind. It just wasn't practical, she told herself. After that, Wandal thought of indulgences that she could earn toward the healing of Cajetan but she did not know how except that she once had a little prayer card that listed indulgences, some six months, some a year and others three and a half years. No plenary. Besides, she had thrown the little card away when she said the prayers to Blessed Mary Help of All Sinners, fervently she thought, and nothing happened.

Wandal even started to ask herself why God was punishing Cajetan with the terrible Plague. What did he do wrong to deserve this? Where did it come from? Who gave it to him? What could she do now to alleviate the situation? She came up with the response of, nothing. Nothing could be done. That's what she came up with. Then the large swellings started to come. Swelling on Cajetan's neck and on his back. They seemed to grow every day, some the size of an egg. Wandal did not know what to make of them. Emmanuel tried several times to see his father and mother but he was refused entry at the door. He worried about them and started to plead with Wandal. "Please let me in, mother. What's wrong? What is so wrong that you can't even see your son?" Until one day, he was given a piece of paper that Wandal slipped under the door while Emmanuel was trying to talk to her. The note read, 'Please do not try to see us. Your father is very sick with a dangerous illness and you could catch it. So please stay away for your own sake. I'm fine, do not worry. I'll send for you when things settle. We love you, Mother - One more thing, your father says to tell you that you are now in charge of the Cathedral. You're the Master Architect responsible for the final phases of completion. Cajetan your father is handing it over to you. God bless.'

Everyone knew that there was something wrong in Cajetan and Wandal's household, but no one knew what it was. No one wanted to pry; no one wanted to intrude, no one wanted to invade their privacy. So, they were left alone by themselves, totally alone. Cajetan had lost a lot of weight; he was practically skin and bones. His buboes got worse until he fell into a coma and lay there for days with Wandal watching over him and trying to do the best she could to make him comfortable. She was exhausted but had not been affected by the disease. She cried a lot but remained calm. One evening in November, while Wandal was sitting next to Cajetan holding his hand, Cajetan looked up at her and whispered with a labored voice, "The stars are coming to get me, Wandal," and then he let out a heavy sigh of pain and letting go as if his lungs were emptying themselves of whatever breath was left. Then he slipped into peaceful death the way saints pass on.

Wandal sent for Emmanuel for she knew that she had to do something with Cajetan's body on account of the Plague. She did not want to infest anyone else, and she knew that he would not be allowed in church that way. Fire was the only cleansing agent she could think of. Late that night a woman wearing a long cloak with hood and a young man wearing black could be seen sitting in a horse driven cart with a long white bundle lying in the back of the cart. Wandal had wrapped Cajetan's remains in a white linen cloth and they were bringing them to the edge of the Évreux forest. Next to the remains were wooden logs and fuel. Enough for a pyre. Cajetan's worn out body would be burned in a pyre to rid it of all signs of the Plague. The fire rose and the two observers stood there as Wandal recited some prayers. Then they sat in the cart until the break of dawn when the fire was turning to ashes. They picked up the bones that were left and placed them in a large basket. As for the ashes, Emmanuel raked them and placed them in a basket to take them home with him. They would become for Emmanuel the fervent memory of Cajetan Stargazer Then, they went home.

Later that day, Wandal went to see the Cardinal to tell him about Cajetan's death and disposal of the body by fire. He told her that what she had done was right and good for the populace. When she asked him about the funeral service, he told her that he himself would preside for Cajetan merited a Christian funeral. She then asked him about the remains of the remains, the bones she had collected, and he told her that the bones would be put in a coffin and the coffin placed on a catafalque in the choir of the cathedral, and no one would know any better. Then she admitted to him that there was no miracle even though she had prayed and prayed for Cajetan to be cured of this terrible Plague. The Cardinal answered her by saying, "There was indeed a miracle, Wandal. You're the miracle. You were not infected by the Plague. Don't you realize that?" Wandal went back home gratified that there was indeed a miracle that had happened. She then hurried to fumigate the entire house with the help of Emmanuel so that it would be cleansed of the remnants of the Plague that had infested her home and taken the life of her husband.

A week later, Cajetan was given an elaborate Christian funeral with all of the mourning pageantry that any well-known figure could get. His coffin lay on a catafalque draped with a black cloth with a large band of sky blue cloth placed on top. Cajetan's medal was pinned on top of the band of blue. His Eminence Cardinal de Champigny led the funeral services and he gave the homily. In it he made reference to Christ as the Divine Temple that He said could be destroyed and then rebuilt in three days. The Cardinal said to all those gathered in the Cathedral that morning that Cajetan had built their temple, this Gothic Cathedral of "Notre-Dame Reine des Cieux," a temple that would last for years and years to come, and would never be destroyed because it would stand in their hearts and collective memory for a very long time. "Yes, Cajetan, Master Architect, can be seen as the builder of this sacred worshipping place that will last as long as the creative genius of a Master Architect like Cajetan will last in the memory of those who proclaim the glory of the Creator God. Adieu, Cajetan Stargazer."

Cajetan was buried in the crypt of the Cathedral. All but one large bone, a femur, was buried there. That bone was given to Abbess Marie Dieudonnée. She was present with two other nuns at Cajetan's funeral. She told Wandal that she would only be too pleased to bury that part of her deceased brother in the cemetery at Fontevraud in the peaceful arms of nature and the quietude of cloistered life. Marie Dieudonnée told Wandal that she considered the femur bone to be like a relic, sacred and precious to her. At the funeral service there was a young man standing in a far corner of the cathedral gently weeping. His name was Gilbert Tendrétoile. Some people noticing this said to one another that this young man must have been very close to Cajetan for he was indeed sad at the passing of the Master Architect. Indeed he was.

A year later, Wandal entered the convent at Fontevraud to spend the rest of her life there. As for Emmanuel, the Master Architect, he lived on to build a Gothic cathedral in Bavaria. His Eminence Cardinal Antoine de Champigny died peacefully in his sleep and his body was placed in the crypt of the Cathedral. As for Bishop Chalumeau, he was transferred to a secluded diocese in the mountains of eastern France where he tends his own little garden and leads a solitary life. Abélard François retired in Paris where he writes poetry and plays. He just published a play entitled "The Stargazer." His poetry is much sought after by the ladies of the court. As for Gilbert Tendrétoile, he went to Germany to further his studies in Gothic architecture and then moved to Croatia on the Island of Visovac under the tutelage of the Augustinian monks to build a small abbey dedicated to the Apostle Paul.

The faithful of "Notre-Dame Reine des Cieux d'Évreux" have just celebrated the tenth anniversary of their Cathedral in the year of Our Lord 1325. Thousands of pilgrims come every year to the Cathedral that Cajetan built, not only to venerate the sacred relics but to gaze at the sculpture of "Sainte Marie de la Belle Étoile" on the tympanum of the southern portal that they like and revere for its artistry and especially for its meaning in their lives. Everyone loves stars in their lives, it seems, particularly the stars that shine so bright in the eyes of children.

Sainte Marie de la Belle Étoile

EPILOGUE

The cathedral of "Notre-Dame Reine des Cieux d'Évreux" stood tall and majestic for over six centuries until World War II when the bombing raids completely destroyed it. Only parts of its foundation remained. Évreux was heavily damaged during that conflict. It was thought by the officials in charge that it would not be worthwhile rebuilding the old Gothic cathedral since there was another church in Évreux, the former Abbey Church of Saint-Turbin. All that's left of Cajetan's legacy is a small granite stone marker on the original *chantier Odelard* engraved with the words: **Cajetan Stargazer lived here and built this cathedral. Évreux, France, 1879.** *Érigé par la volonté généreuse des Dames du Vieil-Évreux.* It is not unusual for some people to leave fresh field flowers on the marker. They remember and they wish to pay tribute to the Stargazer Architect who filled the lives of so many across the ages with the creative power of artistry.

Verba volant, scripta manent

Made in the USA
Charleston, SC
14 July 2012